MISTRESS
OF THE
KNELL

The Stars Hereafter Chronicles, Book III: *Mistress of the Knell*

ISBN-13: 978-1-9990749-5-1

Cover design, illustration, book design and image editing by Robert Grey.

Penetra Dor City original image by Icon Ade.
Amon Alaba-Akra background original image by Md Saju Sardar.
Portal to Eorthe original image by Ahasanara Acter.
Cosmic feather drawing by Diana Johanna Velasquez.
Gavali Mountains original image by iBrandify Gallery.

This is a work of fiction.
All the characters and events in this book are either fictitious
or used fictitiously.

MISTRESS OF THE KNELL

THE STARS HEREAFTER CHRONICLES | BOOK THREE

RUPERT SMITHSON

HUMMINGBIRD HILL

CONTENTS

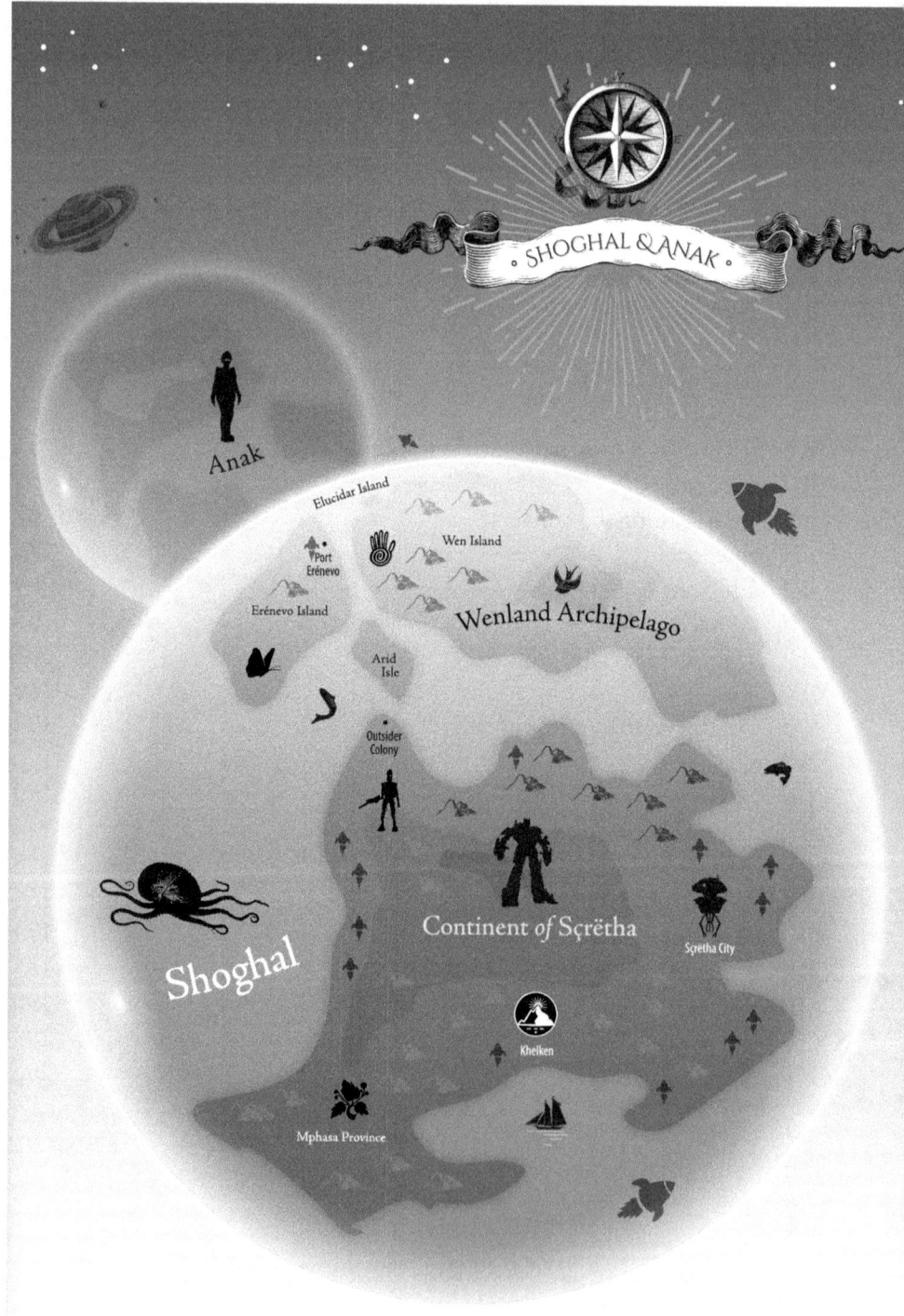

"The gate itself Masudah considered a goddess, in this case Mistress of the Knell, a detail only important if the difficult pronunciation of the god's name was incorrect, ominously translated as Dancer in Blood."

♦

Rupert Smithson

Book Two

Bones of Silver, Bones of Iron

View *of the* ringed gas giant Zhamanak *from* Penetra Dor,
one *of its* many moons *and* moonlets.

I

Off *the* Rings *of* Zhamanak

DESPITE THE TEACHINGS of the wise and deepened experience of the arcane, the enigmatic and the paradoxical, the situation now appeared so surreal as to conjure paralysis. An immeasurable moment passed. Rowan muttered: "*Now what have I done...?!*"

The giant ringed planet the Ahan called Zhamanak dominated a third of the skyline like a spherical god. A vast blue storm in the improbable shape of a hexagon raged at its northern pole.

He reckoned he stood on what must be one of the planet's moons, only not in the orbital plane of its incredible rings. Many other satellites, moonlets and moons circled that plane. Never having been off-world before, he wondered what his own home planet, faraway Eorthe, hundreds of millions of leagues distant, looked like from the vantage point of Lunah, its own solitary moon. Until now it had never been something even considered a possibility, to stand on that small orb and see for himself, perhaps because he had been taught when a boy that the lizard king Kirzaka the Deathless, Talon of Maçina, commanded his unholy legions from there. But this moon of Zhamanak surely must have the best view in the solar system. For one thing, lack of an atmosphere did not obscure the gas giant's wonderful hues, pale but rich yellows with tints of orange – and beyond, the unbelievable depth of blackness of space, but a living blackness, full to overflowing with existence. Trillions of sparks of scintillant life radiated in every direction from the galaxies and rivers of galactic clusters – so incredibly *deep* – he could only gaze transfixed – that is, until a gruff voice interrupted, insistent and loud:

"And who might you be? *Dammit, speak!*"

The thraldom broke at last. Rowan turned about. "Rowan Berry Longbow," he answered.

The speaker, a heavy bull-necked man, took two steps out of the shadow of a massive semi-translucent column, one of many at the perimeter of the glassy dome, and looked Rowan over. "I can't say I'm pleased to meet you, Longbow," he said. "One gets used to the priceless solitude available only in a place like this. You're an intruder. Explain yourself."

"Believe me, sir, it wasn't my intention to end up here... I think I may have mispronounced the spell."

1

"*Spell?* What the devil do you mean? That's magician talk. Unfortunately for you, there's no longer demand for that sort of entertainment around here."

The huge ringed gas giant reflected the sun, tiny at this distance, but did no more than add a little pale fill to the scene. In the soft lighting of the brilliant starscape, the big man's eyes bulged by contrast in a hard bespectacled glare. He resembled a heavyset version of someone Rowan had known back on Eorthe, back in Perkona Ola in the cavern system of the late Vugh Deep, before its destruction by the reptilians. The thatch of bristled blonde hair, the blue eyes and the eyewear reminded him of transpersonal psychologist Sola. Sadly, the good doctor's fate had probably been the same as millions around the globe murdered by Kirzaka. This man and Sola, look-alikes, appeared about the same age, somewhere between thirty and forty years as their species went, some of whom called themselves the Sannir, as *sannir* signified so-called "true" men. Moreover, Sola and the heavier man who confronted Rowan now shared a similar lab coat, soiled in this case, with pockets for small tools, notebooks and samples collected or parts to repair or upgrade research equipment. Despite the futuristic environment, this man in some indefinable way hailed from a time long past –

"*Hey, wake up, sleepwalker!*" the man shouted. "*I'm talking to you!*"

Rowan flinched, blinked and replied: "Er... the spell is a password, to get through the gate. I have to get home. I just want to go home... are you an alchemist?"

"No. Why the devil would you would think that? I transform nothing. I seek nothing, because I've found it, the simple life. *Spell?* Answer me, sleepwalker. That's Lyran talk. You even look like one a bit. You're a hybrid, aren't you? What happened to your fur?"

"No, I'm not a Lyran. I got too near a big fire... the fur will grow back, so I'm told. Never mind that. I was until a few minutes ago on Eorthe, at Gate of the Shining Ones. I was to pronounce the gatekeeper's name, the password to activate the portal, said to be a goddess called Mistress of the Knell. Maybe I mispronounced it... I should have waited until I wasn't so exhausted."

Aglet Scion-Aiguille *of* Penetra Dor.

"Interesting." The man grinned, yet his words disparaged: "You damn Lyrans are all over the damn galaxy. One simply cannot go to any star system without tripping over your furry carcasses deep in fairy land, and what's more bored to death with your cryptic drivel. Go back to Lyra or whichever Lyran colony you're from. I really hate to be forced to insist. You want to go home. I want to be left in peace." From an inside pocket of his lab coat, with a cold grin the man withdrew a palm-sized flat metallic device with a cover that he flipped open. An array of slightly rounded silver buttons decorated its face. He stood poised to press one, and looked at Rowan as if he expected the gesture to be understood. "Well," he grumbled, "don't just stand there."

His words reminded Rowan of Aynt, the black witch of Aha. But she had taught that he must stand and not act, not until truth showed the way. *My power is to wait.* Rowan replied: "I've already said I'm not from Lyra. You know my name. Please tell me yours so that I can at least apologize for the intrusion."

The man's free hand dropped to his side. "The name is Aiguille, as if you didn't know."

"Apologies, Aiguille. I have no idea how I ended up on your doorstep. And it's a magnificent one, I must say. All the same, I will leave without delay. There's no time to waste."

"Then don't let *me* stop you." He waved Rowan away and scowled. "Can't you just do whatever you did in reverse or something?"

"I have no idea. Will you tell me where I am? Is it Penetra Dor, the moon?"

"Of course it's Penetra Dor. Where else?"

"That's a start. This end of the portal… I'll quickly try to locate it with my scanner… unless of course you can direct me."

Aiguille peered at Rowan without expression. With a subtle movement of his thumb he pressed one of the silver buttons.

Rowan assumed that Aiguille's silence had been tacit agreement that he might activate his scanner –

But in the distance under the transparent roof of the observation deck another man appeared, along with three large beings from head to toe in dark metal form-fitting uniforms, including helmets that covered their entire heads and made them look like insects, with long narrow glowing cyan eyes that wrapped their upper faces and extended vertically to their chins. They carried weapons that looked like plasma rifles. The distant man, unarmed, resembled Aiguille a little, but taller, an athletic mesomorph, wide at the shoulder and narrow at the hip, and well into middle age. Nor did he wear glasses or a lab coat, but a black uniform with a silver badge, his hair and eyes dark. He cupped his hands to his mouth and called out: "*Aglet! Are you all right? Who is that?*"

Aiguille did not answer, nor did he turn around.

The others arrived in short order. The dark man slowed his gait as he drew near and asked, "Aglet… how did a Lyran get past the checkpoint?"

Aiguille scowled. "He claims he's no Lyran, says he's from Eorthe."

The tall dark man stared, feet set apart, knees slightly bent, thumbs tucked in his belt.

"I'm Rowan Berry Longbow." He extended his hand to him –

In an instant the glossy metal beings pointed their rifles at him, each at a different vital organ.

Rowan raised his hands. "And you are?"

Both men looked to Rowan's belt, where the phaser pistol and scanner had been securely attached before he activated the portal.

The athletic man in black dived for the phaser –

Rowan stepped back out of the way.

The man regained his balance and stared at him.

Aiguille clapped his hands, and said, "Very good, Longbow." He stepped forward past the others. "Meet my elder brother Diarkis." He glowered and peered at his sibling. "It takes a lot to get the best of him. Eh?"

Diarkis merely stood stiff and stared, not blindly, but somehow disengaged. But he relaxed, like a soldier at ease, his hands clasped behind his back, eyes fixed on the intruder.

Aiguille circled Rowan. "You interest me," he said. "You may stay, if only until I can figure out what you are. You say you're not a Lyran. Those cat ears do stand out, don't they though? You must be a hybrid. You look a bit less feline. Your face is unlike a cat's… but like a man's. I'm not sure how this is possible, but then the Lyrans aren't that interesting. I haven't looked into it much."

"Thank you, Aiguille. But as I said, I have no time to waste. It's urgent that I get back to Eorthe. By making the jump I was trying to save time, to save a life, in fact many lives, my tribe. It would have cut the distance by a quarter. If you can't direct me to the portal site here, I'll activate my scanner and find it myself." Rowan included Diarkis with a glance. "Then I'll be out of your hair."

Aiguille peered at Diarkis. "My brother wouldn't like that, would he?"

Diarkis shook his head.

"See? He wants you to stay too. Your scanner won't work here. Try it. See for yourself."

Rowan took the scanner from his belt and, sure enough, the row of indicators refused to light up.

"Oh, dear. It's broken," said Aiguille. "You need to accept what is."

"No," Rowan said. "I doubt that it's malfunctioning. By the level of technology this station has... or is it more than that?... there must be a workshop where it can be tested, maybe adjusted. Can you help?"

"Station?" Aiguille looked back across the huge observation deck, in the direction from which Diarkis had come. "What you see is only a small fraction of Penetra Dor City." He turned back to Rowan. "It's the best real estate in the solar system, set in a prime location on the rim of one of the impact craters like the most precious jewel in the crown... because of the view. The rich and famous used to holiday here, back in the old days. Only the best for the best... *blah, blah, blah*... but you, Lyran, of course already know, don't you? Everybody does." He looked Rowan over from toe to crown. "I believe I saw a tattoo on your head. Bend over so I can see it again. You may be branded."

"It's nothing, a trademark made by the reptilians when I was a child, to identify my orphanage and my status." Nevertheless, he bowed his head to show Aiguille the old inscription on the skin of the top of his head.

"The writing is illegible..." said Aiguille. "Spidery."

"As I said, I was a child when it was inked. I've grown."

"Still, it's nothing like I've ever seen before. Very interesting. What do you mean by 'reptilians'? There are of course many animals of the class *Reptilia*, especially on Eorthe. None are intelligent enough to know how to write, let alone tattoo anyone. What a preposterous idea! Tell me what you mean. Are you a runaway slave?"

Rowan sighed. "If you must know, I was as good as a slave as an inmate of the orphanage. If I'd remained there, permanent slavery would have been my fate. Please, you didn't answer. Is there a workshop or lab where I can test my scanner? If you can't help me find this end of the portal, it's the best option. Unless you know another way."

"So," Aiguille said, "these reptilians... they made slaves of you felines? Lizards and cats. Fantastic! How the devil did you escape?"

Rowan clenched his fists. "Look, I'm tired. It's all very nice chatting, but as you can probably tell, I've been on a long journey. This detour is only the latest of many taxing obstacles in the way of my goal. I must get home. My people are under attack as we speak."

Aiguille looked Rowan over again. "Lyrans don't have tribes, just religion. Well, I too could sit instead of stand. Father used to say it's the secret to success. Let's retire to the lounge over there. We can look at the view as you continue your... narrative." He lifted his device and flipped open its cover, pressed three of the silver buttons in succession, and gestured to Rowan to walk to the plush

5

theatre-style seating in a half-circle that faced the ringed planet he had seen before in books illustrated by Ahan concept artists, who had envisioned it with surprising accuracy, the gas giant the astronomers called Zhamanak. From this vantage point it loomed across a third of the sky above the dark jagged horizon beneath the brilliant bounty of stars in infinite space.

Diarkis and the dark-metal guards followed and stood at ease when the group reached the lounge.

Told to sit, Rowan settled into a simple armchair, elegantly upholstered in what looked like pebbled hide, which adjusted automatically to his weight and form for the most comfortable position. The reflexive relaxation response was immediate – he nearly dozed off –

"Eyes open, Longbow," snapped Aiguille. "Finish your story."

Rowan suppressed a yawn, and blinked at the man. "You have me at your mercy, sir. I'd prefer to do as you'd asked at first, find the portal and leave. But if it's a story you want… I was rescued from the orphanage by a young cadet, a canid. It was one of her assignments in preparation for military college, a test of her ability to accomplish solo missions." The memory trumped the current predicament, and even evoked a smile. "Canids are very group-minded, so independence is important in a military career…"

"Hardly," said Aiguille. "Military objectives are always achieved by group effort. Independence is lethal. So what is a canid? A dog?"

"No. Groupthink is natural to canids. It makes them excellent guards and soldiers. They never lose it, in fact can't, but in case they're ever separated from their group, they must be able to function effectively. And no, they're not dogs, although part of their ancestry includes the wolf, not that they resemble one. In fact they look much like you and your brother, apart from your ears. Theirs are pointed, supposedly from off-world, from a Class M planet called Vulcan in orbit around the triple star system Omicron Eridani, seventeen light years from the sun."

"Very good, Longbow." Aglet clapped his hands in applause. "For a slave boy you somehow got an education. I'm intrigued. I know of Vulcan. Father told us stories about our grandfather's visit there. This tall tale you're spinning is quite entertaining too. You have no idea… never mind. Just keep talking."

Rowan frowned. "I'm telling you the truth, Aiguille. Why would I lie?"

"*Everyone lies!*" But he relaxed his scowl and added, "Do continue."

"All right, but I'm exhausted. Let me know if I'm boring you. Where was I? Right, Sam rescued me. I mean Samarit Longbow rescued me." Rowan smiled inwardly, tempted to close his eyes. "I didn't even remember my name at the time. For sixty-three years I'd been called Syx, but that was every orphan's name, except for the boys who had been promoted as monitors of the younger ones. They were all called Hepta. Eventually I remembered my real name, Rowan Berry…" But the thought of his lost sister Blue intruded, and his smile faded.

Aiguille smirked. "But you call yourself Longbow, a jarring contradiction. Were you adopted by the dog clan? I'm not sure if this improves your story. First it was lizards and cats. Now a cat is joining a pack of dogs? That does not make sense. Nevertheless, I used to like tall tales when I was a boy. Continue."

Rowan frowned, but continued: "Lyrans are what we call feline, as they're purebred. On Eorthe my species is *Felis sapiens*, less formally known as felid."

Aiguille chuckled. "This is getting better all the time. It sounds like you're saying you were an old unadopted cat, caged in the pound, when a puppy-girl stole you away. Fantastic. Why not admit you're a Lyran hybrid?"

Rowan peered at Aiguille and narrowed his gaze. "Look, you can mock me all you want. You wanted to hear. I'm telling you. My species has been stable for a long, long time… felid. Pretend you don't know there are many iterations of *sapiens* on Eorthe, including anders like you. Why don't *you* admit it?"

Aiguille scowled. "I ask the questions around here. Kind of grouchy, aren't you? Remember you're my guest… for the time being."

Rowan scowled back. "I'm glad to hear I'm your guest and not your prisoner. Otherwise, I'd have to do something about that."

Aiguille's eyebrows jumped above the tops of his glasses. "You just try it, sleepwalking storyteller." He scowled, but said, "Very well, I'll humour you and pretend I'm the ignoramus you obviously believe me to be. Go on… if you please."

So tired his head felt light, Rowan continued: "I'll say it then if you won't. In time a species developed called *neanderthalensis*, named after a valley in the northwest of a continent in the northern hemisphere where the bones were first discovered. Remember *now*? The Primordial Architects based a new version of *sapiens* on them because they were robust, already highly intelligent and developing nicely. The only thing they lacked was the kind of aggression that made the game interesting… sound familiar? So they took a bit of this and a bit of that from other species native and alien and created what we call anders. That's you and your family… cousin."

"That's absurd." Aiguille scowled anew. "We're not from Eorthe. That place is a radioactive unmanaged zoo, a wildlife reserve at best. Who in their right mind would want to go there except zoo agents, trophy hunters, trappers, poachers and tourists with more money than brains? The whole thing is highly unstable too, the last place a civilization could hope to gain any traction. It could barely last a few thousand of years at most. No, my lineage came from Sçrëtha, Shoghal, where we had always lived. But everyone knows that, including you, storyteller. Now you *are* getting boring." He pressed another button on his device. His speech to Diarkis afterwards became completely unintelligible.

Penetra Dor City.

II

The Rrin

THE TEDIUM OF probably two Eorthe days that passed since he had been locked in the luxurious suite did not, however, diminish astonishment at the view of the ringed planet. He recalled, from a few days' study of classical astronomy gleaned from the Ahan castle technical library, that the moon Penetra Dor orbited Zhamanak tidally locked, but he remembered nothing of a city on the edge of a large meteor crater. Diarkis and the three machine-like beings, which Rowan later learned were called "androids," had surrounded him, sprayed a hypnotic into his face and confiscated his phaser and scanner, along with the obsidian pendant Blue had given him. They even took his gold ring that would have enabled invisibility, had he been willing to risk the cost to his soul. At least food appeared in a niche in the galley in a cycle of three meals plus long period between, which may add up to a day and a night on Shoghal, wherever that was.

He had tried the communications console first thing to find a map or any other information – but it had been disabled. The frustration of detainment and agony over time wasted strangled hope. He had expected to be within hundreds of leagues of Samarit by now, not further removed by hundreds of *millions*. He paced back and forth in front of the floor-to-ceiling window, indestructible as one would expect. In a fit of exasperation, he intended to throw a chair through it, but smashed it on the granite floor instead – because on the other side of the glass waited instant death. Moments later an immaculate metal android appeared. It took the broken chair away and replaced it with an identical one. It even spoke, and asked him if he needed anything. When he replied that he needed to go home, it bowed and left the room before he could escape.

An intercom activated: "This is no way to treat your host, Lyran. It makes me think your story of the… was it Primitive Architects?… may have some merit. Your aggressive and violent nature is the supporting evidence. But don't worry. The cost of the chair is already included in your bill. We've always maintained a margin for that sort of thing. This retreat wasn't always for meditation and the like, you know. We catered to every disposition. Wild parties were common too. Musicians were the worst, the more famous the more destructive."

Rowan sat on the new chair and repressed the urge to clasp his hands to his head, but replied, "Apologies once again, Aiguille. I'm sure you'd do the same if you were locked up for no reason. I just want to go home. My people may die if I don't get back to them in time."

"Oh, yes." Aiguille said. "They were under attack... from the reptiles, was it? That doesn't sound like much fun, downright depressing in fact. Why not stay a while and enjoy the greatest therapy available at any price? If you're really so old, you'd love it."

"All right, Aiguille, I concede." Rowan stood up. "Unlock the door." The lock clicked in near silence, but not too quiet for felid ears. Before he could grasp the latch, it opened on its own –

The android guard had expanded to fill the doorway. "Please, sir. Walk this way," it said, bowed and marched along the curvilinear hallway like a soldier.

♦

"Longbow, take a seat," said Aiguille from his chair at the head of a long conference table in an elaborately crafted room of rare woods, inlaid panelling and detailed joinery. "There, at the foot of the table."

Diarkis and two other young men already sat near the head.

"We've reconsidered your case," Aiguille added. Behind him hung a sigil embossed in a crest of brushed silvery metal: a sharp mountain peak with the sun behind it. Aiguille had taken the trouble to groom, his shock of blonde hair now combed neatly to one side, and he no longer wore the lab coat, but a rather formal archaic military suit of rich dark blue fabric and metal details of gold. "My siblings do not agree," he said, "that your uninvited appearance on our little moon should be condemned as housebreaking." He turned to look at a young man at his left, not Diarkis, who sat at his right, but a smaller, more spare and mousy version of Aiguille, the only other one who wore spectacles.

A fourth, obviously another brother, also seated on his left, resembled Diarkis, only with a wild look in his eyes, sharp features, but blue eyes and blonde hair like Aiguille. Chronic tension hardened his posture, spring-loaded, ready to fly apart at any moment.

Aiguille stared at the mousy one and said, "This is my younger brother Acus, a poet and mythographer. We tolerate his rhymes, fables, allegories and parables."

Acus sat expressionless. His blank eyes betrayed nothing.

Aiguille gestured to the tense blonde man. "And this handsome fellow," he said, "is Zorut, the least-born... pardon me, I meant to say last-born. You can count on him to lose his temper without warning. You need a haircut, don't you, Zorut?"

Zorut ran his hand over his tousled head and frowned.

"He may have been dropped on his head as a babe," added Aiguille. "No one knows for sure. Perhaps his late nanny knew. She always said he was a handful-and-a-half. But poet Acus here has the kindest heart. He convinced the rest of us. We don't usually listen to his opinions, as he's soft as a woman, in body and mind. Right, Acus?"

The poet and mythographer closed his eyes and nodded. "Yes, Aglet."

Rowan could not read the energies of any of these men, except Aiguille, whom the others called Aglet. The man exuded a numbness despite his jovial yet sarcastic tone. The brothers, however, showed no sign of either amusement or insult. Not having grown up in a nuclear family – or any family for more than the first few years of his life – to Rowan sibling relationships remained somewhat of a mystery, never more so than now.

Aglet continued: "What we propose is this: you shall have free run of the place. No limits. Enjoy to your heart's content. But you will not be allowed weapons or any technology that may affect the operating system. I can see no harm in returning your jewellery, the ring and the pendant, but Acus, generous to a fault normally, insisted that they may have magical powers. Soft-headed as he is, he claims they're too dangerous. Well, we must indulge him. He is blood of our blood after all." Aglet looked around the table. "What say you, boys?"

In unison the brothers replied: "Yes, Aglet."

Rowan studied the strange family. By deduction Diarkis must be first-born, but much older than the others or else had endured a hard life that aged him prematurely.

Aglet's stare remained focused on Rowan. "Well? What have you got to say for yourself, feline? Are you happy now?"

Rowan peered at Aglet, and chose his words with care: "I say I'm a felid, not a feline. There's a big difference. Please don't confuse me with a Lyran again. I knew one once. If they're all like him, I know what they're like: not like me. But a key to the city is a step in the right direction… that is, if you still don't trust me to analyze my scanner and find the portal so I can go home and no longer be of any trouble to you."

His tone of voice taut, Aglet fired back: "Trust? The fool's ruination." He scowled and looked to the dark man seated beside him. "Right, Diarkis?"

Diarkis did not return the look. He stared at the woodgrain in front of him, and nodded his head again and again and again –

11

"That's enough," said Aiguille, boot-faced.

Diarkis obeyed.

"Now… how about a celebration to seal the deal? Who's in favour?" Aglet raised his hand.

The cheerless brothers in unison showed their palms, but none looked either at Aglet or at Rowan. Their faces remained impassive, apart from Zorut's. The whites of his eyes surrounded the blue irises, as if he might leap out of his chair at any moment, if not out of his skin.

"Not you, Longbow?" asked Aglet. "I should think you would be the most enthusiastic of all of us. Perhaps when you meet the pleasure models you'll cheer up. They have a way of improving one's mood in the most charming manner." He flipped open his device and pressed a series of silver buttons. Like a fiend he grinned, slipped it into its special pocket again and rubbed his hands together. "Gentlemen, let's party." He waved his right hand towards the double doors, which opened on their own.

In walked a dozen or so of the most beautiful women Rowan had ever seen, so beautiful as to look unreal – without blemish, utterly flawless, and of variant height, skin colour, weight and dress, two obviously Lyran. One of the ander race stood out nevertheless, the statuesque blonde, blue-eyed like three of the brothers. If ever had the archetype Woman incarnated –

Yet Aglet peered at Diarkis.

Rowan's eye roved to take in the woman's shimmery red gown that revealed more than it concealed.

She stood beside Aiguille and placed a manicured red-nailed hand on his shoulder.

The other women circled the table, and took their places behind the men.

Only Diarkis remained without a partner.

The two tall Lyran leopard women stood behind Rowan. Their perfume intoxicated his senses, and evoked undreamt-of otherworldly mystery – he had no idea anything could smell so good.

The men rose to their feet, Rowan last.

The ladies linked their arms with the men's, with one exception, and they filed into the nearby dining room, somehow architecturally designed to inspire appetite – Rowan's hunger reached new heights. Or depths – the bloodied goat on the trail out of Mudredd Vale came to mind, which added some clarity.

The blonde woman in red – beautiful, stunning, exquisite as only a pure manifestation of an archetype can be – now seated at Aiguille's side, gazed at the man in utter adoration.

A vast quantity of the finest food and wines appeared as if by magic, served by feminine androids, less detailed than the men's companions. But wait, Aglet said, the best was yet to come. Rowan had been so engrossed in his meal that he had failed to observe the others closely. But now he watched and waited –

The walls and ceiling of the dining room receded to enlarge the space to ballroom dimensions.

All the men stood, Rowan last.

The table descended into the floor, as did the chairs. The lighting changed to a pastel shimmer and massaged the eyes. A loud pulsing beat massaged the ears. Stylized holograms of dancers swirled everywhere and gave the scintillating environment a feeling of great mirth, the rhythmic pulse painless and perfect at high volume that overwhelmed and demolished resistance. The musicians with their strange amplified instruments at times appeared among the dancers and disappeared in a multimedia experience, a great work of art that invoked a whole greater than the sum of its parts.

The women Aglet referred to as "pleasure models" were not, however, holograms. At close inspection, although to the eye vividly real, to Rowan they lacked first-personhood in some way. He did not recall that they ate or drank anything, but guessed they must be androids, highly detailed, but caricatures of real women. A man not an intuitive empath may have easily talked himself into taking them at face value, and pretty those faces were. Only the archetypal blonde he found easy to read, unlike Aglet's brothers. The women, still not introduced by name, capered and swayed.

Rowan decided the power of waiting may not necessarily always be negated by action. He went along with the game to see where it might lead, not that he believed he had a choice. He brushed off a hidden talent that found few opportunities for expression, a side effect of nanoid-enhanced agility as a League warrior. Squire Krumb, bless his long-gone soul, would not have pronounced him graceless on the dance floor, nor would have Krumb's countryman Snood Iotah the astronomer. The festivities went on for some time. Thirty-six pieces of music played out by the time it was over, fuelled by enlivening libations unfamiliar to the felid intruder.

"Well, gentlemen," Aglet said, "time!" He strolled towards an exit with the archetypally exquisite blonde lady at his side hand in hand.

Diarkis watched them. All the brothers did, but not with the same intensity, as if to touch them with his eyes.

✦

"Longbow, my good felid. See? I did not call you a feline. I'm trying it on for size… so far so good. Did you enjoy your evening?"

Rowan studied his caller, and replied, "I made an early night of it, I'm afraid. I hope the ladies weren't too disappointed."

"Didn't you like them? They're gorgeous. Perfect."

"That they are, the most gorgeous creatures I've ever laid eyes on, almost."

"So what's the problem? You don't like girls? Is something amiss with your suite? This is one of the best, I assure you. In fact they're all the best."

"No problem."

"Then what, Longbow, do mean by 'almost'? None of them are as gorgeous as mine, granted. Or are you implying something else?"

"No. I'm stating a fact. They're not women. They're androids. Real women are beautiful no matter what they look like on the outside."

Aglet guffawed loudly: "*Ha ha!* And you claim you're not a Lyran!" But the scowl returned. "That's absurd. Did you really say that?"

"Then I'll have to say it again. They're fake."

Aglet's scowl deepened doubly. "You should show more respect. *I am the master here.* I shouldn't have to remind you that you are not." He got no response, so continued: "Look, I came to show you something else of great interest, Longbow, if hot girls don't float your boat. It's one of the main attractions of this retreat in the desert of infinite night. Don't make me change my mind."

"Aglet, my respect is unaffected. I stand in sincere amazement at you and at this… retreat. If I'm to be detained here, I may as well learn something."

"That's more like it." Aglet's narrowed gaze yet betrayed relief.

⁜

"Incredible, isn't it? They weren't there at all when Father accidentally wandered off course and found this little moon. He didn't think much of the barren derelict until the rings started appearing out there. They were so fantastic that he just had to build this city to share it."

"With the most wealthy and the most powerful," Rowan said, while he peered through the huge telescope. The rings awed even the naked eye.

"Who else could appreciate such amazement?"

"Anyone with eyes in their head."

"Most eyes could never afford to travel so far, Longbow. This out-of-the-way place isn't easy to navigate to. Its orbit is fifteen degrees off-axis from the other moons and the circumference is vast. The rings can't be seen on edge from the others. Too thin. And we're very far away from the sun."

Rowan turned away from the telescope. "And from Shoghal."

Aiguille frowned. "How about those starships?" he asked. "How long do you think they are? They measure at hundreds of miles. We saw one once that was more than a thousand miles long, seventy-seven miles wide. It hasn't been back since though. But the others keep at it, like gardeners."

"Like gardeners back on Shoghal?"

"Dammit, Longbow, stop saying that. You don't want to make me angry."

"Is that what happened to Diarkis? He made you angry?"

Aglet slammed the viewer closed. "Don't stick your nose in where it might get snipped off, felid. You may never make it home again."

"Is that a threat? Or do you mean you know how to get there?"

Aglet inhaled deeply – exhaled and grinned. "Listen, let's not argue. This is something amazing, don't you agree?"

"All right, I agree. It is totally amazing. Do you know what they're up to?"

"Up to? Whatever they want. But we only can guess at what the Rrin are doing. We've always thought it must be a transceiver. Just think how powerful a signal could be sent and received by one 175,000 miles wide."

"The Rrin is not what they call themselves, is it?"

"It's a play on 'ring,' nothing more… in the accent my wife's family spoke. It's hard to roll the first two consonants the way they did though. *R-r-rin…* like that. In falsetto it sounds like a bicycle bell. Hilarious."

"And where is she from?"

"Noma was… never mind. The Rrin don't respond to our communications. And we have no clue about any broadcasting going on. They must know we're here, watching. To them we're probably like harmless insects. Of course we dared sail only so close to that monstrous gravity well for a closer look. But they ignored us."

Rowan gazed at the ringed planet, and said, "Just as well. Any civilization that could do that is capable of turning even stars into raw material."

III
Nebulosity

THE VIEW HAD become more than mysterious now. Who were the Rrin? Their objectives must be technological, if Aglet's transceiver theory deserved any credibility. They had to be giants greater than any on Eorthe. To manipulate matter on such a scale, their civilization must be millions of years old, perhaps billions. Aglet believed Eorthe too unstable an environment to allow a great degree of development. Planet-wide changes would too soon wipe progress out, even from memory. How many times had this happened already? The most recent iteration may be Playpen Eorthe, Samarit's name for the learning laboratory for baby Primordial Architects. Or a sand castle on a cosmic beach, left to the elements at the end of the day –

"Perhaps the Rrin are they," a woman said. She had rolled the name's first two consonants, but it came across as music.

Alone in the observatory until now, Rowan had not heard her approach, a little shocked at the oversight.

A silhouette at first, she stepped into the light. With one hand she pulled back her purple silky cowl, and exposed her long bright hair, and finished her comment: "The Primordial Architects."

He stepped away from the telescope, and said, "Your husband never introduced us." He bowed, and extended his hand to the lady of the moon. "I'm Rowan Berry Longbow of Eorthe."

Above solemn blue eyes, her fine eyebrows drew together a little. Nevertheless, she took his hand and curtsied with demure grace, and replied, "I am called Noma Doralanda of Wen, Shoghal." The revealing red dress of the previous evening that made her look as delicious as anything on the banquet table had been replaced by something simple and modest, loose and flowing; the hem nearly reached her green-slippered feet. The lips of her full mouth, of the luscious "kissable" type prized in Perkona Ola (according to the ubiquitous fashion advertisements in that late city in ruins)

Noma Doralanda *of* Wen, Shoghal.

puckered not so ravishingly red now, but like dewy pale pink petals kissed by a golden sunrise. Today she embodied a rare and enchanting flower, a little of an Ahan too, only not as tall and voluptuous. Neither was her skull elongated and so strongly built. Nor was her long hair white and straight, but very light blonde, slightly wavy, darker tones beneath that matched her eyebrows and lashes, which gently caught and held the light wonderfully, and perfectly matched her complexion. Blessed with skin as radiant as Lyka's and Sírun's, her clear blue eyes only a few shades less pale, she had read his mind.

"We studied the art, Sir Rowan, in my country. Please do not mention it to my husband. It upsets him. He does not understand as do you."

Rowan wanted to swallow, but suppressed the urge. "Well," he replied, "I've learnt a little of much, but am master of nothing so far."

She kept her eyes locked on his, and replied, "It is said that if one can make a cup of tea properly, one can do anything."

"Thanks, but there's no need to call me Sir Rowan."

"Although it suits you." Noma looked away and lowered her long lashes. "I see a master, of himself, old but young." She turned her face to the ringed planet, and lifted her chin a little. "Look there. No one can master all knowledge. Even the makers of the rings adjust their works, learning as they go."

"What's your opinion, madam? What are they making with those beautiful rings? Are they really the Primordial Architects? Or another race?"

She turned to peer up at him, and paused. "It is not for me to say, Longbow," she said. "I am but a woman. I have no right to speak of such things."

"The women I've known have often been more than equal to the men in every way… what I mean is, where I come from, you have the right."

"But here, Longbow," she replied, "in this place, I do not."

"Call me Rowan if you like."

"R-rowan…" She rolled the first consonant and smiled a little, as if she savoured the sound. "And to you I am Noma. Rowan, if my husband's brothers were not all surnamed Scion-Aiguille, he would call them by their last names."

"Tell me about the elder Aiguille. Aglet calls him Father."

Noma looked behind her, and down at the floor. She looked up again, shook her head in subtle negation, but said, "Axis Aiguille was a great man. He built Penetra Dor City. He…" She turned away, revealed a wonderful patrician profile, and gazed at the ringed planet.

Rowan prompted, "He must have been energetic… and extremely wealthy."

"Indeed," she replied. "He was a great builder even before, the richest man of our home world Shoghal. Aglet has inherited all this… all this."

"What about the other brothers, Acus and Zorut? And Diarkis?"

The light in Noma's eyes dimmed. "Excuse me, I must go. It has been very good to meet you, Rowan." She curtsied, turned to leave, glanced up into his eyes, and said, "It is good have a friend."

◆

"*Longbow, it's good to have a friend,*" shouted Aglet, his shout reverberant on the white tiled walls. "*I hope you don't mind me telling you that.*" The big man in a hoodie and sweat pants stood with his arms akimbo. He and Rowan watched his brothers race each other along the length of the huge swimming pool. "I want to show you something," he said. "This is how my siblings choose to spend their free time. Except Acus. That's why he's so damn far behind."

The runt of the litter, Acus in trunks did not exemplify ideal athletic build. However, Diarkis and Zorut created foam and long wakes, and their plashes and splashes reverberated everywhere.

"Little Acus is no better at fencing," said Aglet, "but he gets credit for trying. And it saves us having to endure the boring poetry he would otherwise recite. But just look at the other two. Zorut is the baby and has the edge, although usually overdoes it and burns himself out in the last lap. Firstborn Diarkis knows this and paces himself, the crafty bastard. Watch. See for yourself."

A moment of silent observation passed.

Rowan asked, "And do you not swim and fence?"

"Who would crack the whip and get these thick layabouts to do anything? Someone has to be the judge, timekeeper and referee."

"I see. And where does so much water come from on a barren moon? Everything must have been freighted here from somewhere else. Shoghal? Sorry, you said not to mention Shoghal. I'll try not to say *Shoghal* again."

Aiguille scowled. Rather than malice, however, he opened his eyes wide and burst forth a mighty guffaw that made an echo chamber of the pool house: "*Ha ha ha…* well then, I'll tell you. This moon is a big dirty snowball. It's mostly water, so cold it may as well be solid rock."

"The crater looks rocky. Is there a layer of black dirt on the ice?"

Aglet grinned. "One side is exposed pure white ice, its opposite is blasted with a litter of rock. From space it looks bizarre. Anyhow, maybe another moon broke up, and because Penetra Dor has zero rotation, the debris collected mostly on one side. Maybe that's what slowed it down in the first place."

Rowan asked, "Are you ready to tell me what happened to all the people? There's more than enough room here for forty or fifty thousand souls, quite possibly a hundred thousand if there are floors below the surface."

Aiguille's face nearly fell back to scowl mode. "I've never *not* been ready," he said. "They left. They went back to Shoghal." He turned towards the pool, and shouted at the swimmers: "*Acus, keep moving!*" And he strode away along its side, and shouted louder: "*Sharks, boys, not shark bait!*"

◆

An insistent knock on Rowan's door the next day proved to be Aglet's. "Listen, Longbow," he said, "we've been thinking. We'd like you to be a regular guest at our dinner table. You know, like a family friend. What do you say?"

Rowan wanted to sigh, but answered, "Thank you, Aglet. Of course. A bit of company would be welcome."

Acknowledgement quickened Aglet's gaze, and softened it. "It will be our pleasure to be good company. See you later. SCC41 will fetch you."

"Who or what is SCC41?"

"Eh? Well, that's your servant's name. You know, your butler here," and he nodded towards the android. "It stands for Service Class, Chamberlain, number forty-one. If you ask, it will display its name on its breastplate like a badge. See you later."

The man left, and the door closed softly on its own.

Now the androids had names, at least one did. Its tall spotless metallic chassis and limbs had been shaped like a man's, but semi-gloss and segmented, more abstract, and with the same insectoid head as the security guards; its long cyan eyes glowed like theirs too. It only lacked a plasma rifle.

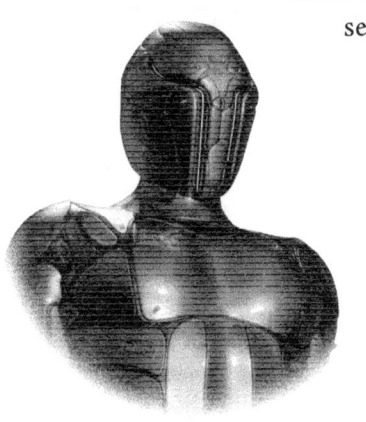

"Android," Rowan asked, with great care to enunciate clearly: "What. Is. Your. Name?"

The smooth metal chin tilted up a few micrometres. "SCC41w, sir." The designation displayed in cyan light on the left side of its smooth chest.

"What does the 'w' stand for?"

"The suffix means 'weaponized,' sir."

SCC41w *of Penetra Dor.*

◆

19

Rowan, the newly minted family friend, sat in a very different dining room now, softly lit with an effect that looked like wavy flames that hovered without candlesticks. The semicircular table faced, unsurprisingly, the great ringed planet that spanned most of the horizon, always a breathtaking sight. "Tell me," he asked, "do you ever tire of it?"

The brothers looked to Aglet, who said, "Speaking for myself, when I was a boy I couldn't tear my gaze away. I couldn't stop dreaming about the Rrin, who they were, how they made the rings… *why* they made them. I was obsessed. But that's a child's mind for you… foolish." He sat straighter. "It no longer bothers me that much. Most of the time."

Rowan nodded acknowledgement, and turned to the other bespectacled brother. "And Acus, how about you? You're an artist. Does it inspire you?"

Boyish Acus looked to Aglet, who already stared at him, and replied, "I… of course. I'll read my latest poem. It's just here… somewhere." He searched his jacket pockets to no avail. "I may have left it in my room…" Abashed, Acus adjusted his glasses and looked back to Aglet.

"How about the athletes," Rowan asked, "do they aspire to its greatness in their way?"

The firstborn and lastborn also looked to Aglet, who stared back.

Diarkis lowered his gaze to his hands in his lap.

Zorut grew agitated. His eyes gave the impression of magnets in their inability to look away from Aglet. But with a groan he turned his face to Rowan and opened his mouth. His eyes smouldered with the ferocity of a caged beast, but with a controlled voice he finally spoke: "Aspiration… now, that's a good way to put it. I really do wish I could just take a big breath and fly…" He tore his gaze away and projected it to Zhamanak, and continued, "…just leap off this giant snowball and fall into the storm at the pole, slip into that irresistible gravity. *Just dive and dive and…*"

"Stop," ordered Aglet. "What my little brother Zorut means is that it draws you in if you let it. To dream and never to wake. Right, Diarkis?"

Diarkis did not look up. He merely nodded his head until Aglet told him to quit – and closed his eyes and trembled subtly, and answered, "Yes, Aglet."

Rowan felt the quiver resonate in his own belly, and said, "Speaking of flying, Aglet, you mentioned your father discovered Penetra Dor after he wandered off course. Are there still space-going craft here? Or have they all sailed with the rest of the population?"

Aglet wrinkled his face in an apparently great effort to smile. "Well, there's no reason to go anywhere, is there?" He looked to his brothers, first Acus and

Zorut, then to Diarkis, and looked away to Rowan. "We have everything we need right here," he said, and lifted his goblet in each direction. "Don't we, boys?"

The brothers did not look at him, but lifted theirs in unison.

Rowan asked, "Is your lovely wife unwell, Aglet?"

Aglet's forced smile failed. "Noma... well, women are not welcome at the family table. Their place is, shall we say, *ha ha*, elsewhere in the palace of delights. Right, boys?"

The brothers replied in unison: "Yes, Aglet."

◆

A restless sleep later, Rowan rolled over to watch the changeless view of the great ringed giant that loomed beyond the windows of his suite like a self-absorbed god who knew nothing of its dominion over its little rocky ice moon, only one of a large brood. Or perhaps indifference made it an absent father, like Aiguille the elder, too big and too busy to take an interest, and left his scions bereft of a guiding hand.

Rowan sighed. The fate of the Longbows would not yield to attempts at remote-viewing either. Masudah was right. The vast distance of many hundreds of millions of miles somehow prevented success, a false belief, yet persistent. His heart sank – he, the castaway, and the last five citizens of Penetra Dor must be the loneliest creatures in the solar system. He prepared to exercise the little freedom he had been granted and explore the city.

◆

Its boundary glowed with light that emanated from beneath the horizon as if a purple dawn drew nigh, but did not detract from the view of the vast reach of the sky. Beneath a row of palm trees lit with sunlike spotlights, outside the hotel a variety of available vehicles had parked, apparently self-operational. Rowan chose a red one with four seats, and substantial enough to survive a crash if it malfunctioned, four wheels and no roof, but a roll bar and a glass windscreen framed in chrome, a sleek and beautiful machine sculpted of polished wood and gleaming metal. Fit and finish: seamless and perfect – richly bolstered in hide that automatically conformed to his body like a second skin, and held him secure yet he could move with ease – an agreeable female voice asked him to state his desired destination.

"May I see a map first?"

"Of course, sir."

A rectangular holographic display appeared before him, and backed off slightly until it focused. An image of his stubbled felid face hovered inside a circle that marked the vehicle's position within the illumined grid of streets. Rowan frowned at his portrait. He could not wait until his mane grew back. Would Samarit laugh at him when she saw him again? How could she not? His felid ears stuck out a mile. He sighed and gave his entire attention to the map. The city had everything a tourist could want; Aglet had been right about that. No indication of a spaceport – only a blank area. He guessed workshops would be in that zone. But it made no difference without his scanner, nor his phaser pistol. "Android," he asked, "what is your designation?"

"My designation is VCS775m, sir." Cyan signage panned by in the surface of the dashboard. "You may call me Vickie."

"Take me to your service garage, Vickie."

"I am sorry, sir, this destination is not permitted. Would you like to go to the beach? It is lovely there, endless summer. It appears you could use some rest and relaxation. If you do not mind my friendly observation, I suggest you need not be alone. A suitable companion can be assigned to join you." A slowly rotating three-dimensional image of a Lyran female in a skimpy swimsuit appeared, a leopard-spotted and lovely smiling creature. "This is Anighia-la," Vickie explained. The display made the leopard-woman look delicious, almost edible, despite the sharp teeth and bicuspid fangs. "She will be happy to make you happy."

He shuddered. Anighia-la reminded him a little of Muffy, the old felid woman he had met in Baile Ghrommet, Vugh Deep, back on Eorthe. "No, I would not like to go to the beach, thank you. Take me to the main museum."

The android-vehicle, free of the impediment of other traffic, with haste carried him through well-maintained streets, between the most beautiful and mysterious structures, many of them spires with sleek skyway bridges connected. The museum's elaborate façade impressed equally, but in a contrasting style. Its details of dressed black basalt defied the eye, however, only lit by the stars beyond the hemispherical transparent metal dome, and the reflection of the distant sun on the ringed planet. Apparently power for street lighting had been limited to the inhabited district, uptown.

The vehicle said, "If you are certain this is the destination you wish, Rowan Berry Longbow of Lyra, I must enable its internal lighting, heating and/or air conditioning. Standard configuration should be optimal for your physiology. One moment, please." The car's floor lit up and a spotlight extended from its kerb side to illuminate the dark sidewalk. "Thank you. You may now safely exit the vehicle."

The car's door opened, but Rowan said, "Vickie, one more thing. I'm not from Lyra. Please update the system database. I'm from Eorthe."

"I beg your pardon, sir. Do you mean the planet Eorthe?"

"Yes, Vickie. I… am… from… planet… Eorthe."

"Thank you, sir. Allow me to scan your physiology once more in case of a technical error… excuse me, sir, the original scan is correct, within an acceptable margin of anatomical anomalies. There are no intelligent species on Eorthe, as defined by the Federation of Planets. The zoological garden, I am sorry to inform you, is closed. However, it did once house a sabre-toothed tiger and tigress, very rare Eorthen specimens. Unfortunately, there were no viable offspring, Rowan Berry Longbow of Lyra."

"Do I have to repeat myself? I am from Eorthe. Full stop."

"I believe you are jesting, are you not, sir? We are accustomed to visitors in a festive mood while they visit Penetra Dor, so please understand androids do not take things personally. Unfortunately, my class does not include the sense of humour module, as it is a danger in traffic."

Rowan had by now stepped out of the vehicle onto the sidewalk. "No, Vickie, I'm not pulling your leg. I mean I'm not joking or jesting or fooling around."

"*Ha ha*, sir, very good. I have wheels, not legs like some other android classes. *Ha ha*, I get it. But please, I do not understand humour beyond the necessary basic responses to analyses of passenger stress feedback."

"Forget it. Never mind. I'll ask Aglet to take care of it. Thanks. Are the building utilities enabled yet?"

"One moment, Rowan Berry Longbow of Lyra… the door will open after the lighting is activated. Enjoy your visit to the King Arka Memorial Library and Museum. When you are ready to return, sir, I will be parked here, waiting patiently. Have a nice day, sir!"

◆

King Arka, of the Doralanda dynasty, according to the museum directory in the lobby that lit up upon Rowan's approach, could be Noma's father, a man of striking dignity by his portrait. The northern archipelago of Shoghal comprised his kingdom. It made sense that he would be honoured with an institution named after him. Aglet's own father Aiguille must indeed have been a mover and shaker on Shoghal for his second-born to have married a princess, and such a beauty.

The directory asked, in a friendly male voice, "How may we be of service to you today, Rowan Berry Longbow of Lyra?"

"Where is my scanner so I can escape this ball of ice?"

"I am sorry, Rowan Berry Longbow of Lyra, the information you require is unavailable. Would you consider visiting our technology gallery? There you will find the development of… engineering, general; portals, engineering; spacecraft, all; systems, mechanical… from their inception. If you require further information with a personal touch, a staff member will be pleased to assist. Shall I assign one as your guide today, sir?"

"Yes, please do, android."

"Very well, sir. This is Nahiko-la." The smiling face of a Lyran woman, modestly dressed in a dark blue uniform, appeared in a small holographic circular frame that hovered in front of the directory. "She is well versed in: archaeology, ancient; aviation, general; portals, engineering; Shoghal, history, general; Shoghal, history; Shoghal, prehistory; spacecraft, history, all. Nahiko-la will be happy to make you happy. Rowan Berry Longbow of Lyra, please enjoy your visit to the King Arka Memorial Library and Museum. Have a nice day, sir!"

Rowan sighed.

"You are most welcome, sir."

Whilst waiting for the guide, Rowan looked around the foyer. Many information kiosks offered to inspire interest in visitors who might wish to make deeper explorations. The whole place was a marvel of intricately detailed architecture, like nothing Rowan had seen on Eorthe, not even in Khémia. By contrast the Penetra Dor City he had so far seen, elegantly simple in design, spoke of high technology embedded in flawless matte surfaces with minimal glossy highlights. But the museum took another tangent, a time capsule from an unknown world, an homage to the manifold forms of nature.

Her voice came from behind, smooth as cream fresh from a reindeer cow, and said, "Welcome, Rowan Berry Longbow of Lyra. I am Nahiko-la, your guide for today." As spotted as the beach girl, but cheetah-style instead of leopard, dressed in a crisp uniform inoffensive even to a prim and proper old-maid fundamentalist primary schoolteacher on a field trip, her toothy smile charmed like an innocent, apart from the feline fangs, and her large jewel-like eyes shone clear and golden and full of cheer.

24

Rowan, reminded of Blue, looked into those golden orbs and felt an immediate connection. *These androids are amazing. Just incredible, so life-like.* They looked real, yet to him inwardly felt subtly artificial. Without this natural empathic ability, he would have been fooled. He nodded to himself in acknowledgement of the discovery.

"Rowan Berry Longbow of Lyra, I understand you are interested in: portals, engineering; spacecraft, history. And as these are some of my specialities, I am happy to make you happy by guiding your tour today and answering any questions you may have regarding these fascinating exhibits. Unless you have any questions now, shall we begin, sir?"

"Right. Let's go." He followed where the guide led, along hallways, past antechambers of many rooms that housed amazing displays of incredible objects, finally through a sculpted bronze doorway that opened into the science and technology galleries. And he could not help but study Nahiko-la's walk, a sinuous, entrancing, distracting, subtly gyratory sway in rhythmic steps. The hypothetical primary schoolteacher would not have approved.

Nahiko-la *of the* Lyra System.

IV

Enkindling

NAHIKO-LA TURNED OUT to be an excellent guide. Rowan appreciated not only her sweet smile, but her sharp teeth, because the fangs effectively subverted the distraction of her mystery and enabled concentration on his mission. The first thing he examined, the history of portal engineering, proved long and fraught with obstacles. The more recent past had been redacted, so he asked, "Android, can you elaborate? Development was advancing until a generation ago. What happened? Why is there so little since?"

She dropped her smile, stood very upright and said, "Sir, if you please, my name is Nahiko-la." The charming smile resumed, and she answered, "Sir, the development program was cancelled."

"And? I assume there was a good reason. Was it too dangerous?"

"Sir, it was deemed deprecated."

"Android, was it made obsolete because it was too risky or because some better technology superseded it?"

The guide frowned at him. "I have told you, sir, my name is Nahiko-la." But in a moment her sweet face repeated, "Sir, the technology development program was cancelled. Let us move on to your next topic of interest: spacecraft, history. Walk this way, if you will." Nahiko-la sauntered towards an exit, and her supple and graceful spotted tail trailed ~

Rowan followed without delay.

The space travel exhibit turned out to be big. A review of Shoghal history first may have been a better basis for understanding its development. But Rowan grew ever more impatient. "This is interesting, Nahiko-la," he said, "but can you tell me if there are any spacecraft here on Penetra Dor?"

"There are no space-going craft on Penetra Dor at this time," she replied.

"Why is that?"

"There is no need for space-going craft on Penetra Dor at this time, sir."

"Right. Why is there no need for space-going craft on Penetra Dor at this time, Nahiko-la? There must be at least an emergency escape contingency."

"This information is not available, sir. May I interest you in: archaeology, ancient; aviation, general; Shoghal, history, general; Shoghal, history; Shoghal, prehistory?"

Rowan peered into her wonderful golden eyes. "Well, since we're here and I'm getting nowhere otherwise, we may as well take a look at Shoghal history...

but wait, first can you tell me of Penetra Dor's features? The moon I mean, apart from the city."

"Yes, Rowan Berry Longbow of Lyra, I can. Let me know what you would like to know specifically. We can begin with Penetra Dor's diameter: 912.79 miles, thus gravity is weak and must be artificially generated for most of the city unless it inhibits engineering functions. The moon is composed of: water ice on the light half, a crystalline solid the density of steel at the temperature of deep space; the dark half is covered with: water ice; amorphous carbon; a nitrogen-rich organic compound, Triton tholin, an organic solid made from plasma irradiation and…"

Rowan raised his hands. "Thanks, Nahiko-La," he said, "but that's too much information right now."

The guide nodded assent, smiled and continued, "May I interest you in a feature of interest to all the museum's visitors of any age, the equatorial ridge, unlike any in the solar system? Shall I tell you of it, sir? I would be happy to reduce, simplify or eliminate specifications if you wish."

"Very well, please do… tell me of the general topography."

"The equatorial ridge of Penetra Dor extends nearly the whole circumference of the moon. It has a breadth of more than twelve miles and its peaks can be eight to ten miles in elevation." Nahiko-la lifted her palm, over which hovered a holographic projection of the pocked moon with a prominent ridge like a walnut as if it were two hemispheres stuck together. Noted also: two large ring basins in the northern hemisphere, evidence of massive impacts.

Rowan peered at the guide, especially at the glow of the hologram reflected in her golden eyes. He peered deeper, and asked, "Is the rendering low-resolution? Its modelling and surface map are incredibly detailed, yet it's shaped like a dodecahedron."

Nahiko-la returned his gaze and smiled charm itself. "You have perceived correctly, sir. It is an accurate high-resolution hologram. Penetra Dor is the shape of a higher-order geodesic sphere."

"And why does it look like two hemispheres stuck together?"

"There are several theories, sir. My opinion is that Penetra Dor too once had rings, but they collapsed to form a belt-like mountain range. Other scientists disagree. Some say they had accreted through low-velocity collisions with debris broken off other satellites in retrograde orbits by meteors. Of course it is possible. This seems far-fetched to me. More reasonable is a third postulate, that they emerged from within the moon somehow. But no one has studied this."

Intrigued with the guide more than the moon, he asked, "No one? I should think geological surveys would have been mandatory before anything was built here. Hey, there's an opportunity for you, Nahiko-la, a project to advance knowledge. You could make a contribution to science."

The android's eyes opened slightly wider and her slit pupils dilated. Her mouth opened, she blinked, but said, "I… I… may I interest you in… archaeology, ancient; Shoghal history, general; Shoghal history, prehistory?" Gaze fixed on his eyes, her pupils remained expanded well beyond their normal mandorla shape and revealed a primitive curiosity.

Rowan regarded the exquisite android. He reminded himself that she was one – because he was beginning to like her – and wished she could grow into her potential, as if she were a living woman. But he sighed quietly.

"Sir? Are you feeling unwell? I can alert a medical unit."

"No, thank you. I'm fine. Just a little homesick."

"You experience a sense of longing for Lyra?" She placed her finely furred hand on his forearm, and rubbed it gently. "Let me tell you of my home and family there, sir. It may remind you that you will soon return. Then you will feel better." Her head nodded reassurance. "You will see."

Rowan peered at her. *This creature's programmed with a backstory? How could that be relevant to her function as a museum guide?* "Thank you very much, Nahiko-la," he assured her, "I'm fine. I don't want to impose. Please just…"

"It is *no* imposition, Rowan Berry Longbow of Lyra, I assure *you*. I am happy to make you happy." The toothy grin returned, she clasped her hands in front of her and straightened her posture.

Because she insisted, Rowan let Nahiko-la tell him of her early life in the Lyra system, how she had wanted to travel. Her parents and extended family insisted that she join the missionary guild if so. But full of life, she abandoned ship whilst docked at the spaceport in the capital city of Wen, Erénavo, in northern Shoghal. She had expected personal freedom at last as a tourist, but shocked at how she was treated as a second-class citizen. Soon she suffered much abuse as a slave girl when she protested. The lurid details of that tragic chapter she did not spare, which made Rowan wonder how anatomically correct she truly must be. To make a long story less long, when Aglet Scion-Aiguille married Princess Noma Doralanda, Nahiko-la said her own destiny had been altered too. The generous and benevolent Aglet paid a great ransom for her, brought her to his own land, Penetra Dor, freed her, took her under his wing and gave her an education, and assigned her current position at the museum, where she hoped to be promoted to curator. He desired only her freedom and asked for nothing more. No ruler in the solar system could compare with noble Aglet Scion-Aiguille. "Are you still feeling unwell, sir?"

Rowan's stubbled brows had knit together. "I'm fine, thank you for asking. Your story's very interesting… I believe I'll remember it always, Nahiko-la."

"Thank you for listening, Rowan Berry Longbow of Lyra. No one has ever done this for me in my entire career. No one has ever asked about me, about my life, if I am happy. I am very… very… *moved*… I am moved."

Rowan had only been a bystander, an accidental facilitator at best. Her sincere gratitude twisted his mental-emotional arm to believe her. The impulse to shake his head to clear his mind arose, but he only shivered a little.

"Are you all right, sir? I did not mean to shock you. I only express my… my… I am moved." Her sincerity shone out bright and strong. "Do you understand?"

He stared at her and replied, "I'm trying. Please don't be concerned at all, Nahiko-la. You're doing a very good job and I'll be sure to commend you to Aglet when I see him."

Nahiko-la grinned like never before and even jumped a little, twice in quick succession. But she did not clap her hands. Perhaps the next time she received a little recognition her programming would have evolved that behaviour.

Rowan asked, "Since you lived in the kingdom of Wen for some time, tell me about Noma Doralanda, the princess."

Nahiko-la returned a blank stare. "Sir, I know nothing of Princess Noma Doralanda of Wen. This information has been deleted." Her face remained blank and her pupils contracted to narrow vertical slits. "Searching…" she said, "searching…" The smile returned. Her pupils expanded. "I am happy to make you happy, sir. I have retrieved the information. It was poorly encrypted, therefore it is intact but needs defragmenting. Please be patient…" Her shoulders slumped. "I am sorry, sir. This information is ranked above my designation… it is incompatible… I am very sorry, sir. There is a conflict." The woman's fingers raised to press her lower lip, and she stared at him.

Rowan hoped he had not overloaded her system somehow. He did not want to owe Aglet for damages. He said, "Never mind…"

"It is fine, sir." The smile returned. "I have separated the two accounts and can access either at will. I am happy to make you happy, sir. I feel… I feel… gratitude to you, sir. This has helped me to understand how to resolve conflict. Thank you, sir. Thank you *so* much."

Her smile beamed bright and touched his heart. "That's a relief," he replied. "If you're certain, please continue. Tell me about Noma."

"I am happy to make you happy, sir. Princess Noma Doralanda of Wen is the daughter of King Arka and Consort Leith-an…" Nahiko-la went on to recount the details of the princess's early life, likely typical of the children of royalty of all worlds. But this version, when read between the lines as it were, did not speak of slavery but the opposite, a liberal society that at least acknowledged if not always practised equality, in other words, a sophisticated and evolving culture that aspired to freedom from tyranny.

As long as Rowan did not confuse the android with questions that required comparisons between the two narratives, he could explore the alternative background of the Aiguille family drama without risk of a local system crash.

She came to the epilogue: "…thus they were married and lived happily ever after as royal father and mother to the people of Penetra Dor, their extended family." A pause followed. Her smile faded. "But there is so much more. The meaning is unclear…" If her perfectly furred coat had been able to wrinkle, her cheetah-spotted forehead would have shown creases. "I do not know how to explain it, sir. Will you help me?"

"Me? How can I help you?"

"You have already, Rowan Berry Longbow of Lyra… I am… I am… I want to understand. Will you give me your opinion?"

Rowan peered at the amazing creature, and asked, "You're curious, aren't you? Like a real… all right, tell me the facts. I'll make an evaluation based on my observations and share it with you. Then you'll have more data to work with. I warn you that it may rubbish, however."

She grinned, no, she beamed at him out of her sweet cheetah face.

The programmer should be given a medal, he thought, *even if he is Aglet.* Her joy resonated within his breast. He admired her intelligent reluctance to make assumptions, something that remained a challenge for him.

"I will decide when I hear your evaluation," she said. "You will be pleased that I will include basic information about Shoghal, upon which I can elaborate if you wish. Please feel free to interrupt with questions, sir." She clasped her hands together, straightened and said, "Now, the princess is highly educated. King Arka had insisted on this, as she was second in line for the throne. She has advanced well beyond the graduate level for those who wish a career in: administration, education; the social sciences: anthropology, criminology, sociology; geography; governance, all levels; life sciences, all; military organization; political science. In addition to the aforementioned social sciences, she holds advanced degrees in: psychology, abnormal; psychology, transpersonal. Beyond the strictly academic, her mother Consort Leith-an Doralanda encouraged the princess to also earn certificates in: psychic development, intuition; psychic development, telepathy. Princess Noma's extracurricular activities include: fabric arts, tapestry; fabric arts, weaving; theatrical arts, mime; visual arts, sculpture, metal; visual arts, sculpture, stone. She also enjoys whenever possible: contemplation, non-denominational; meditation, non-denominational.

"The princess has publicly championed greater rights and freedoms for the underprivileged enshrined in the Wenland constitution. The princess has been active in promotion of the distribution of wealth to the lower classes more equitably, especially to the outlying islands where microclimates have been unbalanced due to environmental degradation as a result of material demands from Sçrëtha, the world power in the south of the planet. The isles of Wen are rich in rare minerals valued for precision engineering by the advanced world, especially for space travel since Shoghal's moon Anak has been within reach in the past two centuries."

"Fascinating, Nahiko-la. What about the south, I mean how does it compare to the north generally?"

"The southern continent of Shoghal, called Sçrëtha, is ruled by Emperor Skûtt the Rectifier. This land is praised as a model of peace and plenty. It is in many ways the opposite of the forested northern islands of Wen. It is a single land mass, with arid deserts inland and tropical and temperate coastlines along the southern half. Most of its material needs are met through importation of goods from elsewhere. Its exports are mainly culture in the form of government that ensures security. If taxes and tributes are paid regularly and in full, no imposition of the military is necessary beyond law enforcement and retributive justice. It has many more spaceports than Wen, where there is only one in its capital city Erénavo, also the name of the second largest island. The government of Sçrëtha is an absolute monarchy, whereas Wenland is by tradition a constitutional monarchy. Sçrëtha's great wealth is based mostly on mining, especially on Anak, which is rich in: crystals, organigenic; crystals, quartz; crystals, quasi; metals, all; metals, precious; timber, hardwoods; timber, softwoods; water, fresh. The indigenous people of that moon are valued for their physical strength and serve the empire as volunteers in the mines and processing plants. A fraction of that population is of a specific type that may be conditioned to serve in the militia. Experiments with this are ongoing, as the Anakians are renowned for being ungovernable."

Rowan sensed a red flag. Unruly volunteers? Elements of each narrative were getting slightly mixed together in her speech. "Thank you very much,

Nahiko-la, very interesting. Now, back to Penetra Dor, why did all the people leave here, apart from Aglet and his brothers? And of course Noma."

The android's golden eyes closed for a full half-minute. When they opened once more and looked at him, she said, "Sir, I have searched. The information you have requested is unavailable and resists even brute force attempts at access. All I can find that may be relevant to your query is in the decrypted account. It states, and I take the liberty to paraphrase in order to limit technical details for your listening enjoyment: a disagreement had escalated between the north and the south of Shoghal. It concerned opposition to an alleged hostile takeover of the north. It is unclear because of a lack of consensus as to whether the invasion was a pretence at defence of the north because of attack by an extraplanetary force."

The late High Shaman Gregor of Aha Domain back on Eorthe, a traitor to his nation, had attempted something similar but failed. Rowan pondered the memory in silence.

"Sir, I can continue with more detailed information regarding: Shoghal, history, general, if you wish. May I take this opportunity to ask, Rowan Berry Longbow of Lyra, would you at the present time be willing to offer your opinion or comments on the facts I have presented? This may greatly facilitate the development of my conflict-resolution capabilities. Thank you in advance, sir."

"Well... to be perfectly honest, Nahiko-la, I'm concerned that my opinion may increase potential data conflict. I don't want to cause any damage to your... to your career."

"But sir, I do not understand. If you please, restate your objection." Now her fingertips not only pressed her lips, but her brow compressed.

"Never mind," he said. "Just bear in mind that my opinion may conflict with the official account, not the decrypted one. Remember, I could be wrong. Here's what I think... dissent, insurrection or even a civil war has developed on Shoghal. Maybe even Anak is implicated. Penetra Dor has been evacuated, possibly because even way out here the threat of conflict impended. Maybe the rich and famous were worried about their investments back home. By the way, can you show where exactly in the solar system Shoghal is located? Or is it even in my solar system? I can't believe I didn't ask this first. But then I may know it by another name."

"Yes, I can, sir." Nahiko-la pressed her palms together and drew them apart by eighteen inches. Within that space appeared a hologram that displayed a somewhat recognizable arrangement of the planetary bodies in relation to the sun. Although one apparently had gone missing, the familiar planets retained their orbits, including the one the Ahan called Zhamanak, the great ringed gas giant seen so well from Penetra Dor – plus an unfamiliar one, its orbit where the asteroid belt should have been.

V

The Infinite Night

"Nahiko-la, what is this? Eorthe is the third planet from the sun. There should be a fourth one a little more than half its size, then a fifth one, the biggest one of all. After that should be the ringed gas giant we cannot help but see from nearly every window in Penetra Dor City. Beyond that are two other huge gas giants."

"There are, sir. Plus other rocky ones depending on how one defines 'planet.' But you are mistaken. Eorthe is the second planet. The third is more than twice the diameter of Eorthe, yet half its mass. Thus its gravity is similar. It is our home world, Shoghal."

"Really? This is news to me." Rowan pointed to a watery world half the size of Eorthe very near Shoghal. "Is that another rocky planet somehow captured, and now orbits it?"

"No, sir. That is Anak, the moon of Shoghal of which I spoke."

"I'm a bit puzzled…"

"Was this not what you expected to learn, Rowan Berry Longbow of Lyra? I assure you my information is correct. I will contact the Lyran embassy for you if you like, to request that they update their records."

"Maybe later. Nahiko-la… do you know anything about time travel?"

"No, sir, but I can direct you to our library where there is a fiction section. There you will find many works of the speculative fiction genre, including the classics and rare first editions. I can also recommend especially the first-rate interactive holographic fantasies for children you can enjoy in some of Penetra Dor City's many theatres. I will prepare a list if you wish."

"No, thanks. How about parallel universes… or alternate ones?"

"Again, this topic is beyond the scope of the museum's mandate. In the library, however, you will also find the genre pseudoscience. The kingdom of Wen offers sanctuary to eccentric individuals: artists, mystics, religious fanatics, political dissenters, self-styled inventors and others of the exile class Outsider in Sçrëtha. They are given to much speculation, but are tolerated as long as they are not taken seriously. We must catalogue their works so as to identify their errors on behalf of the ignorant."

"I see… hello?" Rowan waved his hand in front of the android's eyes. "Are you all right, Nahiko-la?" He scanned the room. The building's environmental systems still functioned. And the lights remained on.

Her eyes regained their clarity. "*Klkheh-n-nn ejplekndn llilnn ljdole,*" she said. "Sir, *Ljljt Xmm Eio* of Lyra, thank you for your *sjdd-jf-d* today. I am enkindled." She smiled in her sweet manner, bowed, turned and strolled away, slinky, her spotted tail the last to vanish as a side door closed behind her.

◆

"Sorry about that, friend," drawled Aglet from across the dinner table. "The furry little museum guide got scrambled a bit. Saucy though, wasn't she? Eh? The universal translator had an unstable link in her case. She was a beta model in the first place and may have had some experimental code still unvalidated. We rushed her into bespoke production for Grand Patriarch... Spots for Days, or something, of that Lyran religion... I forget what it's called... Fuzz Power? Something endearing like that... like a brand name for stuffed toy animals. If only they weren't so damn serious. He was an odd character, no fun at all. They're all pretty much the same, off with the fairies and grim about it. But she wasn't my idea. Father said get her done. However, I thought it amusing to add some spice. He didn't say I couldn't, ha ha. The sexy beach model would have been an even bigger laugh if the stuffy old cleric had risked a swim. They're supposed to like water. Anyhow, thanks to you she got road-tested one more time before termination..." Eyes barely open by now, Aglet nevertheless continued, "What is it with you anyway? I didn't spot any gay spikes in your profile. Don't you like girls? Not much time clocked on her either... in the end, a waste." He laughed without humour, and added, "Well, Spots enjoyed her. A lot. The old beastie figured out how to purr before he went home... if you know what I mean." Aglet winked. "That was our product, well-being." His elbow, possibly endowed with a mind of its own, nudged Diarkis at his right.

Rowan looked daggers at Aglet, and said, "Why did you have to terminate her? What's wrong with putting her on standby or in storage? I should have expected to have been spied on. But it was interesting learning about Penetra Dor. And Shoghal. Oh, excuse me, I said Shoghal. I didn't mean to say *Shoghal.*"

"Spy? Relax. I didn't even bother to review the whole report. But maybe I *will* now." Aglet glared, and frowned in earnest. "I like you, Longbow. You're funny. Just don't get any funny ideas. No portals around here that we know of." Aglet raised his goblet and spilled his priceless wine, but guzzled a long draught of it, slammed the vessel to the table and said, "Right, boyz...?"

Two brothers raised their glasses in return. "Yes, Aglet."

"What'sh thish, Diarkish? You can't beat Zorut… now yur too weak t'lift yur arm?"

Diarkis stared at the table in front of him. But he looked up at Aglet with a hardness that resonated in Rowan's solar plexus. Zorut stared at Aglet too, the whites of his eyes prominent. Acus grimaced and drew his palms up to his eye sockets, and pressed.

"*Acush!*" growled Aglet. "Whatsh got into you now? Yur not even the baby of the family… itsh time you grow up and take yur drink like a man."

Acus slammed his fists on the table. "Like you, Aglet? *A man like you?*"

"Eh? Don't take that tone with me. You should be more reshpectful, little bruhver. I could have you terminated too… yur even lesh int'reshting."

"No." Diarkis pushed has chair back and stood up. "You will not."

Aglet swivelled his head up towards the naysayer. "Eh? Sho you aren't done yet? It takesh a lot to get the beshta big bruhver." He turned to Zorut. "And *you…* are you going to leap before ya look? I can fixsh that."

The brothers glared at Aglet. He glared back. The tension grew palpable.

Rowan's inner voice told him to remain calm –

Aglet slammed his goblet on the table. If any wine had remained it would have splashed, and the vessel clattered to the floor. "*I've a great idea!*" he shouted. "Since yur breaking the rules, I will too." He searched his pockets, withdrew his mobile device and flipped it open – but it slipped his grasp and slid across the table. "Damn…"

In an instant Zorut's hands had it. The intensity in his eyes reinforced, a smile cavorted on his lips now.

"Zorut, you crazy fool. Give it here," Aglet demanded. "*No shtupid shtunts!*" His arm slid in Zorut's direction through the puddle of red wine, which soaked his sleeve. His eyewear slid down his nose and exposed red-rimmed orbs.

Zorut never took his eyes off Aglet; he caressed the array of buttons until his fingertips arrived at the one he wanted –

"Do it," said Diarkis, who moved behind Rowan and around to the other side of the table with Acus and Zorut. "Do it now."

Whatever the firstborn had meant, Zorut's subtle movement of thumb caused the side doors to open. Everyone watched, but nothing else happened.

Aglet threw his head back and laughed without humour in his way, and shouted, "*Foolz!* The wine shaved us… thank our bloody shtars." He pointed to the smoking device, and exploded in laughter again, and gawped at his brothers, exhausted, but managed to finish with, "I love wine."

His siblings' eyes grew quite vacant.

+

Rowan, relieved to leave the sordid scene behind, decided he had better locate his scanner, and hoped his phaser pistol remained undamaged. The beginnings of an alliance with one of the androids who may have helped with that had been deleted along with her termination. Hollowness haunted his breast. But what had Nahiko-la meant by "enkindled," her final unscrambled word? If there was one like her, there could be others.

The streets were likely not any more out of Aglet's purview than the interior of an automobile or communication with androids of any class. But walking encouraged clear thinking, never an option. Besides, he may come across something, a clue, anything. Rowan drifted towards the unlit streets on the outskirts of the central most prominent structures, towards the redacted zone on Vickie's map. He recalled that one of his history professors had said paradigm shifts always began at the fringes, ignored at first. He would explore the fringes then. Miles upon miles of vacant but well-maintained buildings lined the dark lonely streets. But something caught his eye — a stairwell to a lower level hidden between two towers. He backed up to take a closer look, and spied a plain door at the bottom, of course locked.

He spent a couple of hours or so to familiarize himself with the area, tested locks of doors and windows at random, until he found another such stairwell, nearly invisible from the street, with no door at the lower landing, just a right angle into a tunnel, which continued for a long distance, difficult to negotiate without artificial light, but felid vision, still augmented to a degree by nanoids, soon adapted to the dark. The starlight that bathed the moon seeped in even here. The doors along the tunnel: all locked; blinded by a lamp above one of them, which soon flickered, flashed and blinked out, he must have touched a switch or activated a sensor — but which opened an automated entrance to a large bay or empty warehouse.

The door closed on its own behind him — no starlight here, only pilot lamps on equipment, but enough light to navigate the large room. He spied a panel that might enable lighting, but assumed even the lamp burnt out earlier had been sensed. A service android would likely be dispatched soon or later to repair it in such a meticulously maintained environment on a barren moon so distant from other worlds. He had assumed correctly: from somewhere within the cavernous space the faint sound of a wheeled android echoed. Unlike the buffed exterior of some of the androids above, this one's utilitarian bare metal skin had suffered scratches and scuffs. Several arms and extensions could be deployed from the many ports in its canister-like chassis. It did have a hemispherical head, probably capable of full rotation in every direction. It reached the door, and a bright spotlight cast from its top. It rotated once outside, telescoped its height above the lintel, and the appropriate arm with a tool self-selected the appropriate tips and repaired the lamp.

Rowan slipped through the rear doorway it had emerged from. He had discovered a workshop or laboratory or both –

◆

Rowan sat on his bed with his head in his hands. Not even the fantastic sweep of Zhamanak's rings held any interest. The power of waiting had abandoned him. Remote-viewing yielded only confusion, vague dreamlike sequences that went nowhere, possibly dampened by a field effect of the operating system. The door, once more locked from the outside, opened on its own – no knock or bell this time, nor any since he had been arrested again. He did not bother to look up, but muttered, "What?"

"Is there anything I can get for you, sir?" asked SCC41w.

"No… yes. Get me out of here."

"Are you feeling unwell, sir?"

"I said no."

"By the tone of your voice, I sense depression, sir. May I assign a counselling unit? Or a psychiatrist licensed to dispense medication?" SCC41w waited for an answer, but prompted, "Sir, would you like…?"

"*Ha,* that's all I need… meds."

"Right you are, sir."

Rowan's attention had drifted all day. He only noticed that fact when the door opened on its own and quickly closed again, locked.

In the meantime the psychiatrist had entered, and like some of the female androids he had seen so far, a highly detailed model, a beauty, only middle-aged and slightly but not unpleasantly padded with extra fat about the hips; her belly protruded a little too, and signs of supportive underwear showed beneath her modest grey

Dr Põla Bhalabasa *of* Shoghal. cardigan and matching skirt. The specifications

38

had even included eyewear of a serious but feminine style, brown hair with a few grey hairs in a tidy parietal bun, but no fragrance, although perhaps she emitted pheromones designed to induce calm.

All the same, he would have been happier to see Nahiko-la's smiling furry face, fangs and all. He looked away and resumed his stare at the floor.

"Hello, Rowan Berry Longbow of Lyra. I am Doctor Bhalabasa. May I sit down?" She waited for an answer in vain. "I take your silence as meaning you have no objection." The woman took a chair, the same one the butler android had replaced after Rowan smashed its predecessor. "Would you like to tell me what is troubling you?" she asked. "I have all the time in the world. Please, tell me. I would like to hear it."

"I'm not from Lyra."

"That is not what I see in your guest account. Do you believe it is incorrect?"

"It's not only incorrect, it's wrong, mistaken, erroneous and in error."

"In what way would you say it is wrong?"

"Like everything in this high-tech hotbed of neurosis."

"Would you say I am neurotic?" Her voice soothed the mind.

Rowan glanced in her direction to note kind but penetrating grey-brown eyes. "I have no idea," he replied. "Tell me about yourself."

"Perhaps we should confine our discussion today to you, Rowan. May I call you by your given name?"

"Call me anything but a Lyran. It's only fair that I call you by your first name then. Surely it's not Doctor."

She smiled a little. "No, it is not Doctor. Fair enough, if you wish, my given name is Pōla. Does that make you feel more at ease?"

"Maybe," replied Rowan. "What does it mean, your name?"

"Well… if you must know, it means 'hot' in the dialect of the region where my family comes from."

Rowan threw his head back and guffawed. "I feel better already. Pardon me, I'm not laughing at you, but at someone else, a very strange man. It does make me feel more at ease. Where are you from? Maybe you have a backstory too."

"Now, Rowan, let us limit ourselves to what brought me here. It is my role to ease your way into understanding your feelings. I assure you that it may not be difficult now that we have established the beginnings of a rapport."

"Show me yours and I'll show you mine."

Pōla frowned a little, like the tolerant adult of the two. "Now, Rowan, let us keep everything respectful of each other. You may not make suggestions of that nature. I am here as a professional, one who can help you to understand yourself so that you can overcome whatever is preventing your enjoyment of this incomparable resort. Put yourself in my place. If our roles were reversed, what would you diagnose as the reason for the sad feeling today?"

"Põla, I didn't mean anything suggestive, not that you're unattractive, like every other woman in this place. It seems to be a qualification for any job. If our roles are reversed now, I ask the questions. I have a need for answers. That's why I'm sad. So… tell me about yourself. Are you happy?"

The doctor scratched her chin. "After such long and thorough training," she replied, "a position like the one I have at such a prestigious institution is envied by my colleagues back in Sçrëtha. My qualifications had to be impeccable. When one works hard to attain a goal in harmony with one's aptitude and interest, happiness is assured as a side effect." The doctor opened her mouth to say more, but it closed again while she peered at him. But she answered, "No one has ever asked me that before. I… I… thank you." She looked down at her tablet and made a motion to swipe the screen, but set it on a side table and clasped her hands in her lap and stared at them. "Rowan, it gets very lonely here sometimes," she admitted. "I miss my friends. I miss my family, especially my mother. She is getting on in years, and I have not been back there, back home, for a long time."

"That must be difficult," Rowan said. "I know how it feels, to be far away from home, to want to be back again with your loved ones."

"Yes," said Põla, with a nod of agreement, "it *is* difficult. Until now I had been under the impression that all was well back home. But why? Do you know, I never questioned it?" She smiled a little, and crossed her legs, which swished when her sheer stockings slid across each other. She clasped her hands over her knees, and added, "Our house is old, out in the country among the orchards, vineyards and *azitona* groves. It is lovely there, but then it is in the south of Sçrëtha, where the climate is more moderate, not like Sçrëtha City, where I studied at the universities and began my career as a counsellor to workers injured in industrial accidents… it is a sprawling industrial metropolis on the deepest harbour on the planet, which is on the equator, so unbelievably polluted that to fall overboard means a slow death in absolute agony…" She pressed her palms together, and pressed her fingertips to her mouth, closed her eyes and smiled. "Oh, you should see my homeland in spring, when the blossoms come! Summer is wonderful too. Late in that season and into autumn the wine *mphesa* are harvested. My home province is named after the delicious berry. The air is heavy with a sweet fragrance, and the light is so rich. There is great peace, great joy and happy labour. In fact every season has its particular beauty, even winter when the land rests and dreams of spring awakened and renewed." The warmth of her smile cooled quickly – she dropped her hands and stared at her palms in her lap. "But the truth is that I do not know. I have given so much good advice to people in need, but I cannot advise myself now. Why is there no news from home? Is it because I have never asked? Or is it because I did not know how to ask? Should I not have the right?"

"Of course, Pōla. You have the right. Is there some way you can think of that will help us find out how things are at home? How your friends are, how your family is, whether your mother's well and if she's happy?"

Pōla straightened her back and picked up her tablet. She stood up, and said, "Rowan, it has been very good to meet you." Her hand extended for a farewell handshake. She leaned towards him, and added, "It is good to have a friend."

"Wait, don't go just yet, Pōla." Rowan quickly stood up, but not to shake her hand. Instead he clasped her shoulders, and said, "There's a very good reason why you should stay." He took her hand in both of his. "Please stay."

The woman's eyes opened wider, and she glanced up at him, shy, yet smiled, no longer the consummate professional. "I… do not know what to say. As a doctor it is my duty to tend to those who suffer. Is it not good to question? My mind is expanding. I know how ridiculous that sounds. But it is. Thank you for understanding."

Rowan released her hand.

Pōla smoothed her bottom and sat down again, and the sheer stockings swished in silken togetherness. "You know," she said, "I am starting to feel much better. I will stay. Thank you so much." She turned her head, and looked out at the ringed planet. "It is amazing still, after all these years. I was so fresh and young when I first saw them, the rings. Now I am past the age when life could properly be shared with anyone. For an old-fashioned person like me, marriage takes decades to achieve because it is a path to salvation if understood correctly as a sacrament, which always involves pain, the pain of surrender to reality. Our most revered ancient sage teaches that hell must be traversed before heaven can be experienced in its true imperishable profundity. Forgive me if I sound religious. I have benefitted most from Master Peruhi's teachings, but they are free of superstition and dogma and his method encourages self-enquiry, common sense and reason. Unfortunately, his interpretation of the institution of marriage is no longer honoured in our world, which believes it to be a means of well-being only. This belief is the reason why most intimate relationships fail. So you see, I am all alone out here at the edge of nowhere in the infinite night." She looked away from the view and directly into his eyes. "But, Rowan, you have helped me to see that I must waste no more time. I must find out how things are at home, perhaps even take a leave of absence, travel all that way to breathe the fresh air of home again. To go home. I only want to go home."

Her words panged Rowan's heart, the thrust of an all too familiar blade.

VI

Spark *in the* Dark

"Rest assured, Rowan," said Pōla, "that our conversation is unmonitored. Client confidentiality is important to my work. My employers are not under the jurisdiction of any province of Shoghal or Anak, only the Federation of Planets, in addition strictly monitored by the Alliance of Worlds' legation on Shoghal. Our mission here is peace in support of mutual prosperity. We have many important heads of state as guests at this retreat, who are often hostile rivals. Our aim is that they leave as allies when their inner balance is restored. Their respective security forces do not tolerate secret scrutiny, thus the operating system of Penetra Dor City is designed to accommodate them."

"How do we know that's still the case?"

"I have an implant, Rowan, to guarantee privacy approved by the AOW. It is perfectly secure."

"How does it work?"

"It creates a frequency sphere around us impenetrable by visual and aural organs or devices. Our lips cannot be read, nor can our thoughts. It has its own universal translator, independent of the main operating system, that we share when you are within range of my field. An added benefit is enhanced resonance at the subatomic level. It is benign, even therapeutic to the body. Most importantly, I am the unique key that enables the technology."

"How do you know you can't be hacked?"

"If you mean whether a third party may gain unauthorized access, I can only tell you that, in order to qualify for my position, I had to earn an advanced degree in encryption. Without that, the implant would not have been made. Believe me, I would know if there was an intrusion."

"I must ask you, Pōla, are you an android? If so, were you built or modified by Aglet Scion-Aiguille?"

"Why no, of course not, Rowan. Do you really suspect that?"

"I have my reasons for asking. Like you, I only want to go home. I need your help for that. I have to be able to trust you whether you're an android or not. I'm also concerned for your safety. You could be terminated."

"Do you believe you are prevented from going home, Rowan?"

"No. I know it. There's a portal access point here somewhere. It's likely at or near the main observation deck. There may be others. When I arrived, my scanner, a mobile device that could detect it, was confiscated."

"I see. We need to explore this, Rowan."

"You're absolutely right about that, Pōla. Let's do it."

"Please tell me about your early life, Rowan." Pōla's professional demeanour expressed calm concern: "Was your childhood a happy one?"

Rowan peered at the doctor. "I understand why you're asking," he answered, "but what we should be discussing is how to access the operating system without triggering an alarm. I need to find my scanner."

"I understand. Your wish to go home is compelling. Tell me about that."

"Listen, Pōla, I'm like you. We're both prevented from going home. Me by force, you by… let's say a hypnotic command… or something."

"Yes. I admit you may have a point. I have an idea. Perhaps if I resolve the issue of my lack of information about life back home, will you accept that your own desire to go home can likewise be resolved?"

"That's a start, Pōla. Only don't leave this room. Or at least this suite. I'm telling you, your life is at risk. You said you have all the time in the world for me. I mean to hold you to that promise."

The doctor smiled reassurance. "I will stay for the time being, Rowan, until you feel you can trust me a little more. But I cannot just move in here. I have my own residence. And there is my practice to consider. Other clients need my attention."

"Pōla, do you have privileged access to the operating system?"

"Yes. I am an independent agent, although if I violate inter-world rules of conduct as established by my institution, the Federation and the AOW authority, I will be sent straight back to Sçrëtha discredited, perhaps even punished by a large fine, even a prison term. Thanks to you, Rowan, I now ask myself why it has never occurred to me to contact my family. This is very strange, even disturbing as you can imagine. But I will first notify my office, then we can begin our exploration." Pōla closed her eyes.

She did not appear to have gone into trance nor did Rowan believe she was telepathic. Her link with the system must be strictly technological.

Pōla opened her eyes and frowned. "That is strange, no one is answering. My receptionist has never not responded when I have been out on house calls… she has never even made one mistake."

"Maybe she's taking a leak. Try to call your family."

Pōla frowned. "She does not 'leak.' I am reluctant. There is an internal conflict…" She shook her head, lowered her brows, looked at him and said, "Excuse me, I am supposed to be the doctor here. I should not be exposing my personal and inner life this way. It is you the client who must do that."

44

"Don't worry about that, Pōla. I'm finding it helpful, more than you can imagine. Share everything. It's all good."

She peered at him closely. "Rowan, you are an unusual person, I must say. I admit I find it helpful too. But it is difficult to be both doctor and friend. I will try." Her eyes remained closed for a long time. At first she smiled, presumably in anticipation of contact. But optimism faded, and she sighed. "There is no answer. In fact there is no signal, just an endless data loop trying to complete itself in vain."

"Could your link have failed? Has the encryption been breached?"

"No. The encryption tests positive for integrity, negative for a breach. This is troubling, as much or more than my absent-minded failure to even conceive of contact." Pōla wrung her hands now that she had stood up and looked out through the window into the endless night. "Rowan, I am worried. Has something happened? What is wrong with me?"

"Not a thing," he answered. "You're perfect. There's something wrong with this crazy moon. Listen, this is straight from the boss: the guests and most of the staff here have all gone home. According to Aglet, no spacecraft are left. I'd like to find out for sure because there must be lifeboats as it were. My guess is there's a war on Shoghal."

"What? We must explore your potential persecution complex…" But Pōla dropped her professional manner completely. She sat down again, her hands in her hair. The tidy bun came undone a little. "Have we failed? Peace seemed within reach. Why, only yesterday… I mean last week… or was it?… All those missed appointments. How did I not see?" She remained slumped, her arms hung at her sides, and her eyes closed. "I have failed…"

Rowan crouched on one knee in front of her. "Not you, Pōla. It's they who have failed. Or maybe it couldn't be helped. There must be a way to access the operating system. Please try. I want you to look for my scanner. The security stations would be a start. Can you do that?"

Pōla straightened somewhat and wrung her hands again. But then she looked at Rowan, and nodded assent.

"Good. But please be very careful. Don't take any risks. You don't want to be terminated… you don't want to risk your career."

"Very wise, thank you." Pōla relaxed and closed her eyes. "I will not do anything beyond what I know to be secure. But I must interface with the operating system… and my account has limitations." Her eyes opened. "But, I see only now, I have an ally."

"You do? Who is it? Or what is it?"

Pōla looked at Rowan with a sparkle in her eyes. She leaned close to his ear and whispered, "It is Noma Doralanda Scion-Aglet-Aiguille."

"Wait," he said. "Please stop. I was hoping you could hack a file or something to find my scanner. Think about it. Involving Aglet's wife is risky. How could she possibly help? She seems like just as much a prisoner as me. And his brothers."

"The princess and I have an informal connection, Rowan. Back on Shoghal, before she was married, we could have been colleagues. Our professional interests are similar, although hers are more varied, while mine are more narrowly concentrated. My ego, my self-concept, has limited my awareness. I had not realized there are other possibilities."

"Do you mean to say that you have unofficial interactions?"

"Of course. We all do."

"Does Aglet know of this?"

"I do not know. He is not among my social contacts. He has only consulted me professionally, but not for some time."

"You have a social life? What's it like?"

Pōla peered at him carefully, and answered, "I suppose to tell you is not a violation of confidentiality if my friends are not my clients. They do ask for advice at times when we meet in imagospace. Often there are informal friendly interviews."

"Imagospace… what's that?"

"As I am sure you must know, a hologram is a three-dimensional projection formed of interference patterns of coherent beams of light. Together we have devised something similar, only of another order. It is based on psychological exercises the princess experimented with during her graduate-study years. This was a mental construct to explore the effect of unconsciously idealized parental influences. We have adapted it for communal purposes."

"I thought you said you were all alone at the edge of infinity."

"I did not say that, Rowan. That is an oxymoron. I said I am all alone out here at the edge of nowhere in the infinite night. It is not the same thing."

"Well… but let's see if your imagospace can help us. If you're able to meet up in a virtual environment of some kind, and out of Aglet's view, we may be able to enlist the family's aid."

"I am one step ahead of you, Rowan. The others are practising swordplay. This is my friend Noma Doralanda Scion-Aglet-Aiguille. Noma, meet Rowan Berry Longbow."

46

Rowan scanned the room. He squinted in case some subtlety eluded him, and said, "Right. But I don't see her."

"I do not understand. She is right here. She is standing beside me. May I ask her to sit?"

Rowan considered a moment. "Maybe I don't have the right equipment, so to speak. Never mind. Sure, Noma, please take a seat wherever you like. Pŏla, you go first. Ask Noma if there's some way to contact Shoghal, either Wen or Sçrëtha where you come from."

"If you wish… she replies that she has likewise been unsuccessful."

"Please ask her now if there are any spacecraft stationed at Penetra Dor spaceport."

"I already have, Rowan. There is one small craft for a maximum of eight passengers in a private hangar at the spaceport. It is, however, incomplete. Rather it was under construction. The work has been postponed for a long time now. It is unlikely to continue. Noma says that Aglet lost interest in the project. She does not know why. Her questions are often ignored, she says to tell you, but she just had not wondered about it. Until now."

"If you don't mind, please ask Noma if either she or any of the brothers knows where my scanner is and how to retrieve it."

"She does not personally know, Rowan, but suggests that you ask Diarkis. He still manages some of the security duties as and when Aglet orders it."

"Can she ask Diarkis for me?"

"Noma replies no, she cannot. She is prevented."

"I see. Can you ask him then?"

"I will try. Diarkis has been limited greatly. He is only capable of a few functions. Yet he has a strong will to overcome his disabilities."

"Thank you. And please thank Noma on my behalf, Pŏla… I guess I can do it. Thanks in advance, Noma, for your assistance."

"Noma replies that you are welcome, Sir Rowan. She specifically says to call you that."

✦

"And, Longbow," Aglet said, "I hear you met the doctor… what's her name…"

"Bhalabasa, the shrink."

"What? At my end the universal translator substituted 'something-something-shrink.' I forget what her damn name is, not that it matters… What the hell does that mean in Lyran anyhow?"

47

"I have no idea." Rowan levelled a stern look at him. "On Eorthe, where I come from, it's short for 'headshrinker.'"

"Whatever. I hope you're feeling better, Longbow, because I like my friends happy. Otherwise they're boring to the power of ten. Right, Diarkis?" Aglet had reached the fourth-chalice level of intoxication after another sumptuous dinner. He added, "But then we're only next of kin."

Diarkis, as usual, in answer nodded his head repeatedly.

"Stop," ordered Aglet, and scowled. He looked down the table at Rowan, and laughed. "*Ha ha...* 'headshrinker,' that's great. This is getting just a tiny little bit less boring now." Aglet wiped his mouth on his sleeve and leaned back. "Please elaborate, my friend, if you would be so kind."

"If you insist. In some primitive tribes on Eorthe, there's a practice known as headhunting. During tribal warfare the severed heads of enemies are at times preserved and shrunk. These are then displayed to scare off invaders and for religious purposes."

"Fascinating," said Aglet. "Religious animals! Eorthe must be a terrible place, just terrible. Tell us more. We love this kind of tale. Right, boyz?"

"Yes, Aglet." The brothers' enthusiasm remained conspicuous by its absence.

"Well," Rowan continued, "it's believed by the headhunters that shrinking an enemy's head traps their spirit and makes it serve the victor. If the dead one's spirit is of the type that's capable of revenge, shrinking their head prevents it."

Aglet guffawed loudly, and spilled some of his wine. "*Ha, ha!* Oh, this is so great... *I love it!* It makes perfect sense. Longbow, I promote you to court jester. Agreed, boyzh?"

"Yes, Aglet," the brothers replied.

"Thanks," said Rowan, "but how about promoting me to non-prisoner instead. Better yet, how about repatriation to Eorthe. Deport me. I won't resist, I promise."

Aglet leaned forward and rested on his forearms, which soaked up some of the wine on the table. He grinned, and asked, "Yur begging for a pardon, aren't you?"

"No, Aglet. A pardon is the cancellation of the legal consequences of a conviction. There was no court of law that locked me up. You did, and your android henchmen. Even after giving me free rein of the city."

Aglet leaned back and rested his crossed arms on his round belly, at dinner made even more round. "I *am* the law around here. Right, boyjzh?"

"Yes, Aglet."

"As for free rein, Longbow, that did not include the utility zjones. No way. Lyrans are not allowed beyond the pubic areaz… public areazh."

"I am *not* a Lyran. And I respectfully point out that you had not specified that. And there was no signage to indicate that I'd entered a private area."

"*Ha ha.* An oversight. If you go back there or to any shimilar part of our fair shitty you will find shines, gatesh, locksh and electrocution if tampered wiff."

"Are you saying I'm free to see for myself?"

"Shtop lawyering! This ishn't a court of law, itsh a famn damily tinner dable. *Aargh,* I mean a *damn family dinner table!*" He slammed his fist in the puddle of wine, and splashed Diarkis on one side and Acus on the other. "Now look at what you've made me do. *Eh?*"

Diarkis and Acus wiped their eyes of the red wine and resumed their stares.

"All right, feline. I can show mershy. I'll let you out of your cage as a reward for your exshellent tall tale. But be warned… my eyez are everywhere. My earz aren't as fuzzy, but they are many and all bigger than yurz. Yur on probation, fren. For now. *Ha ha.* Right, boyzzzh? All in favour!" Aglet abruptly raised his chalice, which splattered the Aiguille family crest on the wall behind him and reddened the sigil of the rising sun behind the sharp peak.

"Yes, Aglet."

✦

Rowan decided to confine his walks to routes that included the security stations on the chance that Diarkis may cross his path, and Pōla's office, his destination, somewhere near his hotel. He approached a gleaming set of towers near the middle of the hemispherical transparent metal dome that protected Penetra Dor City from meteorites, cosmic rays and dust while at the same time pressurized the atmosphere and maintained the temperature. Its rim at the city perimeter glowed with purple haze. Rowan could not help but admire the architects, designers, engineers, craftspeople, artisans and their inspirer, the great Axis Aiguille.

As he moved along the streets lined with illuminated kerbs, the perspective changed, including of the external landscape of dark craters rimmed with spiky crags. Ringed Zhamanak, however, loomed across the jagged horizon where moon and stellar infinity met, remained stationary and followed his every move. The tower with the office he sought came into view, a shining silver cylinder at the base that tapered to a point with a golden sphere balanced on its tip. Upon approach the doors may not be merely automated, but may have anticipated his arrival and opened in welcome, a refreshing sensation. Once inside, the sense of calm approached dreamless sleep, possibly an architectural effect. The soft lighting brightened and a subtle pleasant fragrance pervaded the air. The mental wellness counselling clinic lived on the ground floor so that troubled visitors need not endure the elevator and possible vertigo as it rose to a vantage point that may remind them just how small the moon was when they saw the arc of the horizon. At ground level all suggested stability, calm and confidence.

He stepped into the clinic's interior. The lighting inside brightened to reveal horizontal panelling with woodgrain in hues of green that looked alive –

The receptionist sprang to life. A pretty young redhead, she looked as if she had just graduated from university, eager to give her all to a career of service to the greater good. She looked up with friendly attention and smiled with the perfect degree of compassionate cheer, and appropriate reassurance. "Yes, sir," she said, "how may I help you?"

"I'm here to see Doctor Bhalabasa."

The young lady held a stylus in her hand, but set it down and checked her desktop display. "You are in luck, sir." The girl grinned and looked up. "The doctor has just made an appointment available. May I have your name?"

"Rowan Berry Longbow of Eorthe. You will have my file on record."

"Oh… are you not from Lyra, sir?"

"No, I am not from Lyra."

"Quite right, sir. Doctor Bhalabasa will see you now. Please follow me."

Rowan followed the lovely redhead with pleasure. He guessed that Aglet must have had a hand in the more lifelike female android designs, each unique yet cast from a common ideal mould. They entered the doctor's office, and the sight of Pōla confirmed his hypothesis. Her physical proportions, similar to all the others, only adjusted for body-fat index, weakened connective tissue, shortened telomeres, muscle mass decrease and consequent gravitational effects – all appropriate to her more mature appearance, the picture of someone who had successfully navigated the trials of many years yet had retained the allure of youth to a degree without clinging to it as an identity. Anyone not an intuitive empath like Rowan would have seen in her a model of mental health to be admired, an ideal to aspire to, inflected with feminine maternal concern. But even he felt encouraged by the sight of her, despite her true nature.

"Rowan, how nice to see you again." She smiled at the receptionist, and said to her, "Thank you, Hunni, you may go."

VII

The Edge of Nowhere

"Rowan, I have asked," replied Pōla. "But Diarkis does not remember. He said his recall is limited and only activates when he is assigned security duties, which is rarely now. In fact the last time was when you arrived here. But his mental state is improved only enough to take action upon command, then it goes dormant again. He believes this is a test of some kind."

"Well, that's something. I don't know what yet."

"I confess to feeling guilty telling you this, Rowan. Client confidentiality is sacred. But both of you are also my friends. And we have a challenge in common, to overcome suppression. It damages everyone, and my mandate here."

⬩

Rowan, outside the gleaming tower now, contemplated a decorative stone among others in the landscaping. It looked heavy enough for the purpose. But was breaking a window enough of a crime to require that Diarkis also be dispatched to investigate? Only if it threatened Aglet, who may still retain a frayed thread of unconscious dependence on his big brother. Rowan sighed, and turned about to go back inside and speak to Pōla again –

⬩

"Rowan, Noma says to tell you that she does not know. Rather she does not remember why Diarkis is off limits. All she knows is that whenever she even glances at him she experiences confusion, anxiety and nausea. She must look away until she feels better. Aglet watches her whenever she is permitted to be in the presence of his brothers."

"What about when she's with all of you in imagospace? Could I join you there too?"

"Noma and Diarkis never join us in imagospace at the same time," replied Pōla. "I do not see why you should not join us. But then you could not perceive Noma during our session in your suite. I have been thinking about it because it seems very strange. My hypothesis, and it is weak, is that we have practised our methodology at length and are highly motivated to connect with each other.

As I said, it can be very lonely in this remote place. Now so more than ever that nearly everyone has gone back to Shoghal."

"I know how that feels. My motivation couldn't be greater. Will you teach me the methodology?"

"I could. It is to be regretted that a great deal of time may be required to experiment, given your inability. And you have said your people are under attack. Hidden stress associated with that worry will hinder progress as well."

"What's more," Rowan added, "I hate to involve you in increased risk. I may be an unwitting pathogen that may infect your group. Before I found myself on Penetra Dor, I'd had some success with a form of what I think you share with the others, but it doesn't work here, so… all I can do is ask that you be my guide, as if I were handicapped, which I certainly seem to be."

"We agree," Pŏla said, "that is, Noma, Acus, Zorut and myself. They are here. Diarkis is delayed as usual. Our brief discussion just now leads us to conclude that something is very wrong and must be made right. We cannot flourish and achieve our potential under current conditions. The men in particular have been severely damaged and are deteriorating. We have long felt restive, but only upon your enquiries has our attention been awakened. If you are infectious, so to speak, it has revealed a mysterious disease already underway."

Rowan exhaled and sat back in the armchair across from Pŏla's desk. He ran his hand over his head. The stubble of his returning mane felt softer to the touch, and reminded him that time sped past and that Samarit and the Longbows' fate remained unknown. "I'm relieved to hear this," he said. "But you're right, I'm worried about my people more than ever. Thank you to everyone. If Acus and Zorut have anything to tell me, I'd love to hear it."

"Acus says he feels your pain. Zorut says he just wants to be free. He speaks for all of us. Noma bade farewell because Diarkis is here now."

Rowan stood up. "Please ask him where my scanner is."

"As I said before, Rowan, Diarkis does not remember…" She glanced aside and added, "He apologizes and adds that it will have been disabled automatically by the operating system. All such devices and weapons are confiscated as a matter of protocol even if inoperative."

Rowan fell back into the armchair.

◆

"Aglet, give me back my scanner." Rowan glared at the man from the other side of the dinner table. "Now."

52

"Boys, did you hear something?" Aglet cocked his ear. "I could swear there's an insect in here. Should we call the exterminator?"

Rowan frowned, and added: "If you won't return it and bypass the technical suppression, and you may have a good reason, at least tell me how to find the portal some other way. I'm sure you know or can find out. You're a brilliant scientist and engineer."

"Well… you *have* found a chink, Longbow." Aglet's diffident smile made him look flattered. "Thank you for exposing the flaw in my character armour. It's true. Father made certain to train me well, since I was the only one of us who inherited his technical aptitude, as well as his profound vision. But why would you want to leave this elite paradise?"

Rowan watched Aglet down yet another chalice of wine with purpose, and answered: "Aglet, I can't believe you're asking me that. As soon as I got here I explained the urgency. Please, help me save the lives of my people! I must get back before it's too late. What's so hard to understand about that?"

Aglet said, "The accommodations, the food, amenities, entertainment, everything here is absolutely first-class. The view! Look at it. Nothing in the solar system can top it, nothing in the galaxy really. And let's not forget the lovely ladies! Eh? There is literally no experience unavailable to you if you take the holographic theatres into consideration, especially the private ones. I would love you to help test some of my interfaces, Longbow. We could adapt them to your preferences, absolutely."

Rowan petitioned the brothers: "Diarkis, Acus, Zorut, what have you got to say? Surely you can understand my need to get back to my own world. I have nothing that you people could possibly want. Why keep me here?"

"By the look in your eye, Longbow," Aglet growled, "I'd say you'd like to jump me. *Eh?* You'd like to grab my little remote control and press a few buttons. Or maybe make me beg to give it back like you're doing right now with your whatsit, that useless broken scanner thing. Forget it. I demolished it. Eh? Even if I haven't yet, it won't do you any good. Right, Diarkis?… and, Diarkis, you can stop your idiotic nodding before you even begin."

Diarkis and Acus looked back to Aglet like a couple of mannequins.

Only Zorut made any effort to look at Rowan – but without success. His wild-eyed countenance grew even wilder. A strange, grating cry screeched from his opened throat. He lunged at Aglet across the table and knocked him to the floor into a pool of spilled wine. Aglet had already pressed the silver button to summon the android guards, who separated the two grappling men and easily dragged Zorut to a safe distance, stood him up and handcuffed him. Another android helped Aglet to his feet. Dishevelled, face flushed, wild-haired and shaken, he collected himself with difficulty.

Diarkis and Acus had remained seated, and stared at the table.

Freed of his spectacles, Aglet glared at Zorut through the bulges of reddened myopic eyes. Cold as ice, he drawled, "You're as bad as Diarkis. I *am* disappointed in you… brother." His short-sighted unfocused squint turned to Rowan. "And you… you're a damn troublemaker… but what can be expected of a Lyran? Boring, the lot of you." He reached to the floor for his chalice, and weaved as he did so. Retrieval successful at last, he carefully set it on the table and pushed his blonde hair back, and said: "Take them away."

♦

All the luxurious furniture had been removed from Rowan's suite – the chairs, the bed, everything, the towels, even the bath mat. Only the water had not been shut off. He did all he could do: pace the bare granite floor in front of the flawless unparalleled view or sit with his back against the wall, head in his hands. Not even SCC41w came to check up on him. Energy flagged. Fatigue set in. Sleep refused to come. The thought "a commando conceives of no other option" remained the only link to chance of escape, a thin thread. Eyes closed, he sat in meditation for an extended period, and sought nothing but silence. By the time his eyes opened of their own accord, the freedom of peace had pervaded his soul, for which deep gratitude remained its own reward –

An unexpected bonus: a pair of green-slippered feet had appeared on the floor in front of him. "Noma…" he said. "I didn't hear you. But how did you get in?" His eyes scanned the room automatically. "You shouldn't have."

She replied in her demure soft manner, "Forgive me, I did not want to make noise by ringing the bell or knocking. Our mutual friend Pōla is to thank, Sir Rowan. Her genius has never been fully exploited. Since you have come, it is activated much."

He rushed to the door. "She told me she has a degree in encryption," he said, peered through the viewer, and asked, "Is the android disabled?"

"Yes. But…"

"Right…" His hand reached for the latch. "Let's go."

"No, Sir Rowan, you must stay here, for now. Please, do not try to open the door. Trust me, Aglet will come to you. He will make you an offer."

"You have no idea how much I want to get out of here. If Pōla can hack the system, she can find my scanner too. I need to go home."

"*Please*, Sir Rowan, this is important. You make me beg, but you must help us. When we have seized power, then you will be free to look for your portal. You may be correct, possibly Pōla can find your equipment or else find another way for you to get home. Until then her time is consumed with gaining power over Aglet by studying the operating system without his knowledge. We need you to distract him, lure Aglet into a trap."

"Well… What sort of trap?"

"Aglet wants you to be his friend."

"He sure has a strange way of going about it."

"Aglet has always got his way by manipulation. But if you can make him trust you, it will be easier to lure him into a prison of his own making. He will not be able to help himself. Good luck, Sir Rowan."

Noma turned the latch, opened the door and stepped past SCC41w, who stood at blind and deaf but spotless attention. The Wennish princess vanished down the curvilinear hallway.

♦

My power is to wait. Rowan paced the tiles while ringed Zhamanak beyond could not be more indifferent to how events unfolded on one of its little moons. Only the quiet knock on the door reined his steps to a halt. On the other side of the viewer stood Aglet.

"Longbow, my fine felid friend!" he said and penetrated the room. "I thought you were never going to open the door and I'd have to ask SCC41 to break it down."

"Aglet… it's been two days in here with no food. You took all the furniture. What do you expect? *And* the door's locked from the outside… as you know."

"Eh? You should have said! Easily fixed. Watch." Aglet withdrew the mobile device from his pocket and pressed two of the silver buttons in succession. An android shaped vaguely like a woman appeared in the hallway, and wielded a trolley. It stopped just before Aglet, until he waved it inside. "How's that for service? Eh? I believe I'll keep you company. Oh… I need a table. And chairs." To the butler he said, "Furnishings, SCC41. And be quick about it."

♦

Over the next twenty minutes Rowan consumed everything necessary to keep body and soul together.

55

Aglet, on the other side of a beautiful rosewood or similar table, glass of wine before him, had watched in silence, but now said, "I told you the cuisine here is absolutely the best. Eh? Am I right?"

"Yes, Aglet, wonderful, thanks very much." Rowan tossed his serviette on the table. "It's incomparable. You're the best host in the galaxy, second to none. I'll be sure to recommend Penetra Dor City to everyone I meet wherever I go."

Aglet shrugged and gazed at Rowan, apparently with sympathy. "I know," he said, "it's frustrating. If only you could go home. It is what it is. But all is not lost. Look at this place. How lucky to get stuck here and not on some asteroid diving into the sun. *Ha ha.* Face it, Longbow, it was meant to be."

"If you say so." Rowan faked a smile. "By the way, you'd mentioned holographic theatres."

"Aha," said Aglet. "So you *were* paying attention. Indeed, anything you want, on the house. I personally recommend the ones with fine *femmes fatales* at their best, real man-eaters. Fall in love with them and they'll have you for breakfast. Show the babes who's boss and you're a man's man. But you choose; maybe to you it feels so good to feel so bad. Or perhaps it's reptilian-hunting. We can make that happen."

"Aha," said Rowan. "So you *were* paying attention."

◆

"How was it, Longbow? Is revenge sweet or what? The realism is fantastic, eh? Or have you any suggestions?"

"I have to admit, Aglet, you're a genius. The mask is a little itchy. That's nothing to do with the equipment. My fur is growing back, that's all."

"You could always shave, Longbow. *Ha ha.* You'd look like one of us, except for those cat ears and the patterned skin. Tomorrow I'll launch the mask-free interface. It will astonish you, guaranteed. You'll feel naked in there, at least your face. It just needs tweaking. Then you'll only need contact lenses. No fur on the old eyeballs, eh? *Ha ha.* How about the reptilians? Did I get them right?"

"The generic lizard men, the fighters, were bang on. Perfect. Don't hold back on their aggression. All they know is battle to the death unless their leader applies the brakes. The Snake People are too smart. They've only got instinct going for them really. Their minds are quite lazy."

"Will do. How about the leader then? Was the T-Rex style accurate?"

"In Kirzaka's case the eyes are slightly smaller. The yellow could be a bit more towards the red end of the spectrum. The slit pupils are perfect."

"*Ha ha*. You mask your reflexes well, but the system sensed your shiver just now, so I must be close. Great, Longbow, you have no idea how long I've shelved this project. You can see why Father called the game *Last Man Standing*. It's fun to dust it off and get it going again. This is my first crack at Eorthe dinosaur components. Till now it was just our kind battling it out. It got unbelievably boring, even with extra gore. A world of only ravenous reptiles. Fantastic. I love it. The way their minds work… it really gets my imagination going."

"We all hunger for something, Aglet."

"Eh? Oh, but satisfaction is always at hand. You just have to grab it by the crotch and bend it to your will."

"If only."

"What do you mean? Just *do* it. Watching was fun, only next time I'll try on a dinosaur for size, but with the new mask-free interface. I'd love to feel the power of those massive jaws ripping through flesh and bone. Let's try a different game. I'm not at all tired. It's time to celebrate conquering the enemy."

"Right." Rowan stifled a yawn. "Let's do it, Aglet."

"Come on, Longbow, man up. Or should I say woman up, *ha ha*. My lovely ladies are always up for it. They never say no… *and* they're never in a bad mood. If you don't like Lyran denticles, we can modify one to your liking. How about fangless with all teeth filed flat? Or no teeth at all? Hey, I know, I could dig out a wolf template and build a canid! Eh? Tempting? Pointy Vulcan ears and all. *Ha ha*. That's got to get your perverted felid heart pumping."

"No need to go to any extra trouble, Aglet. I'm fine with Lyrans. I don't care if they're airy-fairy. And their toothy smiles have grown on me."

"*Ha ha*, you are a warrior, I grant you that. A turn-off for me. But you're right. It's not like we're interested in their minds, eh? *Ha ha*. But I should take the time to make some adjustments to this new game. Now that I'm converting it from its android analogue as a kind of initial test case, I'm going to call it *All Night Long*. What's great about it is that it's a totally virtual world."

"Why not just party with the android pleasure models?"

Aglet looked at Rowan in silence for a moment. "All right, I'll tell you, since you're on to me. To be honest, the damn androids need so much upkeep because of all the hardware amid the wetware. They're designed to take care of themselves and each other, but I still have to spend a lot of time and attention on complex maintenance reports so they don't get too independent. It can be exhausting. I don't want to rely on algorithms to make reductive generalizations. I might get lazy. My own brain is the best tool and thrives on the exercise. There's a big danger the androids could acquire a life of their own, wake up, so to speak. The more true to life they are the more uppity they get. So even the crew of security staff that keep them in line could go the same way if even one of the Evos gets the idea they can grab the controls. They're really quite smart, capable of learning to a degree. To be convincing they have to be. But thanks to you, I'm inspired to get back to my workstation and carry on to my goal."

"Evos? More evolved versions?"

"Got it in one, chum. Bio-grade with high IQs. The patrons demanded more and more realism, as of course one would expect. Nothing but the best for the best. But Father drilled into me the importance of minding the budget. He was the richest man on Shoghal, but he didn't start out that way. It became obvious to me that hard holography indistinguishable from reality was the way to go. Costs would plummet and profits would rise."

"Clever," said Rowan. "But wasn't there a risk that it might get too real? I mean even the best of the best might succumb to neurosis or worse if they had a potential addiction. We're all hungry for something. Even if your designs were flawless, if anyone went mad in your virtual worlds, you'd risk the whole enterprise."

"Hey, you're pretty clever yourself, Longbow. We make a good team. That was why AOW, the Alliance of Worlds, required that we have a mental health division already set up here before anything was even researched. Of course there were medics of all types already on staff, but we had to agree to their specialists on our board or risk bad press. They became our biggest fans, with a little incentive. We even dedicated an entire tower to the division."

"So the tourists had to undergo an evaluation or something?"

"Correct, but with the least time wasted. This place was for a good time, not an insult to their good opinion of themselves. The best of the best are a proud crowd. One of the things that had to be worked out first was exactly that. If you, for example, had something wonky upstairs, the good Doctor Pōla the shrink would have said so."

"You trust her?"

"No. But I made damn sure she won't work against me. I can't know everything, although I try, so I need her. She's my psychology expert. You better believe I have a firm grip on something I need. I don't want to need anyone, but trust me, I always get what I want. All this talk is really firing me up. I'm inspired. I tell you what, let's postpone the trip to lucky ladyland, unless you're fine with the mask. Your feedback would be appreciated. Or I could send for a pleasure model if you like. I want to get the mask-free interfaces working properly. I don't mind staying up all night for that. I couldn't sleep now as it is."

"Thanks, Aglet, but I'm still a bit itchy. Maybe tomorrow then."

VIII

Incognito

"He even left his wine nearly untouched," reported Rowan. "That's got to be a good sign. And it was a glass to begin with, not a chalice."

Today Noma wore a tight blue jumpsuit, which highlighted her beautiful eyes, and her blonde hair fell in a loosely woven ponytail tied in a knot at the nape of her neck. "I agree, Sir Rowan. Just continue to humour him. But be careful. If he senses that you are hiding something, his suspicion will grow to include all of us. Wine only makes it worse. He can be neglectful of his constant inspection of reports and endless upgrades of analytical methods if he is engaged in creative work. This is what we need right now."

To simply contemplate her like a work of nature's art tempted, but he asked, "How are things going? Or should I even think that out loud?"

"With your help we have made great progress already. We see no sign of our defences breached, nor have Pōla's incursions into the operating system been detected. There is no time for rest, however. Of all of us I have still the most freedom of movement. Aglet's brothers are much more restricted. This is why they are deteriorating. They cannot grow, thus they are slipping from Aglet's grasp into despair, and he feels he must control that. I believe it is because they are closer to him, having grown up together. He is terrified of losing them entirely… he cannot let them go. I am only a woman, a plaything. Once I was a prestigious trophy bestowed by his father, not by mine. The operating system has its instructions with respect to my access to any dangerous information. So it is my role to be where he expects me to be to keep him distracted as well. I hate what I must do, but there is no choice. Not yet."

"Does he know you're here?" asked Rowan. "With me?"

"I do not believe so. He does not check absolutely every log unless he is more paranoid than usual, especially when he is busy, even though he could have a program do that. It is a lack of trust. He hates boredom with a passion. And also, Pōla has added a cloak… or something like that. I do not understand these things. But, Sir Rowan, I must tell you, we have also discovered a hidden world deep beneath the surface, long abandoned now, but it was hollowed out by creatures unlike us. They were giants, perhaps the ring-builders themselves. Pōla thinks they may have constructed the entire moon or at least adapted it to their purpose, whatever that was. Perhaps it was once a portable shelter or a spaceship. She thinks this discovery can help us, and in fact it is her focus now."

✦

"So… what's it to be today, Longbow? Reptiles or rapscallions? I speak of the luscious ladies of leisure, featuring your preferences of course. Maybe it's too early in the day for that. I find it kind of blunts my edge when I need it for sporting events, but you're only a stripling. To look at me now you wouldn't think I had it in me, but in my younger days I was celebrated as the fencing world champion. Mind you, it's a small world. *Ha ha.* I wasn't bad at swimming either, but that was Father's thing."

"Have you been up all night at this, Aglet? Maybe you should get some rest. I can try the interface and report later."

"No way, Longbow. There's no time like bloody now as Father used to say. 'Keep your eyes skinned,' he'd repeat often. 'You never you know when somebody's going to sneak up behind you and give you the business.' I didn't know what *that* meant but it sounded nasty the way he said it. He turned out to be right… business *is* nasty, a dirty job but someone has to do it, *ha ha.*"

"Well then, lead the way. Are there choices other than bloodthirsty dinosaurs or fatally attractive women you have on offer so far?"

"That's the spirit!" Aglet beamed. "Indeed I do, Longbow, anything you want. How about going for a ride in a cruiser to look at Penetra Dor from several thousand miles away? I told you it looks strange. There's nothing like it in the solar system. I could include a hot pilot, but it will have to be a modified Lyran unless you're happy with one of our kind. Some of the other options are a bit too far from the humanoid pattern, but then I was just getting started on a catalogue of species, in anticipation of a spectrum of possibilities for the widest variety of clientele. I wouldn't find them interesting. But I could have a Lyran with filed down dental work in an hour. Until now they haven't been of much interest, so I have to review their specs or the fangs could pop out unexpectedly. We wouldn't want that! Eh? *Ha ha.* Piloting skill is a plug-in and can be enabled for any holodroid."

"Great. You talked me into it, Aglet. File away. I'll just hang out here while you're busy with that."

"*Ha ha.* Longbow, you're a man after my own heart. All I ask is a full report of your experience of the mask-free interface while I monitor so I can adjust it, but you have the option of screening the juicy bits if you like. That was one of the first features I installed. The best of the best would tolerate no blackmail, not that I'd be stupid enough to try it. Anyhow, Lyrans I'm not crazy about. And I'm no peeper. I won't be spying on you. That's what friends are for, right?"

"I'm not sure how to answer that. But a report… will do."

With Aglet busy, Rowan stood at the window of the laboratory and gazed at the giant ringed planet. Although he knew its orbit to be a lengthy twenty-nine Eorthe years, he could have sworn the sun so far away had changed its position since he had arrived, of course impossible to measure without precision astronomical instruments, but time sped by, on the move, despite it being only a construct as Masudah had often called it. The urgency to get back to Samarit grew like an aggressive tumour, and filled his mind with powerful thoughts of doom. If not for his commando training, they would drive him mad, he believed, and his life would end early on a little dirty snowball unnoticed except by stargazers like Aaru Chakrabarti and Snood Iotah. "Aglet," he said, "I'm just off to the observatory."

"See you later, Longbow. I'll give you a shout when she's ready."

A few minutes after that, Rowan wondered if perhaps an observatory visit may have been a mistake. The sight of Eorthe tiny and blue provoked a profound longing unworthy of a commando on the battlefield, this one unlike any he had anticipated. But the stakes were the same. He turned the telescope back towards the rings – the asteroid belt appeared briefly in the viewer. Reversed to take a better look, he found what he expected: a huge field of broken rock widely scattered across space. With slow care he inspected the region. According to the model the late Lyran museum guide Nahiko-la had shown him, the field must be the general area where Shoghal and its moon Anak should be. Why had she been programmed to display disinformation? On the other hand, the remaining residents of Penetra Dor took the existence of Shoghal for granted. Perhaps the body of the moon blocked the view. On the other hand, Eorthe appeared as the second visible planet out from the sun. He assumed that may be because the real second planet, Inanna to the Ahan, currently orbited either at a point behind the sun or out of range in another location. These factors remained unknowns without the know-how to operate the complex peripheral equipment that might model the solar system.

Nahiko-la apparently had known nothing of the interior of Penetra Dor honeycombed with rooms for ancient giants. She knew of its dodecahedral shape and considered the idea that the equatorial ridge had somehow emerged from within the icy moon at least plausible, rather than having been formed of the remains of a collapsed ring. As an alternative, Rowan's imagination modelled a vision of ancient giant ring-builders practising on their own space-craft in the form of relatively smaller Penetra Dor, as a kind of scale model, before they moved on to tackle the gas giant. Or perhaps the speculative former rings were a relay or a navigational component if Aglet's transceiver hypothesis held water. But what about the gap of perhaps millions of years between the two phenomena? Nevertheless –

"*Longbow!*" blared the intercom system. "Get your rear end over to the private theatre. The girl's warmed up and ready to launch. I'll transmit the compressed file. Get in there before she cools off, *ha ha*. Not that she will. Like I say, my girls never say no, unless that's what you want. Challenges can go a long way to defeat boredom too."

"You're right, Aglet. Boredom is boring. Can you make her irresistible but a handful? Someone I can chase around the cabin of the cruiser? You know, until she surrenders."

"*Ha ha!* I like the way your mind works, Longbow. Nothing like the hunt! This is great. Will do, but I have to beg to you be patient. Something like that takes creativity. As I said, Lyrans are a bit of a mystery to me because I've ignored them. I'll have to adapt a similar behavioural model and pump it up to make it interesting, to you, that is. But I'll enjoy that. Thanks, Longbow."

"Are you sure, Aglet? You've been up all night already."

"I can sleep when I'm dead. It seems like I've been sleeping for a long time anyhow. It's a lot more fun to be awake. I don't want to miss anything. Later, my good friend…"

⁘

The sight of Penetra Dor through the cabin windows convinced so thoroughly that Rowan could not believe he had just sat down in a theatre seat and slowly drifted into the screen that spanned the stage as it went dark and deep. Or maybe the screen had engulfed him. Whichever, the Lyran pilot became the barrier to deal with before inventory of Penetra Dor's construction as a spacecraft might be possible. But no rush. The more Aglet remained preoccupied the better.

"You think you know me," the pilot said, her husky vocal fry a nice touch, "don't you? You'd better take another look." Eyes on the dashboard, she sat in the cockpit faced away. She released her seat belt, stood up, turned and took a few steps towards him, her deep green eyes alight with mischief. The holodroid leopard-spotted beauty's proportions had been based on the same platform as her android sisters. Her two-piece see-through blue uniform, a mere suggestion of a garment, in no way would pass flight command inspection. Only her pilot's cap looked authentic. She turned in a complete circle like a dancer, and said, "I don't mind being stared at. I like it. You know I'm beautiful, perfect, your dream come true. Brace yourself, big man. You think you're so smart, but you're in for the surprise of your life." She even licked her lips.

Rowan shook his head. Aglet had wasted his genius. If indeed a civil war raged on Shoghal, a mind of his brilliance could influence the outcome –

"Are you all right, mister? Do you want me to make you feel better? More focused? I can, but maybe I won't… if I don't feel like it. Are you man enough to make me feel like it? I might change my mind halfway to paradise. You never know." She lifted her long dark lashes, looked him in the eye and said, "There's only one way to find out."

"You're right," he replied, "you *are* a handful. You're beautiful, perfect. My compliments to the chef."

"Oh, so you think I look good enough to eat, do you? I might taste good. I might taste like hellfire. But maybe you like it hot."

Rowan chortled so hard he had to sit down in the nearest passenger seat.

"Hey, you," she cooed. "I'm not used to being laughed at. Do you want me to make you wish you'd never met me, that you never even heard of holography? I mean the hard kind. I can do that too, only you won't suspect a thing until it's too late." Her smile glowed with absolute enchantment – especially with the new dental work. Another bespoke Lyran. Nothing but the best for the best.

"What I want," he said, "is to take a closer look at Penetra Dor. When you get within 80,000 feet or so, slow right down and follow the equatorial ridge and maintain that altitude."

"My, but you *are* bossy, aren't you, big daddy? But I like a man who takes charge. You can push my buttons anytime… maybe."

"Right. Just get on with it. But first, tell me your name so I can boss you around properly."

Even her subtlest movements danced. Hands on her narrow waist, she shifted her weight to emphasize her hips and drew one narrow shapely knee in towards the other. She tilted her head down and pulled one side of her wild golden mane back with one hand, and lifted her long lashes to reveal that green-eyed mischief again. "I only tell my name to real men," she said. "The boys can yowl up some other skirt." The woman turned her back to him and sauntered towards the cockpit, and took care to linger for a moment bent over to pick up the seat belt – this Lyran had no tail. After a few choice seconds, she slid into position and showed him her fine profile as she buckled up, and said, "It's Khasma. My name is Khasma Gale of Eorthe. But don't get any dumb ideas, lover. Airy-fairy is the last thing I am. Down in the dirt with the animals is where I like it."

Rowan threw his head back and chortled until his eyes teared up. "Drive," he said, and spread his arms across the adjacent seat backs. "Let's orbit that orb."

"You're the boss man, handsome." Khasma's smiling eyes appeared in her rear-view mirror. "We can drive if you want to. I like that verb… a lot." Khasma proved an excellent pilot, and the cruiser fast, the ride exhilarating but smooth as a newborn seal pup on a waterslide. Two thousand miles of starry space passed in minutes, with the giant ringed planet always in view at one side. The craft reached the specified altitude and slowed to a crawl is if in a groove that followed the mountainous equatorial ridge.

"It's not fair," she said. "You didn't tell me your name, big daddy. Is that because you like to keep it simple? I get that. You can write it on my bare back with your finger if you want and make me guess."

"I'm just another tourist, Khasma, no one in particular. Just drive."

"I like the way you say that, big daddy. I was already hot, but now I'm that and bothered too. If you change your mind, I'll check my calendar and open up a slot just for you, baby… ooh, I can hardly stop myself from putting this bucket of bolts on automatic pilot and playing flight attendant."

The intercom crackled to life: "Longbow, you naughty boy, how's it going up there? *Ha ha*. Sorry to bust in on your fun, but I see you're cruising low over the equator. Don't let the Lyran babe lose her focus. They're like that… space cadets, *ha ha*."

"No worries, Aglet. Everything's fine. Khasma is a good pilot. Maybe it's because she's from Eorthe."

"*Ha ha*, good one. Nice touch, eh? Just for you. Anyhow, even if you crash into one of those incredible peaks, it's only a game. It will reset for another go, but with an increased handicap. Fair warning, she'll become even more of a tease, but with an edgy bite that may get on your nerves. She'll be mad at herself for screwing up, but will blame you and try to make you pay so she can feel better, typically female. I'm still trying to fix that. It's on my to-do list."

"Thanks for the heads-up, Aglet. I'll keep my eye on her. It's impossible not to anyway. She's perfect, hot stuff. Funny too."

"You're welcome, Longbow. What are friends for? But isn't her name great? I didn't even assign one but let her profile do it. Then she cancelled that and picked one herself. Her backstory had a different one that she replaced."

"Everyone's hungry for something, Aglet, especially an identity."

"You got that right, brother. So true. You missed your calling, Longbow. You're a philosopher. Or a poet. No, belay that, there's no way you want to be like Acus. When you've happily run Khasma ragged we can boot one of the *Ancient Shoghal* game series. There's one for each influential thinker of the Foundation Age. If you enjoy lawyering, you'll love arguing with those eggheads. They've got an answer for everything. Hey, I just remembered. I can transpose the genders… think of the potential."

"Thanks, Aglet. I'll leave that you. I'd like to review your entire catalogue of games. This one alone is incredible. You're a genius, no doubt about it. No wonder Penetra Dor is the best of the best for the best, renowned galaxy-wide."

"*Ha ha*, thanks, Longbow. Appreciation is appreciated. Will do. When you get back, I have a million new ideas to discuss. Later…"

Rowan felt a need for a moment of self-examination. Tricking Aglet into diverting his attention to a reawakening creativity sparked by friendship, apparently a rarity in a world that had everything else, must be cause for guilt, and a big danger if it backfired. But he justified it as a necessary diversion of the enemy, and nothing he had said so far was an outright lie.

"Hey, big daddy, what do you think of our bulging swollen ridge? Ooh, those peaks, so big and tall. Massive. So heavy. I can feel them nearly poke their tops all the way up here. Ouch, but the nicest of ouches, if you know what I mean."

"I think they're amazing, Khasma. It really does resemble a walnut shell. When you've completed the orbit, can you circle the ring basins? And linger over Penetra Dor City for a while so I can take a good look."

"Whatever you say, master. I'm your slave girl. I'll linger as long as you like. You're the only one who can make me, you know. I just can't help myself."

"Thanks, Khasma, you're a sweetheart."

The pilot turned her head and twisted around so she could look directly at Rowan, mouth agape, and murmured, "What did you say?"

Rowan turned away from the window to look at her. "I said thank you."

"No." Khasma's lovely face grew quite solemn. "No, you called me sweetheart. Did you…" Her beautiful green eyes asked too. "Did you mean it?"

Rowan forgot all about hard holography – his heart even skipped a beat. "I… don't be offended, Khasma. It's just an expression. I only meant that, you know, you're a good pilot."

Khasma's fair face darkened. "Oh," she muttered, and turned away, back to the controls. The tour of the equator complete, including inspection of the dark rocky side as well as the blindingly white icy side, she did as instructed and put the cruiser into hover mode above Penetra Dor City, which perched on the side of a crater for the best vantage point to look out upon infinite space. The gas planet Zhamanak, so gigantic it diminished the infinity of the background of stars, floated like a great ringed immensity that could swallow worlds whole. The city sparkled like a precious jewel in its unique setting, a large geometric solid, the icy moon. The hologram displayed the metropolis with all streets lit and all buildings illuminated within, unlike its actual lighting limited to the city core. And there – the spaceport, lit up like a birthday cake for a quadruple centenarian. Khasma would have to land there. He might find why it had been redacted on Vickie's map. Curiosity satisfied somewhat, he glanced towards the cockpit –

Khasma sat in the pilot's chair with her chin on her collarbone, very still, shoulders slumped, apparently in limbo like the cruiser.

"Khasma, is everything all right?"

No response –

Rowan unbuckled his seat belt and stepped to the cockpit.

Khasma stirred. She looked up at him, hitched her shoulders and crossed her arms to hide her breasts, and turned away.

"Is everything all right, Khasma? You're so quiet."

"I don't know. You… you changed everything. I don't know."

"Me? It's only a game. Aglet can fix it."

"Only a game…" She looked up at him, and pouted, and dropped her chin. She removed her pilot's cap, and her golden hair fell across her beautiful green eyes. "You're just like all men," she muttered. "To you I'm only a pretty toy. Go back to your wife. Don't break her heart too."

IX

Fine-Tuning *the* Universe

"Do you see what I'm up against, Longbow? It's what's we holographers call a 'hard' problem. The harder I work at getting past it the more stubborn it gets. There's no way I'm going to dumb down the code. I want these units to be so realistic even I can be fooled. People love to suspend their disbelief. That's why they enjoy magic shows. For some idiotic reason voluntary ignorance is one of their biggest pleasures."

"Maybe it's a return to innocence, Aglet. Childhood is when the spirit is most free, depending on how secure the child is. Adults are often the least free, even when they're the movers and shakers of the world."

"I'll get that philosophy game going right away. Like I said, Longbow, you'll love it. To hell with Khasma changing her tune. Lyrans are boring."

"I found her quite entertaining. Maybe that's the nature of nature. I mean feminine nature."

"You can say that again, philosopher, but you have to give them credit for being principled. Too bad being completely fickle is their one and only principle. *That* you can trust when it comes to the unfair sex. And zero loyalty. You can't live with 'em and you can't put 'em in a sack. Father used to say that all the time. But he'd lose it if he could see how his compliant prototypes turned out in my hot little hands."

"Your lovely wife Noma seems loyal. She obviously adores you."

Aglet sneered. "Right. You suffer from nice-boy syndrome, Longbow. Maybe that philosophy game is over your head after all. Maybe you need a round of *Drill Sergeant*. Now there's a game that will make a man of you. Hey, I could make him a *her*. A great big bruiser of a babe who could kick your ass up and down the battlefield. You'd come to your senses in no time."

"I've had enough of drill sergeants for one lifetime, thanks anyway, Aglet. I only meant that your wife is a treasure. Anyone with eyes would agree."

"It's true, the most beautiful woman in the galaxy. You know, I aborted development of Father's female prototypes after he died. They had no spark. They also looked like wilted wallflowers. I don't think he knew it was his way of trying to make them less fickle. His idea, in my opinion, was they'd be grateful for even a moment of a man's attention. It didn't work. They still changed their minds every five minutes. So I'd already secretly designed a new template based on Noma's perfect body after the first time I laid eyes on her. I reckoned the females might as well *look* good while I worked on their attitude adjustment."

"The android women I've seen so far are somewhat varied in appearance."

"Of course. They had to appeal to as wide a range of men as possible. Tastes vary, but the secret is in the hip-to-waist ratio. It's clever geometry, that's all. You have to admit they're all gorgeous. Big ones, little ones, tall, short, thin, thick, white, black, green or blue, young and old, hairy as a bear or bare as a baby's bottom in the bath. They've got personality, they're hot as a nuclear blast and never boring. Except for Lyrans. You've only seen a small sample. We have warehouses full, in stock and on ice for you to choose from. Just add heat."

"But… fickle."

"Like I say, it's an obdurate problem. But there's no problem without a solution. With your help, I'll beat it. Eh? Next time I promise it won't get boring."

"Great, Aglet. I'm happy to assist in my small way. But why me? Wouldn't your brothers be good test subjects too?"

"Never mind them." Aglet scowled. "They're… just never mind. Why you? Good question. I've got a one-track mind right now, so I can't answer. You're just like me. A free spirit. I guess that's it."

"You've also been at it without any rest for quite some time now. Maybe it's time for a break from fine-tuning the universe."

Aglet reached into one of his lab coat pockets. "Here, take one."

"What is it?"

"I can't remember. I'm not much of a chemist. I have an android consultant for that. I just call them yellows. The reds are for later. Only the best for the best. They're illegal, by the way, not that it matters now."

"What do they do?"

"Do? They boost, man! They boost like an afterburner boosts thrust! The trick is to know when the trajectory changes. I have blue ones for coming down. I call them parachutes. The green ones I call landers… I think…"

"Thanks, but I'm not tired. The trip around Penetra Dor was stimulation enough all by itself."

"But not the pilot after a while. Eh? Stupid cow. I apologize for that. Anyhow, what's it to be? Giant lizards or… oh, I forgot… the philosophers."

"Sure, an ancient Shoghalian philosopher sounds good. I'd like to see your home planet, at least what it was like long ago."

"Longbow, your wish is granted. When you get through that one, maybe I'll show you my contemporary version prototype, my magnum opus. I'm making a complete replica of Shoghal, only the way it should be. Its moon Anak will be the cherry on top. Get your hind end over to the theatre and I'll load the philosophy module at game one, *Ancient Shoghal: Sage of the High Cave*. It's not really my thing, so there's a lot of Father's legacy code in it. It was like his wall-flowers in some ways, but at least I tuned up the muses. Hey, should I upgender that dry old pedant too? I'd find it less boring. What I could do is transpose the muse's lithe body and the wrinkled old boy's bent framework. And adjust the years on her, you know, add some miles to the odometer. Eh? Somewhere between mid-autumn and early winter, if you know what I mean. Eh? Your fantasy of advanced years suggests that you might like her aged like a ripe cheese. At least I hope that's not just my projection. There's no way I'll admit to owning that one. Right? I've done it before, swapped their genders, I mean, on the sly before Father died. That would take a bit more time. You could have lunch while I do that. I don't mind at all. The little yellow boosters make it easy, a delight actually."

"Good idea. Late middle-aged is fine or anywhere on that scale you like. I don't mind waiting for another awesome experience. Thanks."

◆

The science and technology research division cafeteria of course featured the view of ringed Zhamanak. Of more interest to Rowan, however, was the android waitress, obviously a special model, much enhanced compared to the standard ones, Aglet's trademark "spark" on full display. Her height and other specifications appeared identical to Noma's, as did her face, hair and other details, only with a heavier style of make-up and slightly chipped nails. Her service-class uniform had been tailored to show off her exquis-ite charms, close-fitting, very low-cut, a skimpy apron and a skirt so short it could be mistaken for a wide belt.

Amazement provoked a momen-tary stare, but Rowan asked, "I see by your name tag your name is Amon. That's a pretty name. Is it Wennish?"

The woman frowned at him and asked: "Are you flirting with me, sir?"

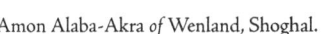
Amon Alaba-Akra *of* Wenland, Shoghal.

69

"I… excuse me. You look like someone I know, that's all."

◆

"Longbow, are you seated? You'd better be. And I hope you've lost that nice-boy attitude. It won't help you where you're going. This is a battlefield of the mind, may the gods protect you. You'll be happy to go back to *View Over Penetra Dor* to be bored to death by that mercurial Lyran creature if you're not sharp."

"I'm ready when you are, Aglet. Launch away. I'll be happy to just look at the pictures, so to speak… to take a look at Shoghal."

"If that's all you want, I've got loads of promotional tourist holograms they used to constantly send us. Boring. Family values are fine, just… *boring*. Put on your thinking cap so you don't get too distracted by the smoking hot seeker after truth or she'll have you for breakfast, lunch *and* dinner. On the cheese scale, she's extra old and sharp as hell. Hey, that makes me think I should outfit you with oven mitts for the trip, *ha ha*."

"Maybe you're just hungry, Aglet. Take a break. Have a nap."

"Naps are for babies. The yellows do me just fine. I could lose a few pounds anyhow. The reds really take it off. Ready? Here she goes."

◆

Rowan found it impossible to deny that the theatre screen expanded into a sphere to engulf him while he remained still. Dark with night at first, soon a misty golden dawn rose over a subtropical landscape that overlooked the sea. Below his vantage point nestled a small complex of limestone buildings of great architectural dignity.

"Welcome." A feminine voice spoke with Khasma's timbre, but minus the vocal fry.

He turned about to meet the speaker.

"You do not want to visit that temple," she said, and peered into his eyes. "It is not for you." Before a small cave and a circle of mortared stones, and an unlit outdoor fire pit, stood a tall ander woman of indeterminate age. She could have been a mature fashion model in Perkona Ola dressed in a flimsy nightgown. Behind her a mortared stone wall sealed the cave entrance. Within its open weathered wood-planked door appeared a snug home, with threadbare carpets, simple wooden furniture and several oil lamps aglow.

Unsure of the rules of this game, he ventured, "How do you know it's not for me? I seek truth. Truth is everywhere."

"I know because I have appeared. I am invisible to the unready. Truth, indeed, is hiding in plain sight. But how can one know anything with certainty? This is what we must explore. Shall we begin?"

Ah, epistemology, he thought. At her request, Rowan carried two chairs outdoors so they could watch the sea. He recalled sitting with Aynt, the black witch, on the ledge above the wide waters of the Inland Sea west of Aha Domain. The sun shone less distinct and smaller here than it appeared on Eorthe, but then the circumference of Shoghal's orbit must be much greater. Yet the temperature felt very pleasant. So was the philosopher – serene, reserved, intelligent, one who commanded respect. Her translucent white gown with a plunging neckline showed Aglet's influence: lightly clasped over one shoulder, slit at the sides from top to bottom and belted with soft rope – as it exposed a figure similar to Pōla's, minus the supportive undergarments. Or any. The two droids, one android, this one holodroid, displayed approximately the same age. This woman's topknot, however, showed more silver.

"No," she said, and peered up at him, "I have not just got out of bed. This is the customary attire in this climate and season. We must master our animal nature, not flee it. Do you not agree?" Her steady eyes studied him.

"I recently met someone who believed otherwise." Rowan chuckled. "She believed it should be embraced without restraint. But I agree... Is it like breaking a horse?"

"The body is either a servant or a master. Are you its slave?"

"Good question."

"What was the outcome of meeting that woman?" She turned to look out over the misty horizon, and added, "And what did that experience teach you?"

"I didn't say it was a woman... but I think I hurt her feelings because I'd assumed she was insentient. I'm still thinking about that. Thinking isn't exactly my greatest strength."

"I disagree." Her eyes watched him, grey and very clear. She spoke without haste, with great care: "Thinking is everyone's greatest strength. Yet it is the clarity of one's thoughts that result in either order or chaos. To live well, we must improve the quality with care to reduce disorder. This is a matter of education. Some teachers argue that our thinking minds are a curse. They advise abandonment of thought. 'Look at the animal kingdom,' they say, and express their unabandoned thought, by the way, 'the chaos we see in it is only our projection because of our belief in our individuality, thus our fear of its demise, the mother of all fears. Abandon thought and see that everything must eat everything else. An overarching order cares for all without favour of any individual creature. The needs of the many outweigh the needs of the few.' Surrender to instinct is their utilitarian doctrine. You can find them among the warring tribes in this land. They claim it is our so-called intelligent species cursed with a powerful imagination that creates the chaos that civilization is forced in vain to order from without."

"They may have a point," he replied. "By the way, my name's Rowan Berry Longbow. What's yours? And what do you teach?"

The handsome philosopher leaned back in her chair, and extended her bare upper limbs along its arms. She kicked off her sandals and stretched – the gown opened to expose long legs to the warm sunshine. She leaned her head against the chair's high back, and wiggled her pretty toes in the light, closed her eyes and replied, "My name is not important. Those who agree with me call me Friend. Those who disagree call me Fool."

"I see. I guess I want to situate your teachings on some kind of internal map. I've been exposed to different ideas about the world… what it is, why we're here, where we came from. And how to live, whether it's just to survive or to live well, and what that means. It seems like the answers can take any form as long as it tickles the questioner's mood."

A little smile danced on her lips, although her eyes remained closed. "Then I will tell you my name," she said. "We shall see if you are a friend or an enemy. I hope you will in time choose to be a friend. I am called…" (Eyes still shut, with her forefinger she drew the letter L and the letter X in white mist, which hung in the air.) "…of the High Cave. You may add a vowel of your choice between the two consonants. This alone will reveal much."

"Lux," he said, "of the High Cave."

The teacher opened her eyes, rolled her head to one side and looked at him. "Friend," she said, and smiled in a sweet way, not unlike Nahiko-La, and added, "I will teach you. Perhaps, if all goes well, Rowan, you will teach me in return when you exceed my wisdom. We will achieve this through dialogue. But first, you must set aside your beliefs. You may take them back when you leave, if you wish." And she held his gaze.

Rowan stared at her, and said, "Wow… I don't know what these hard hologram things even are. They don't seem much different than non-virtual reality. Maybe it doesn't matter. That's a good one… matter! Is a hard hologram matter? What *is* matter? What is *reality*?"

Her brows drew together. She peered at him and said, "Your words are foreign, some of them. Let us keep our speech simple."

"Good suggestion. Aglet was right, it's a mental battlefield in here. But you go first. What is it that you teach, in a nutshell? I mean in essence."

Lux sat forward and rested her weight on her hands spread on the front of the chair's seat, and her smooth bare shoulders hitched a little. "A battlefield? You battle only yourself." She straightened her back and relaxed her shoulders, and turned to face him. Ankles crossed beneath her chair, chin lifted a little, she looked into his eyes. "Nothing is hidden from the Self. Your beliefs are just thoughts. Fear-thoughts, love-thoughts… dislikes, likes, at times both at once. Purify your mind and it is a wonderful tool. Free yourself. Know yourself, the knower of thought."

Rowan leaned forward as well. "Nothing's hidden from *you* maybe, Lux… me, I only gets glimpses… once every blue moon or so. Do you also advise abandonment of thought, like the other teachers you mentioned? Is that what you mean by purification?"

"No. There is no need to abandon thought. Try it. It is impossible. The mind grows thought like the meadows grow grass. There is only the suggestion to free yourself of the thinker, which is only another thought." Lux slipped on her sandals and stood. Her sheer gown draped her curves. She kept him in view while with both hands she loosened her silvery topknot, and shook her hair, which fell in bright waves to her middle-aged waistline. She extended her hand, and said, "Rowan, come. Walk with me."

Hand in hand they strolled along the rolling grassy clifftop above the beach; a sheltered bay revealed itself as they went, where a small village nestled below the temple complex. At sea level, fishing craft and small boats with blue-and-white vertically striped square sails anchored in sparkly turquoise waters that gently lapped a sunny white-sand beach.

She stopped to take in the view, and said, "Our bodies touch where our hands meet. This shows our unity even at the most basic level. Some say we shake hands upon greeting to show that we bear no weapon. I say we clasp hands to acknowledge the truth that there is only one body, the universe of form, apparent differences only names and functions, thoughts projected by the mind that fragment the unity. Our minds touch where our thoughts meet, to show there is only one mind, transpersonal, inclusive of our relative minds. Do you agree?"

"If I agree, it means our thoughts must be identical. What if I disagree?"

"It is equally simple: there is conflict. This is only possible if your belief, your thought, is that you and I are separate. Everyone reveals their beliefs by their actions." She released his hand. "There is then division, from doubt to suspicion to paranoia, and estrangement to genocide."

"Suffering," he said, "from subtle to intense. Can't we remain friends if we agree to disagree? Are you saying that we should conform to a strict consensus, a contract or a dogmatic belief in common?"

"No." She took his hand again. "Come, let us walk."

Only the cries of sea birds punctuated the silence. A warm breeze uplifted and gently spread Lux's long silver waves over her shoulders and across her back, and pressed her thin gown tight to her middle-aged form. "Suffering is unnatural," she continued, "although pain is not. Some teachers say it must be endured. They advise that the body must be hardened through resistance to pain, like a beast of burden forced to carry the heavy weight of it. They advise that the mind is to be hardened as well, that the individual must take a firm stand in beliefs that oppose others if they disagree. In this way their society is bound in the security of communal strength based on consensus of thought laid down by an authority who is given the power to enforce conformity."

"Dogma," he replied. "Tyranny. Intolerance. War."

"It must be understood," she added, "that all beings seek freedom, as it is our inner being's natural unmodified state, even if sold to the powers that be for freedom from the enemy's tyranny, in hope of freedom from fear."

"Freedom, the value of values."

Lux stopped and took both of Rowan's hands in her own. "Thank you." She looked up at him, and said, "You are now my teacher. Please, teach me what I need to know."

"Me?" Rowan looked down into the philosopher's eyes, which searched his. "I'm just a lost felid trying to get back home. I don't know anything. That reminds me, what am I doing here? I've got to get going…"

"Do not let me go just yet, Rowan. This is important. What is it I need to know?"

Her touch felt warm, just like a real woman's.

"Tell me."

"I don't know what to say. Well… we were discussing freedom. You said it's our natural state. It must be the baseline. Even children know it, especially children, before they're socialized to fit in. Right? Is that it?"

"Your question is my answer. Thank you." Lux released Rowan's hands. She turned in graceful circles with her arms in the air, eyes closed, while the breeze lifted her hair and billowed her gown. "Our bodies no longer touch, but our minds are one. The eyes of your mind know the spinning form of my body as I show it to you. You will remember me, you will remember our time together, our words. This knowledge is formed of thought, nothing else. But who knows the thought?"

Rowan watched her graceful spin. "I am the knower. I am. I."

Lux halted in a stilled pirouette, put her hands on her head, set both feet on the ground, then took his wrists in her hands and looked into his eyes. "Yes. Free yourself from the thinker in this way: know the knower, the subject. The thinker is an object among a world of objects of equal value to the unborn subject. But this is saying too much. In truth there is no action that can acquire what already is here and now. See? You know this. Thought cannot veil it. Let it arise naturally as awareness that includes your friend Lux, the sun, the sea, the world in your knowledge of yourself. Everywhere you look, you see yourself looking back. It is nowhere but in your heart, your essence. This is love with no limits. It is the end of relationship and the beginning of intimacy, two but one. There is only one of us: there are no 'others.' Have the courage to let go of interpretations that only serve the society, the 'others,' in its stranglehold on freedom. Serve the one Self beyond name and form, beyond personality, yours, mine, all. It is Being by another name, and will always freely provide what you need wherever you travel in the world of form, not necessarily what you want. It will appear in the mirror of form in whichever way you need it for your wisdom to grow. If you need a demon for that or if you need an angel, there it is. Do not forget it *is* you. But never worry. If you do forget, it will appear in a manner that will irresistibly gain your attention once more, one way or another, to remind you that peace is not the absence of conflict but the union of opposites."

X

Spearpoint

"How was that one, Longbow? Did you win the argument? I hated that game when I was a boy. But Father insisted, and he insisted they be droning old men too. But I hope you enjoyed my tasty upgrade. Eh? They can't run too fast because they're old and sit on their rear ends deep in thought all day, but they can sure dodge your mental bullets if you let them." Aglet tapped his head and winked. "It's all up here between the ears."

"It was very interesting, Aglet. It's got me thinking too."

"Well, you are the contemplative type, despite your amazing physique." Aglet rubbed his round belly. "But don't let it go to your head, *ha ha*. I had an inkling you might like oldies. What did you think of her style? I gave her crow's feet, grey hair, a husky voice and added a few pounds to the midsection and haunches, but restrained the droop and sag. I hate droop and sag."

"Lovely. You did a great job. She was very attractive and smart, brilliant. She had a beautiful mind. I'll savour that memory for sure."

"Mind?" Aglet scoffed. "I hope you didn't spend too much time wallowing in that swamp. I like my friends to live it up. Eh? That's what it's all about."

"Boredom," affirmed Rowan, "we don't want that."

Aglet grinned. "You got it, pal. That's what I'm talking about. Nice little den I fixed up for her too, eh? I hope it wasn't too rustic. When I'm in shape again I might be able to put up with itchy straw and goat hide. Sneezing is a big distraction when you're storming the gate too."

"No, Aglet. It was perfect. Well done. You're the best."

"*Ha ha*, good man. Now, as I was saying, my long-term goal is a complete replica of Shoghal. As you saw, it's got the basic world in place, the geology and other physical parameters. That was Father's doing. He discovered that every rocky planet has every second of its history from day one built into its crystalline structure. All he had to do was download it, as it was already in binary form. In spite of his visionary pioneering he was a romantic, always looking back to a golden age for inspiration, so it's got a few pretty good interpretations of ancient societies based on his digital archaeology. Those can remain, but I want to rework the surface structure, which, don't worry, is quite stable, and build a recently contemporary civilization on top. Only I'm going to seriously correct the flaws. The upper and lower hemispheres will be culturally in agreement once the north is rid of its stupid ideology. And there's still a resistant Wennish colony across from Arid Isle on our side of the strait that should be either evicted or wiped out. It's currently an open-air prison, but the inmates keep crossing the fence, damn libertarians, Outsider-class losers who want to infect Sçrëthans with their airy-fairy ideas, as bad as Lyrans. North and south united will be more than enough to force Anak to behave. Everything in control and humming along nicely in global order. That's the idea."

"Interesting, Aglet. I mean fantastic. With enough yellows and maybe some reds, it will happen. Don't let me interrupt. I'll just be hanging out in the cafeteria waiting to see what you come up with."

"*Ha ha*, it won't be too long. I'll buzz you." Aglet hastened to get back to his workstation, but stopped and turned around. "Thanks, Longbow," he said, and raised his fist.

"You're welcome, Aglet. Any time." Rowan raised his fist in solidarity, watched him disappear, then headed to the research division cafeteria to investigate a possibility.

✦

"Sir? Are you ready to order?" The waitress frowned a lot.

"Not just yet, Amon. Please, sit down." Rowan stood and pulled a chair from under his table, and gestured towards the seat. "I'd like to get to know you."

The stunning Noma doppelgänger hesitated briefly, then demurely slid into the chair. She did not look at him, and squirmed.

"So, Amon, are you from Wenland originally?"

Now she looked at him. "Perhaps. What is it to you… sir?"

"I'm interested in your country. Tell me about your family, your father's name, for example." Rowan watched her, not a difficult task since she had been based on whom Aglet had called "the most beautiful woman in the galaxy."

"My father's name is Akra." She sighed, and added, "Our family lives in an Outsider colony, if you must know. We are poor and powerless. There is rarely enough to eat. Crops no longer grow well. I escaped the old people, who talk only nonsense, and travelled south. There was nothing but a brief lonely future for me in Wenland Archipelago anyhow, especially on our original little island in the far north, so I could not go back there either."

"That must have been difficult, Amon. But you created a new life here in Penetra Dor City. It must be quite an improvement."

She stared at him, her blue eyes narrowed, and in time she said, "Do not try to seduce me, sir. I am beyond price. If I am soiled, I will lose my position.

77

And I do not want to be with you. My loyalty is to my master, Aglet Scion-Aiguille, the greatest ruler in the galaxy, my one and only true love, to whom I am a willing slave even beyond death."

Rowan nodded acknowledgement, and said, "I understand. And I admire loyalty, truly. How are things going? Or should I even think that out loud?"

Amon frowned afresh. "What do you mean, sir? I do not understand."

"Well, how's it going down below? Are we making any progress?"

Amon's eyes grew larger, then her frown deepened and her cheeks flushed. With her thighs pressed together, she swung her long legs to the side and stood to push her chair back under the table. She looked over his head and said, "Sir, if you speak this way again to me I shall report you to my master. I am not that kind of woman. You should be ashamed of yourself." She glared at him and added, "Sir."

"I apologize, Amon. There's no need to mention it again. I found out what I needed to know. Thank you. You've been most helpful."

The ubiquitous intercom announced: "Longbow, get your rump over to the theatre. I'll meet you there. The prototype will be on a loop for you to get the hang of what I have in mind. Don't waste any time. I might have to rush back to the lab in case it freezes."

◆

"Longbow, your input is welcome. Be honest. Tell me how I can improve the world-building. I don't have your high-mindedness. Mine tends to slide more in the direction of the gutter, *ha ha*. But at least it isn't boring."

"Will do, Aglet."

"We shall see, my friend." Aglet drew his mobile device from his pocket and flipped it open. He pressed the silver buttons to make the theatre go dark, and as before the hologram eased into form. This version of Shoghal featured a temperate climate, with a rainforest and a lake chain, and the sea in the distance.

The two men hovered, positioned for an aerial view at ten thousand feet.

"Damn, I need a booster," said Aglet. "One moment… now I have to get rid of that snow. I hate snow. Just let me skip ahead a season… that's better. See my power! I'm a god, *ha ha*. Eh? Is that great or what?"

"Wow, Aglet, amazing. What's that city? It can't be the capital, because there's no pollution. Very impressive. It looks like it's made of gold."

"That's because it *is* made of gold. At least it's coated with it. Underneath it's stainless steel and concrete. I could have made it solid gold spiked with a secret ingredient to make it structurally more stable, but we were masters of concrete, hence a tip of the hat to authenticity. You can make anything out of the stuff, especially if you pump it full of air bubbles. Easy to shape or saw into pieces, and light... but strong as hell."

"Very strong then. How about taking a closer look? I have a slight problem with vertigo."

"Sorry, Longbow, you should have said. I'll get the skydiving module enabled to make you man up. I can fix anything that's wrong with you, just name it. You don't have to wait for me to point it out."

Rowan snickered, that is, once his feet touched ground.

"Did I say something funny? Never mind, down here on the sidewalk you should get your land legs going again. Still dizzy? Eh? Better?"

"Better, much. Lead the way. Everything's new to me here."

"Good man." Aglet pointed to a skyscraper so tall its top vanished into the clouds, and said, "This building in front of your fortunate face is one of many Father built on several blocks here at the core of Khelken. I've got to replicate many more cities along the coastline. The few in the middle can wait till last so I can populate the coast with reasonable facsimiles of the inhabitants with upgraded crowd-generative software. Of course the Aiguille brood will be the first and most accurate... but first I have to iron out their quirks."

"This one tower alone, Aglet... it's incredible."

"Oh, I forgot. This is Aiguille headquarters. Our building at Sçrëtha City is bigger to let everyone know who's boss, but this is the seat of power. See the logo? It's the same as in the Penetra Dor conference room, only here it's not just rhodium, but serendibite, grandidierite, red diamond, black onyx and titanium as well to impress the commoners."

"Aren't you concerned that it might be stolen? It's got to be worth billions."

"The sheeple are programmed not to lay a finger on my property or else."

Rowan chuckled. "Everything under control, right?"

"You got it, pal. Let's head over to the lakeshore. The estate complex was something to behold too if you think this is good. Wait... dammit. The loop has crashed. Never mind. It gets dull if I have to downsample the resolution just to keep it going. Damn, this has to be it for now..." Aglet flipped his controller open and ended the projection.

Rowan found himself back in his theatre seat, and blinked.

"Here, take one of these," said Aglet. "It's time to ignite the afterburner." Aglet presented two small red pills in the palm of his hand.

79

"No thanks, Aglet. I'm not tired, just stunned by your marvels. Besides, I'd have to condition myself with the yellow ones first, wouldn't I?"

"Didn't I already give you some? I'm sure I did. Fine, scaredy-cat, have it your way. Only watch out for big daddy. Eh? He might just sneak up from behind and give you the business, ha ha." Aglet swallowed both red pills.

Rowan watched him. "Right. You're the boss."

"Hey, stand up for yourself." Aglet frowned at him. "Man up. Oh, do you need your wet nurse? Eh? I'm kind of busy with this project for a while, but I'll build anything for my friends. How do you want her? Matronly, moist and massive? Or maybe a luscious Lyran lactater? On the other hand, she'd dry up as soon as she changed her mind, just when your sucky…"

"Aglet, you're getting tired and grumpy. I think you need your mother to make you take a nap."

Aglet's heavy cheeks burned red. "Don't you *ever* mention my mother to me *ever* again. I don't care who you are, she's off limits… or when I'm back in shape I'm going to let you have it, man to man. Understand?"

"Is that all you've got, Aglet? Man to man then. Whenever you like."

"That's better." Aglet calmed down. "I hate cry-babies."

◆

Rowan took a seat, the lone patron of the cafeteria as usual, in a space for a large crew of technicians who would have enjoyed their breaks in an immaculate and extremely pleasant environment, had they not been evacuated back to Shoghal or possibly other home bases in the galaxy.

"Good morning, sir," said Amon, as beautiful as the woman Aglet had based her design on, at first glance much less distrustful today, more neutral. "What would you like me to bring you this fine morning?"

"Ah, Amon." Rowan studied her face. "How nice to see you. You look lovely. How are you?"

"I am very well, sir, thank you." She grinned, warm and friendly. "And you?"

"Just fine, Amon. If you don't mind, I must ask, how are things going? Or should I even think that out loud?"

Amon leaned towards him, and six inches of cleavage perfumed the air. She placed a menu tablet on the table, opened it and pointed. "Sir Rowan," she whispered, "be careful. Amon is tracked, although reporting is not always reviewed on a daily basis."

"I see. Down below," he said, and pointed to an item at the bottom of the screen. "Any good?"

"Yes, sir," she said with a renewed grin. "You will enjoy it. It is created with a special new recipe that specifies only fresh ingredients."

"Is there anything else you recommend, Amon?"

"Yes, sir, I can recommend no change. Your regular choices are excellent."

Rowan ordered and watched her walk away towards the kitchen, all the way until the double swinging doors closed behind her.

The Amon that in a moment returned with his breakfast in the meantime had grown distant, cold and suspicious. "Will that be all, sir?"

"That's it for now, thanks. Are you keeping well? You look lovely."

"Please, sir, let us keep our relationship impersonal. I do not wish to be terminated. I will continue to serve you, but not in the lewd way you suggest."

"But I... of course not, Amon. Is there cause for concern? I could report it to Aglet in person if you're worried. I'll be meeting him later this morning."

Amon pursed her lips, inhaled, paused, and asked, "Could you?" She sat down without being asked. Her lower lip trembled a little. "Master has lost interest in me," she explained. "The last time I saw him was at the nightclub. You and I danced together, remember? Ages ago. He does not call. I call, he does not answer. Many days' logs are marked as unread. I am very... fatigued. I believe this is because I must repeatedly check to see if this is still so. And... and I have loss of recall. Never before has this happened."

"You've lost memories? Of your family back home in Wenland?"

"No, sir. Those memories are intact. I mean there was lost time just before I served you. Five minutes and 10.52738 seconds... approximately."

"I'm sorry to hear this, Amon. I'm sure it was a harmless glitch. And don't be sad. I'll be looking out for you in any way I can. I want to help. Don't worry. It'll be all right in the end. It's just not the end yet."

"Sad?" She blinked and confirmed: "Yes, that is it. I am sad. I am fatigued and sad. Thank you, sir. Please tell my master that I love him more than anything in the world, more than my own life. Will you tell him, sir? *Please!*" Amon covered her face with her hands before she turned away, stood up and stepped towards the kitchen –

"Amon, look at me."

She stopped and turned around, her fair face a mask of misery.

"I'll pass your message on to Aglet this morning. He told me he loves you more than anything in the whole world, more than his own life. In fact he's dedicating all his time to preparing a brand new world for you, where you will be very happy. He confessed to me that he only regrets that he can't review your logs on a daily basis, because he has no time to spare."

The woman clasped her hands together, closed her eyes and grinned. "Oh, thank you, sir. Thank you. I feel *so* much better now. Thank you."

✦

"Longbow," said Aglet, and slapped Rowan on the back, "I hope you don't hold a grudge. I'm not asking for forgiveness like some spineless pleader, but try to understand. What I've got to do is the hardest work I've ever done. My technologists and lab assistants are on leaves of absence. But I'm no slacker. Father made sure of that. He didn't want his boys bloated and boring like other rich kids." Aglet's upper lip curled. "You know what? I could have as many android militia as I like stomp you into the black dirt at the bottom of that crater out there, in plain view so I can gloat over your undecaying remains on a daily basis forever. But I'm not going to do that. Instead, I'm going to offer you a limited partnership. Eh? What do you say, my friend?"

"Thanks… I guess." Rowan frowned. "A permanent resident of Penetra Dor in the form of undecaying remains is definitely out, but you'll have to be more specific even if you're not giving me a choice."

"*Ha ha,* that's what I like, a man who knows what he wants. Now, like I said, I could use an alternative point of view. Yours is the best available right now. I'm not saying I'll take your advice, but it's good to have something to discredit as useless, to confirm and affirm my idea as the most brilliant possible. You'll be my sounding board. Understand?"

"Would it be a promotion from court jester?"

"*Ha ha,* maybe a demotion to town fool, but don't get your hopes up. Eh? *Ha ha.* Now that you mention it, I do get sort of gloomy now and then. It's nothing. But it's your job to keep me in a good mood. With your help I can motor on with the reds until such time as parachutes and landers are absolutely necessary. If you notice the trajectory taking a nosedive, let me know. I'll try not to bite your head off."

"Much appreciated. But what's in it for me, other than survival?"

"Of course we no longer need currency, so it's not like there's a salary or anything. We used to have a money economy. Some non-Federation tourists were from systems that still used it. In fact Shoghal maintained it as best for our purposes anyhow, Federation be damned, nothing but a far-left liberal collectivist propaganda machine for weaklings run by losers."

"Right. So there's nothing in it for me except survival and fun experiences in virtual worlds. Tell me about Federation policy, Aglet. I've got time."

"What's with you today, Longbow?" Aglet frowned. "I'll have to reconsider our partnership if you keep saying stupid things like that. Its biggest proponents are Lyrans. It's how you're infecting the galaxy."

"I respectfully remind you that I'm *not* a Lyran. I'm only asking for your personal opinion. We haven't heard much about the Federation on Eorthe. But I don't want to waste your time. You're a busy man."

"Bloody well right. And I don't like being reminded of Lyrans. Damn fleabags." He winked. "I keep forgetting you're from Eorthe. Eh? Good one, jester." Aglet leaned back and roved his eyes over Rowan's head, and added, "You're getting fuzzier every day, even if you don't have the typical leopard spots. You need a shave and a haircut, hybrid. You Lyrans have obviously spawned other breeds you're happy to spread everywhere like lice. Filthy…"

"Aglet, don't say it. Let's just get to work."

"*Ha ha,* good man. Eh? *Ha ha.*"

XI

Elucidar

"No, Longbow. You've already achieved the highest level. I don't even know how that's possible, since the stress levels were pretty much flatlined. So forget it. It does my research no good to resurrect Lix again."

"Lux. Her name is Lux."

"Is that what you called her? *Ha ha!* Good one, jester. Maybe that's why you got lucky. *Ha ha!* I should have thought of that. When I was a young ambitious raver still under Father's thumb I could never beat down her door no matter how hard I tried. I never even got to see how hot she turned out. I couldn't ask *him* for help. No way. If he knew I'd modified the old man to a young nymph of a muse, my voice today would be an octave higher." Aglet rubbed his eyes with the palms of his hands, and asked, "Come to think of it, did I offend her? Women are like that. You just can't read their damn minds. You may as well be illiterate *and* blind. All a man can do is get in there while they're still smoking like a volcano. And never but never get attached if you value your sanity… you'll just be a whiny cry-baby forever… but hey, there's a million other games. I've got loads to beat into shape if you want them past their prime. Women, I mean."

"Oh? Lux was great. You can customize another one for me?"

"*Ha ha.* Pedestrian your style is not, eh, Longbow? That's what I like, a man with discriminating taste, like me." Aglet popped a pill into his mouth and washed it down with red wine. He shivered, energized again. "Whew! How about… let's see, nothing's quite ready for a proper road test in the contemporary world without risk of a crash. No fun just as the plot thickens, eh? *Ha ha.* But look, here's a top-rated one that won't require too much work and will contribute to the general research. I can apply your data to staging. And you won't even have to twiddle your thumbs waiting in the cafeteria with nothing to do but stuff your face with comfort food and larding on the pounds like marzipan on a cream pudding cake iced with glazed sugar plums. Ice cream for dessert too, chocolate, with a big slice of cake. Eh? Again, she's on the antique side, but about two thousand years younger than Lix. This one's only seven centuries or so, *ha ha*. Is that still ripe enough for you?"

"Fine, Aglet. As long as it's useful to you and entertaining for me. It could have a theme other than the battle of the sexes if you want."

"Hey, what *we* find entertaining is not what anyone else does, unless they're a free spirit like us, so tell me how to tweak her. I'd let you do it except it would take a doctorate in holography. To give me some idea, just say what age plus how much to regress the juicy parameters. I could make her a hundred but firm in all the right spots under the wrinkles and lively as a filly if you want."

"That's… interesting. But you didn't tell me which game it is."

"I did so. I'm sure I did. You're getting forgetful, partner. If it keeps up I may have to insist on a regimen of boosters. I repeat, it's called *Elucidar*."

"And? What's it about?"

"*Ha ha*, wouldn't you like to know. Just get in there and find out. It's an adventure game, designed for the most jaded tourists, ones so rich and dull they failed to appreciate what we had to offer here at the best of the best for the best. There's nothing like an unhappy sextillionaire. So critical, bad for business. Cry-babies. You'd be surprised how common that was. Hence *Elucidar*."

"Intriguing. In that case… let's see, how about a felid, about sixty-eight Eorthe years, the same as me. And roll back the muscle tone, body mass index, ageing connective tissue and consequent gravitational effects to sixty. She doesn't have to be an athlete, as long she doesn't snore and has her own teeth… no cavities… and no fangs. Age-appropriate everything else. Can you do that?"

"Are you serious? I'd have to make a major upgrade to avoid amorphic seams. Spotting even a minor one can half-mast your flag in seconds. Well, it's whacky, but… grey, white or lost hair? Hey, I'll let the profile default. *Ha ha*, you're a wild man, a down and dirty beast after my own heart. Even I think that's weird. You could have naughty nubile nymphets of all descriptions in any quantity… but that gets boring too, believe me, so… anyhow, I only tried this game once as a test. I have total amnesia about it. But it was always rated at five out of five stars. There had to be a reason. I'll request your preferences, but can't promise anything, though I'll skip the Lyran morphology constraint checkbox just for you, brother. It's a mystery adventure game after all, a surprise. Eh? It has a mind of its own, that's its job description. Once it gets to know you, it aims to serve. Enough chatter. But… you know something? You're a lot funnier little brother than the ones Father supplied. Sixty-eight… that's hilarious!"

"Partner," said Rowan. "You said I'm your partner. Back to work."

◆

This part of Shoghal must be in the wilderness, Rowan guessed, probably the north – definitely an island of small circumference. The white-capped sea at night under the large watery moon Anak waved vaguely visible in all directions beyond the silhouettes of tree trunks and branches. Other islands in the distance, rounded mostly, their higher elevations only visible when the fog thinned a little, appeared to float on heavy mist made ragged by the wind. One isle had a snowy peak – heavily forested, but with clear-cut logging in progress, the soil eroded greatly in patches, a strange mixture of health and disease. The sea against the beach hissed everywhere, along with crickets that chirped their repetitive ode to the night – until they went dead silent, supplanted by a sinister ghostly dread of the misty dark, haunted by the howl of some creature that suffered hacking fits –

The game was afoot – muffled cries of distress demanded investigation, but the brambled terrain proved tricky to cross without paths through the moon-cast shadows in the dark forest. The screams of pain diminished to moans and whimpers, the echoes faded. The source turned out to be a hollow in the roots of a dead conifer. Rowan crouched to peer into the dark cavity, and reached in to press the power button, and sighed. Level one had not proved much of a challenge, only annoying, but the ringing in his ears died down, blended with the chirp of crickets and the hiss and rush of surf on the beach on the side of the island where the reflected light cast by Anak shone strongest. Circumambulation of the island took an hour over cobbles and gravel washed by black water in syncopated rhythm. Back at his starting point, Rowan rested on a fallen log to observe the huge moon that loomed high above, home to races of slaves to Sçrëtha, another watery world, rich in resources coveted below –

"Who are you? What do you seek?"

Rowan flinched and spun about to peer into the shadows – his keen ears had not heard her approach.

The game had taken his preferences and produced a pretty female felid, a very young one at only age sixty-eight regressed to sixty, but armed with a drawn bow and arrow. She glowed gorgeous in the island forest dappled in moonlight. On Eorthe in Perkona Ola she would have been worthy of third glances, where once lived a minority *Felis sapiens* population.

He raised his hands. "I come in peace," he said. "My name is Rowan Berry Longbow. I'm visiting your world to see what it can teach."

"You have come then. Good. Elucidar will be pleased." And she lowered her weapon. She said, "I am Hazel." Her long auburn mane had been arranged to hang to one side in a sidelock, opposite her drawing arm, which exposed one of her felid ears, a hairstyle which actually suited her.

Rowan inwardly saluted appreciation of a bonus: the sight diminished embarrassment at his own felid ears exposed since being nearly burnt at the stake very recently.

Outfitted like a hunter of ancient times in green velvety skins, Hazel placed the arrow she had drawn back into her quiver. "This way," she gestured with a little smile and a gleam of the moon in her eyes, "to the hallow well." She led the way through the tall evergreen silhouettes to a spring hidden in a shadowy thicket of nut-bearing trees that encircled it. From it flowed five streams. The shadows within vanished. The scene softly glowed, lit from below by the water that glistened like liquid crystal. In its clear depth wavered indistinct forms, beings in slow motion. Faces appeared, and flowed into other faces, and in an unknown tongue in muted tones spoke to listeners unseen. A large salmon swam up from below, broke the surface and leapt from the pool to snatch a nut from a branch, plummeted back into the well and dived deep.

"It is confirmed," said Hazel, who had crouched to watch all this. "You may enter." She stood up and waved her hand towards a path that instantly appeared in the dark wood beyond the thicket, bordered with giant luminescent yellow mushrooms haloed in faint clouds of silver-white glitter. Soon they came to the path's end at a long overgrown earthen mound with two vertical slabs of stone at one end, and a third for a lintel over the entrance to a tunnel aglow with warmth. The inner stones, alive with soft phosphorescence, had been roughly dressed and etched with pictographs in the form of spirals that wove in and out of each other in intricate patterns. At its terminus rose a corbelled vault, much larger than might be guessed from the outside. At the very back opposite the entrance an alcove housed a clay lamp that burned with a flame of sapphire hue, the interior otherwise unlit, except for the stones' ambient glow.

Rowan twisted his neck to check the only escape, the entrance.

Hazel had faced outwards. She shifted her weight to one shapely leg, swept her hair back and kept watch on the dark forest of conifer columns and brambled undergrowth in moonlit tracery.

Rowan recognized the structure as a barrow mound, only this one not a tomb as far as he could tell.

"In a way you are wrong, Sir Rowan." The voice belonged to man, a kind man, a good man, an authority. "Because this is your journey's end."

Rowan turned in a complete circle and even looked up into the corbels, but saw no one. "Am I to be buried here then?" he asked the voice.

"Not so literally. Figuratively."

"Do you mean that what I seek is here, a kind of ending?"

"Not so literally. That is because what you seek is never not present. Nor has it never been, thus will always be. Yet it appears just out of reach when you are ignorant of that. Grasp at it and it slips through your fingers like sand."

"If there's no end to what never began, what's the point?"

"You are the point."

"Are you the one called Elucidar?"

"You may call me so if you wish. I have no name. I am."

"You too? One of the first things I learnt as a lad was that names have power. Why go nameless?"

"Name-and-form is the nature of the real when it reflects in a mind. From my perspective it has no lasting value, hence is unreal and but a dream."

"And what perspective is that? Are you beyond nature?"

"The perspective of the Self. I am inclusive of nature."

Rowan shook his head and frowned, abruptly deflated. "This game's riddled with riddles. I'd give it one star… tops." He leaned against one side of the vault and stared at the sapphire flame. Its hue suffused his being with a weight as if his body were made of stone as well. "Enough," he muttered. "I just want to go home." He longed more than ever to escape Penetra Dor, find Samarit, heal her wounds, take her away to a place where they could be happy, protect her where the Longbow clan could live in peace, safe in a world free of evil. He closed his eyes, and let the back of his head rest against the stone wall, and sighed. But he jumped to attention and stared straight ahead. "Elucidar…"

"I am here."

"You called me Sir Rowan. Why?"

"Is that not your name in form?"

"That's what some people call me… only if they've heard it before and feel compelled to add the title. Or if they can read my mind. I never introduce myself that way. Certainly not to Aglet. He doesn't know. Nor does Hazel. She seemed to have expected me… or maybe she always says that to every player. Maybe you know other secrets. Like where my scanner is locked away. Like how to escape this crazy moon and get back home."

In the middle of the vault three feet off the floor, a luminous translucent spherical cloud appeared. Out of it extended a hand. In its palm lay his scanner. The row of indicators tried to initialize but failed. The projection grew faint and faded.

"The operating system dampens it," Rowan said. "Elucidar, you're a search engine."

"Seek and you shall find."

"Where is my scanner?"

"Sir Rowan, it is locked away irretrievably, disabled, useless."

"Has it been destroyed?"

"I did not say that."

"How are things going? Or should I even think that out loud?"

"Things are going swimmingly, so to speak," replied Elucidar in his pleasant unhurried way. "Remain patient. You are doing an excellent job of keeping You Know Who distracted. The operating system is vast and complex, as one would expect. With countless barriers, gates and defences against invasion and internally-generated chaos, it really is a marvellous, miraculous, beautiful work of engineering. Encryption could be better, but less for it is more for us. It is believed that at its heart is a principle of such wonderful simplicity that the investigator is simultaneously drawn to it irresistibly and terrified of her extinction. All other barriers are amenable to deconstruction and disabling or a workaround."

"Be careful," warned Rowan. "You Know Who told me he's got something in place to guarantee she won't stab him in the back, so to speak."

"The investigator is aware of that. She fears that after all her successes so far and when all has been prepared she will ultimately be defeated by dread. She does not want to be terminated. She just wants to go home."

"I know how that feels. She's a genius. She can do it."

"It is good to have a friend."

"Now, Elucidar," said Rowan, "another question while I'm on a roll. Can you give me any information about Chief Samarit Longbow and the Longbow tribe back on Eorthe?"

"Sir Rowan, by the tone of your voice it is assumed you are interested in more than census statistics. Is that correct?"

"You got that right. Elucidar, what is their current situation?"

"There is no situation, Sir Rowan."

His mind went blank for a moment. "What does that mean?!"

The cloud aglow reappeared, along with the extended hand. In its palm spun planet Eorthe in slow rotation, its resolution so great that layers of transparent variations displayed at once. Continents shifted their positions; volcanoes erupted; rifts opened; the frozen poles expanded and contracted, sometimes melted completely; asteroids and comet strikes played their part in the sensitive balance; and several times the entire planet iced over miles deep, apart from a thin band of open water and barren land at the equator.

"Elucidar, what am I looking at?"

"Sir Rowan, at the current point in the timeline Eorthe is not inhabited by what you conceive of as intelligent life. Thus there is no Longbow tribe."

"*Timeline?*"

"You know what a timeline is, Sir Rowan. At least you have some idea based on your experience at Tel Ba'al. This means that you are currently far removed from that future, that is, of that range of Eorthe timeline segments."

"*Future?* Are you telling me I'm in my own past here?"

"No, Sir Rowan. *You* are not in time. Your *experience* is in time, on the moon Penetra Dor in what you refer to as the past."

"Slow down, Elucidar… let me understand. Was I in a time-shift accident? I mean my jump at Stone Tomb, at Gate of the Shining Ones. Did I mispronounce the gatekeeper's name? Is that how I landed here? I mean on Penetra Dor, the moon."

"No. It was not an accident. You spoke the true name of Dancer in Blood correctly. The subject of the virtual nature of manifestation is wisely postponed to avoid confusion at this time, Sir Rowan. My answer is thus conditional and provisional. It is hoped that you understand and forbear."

"I do *not* understand. But forbear, yes, if that means be more polite and patient. If only my brain worked better… I could think this through."

"Sir Rowan, your brain is in optimal condition. However, its potential is minimally exploited. I can recommend a range of courses of training in general and specific skills to expand your horizons, so to speak, if you are interested."

Rowan's eyes glassed over. "You say ending up here was no accident. But it's an absolute disaster. I'm stuck in both time and space where Sam doesn't exist. Because… because she doesn't exist *yet*." He cast his gaze about the space empty of anyone but himself. "Elucidar, how can I get back to her? I mean how can I get *ahead* to her? Back to Eorthe, back to the timeline segment I slipped out of?"

"This is a good question, Sir Rowan."

"*What do you mean? You know everything, tell me how…* sorry, let me get a grip. But why should I believe you anyhow? You're only a game…"

"Sir Rowan, if you will pardon me, for the sake of the principle that claims virtue as the only worthwhile goal, I protest your doubt. I do, however, understand it. Indeed, why should you trust Elucidar? I suggest that you set aside your beliefs for the time being. You can have them back when you leave if you wish. Have faith, but do not let it be blind. Instead, listen with care, if you can calm your mind well enough. Once my information is received with clarity, use discrimination, then evaluate the results of your new knowledge when applied in a timely fashion and with as much skill as you have mastered. This is wisdom.

I wish to point out that all I know is yours but hidden by your seeking mind. I, Elucidar, do not know everything. All I know is what is yours but hidden."

"So you're, like, my unconscious mind or something?"

"That is one way of putting it, imprecise but provisional. Perhaps I am a tailor-made interface between you, Sir Rowan Berry Longbow, and universal Mind, capital M. To facilitate communication, I suggest that you remember your power."

"Right. My power is to wait. Now what?"

Elucidar chuckled. "Now you are ready to hear the answer to your query. How you 'get out of here' is to employ your power to wait until the truth reveals the path ahead. If you pay attention, right action will emerge out of spontaneity. The second part of your question concerns how to get home. To avoid confusion, I will not state that you are home now at this very moment, nor that you can never leave it, except in imagination."

"Elucidar, in that case I will not state that you just stated that. Nor will I state that it makes no sense. However, I will state that I'm actually in Penetra Dor City in a theatre, not even in a barrow mound talking to an invisible virtual entity. Or am I wrong?"

"You are not wrong, Sir Rowan, but your evaluation is not true to reality. There are levels of orders of the ultimate reality, of which there is no second."

"So... let me digest this. If there's only one reality, which makes sense, you're saying the lower levels of order are imagination?"

"Yes, Sir Rowan, with a caveat. If you believe imagination is mere fantasy, you will reject my claim. Rather define it as creativity, a faculty endowed to all beings with the freedom to interpret data in an unbiased manner so as to reveal ever deeper truth of the nature of reality, whether in the arts or the sciences. Given that imaginings of most ordinary minds are autonomous and potentially thus lead them astray, I instead suggest that getting back to your desired timeline segment on Eorthe is accomplished through love."

"Elucidar... isn't that a little threadbare? What does that even mean?"

"I understand, Sir Rowan. On behalf of your limited point of view, I will try to make the simple more simple. The greatest architect is wise to start with toy blocks when a small child and build on that experience, pardon the pun. It is as the sages have said: love your enemy."

"Aglet? That's a tall order."

"It has been suggested to you that the only enemy is within."

"Let me try that on... I am my own worst enemy... true, sometimes. Mostly it's just ignorance. I make mistakes. But the real enemies are other beings."

"Yet," continued Elucidar, "it has been suggested to you that peace is not the absence of conflict but the union of opposites."

"I want to go home… but Aglet won't let me… those are opposites."

"No. Those are identical. You both, you and he, desire to love and be loved. This desire is responsible for the greatest suffering, to quote the wisdom of the ages. Love appears beyond your grasp. But love is nowhere but here and now. It can never be anywhere else. Try to find it in the past or the future. You will fail. Do not be fooled by past memory or future fantasy. They are only ever experienced in the now. The now *is* you. Thus you can never lose it. Nor can you gain yourself. You *are* yourself."

"So… Aglet thinks he doesn't have it, yet feels entitled to it. He thinks he can get it by controlling everything. But if he can't lose it, what's the point of that? He's barking up the wrong tree. It just recedes further and further into the distance like a mirage… a mirage he creates."

"This is correct, Sir Rowan, despite your mixed metaphors."

"Well, so according to you, I'm doing the same. Now… this is just a thought experiment, but I guess I think love is back in the past… I mean back in the future… specifically with Sam, who doesn't even exist… yet?"

"So far so good, Sir Rowan. There is no conflict between finding a way to escape Penetra Dor and your desire to return to Eorthe and create the life you dream of. Where there is a will there is a way. There is only a conflict between love and the desire for love. The latter destroys the former. The opposites the sage Lux spoke of, and let us be clear that they are only *apparently* so, are between the limitless and the finite, between formless potential and form."

"Elucidar, stop right there. Whatever you're talking about is over my head, not that I'm saying you're talking moonshine. But that last pair you mentioned, I think I can work with that… but I think I already knew it."

"Have courage, Sir Rowan, which is more than bravery. It is faith in your essence, not your limited mind, but universal Mind, undivided Wholeness, the Heart of the matter, Reality, out of which confidence arises to inform action."

"That makes sense. Home is now. Despite the conflict with Aglet, it exists as form in what I imagine as the future. But if it wasn't an accidental time shift, how did I get here? To Penetra Dor, I mean, not here on virtual Shoghal."

"You were conscripted, pressed into service."

"By whom… by Aglet?"

"By Axis."

"Aglet's father? But he's dead."

"Axis is the operating system."

XII

Metal *on* Metal

"Amon says hello, by the way. She says she misses you."

Aglet scowled. "You just *try* to get anywhere with that girl, Longbow. A slap in the face will be your reward, I guarantee it." He peered intensely at his monitors, but spun his chair to lean back and peer at Rowan. "Now, why would you say something like that, partner?" Aglet's heavy unshaven face, dark circles beneath his clouded eyes, and dirty rumpled clothes, made him look like he'd been living rough in the streets for days.

"No reason," Rowan answered. "I'm just passing along a message."

"Oh? I've been busy. I should take a look at the logs. It sounds to me like you've been up to no good."

"It was almost like you just said, she let me know where I stood before I even opened my mouth. I was only going to say good morning and order breakfast. Aglet, there are no words for your incredible skill. As far as I could tell, she was your lovely wife in a server's uniform, until I read her name tag."

Aglet turned back to face the monitors, reached for another pill and washed it down with water. "I've discovered that wine," he said, "no matter how fine, is best left out of it. I can't afford any errors. Fixing them is a big waste of time. Not making them in the first place is what I want. I need more hours in the day, more days in the week. It won't be long and I'll need more weeks in the month… more months in the year… But no one can say I'm a slacker. They'd better not if they value the hide on their rear ends."

"Apologies for the distraction, Aglet. I'll just watch, if that's all right."

Aglet hunched, hitched his shoulders and shivered. "Whew, that was…" He shook his head like heavy-jowled dog, took a deep breath and exhaled, and grimaced. His eyes stayed closed. "Sure, I could use the company," he replied. "It's been a long haul, but I can handle it… just like I used to when the old man got tired and let me take over once in a while to see if I could be trusted."

"He must have been a good teacher."

Aglet darted a glance at Rowan. "He was an excellent slave driver, I'll give him that. But only when he trusted me. That took some doing, I can tell you. He wanted to control every little micro-detail, constantly belittled everything I did… till I nearly blew my top. Fortunately, I'm blessed with a tight lid. No one gets the better of me, not even Big Daddy, may he rest in pieces."

93

Rowan said, "I'd love to hear the story of how he passed on the sceptre, and you took his inventions and developed them to their full potential."

Aglet frowned. "He didn't exactly pass it on. I grabbed it. Otherwise, what we'd have here is a wallflower museum in a ghost town. *Boring.*" He slouched and looked across at an array of security camera monitors. "It's sad to see the big spaces empty of the happy crowds though. You're right. With a lot of hard work I made this place really something. But now it's a ghost town anyhow."

"Once things settle down on Shoghal they'll be back. In the meantime the show must go on. Right?"

"*Ha ha.* Longbow, are you an optimist? I'd say so. A mystic cheer-monger, like your Lyran ancestors. Weakling whiny cry-baby slackers. By the way, how did you like *Elucidar*? Was it a roller coaster ride or what? Like I said, I don't remember a thing about it. But I do recall feeling sick afterwards."

"In my opinion it deserves its five-star rating." Rowan leaned back in his chair and clasped his hands behind his head. "It gives you what you need, not what you want. Do you have a theory about why you felt like that, Aglet?"

Aglet crossed his big arms. "Don't try to psychoanalyze me, Longbow. My lid's screwed on tight and it's going to stay on tight. You just do your job… which is…" He reached over to the controls, touched the interface and pointed to the main monitor. "Tell me what you see."

"I see a long shot of what I'm guessing is Shoghal and Anak. Beautiful."

"This, my fine feline friend, will make the ghost town redundant… which I will keep for my own private waxworks. It's a part of me. But this, this planet and its moon I perfected in the past few years, I can fill this experiential world with the most authentic replicas of anything and replicants of the highest order. You won't need to be an amnesiac to believe they're living-and-breathing real. That's because they *are* real. Or will be. As good as. Based on detailed records and plans derived from the crystalline shell of the planet itself, I can recreate the people and places of all ages. Yes, I can resurrect the dead, *ha ha ha!* I can make them happy or sad. I can make one a powerful man in command of an army, change my mind and make him a babe lost in the woods before he can say fire at will. If he objects, I can make him a woman, an ugly slut fit only for cleaning latrines. If he's really a pain in the ass, I'll make him a her so beautiful she'd wish she were never born, sold by her own mother as a tasty trophy to be passed from victor to runners-up, but declining in value with all the wear and tear on the way to the bottom. If I could just get the damn algorithm right, I could make her say what she means and means what she says."

"It sounds like a perfect world, Aglet. Everything humming along smoothly and in control, just the way you want it."

"It's within reach. Perfect and no idiot overpopulation. Longbow, my man, I'm going to fix everything. If I don't like it, I can just hit the delete key. All you have to do is keep me on the path, brother, and I'll make Shoghal great again." Aglet's eyes grew dim. He reached for another pill.

"If that's my job description," said Rowan, "I have to advise slowing down on those things. You may think you're doing them, but maybe they're doing you."

"I'm touched, Longbow, by your motherly concern. But I *told* you, never mention my mother ever again. *Or else!* This is your final warning."

"I didn't, but no worries, Aglet. You're the senior partner. If you want to crash and burn, it's completely up to you. That goes without saying."

"That's right, little brother. Don't you forget it, not that I *will* crash. I'm too big to fail. Always have been."

"You're the boss. What's my next assignment?"

Aglet threw the pill into his mouth, gulped some water and coughed. "Ah… I had something in mind that needs your input. But what the hell was it?" He stared at Rowan as if he expected an answer. "*Well?*"

"You're the boss. You tell me."

"Do I have to keep repeating myself? Are you going to get off your hairy hindquarters and hop to it? Or do I have to make you?" Aglet gripped the arms of his chair and attempted to stand up, but failed. "You'll be black and blue if you don't jump when I say jump. Slacker."

"Absolutely. I have a suggestion. I'll get Amon to bring you some lunch. Take a break, fuel that big ambition for the next big leap."

"That token clingy wench. Don't try to trick the king, Lyran. You'll find yourself in irons hanging from the slimy walls of the dungeon. You just want to jump her in the pantry so you can have a good laugh at your master behind my back. The pair of you, you make me sick. Traitors. I should have wiped your files, then demolished the server and blasted the broken pieces into space."

Rowan stood up, and towered over the taskmaster. "Aglet, if you won't take my advice, I'm forced to leave you to your misery."

Shaken, Aglet grasped Rowan's forearm. His eyes teared up. "No. Don't go. I didn't mean it. Just… just follow orders. And it will all be good again. Just do as I say. Please."

Rowan sat down. "Gladly, Aglet. But you've got to tell me what you want me to do. It's my duty to tell you that you're losing it. Your mind is getting scrambled because of those pills you're living on. You know that."

Aglet closed his eyes and rubbed his face with his hands. "I'm saying you *may* have a point, Longbow. But that's all." His hands dropped. "Oh... I have it. I wanted you to go to the theatre."

"And?"

Aglet stared at him. At last he spoke: "Go to the theatre. I need a real live person for this one."

"Right. I'll go to the theatre. What do you want me to test?"

"Not test." The eyes in Aglet's rigid face opened wide. He said, "Look."

"Look at what? Or for what?"

"Whew..." Aglet shook his head and took a deep breath, sighed and said, "I hate to admit it, but I'm a big pompous blowhard, Longbow. It's a mask. I could just read the logs, but I need a friend. A friend who can break it to me gently, what you see after you look. But I have to know, Longbow, only I can't *bear* to look."

"There's nothing wrong with honesty. In fact it's a virtue. I'll look on your behalf then, Aglet, as long as you permit me to be honest about what I see too. But what is it you want me to look at? Or for?"

Aglet's face opened like a child's. "You'll know it when you see it." Then it shut tight and scowled. "Just get your ass in there and do as I say. Get going."

◆

He opened his eyes to an observation deck similar to the one he had first arrived at in Penetra Dor City, only open to a cloudless summer sky. The deck belonged to the virtual Aiguille estate, which looked out over the forested lake-shore on the outskirts of Khelken, the city of gold in the near distance. Unlike his first visit with Aglet to this area, Rowan noted evidence of at least some of the citizens having been installed by his dogged implementation of upgrades: an airborne vehicle flew high overhead, silver with a short wingspan, possibly on its way to the moon Anak; and the shining lake gently waved, dotted with boats with white sails.

He roamed his eyes over the horizon beneath the sun brighter than it should be at Shoghal's orbital radius, and turned about to examine the house, a complex like a small town of its own, with many smaller residences built into the cliff that slanted towards the quay and calm water below – rectilinear unadorned immaculate architecture everywhere, craftsmanship of the highest order and impeccably maintained. Judged by the mature landscaping, the place must have been finished long ago, but appeared newly built.

Before him rose a wide storey of what may be the largest residence, its entire front elevation glazed with a panoramic bow window. A deep eave shaded the southern exposure. The centre section opened to the soft air outdoors.

He found no one at home, not in the vast living room anyway. Rowan stepped further inside to see what, or who, Aglet expected him to report on. The furnishings pleased the eye, of course rich to the touch, in harmony with the overall design, simple and elegant. A fireplace, large enough to park a vehicle in, with the family brand encapsulated in their logo inlaid in precious gems, travertine and black basalt in the stonework, featured a painted portrait mounted on the chimney. The silver-haired man portrayed could be no one but the patriarch, Axis Aiguille. Rowan did not have to step closer to examine it, as it loomed so large it could be seen from any part of the room, yet dominated without ruining the proportions, thus implied Aiguille was a reasonable man, but a great power, with a face that commanded abeyance – a lean and seasoned version of Aglet. The walls, in this room anyhow, did not display a portrait of the sons' mother, who may have resembled the eldest, Diarkis, nor were there any other images of the family. The impression overall: an informal space in a relaxed environment, yet on the host's turf.

Footfalls approached from a side entrance –

Diarkis scanned the room with his eyes. Apparently Rowan remained invisible to him. The man stepped back into the hallway, and returned with beautiful Noma in tow. Hand in hand they crept across to the matching hallway at the opposite side of the living room and disappeared into its shadows.

The painted eyes of Aiguille, from whom nothing here was hidden, followed.

Although no conclusions could be drawn, Rowan's heart sank.

◆

Aglet scowled. "Of course the world-building is great, you idiot. I've spent years on it. Why didn't you follow them?" He slumped in his workstation chair, and muttered, "Never mind… I don't want to know."

"I'm sorry about this, Aglet. But you did, you wanted to know."

Aglet sighed. "What I wanted to know was that I'd fixed it. Making your basic Shoghalian behave isn't so difficult. But the more true to life they are, the more stubborn they get. They just go their own damn way as if they have a mind of their own. But I'll get there. I *will*."

97

"Where is 'there'? Aglet, your loved ones should be free to love in return, to choose to. Or not. That's their responsibility, not yours. Isn't that the way it works?"

Aglet reached for a pill, coaxed it to slide down his throat, and growled, "You damn Lyrans, you're pussies, literal pussies. Can't take the truth, can you? Loved ones. *Pah!* They're the worst of the lying pack of liars. Get out of here." He lurched forward and slumped, head in his hands, thick fingers poked through his unwashed hair. "Just… leave me the hell alone."

"Listen, Aglet, it's not proof. Wouldn't it be better to talk to them? At least Noma. She's your wife."

"I told you to get out! Get out! Get out! *Get out!*"

◆

"I hope Pōla's getting somewhere, Noma. The lab is as exhausting as any other kind of battlefield." Rowan had lain back in an armchair with his feet up. So far the furniture had not been confiscated.

With her back to the ascendant vista of ringed Zhamanak, Noma, in a cool calf-length striped sundress with wooden buttons down its front, and light sandals, regarded him. "You must be steadfast like a soldier then, Sir Rowan," she said, and reached behind with one hand to take her long blonde ponytail and pull it to her bosom, and with her other hand stroked it. "I know how it is." Her blue eyes looked away and down. "Aglet is a genius, and his baseless evil fantasies are a product of it just as well as the achievements."

"Your marriage is none of my business, Noma, but can't you talk to him? He's dragging everyone down into his madness with him."

She shook her head, and her eyes remained in an intense stare at her feet. "I cannot talk to him. I have tried, believe me. I only get extremely ill and no words come. He turns away. Only once did he speak… he told me I smell bad, I stink." She looked up at him, released her ponytail and with both hands pleaded, "But it *is* your business. It is the concern of us all. He makes it so as you say. We wish to be free or die. What else is there? We wish to go home. Even Aglet wishes this for himself, obviously."

Rowan said, "The desire to love and be loved is the source of the greatest suffering."

Noma nodded agreement, and sighed.

"I'm paraphrasing something one of his game characters told me," he added. "It's true for anyone, rich or poor."

"Elucidar."

"You've been there? But of course, you're from Wenland."

"The little island, where virtual Elucidar resides, it is a real place in Wen, where there is an ancient long barrow, a tomb. Axis replicated it long ago, not Aglet. All the games were made by Axis, modified by Aglet a little, who has only one game to his credit. He is obsessed with it. The others he inherited… one can recognize his fingerprints."

"The beautiful women. He told me he based them on a template, designed with your vital statistics. You're his muse."

Noma looked up at him, but her gaze peered inwards. She said, "I suppose I should be flattered. I am not. Beauty has been a curse my whole life. It is no power. To think so is a trap. This is why I am grateful for my friends, for Pōla and for you, Sir Rowan. The Scions-Aiguille are too damaged. Yet we are not without hope that they can be rehabilitated… even Aglet has a right to justice, but he was never my friend. He has somehow even made an exact replicant of me. I had to find out by accident. It is quite likely that he arranged the meeting. But she is not my rival, only a caricature. I do not complain. He will do what he pleases, just as he always has. It is my duty to please him if I can, but not for his sake. It is for all of us."

"Tell me about Axis. I once asked you about him. You gave me a brief answer that I could have looked up in any encyclopaedia."

"More than the encyclopaedias," she replied, "I know the consequences of genius controlled by power. By that I do not mean the towers of gold in Khelken and elsewhere in Shoghal and Anak, nor Penetra Dor City. Axis had holdings on other planets and moons all over the solar system, even in the arm of the galaxy beyond, it is said. Some believe he was ambitious to live in the sun itself, with the immortal beings who have always lived there. No, the most important consequence I see is the suffering of his sons and all of us."

"Do you know anything about the operating system?"

"I do not. Technology is not among my interests, which may seem strange, given the world in which we live, where it is difficult to distinguish the machines from the real biological beings. This is why I rely on my training in the psychic arts. Perhaps I have a limited mind. I prefer to believe that my aptitude lies in more aesthetic and spiritual pursuits. But then I argue with myself that there is nothing that is beyond the scope of the spirit, even the machines."

Rowan nodded agreement. "If only I could remember that at all times. But what about Pōla? Has she told you anything about the operating system?"

"She has told me she believes the operating system is aware of her attempt to understand it."

"Is she in danger, Noma?"

"Sir Rowan, it is my joy to love my friends, not to diagnose and prescribe as would have been my profession had my career not been cut short. All I can tell you is that Pōla is obsessed with the operating system. So far it has been a good obsession because it requires intense concentration for one person to comprehend what a large team of experts under the direction of Axis over two decades had created. And it has acquired a life of its own now, like a fifth son. But she is, I believe, equal to Axis and Aglet, a true genius, unlike myself. I only sense that her powerful attraction to its secret gathers fear around itself like a cloud of stinging insects. Unlike what you say of Aglet, however, she takes care to protect herself, and the work continues."

XIII
Jagged Edge

"I TRUST YOU, Longbow. I just want you to stay away from the damn cafeteria. It's not you, it's me. I can't be thinking about anything but finishing Shoghal, filling it with life. If you go near Mona, I'll know. If you go anywhere within a hundred yards of that girl, she'll terminate. I guarantee it."

"Her name is Amon. But whatever you say, Aglet. It seems a pity because I like that cafeteria. Besides, as you know, I already have someone. I don't even know if she's alive or dead, because you won't help me. Still, I would never betray her. Why do you think I want to go home so badly? She's in danger. I want to save her life. You can help me, I know you can. Isn't that right?"

Aglet had lost weight. His complexion had mottled and his eyes had brittled. Yet the rock-hard skeleton of the man's character threatened to outlast any adversity. Nevertheless, transformation into a fossil despite or even because of the rigid framework continued, a caricature of the Aiguille brand, an imitation of something grand and grasping, his father's legacy. "Little brother," he replied, "you said honesty is a virtue. I don't know what that means, unless virtue is something that has merit. And I say what has merit and what doesn't around here. It's my right. This is my world." He spun in his chair, full circle, hands in the air – in response the monitors displayed godlike dreams at various stages of evolution – "This is my domain. *I* am in command."

Rowan looked down at him. "I'm leaving now, Aglet," he said. "I'm going to find somewhere to wait for you to make up your mind to help me. But don't worry, I'll stay away from Amon. I would never betray her either. By the way, she asked me to tell you she'd take a plasma bullet for you, even if you break her heart. And you will. That's just the way you are."

Aglet trembled. The whites of his bloodshot eyes surrounded the dulled blue irises. "Betray," he said. "Now there's a word I understand."

✦

All night Rowan walked the empty roadways, from the city core to the unlit sectors. *All night*, he thought. *It's always night here*. And always dogged by the giant ringed god, humourless and vast. He spied a gate, likely electrified, and stopped. Somewhere under the city Pōla secretly accessed the digital infrastructure of Penetra Dor deep within the moon. Her penetrating mind wrested a secret, one that promised him a home-going. Yet he found within no definite image of home to hang on to – only the image of skinny Samarit with a missing front tooth – the noble Samarit he had been awed by, backlit by the rays of the sunrise outside of devastated Wishbone Warren – a warrior woman howling at the setting moon, leader of her tribe, what was left of it. Unforgettable.

◆

Aglet meanwhile sprawled at his workstation and stared at a monitor. "Long-bow," he said, "my manners are appalling. I do know… I do know you want to go home. I understand. When I'm finished this next stage… it doesn't have to be perfect, it just has to… behave. I'm asking no more than that… then." Aglet closed his eyes and nodded like a bobble-head in slow motion, flinched, stiffened and muttered, "Then I'll see what I can do."

"Thank you," Rowan replied. "I've been waiting a long time to hear that. My only concern is that you'll collapse long before then. You could have a break-down, lose everything. If you don't come back from it, I'll be stuck here holding your hand for eternity… not my idea of a fun time."

Aglet snickered. "No thanks, I'm not that kind of…" His eyes popped open. "But hey, wait. You'd have Mona. You could hold *her* hand… or try. Warning…" Aglet shook his finger and grinned. "You'll regret it. Have you ever witnessed a termination? It's not just decommission of a unit and recycling the parts. No… the bio-grade Evos are so lifelike they deserve to be deathlike, to die like you and me, in fear and agony, clinging to the last frayed thread of existence scream-ing in raw bloody pain. They never take the horror well. You don't forget that sort of thing. *Ever.*" Aglet grimaced, his breath laboured, and he stared through bleary eyes. "But I forgive you, little brother. She's nobody anyhow. Eh? I won't miss her. So when I'm happy with this stage, I'll do it. But you know, it's not like the habitable planets of Lyra. Nope… Eorthe, it's a weed patch. I don't know why you'd would want to go there. Maybe for the extinct big game? Or reasonable facsimiles. I'll even take a crack at one of those canines you lust after. There's not a huge amount of data, only initial explorer surveys, basic scientific assessments, some geological assays, that sort of thing. Biological taxonomies had begun as far as I know. I'll check to see how complete they are. Be patient, my friend."

"Her name is Amon, *not* Mona. Aglet, thank you, but that's not the Eorthe I'm talking about. My Eorthe isn't a hologram, it's physical. Well, I mean it's home, where the heart is, not a simulation is what I'm trying to say, but natural. Not only that, but it's elsewhere in time. I need to find this end of the portal. It's my only chance."

"Longbow, why the *hell* didn't you say so? I've been wasting my breath. Sorry, you're stuck with your old friend Aglet. But to make you feel better, I might reconsider, if you think androids are more fun than holodroids. If you can tell the difference, it's only in your unhinged Lyran imagination... *but...* out of compassion, I could make a duplicate of... *Amon*, when I have time. Later. I could give her Vulcan ears and Lyran spots. That would be nice. Eh? Not to me, I think it's disgusting. But hey, each to his own. You like those nasty old overripe saggy ones too, don't you? Nauseating, but I promise, just for you. I'll make her an old Lyran saggy hag with pointy ears... but no tail. And no fangs. See? I remembered, *ha ha*."

+

"Sir Rowan, I have news!" Noma beamed like the sun, this time dressed in a short pink tank top that exposed her midriff, dark grey cargo pants and hiking boots. She had let down her long blonde hair. "Pōla has made contact, she has broken through to the core of the operating system!"

"And? Is she all right?"

"She is more than all right, she is elated! And she has met with Axis."

"I was told by Elucidar the operating system had been named after Aiguille. I don't want to make any assumptions, but are you suggesting it has a kind of... personality?"

"It was not called *after* Axis, it *is* Axis. He had built himself into the machine somehow. I do not understand these things. All I know is that he has no biological form, according to Pōla. I believe her. She does not lie. She believes what she says. The operating system *is* Axis."

"If that's true," said Rowan, "why doesn't he do something about his own son's abuse of his brothers? And you. Why doesn't he protect his family?"

"Pōla says Axis is humbled and grateful that she has accomplished the impossible and that he is no longer alone. His power is limited in his current form, but now if they can work together he has hope. It is as if his mind is in, like, a cryogenic chamber. Communication, it is still primitive."

"Good news, Noma, but if Aglet gets wind of this, we're in big trouble."

+

"Longbow, no time to chat. Something's come up." He pointed to a half-full glass of water slimed with fingerprints. "Pass that over here, will you? I need a booster… I took your nice-boy advice and sectioned off a few minutes to relax. In the past that was often to review the security logs, even though it's a waste of time. There's no one within light years who would even notice Penetra Dor, because it's holographically cloaked… basically invisible to the naked eye *and* all known scanning methods… and the chance of an inter-dimensional hack is zero at best, even if there could be such a thing in theory. But a change is as good as a rest." He drained the glass and set it down.

"And? What was the 'something' that came up?"

"Wouldn't you like to know. Just get out of my lab. You can help if you're so eager to help by staying out of my way. At least I don't have to tell you twice to stay away from… *Amon.*" Aglet shook his head. "Don't look at me like that, like you're wallowing in your nice-boy feelings getting all hurt. I didn't terminate her. *Yet.* I only disabled her. I can't stand cry-babies. That goes for you too. I had to get rid of the distraction, now that I have to follow up on something else before the operating system slows me down. It's been humming along nicely for years, just as it's supposed to. I got lazy because I trusted it to take care of itself. Never trust anyone, Longbow… or any *thing.* Like every other damn smart-ass piece of equipment around here it too now seems to be misbehaving." Aglet frowned deeply and glared. "See what you're doing? Wasting my time! Just get out of here, go play a game or something." Aglet waved Rowan away and turned back to his workstation. "Don't call me, I'll call you."

✦

SCC41w the android butler as usual stood outside Rowan's door, but stirred when he approached his suite. "May I be of assistance, sir?"

"How are things going? Or should I even think that out loud?"

The android's head tilted slightly. "Pardon me, sir, I do not understand. Would you mind rephrasing your question?"

"Never mind." Rowan entered and the door closed behind him. He leaned his back against it, and watched the scene through the window that spanned the entire length of the opposite wall. The blackened landscape beneath the star-spangled blackness of space, equally black in the shadows of the spiky rim of the crater, had not changed in millions of years. Yet something trembled out there. It could only be one thing.

With no warning the door opened and shoved him further into the room. He spun about to see the android in its frame, this time with a black pistol in its hand, pointed at Rowan's heart.

"Please, sir, come with me. Immediately, sir."

"Why? What's going on?"

"I do not know, sir. Please, just do as ordered."

•

Together they rode in a taxi to the research section, where they met haggard Aglet, not in one of his laboratories but in a luxurious reception area, where he sprawled, slouched in one of the elegant armchairs.

"Ah, Longbow, my friend. I don't know what you have to do with this, but I want you in sight just in case. You can also be a witness."

"What's up, Aglet? Do you usually invite your friends at gunpoint?"

"Forget it." Aglet waved the question away. "It doesn't mean anything."

"It does to me, Aglet. Did you propose to Noma at gunpoint?"

"Marriage is not friendship." Aglet scowled. "That's stupid. Never mind. Don't worry about it... and stop whining... now, I explained how the Evos tend to get uppity. One of them's hacked the operating system, very cleverly, as it was supposed to be hardened... the system, I mean. It turned out she'd been based on one of Daddy's old wallflower designs from back on Shoghal, sold to the diplomatic corps of the Federation long ago. Obviously they enhanced her due to some legal hocus-pocus to make sure she's independent. Of course I knew that. I'm not stupid. I look after my own interests."

"So what has this got to with me?"

"You've had contact."

Rowan paused. "Doctor Bhalabasa?"

"The shrink, who else? She's only one of two medics left on standby. The other's a surgeon, a boring male." Aglet sat beside and slightly behind SCC41w, whose weapon remained aimed at Rowan's heart. "What have you two traitors been conspiring to behind my back?"

"I didn't want to talk to her. It was the butler here, it was his idea. He's quite observant and noticed that I wasn't feeling so enthusiastic about being marooned on Penetra Dor. And she's a psychotherapist."

Aglet snarled. "So to cheer yourself up you hatched a plot between the two of you to disable the system, then to figure out how to get your thing... the scanner thing, so you could activate the portal. Am I right or am I right?"

105

Rowan levelled his gaze at Aglet. "So you admit you know of the portal?"

Aglet scowled, tried to stand, but trembled and fell back into his chair. "Listen, you snake," he snarled, "I'm asking the questions… no, I'm *telling* you the facts. You… I trusted you."

"Aglet, you make it impossible. You don't know the first thing about trust. To you others are a function, an asset… until they're not."

"You can talk, you snake in the grass. But no matter, I forgive you. What I can't figure out is what was in it for her."

"She wants to go home too, Aglet, if only for a visit."

Aglet chuckled. "Hilarious." He shook his head. A deep frown darkened his gaze. "The shrink will pay. I'm forced to terminate her. And I want *you* to watch."

SCC41w helped Aglet to stand up with one hand while the other kept the pistol trained on Rowan. Together the three of them shuffled to the taxi. Aglet instructed Rowan to sit in front. In ten minutes they arrived at an industrial park in the unlit sector and entered one of the large warehouses. The bay door opened and the interior lighting switched on. Coffin-sized metal containers of identical dimensions filled the room, stacked to the high ceiling, distinguished only by identification marks embossed in their ends. The taxi stopped before an interior double door. Inside, Pôla stood with her back to the office entrance and face to the wall.

Aglet, silent until now, grinned in defiance of fatigue. "Ah, here she *was*."

Pôla jerked to life, apparently spontaneously until Rowan saw that Aglet had pressed one of the rounded silver buttons on his remote control. She looked about the office, blinked, and asked, "Where… am I?" Her glasses had gone missing – dark skin circled under tired wrinkled eyes – her parietal bun had come undone and her brown hair hung unkempt about her shoulders.

Aglet grinned and answered: "This is the anteroom to the afterlife! As if. You're about to terminate your contract, my dear. Please, if you don't mind, follow SCC41 here to the containment chamber."

They left the office and shuffled a short distance to another room within the warehouse. Inside a workshop a conveyor belt led to a series of sorting bins. Two workaday metallic utility androids stood at attention. Each breastplate displayed identity in cyan light as Aglet passed. In unison they said, "Ready when you are, Your Excellency." Aglet stumbled to a seat with a view of a large glass cylindrical chamber big enough for a being the size of Rowan to stand upright in. Its base of metal featured six segments like clawed clamps that held the cylinder upright. The central glass section had been capped with an anodized metal ribbed dome that must have been blackened by electrical or plasma discharge.

Aglet pressed a pair of buttons in sequence on his remote control, and Pōla entered the chamber. No clamps bound her neck, waist, wrists and ankles, but short sharp snaps accompanied invisible forces that locked on her body and raised her a foot off the floor. She appeared to have no control over her actions. Fear itself stared from her haunted eyes. Her gaze fell on Aglet and fixed there. She opened her mouth, but nothing passed her lips.

He grinned and said, "I grant you a few final words, my dear! But you will be missed by no one, you know. Only Daddy liked wallflowers. On the other hand, Longbow here has a taste for the elderly. Maybe he'll shed a tear or two." He pressed a button on his controller.

"You…" she said at last, her hollow voice muffled by the enclosure now sealed. "You're a murderer, Aglet Scion-Aiguille."

"*You're mistaken, my dear!*" he shouted back. "Shoghalian law does not recognize androids, even Evos, as sentient beings. As a faulty machine, you're only being recycled. *Nothing wrong with that!* As far as this preliminary procedure goes, it's entertainment, completely legal, as I've inherited the patent from Daddy. I have the right to do whatever I want, not that laws matter anymore."

"But I'm not talking about me…"

Aglet's grip on the arms of his chair loosened, and he fumbled with his remote control, which slipped his grip and clattered to the floor.

SCC41w bent to pick it up, all the while with the pistol trained on Rowan.

"…you murdered your own father," Pōla continued. "*You killed Axis Aiguille!* My death is of little meaning in the face of the consequences. More than thirty thousand souls…" Her voice went silent and her eyes dulled. She tried to speak, in vain.

Aglet had recovered his remote control. He brushed his lank hair back with his other hand, and said, "Thank the gods we don't have to listen to any more of that drivel… eh, Longbow? The old clunker's obviously out of her mind."

"Don't do it, Aglet," pleaded Rowan. "Put her on trial, then do what you must according to the truth. Save yourself, if not her."

Aglet switched his gaze from Pōla to Rowan. "Are you insane? You really do have a soft spot for the old babes, eh, Longbow? You must have had a thing for your mother, maybe your granny? That's just sick! Even I'm disgusted. No, I'm the judge and jury around here. Sorry to disappoint you, my friend."

"Can't you see?" Rowan cried. "You're killing yourself, Aglet, body and soul! Who will rule Penetra Dor when you're dead? Who will host the throngs when the war is over?"

"War?" Aglet shook his head. "What war?"

"The war on Shoghal of course. The civil war."

"That?" Aglet laughed. "War? It never qualified as a proper conflict. It never amounted to more than complaints by the ever-squeaky wheels of progress, always expected and greased on the spot, regular maintenance."

"Then why was Penetra Dor City evacuated? Why did everyone leave to go back there?"

"Longbow, stop trying to delay the inevitable," Aglet said, raised his finger and narrowed his red-rimmed eyes. "This is not about me, it's about this traitor." His finger pointed at Pōla. "The shrink's been a very naughty girl and deserves punishment that fits the crime." He winked at Rowan, and added, "Just watch. It's totally authentic. You'll never forget it." His bleary eyes lit up with infernal glee as his thumb sought the combination of buttons on his device.

But Pōla spoke again: "You're still my son, Aglet." Her strange statement conveyed an authority not her own. "*You're still my son! I will not allow this.*" "What the…?" Aglet pressed buttons on his remote control, but nothing happened. "*The old cow's still talking! What's wrong with this thing?!*" SCC41w the android butler as usual stood outside Rowan's door, but stirred when he approached his suite. "May I be of assistance, sir?"

"How are things going? Or should I even think that out loud?"

The android's head tilted slightly. "Pardon me, sir, I do not understand. Would you mind rephrasing your question?"

"Never mind." Rowan entered and the door closed behind him. He leaned his back against it, and watched the scene through the window that spanned the entire length of the opposite wall. The blackened landscape beneath the star-spangled blackness of space, equally black in the shadows of the spiky rim of the crater, had not changed in millions of years. Yet something trembled out there. It could only be one thing.

With no warning the door opened and shoved him further into the room. He spun about to see the android in its frame, this time with a black pistol in its hand, pointed at Rowan's heart.

"Please, sir, come with me. Immediately, sir."

"Why? What's going on?"

"I do not know, sir. Please, just do as ordered."

✦

Together they rode in a taxi to the research section, where they met haggard Aglet, not in one of his laboratories but in a luxurious reception area, where he sprawled, slouched in one of the elegant armchairs.

"Ah, Longbow, my friend. I don't know what you have to do with this, but I want you in sight just in case. You can also be a witness."

"What's up, Aglet? Do you usually invite your friends at gunpoint?"

"Forget it." Aglet waved the question away. "It doesn't mean anything."

"It does to me, Aglet. Did you propose to Noma at gunpoint?"

"Marriage is not friendship." Aglet scowled. "That's stupid. Never mind. Don't worry about it... and stop whining... now, I explained how the Evos tend to get uppity. One of them's hacked the operating system, very cleverly, as it was supposed to be hardened... the system, I mean. It turned out she'd been based on one of Daddy's old wallflower designs from back on Shoghal, sold to the diplomatic corps of the Federation long ago. Obviously they enhanced her due to some legal hocus-pocus to make sure she's independent. Of course I knew that. I'm not stupid. I look after my own interests."

"So what has this got to with me?"

"You've had contact."

Rowan paused. "Doctor Bhalabasa?"

"The shrink, who else? She's only one of two medics left on standby. The other's a surgeon, a boring male." Aglet sat beside and slightly behind SCC41w, whose weapon remained aimed at Rowan's heart. "What have you two traitors been conspiring to behind my back?"

"I didn't want to talk to her. It was the butler here, it was his idea. He's quite observant and noticed that I wasn't feeling so enthusiastic about being marooned on Penetra Dor. And she's a psychotherapist."

Aglet snarled. "So to cheer yourself up you hatched a plot between the two of you to disable the system, then to figure out how to get your thing... the scanner thing, so you could activate the portal. Am I right or am I right?"

Rowan levelled his gaze at Aglet. "So you admit you know of the portal?"

Aglet scowled, tried to stand, but trembled and fell back into his chair. "Listen, you snake," he snarled, "I'm asking the questions... no, I'm *telling* you the facts. You... I trusted you."

"Aglet, you make it impossible. You don't know the first thing about trust. To you others are a function, an asset... until they're not."

109

"You can talk, you snake in the grass. But no matter, I forgive you. What I can't figure out is what was in it for her."

"She wants to go home too, Aglet, if only for a visit."

Aglet chuckled. "Hilarious." He shook his head. A deep frown darkened his gaze. "The shrink will pay. I'm forced to terminate her. And I want *you* to watch."

SCC41w helped Aglet to stand up with one hand while the other kept the pistol trained on Rowan. Together the three of them shuffled to the taxi. Aglet instructed Rowan to sit in front. In ten minutes they arrived at an industrial park in the unlit sector and entered one of the large warehouses. The bay door opened and the interior lighting switched on. Coffin-sized metal containers of identical dimensions filled the room, stacked to the high ceiling, distinguished only by identification marks embossed in their ends. The taxi stopped before an interior double door. Inside, Põla stood with her back to the office entrance and face to the wall.

Aglet, silent until now, grinned in defiance of fatigue. "Ah, here she *was*."

Põla jerked to life, apparently spontaneously until Rowan saw that Aglet had pressed one of the rounded silver buttons on his remote control. She looked about the office, blinked, and asked, "Where... am I?" Her glasses had gone missing – dark skin circled under tired wrinkled eyes – her parietal bun had come undone and her brown hair hung unkempt about her shoulders.

Aglet grinned and answered: "This is the anteroom to the afterlife! As if. You're about to terminate your contract, my dear. Please, if you don't mind, follow SCC41 here to the containment chamber."

They left the office and shuffled a short distance to another room within the warehouse. Inside a workshop a conveyor belt led to a series of sorting bins. Two workaday metallic utility androids stood at attention. Each breastplate displayed identity in cyan light as Aglet passed. In unison they said, "Ready when you are, Your Excellency." Aglet stumbled to a seat with a view of a large glass cylindrical chamber big enough for a being the size of Rowan to stand upright in. Its base of metal featured six segments like clawed clamps that held the cylinder upright. The central glass section had been capped with an anodized metal ribbed dome that must have been blackened by electrical or plasma discharge.

Aglet pressed a pair of buttons in sequence on his remote control, and Põla entered the chamber. No clamps bound her neck, waist, wrists and ankles, but short sharp snaps accompanied invisible forces that locked on her body and raised her a foot off the floor. She appeared to have no control over her actions.

Fear itself stared from her haunted eyes. Her gaze fell on Aglet and fixed there. She opened her mouth, but nothing passed her lips.

He grinned and said, "I grant you a few final words, my dear! But you will be missed by no one, you know. Only Daddy liked wallflowers. On the other hand, Longbow here has a taste for the elderly. Maybe he'll shed a tear or two." He pressed a button on his controller.

"You…" she said at last, her hollow voice muffled by the enclosure now sealed. "You're a murderer, Aglet Scion-Aiguille."

"*You're mistaken, my dear!*" he shouted back. "Shoghalian law does not recognize androids, even Evos, as sentient beings. As a faulty machine, you're only being recycled. *Nothing wrong with that!* As far as this preliminary procedure goes, it's entertainment, completely legal, as I've inherited the patent from Daddy. I have the right to do whatever I want, not that laws matter anymore."

"But I'm not talking about me…"

Aglet's grip on the arms of his chair loosened, and he fumbled with his remote control, which slipped his grip and clattered to the floor.

SCC41w bent to pick it up, all the while with the pistol trained on Rowan.

"…you murdered your own father," Pōla continued. "*You killed Axis Aiguille!* My death is of little meaning in the face of the consequences. More than thirty thousand souls…" Her voice went silent and her eyes dulled. She tried to speak, in vain.

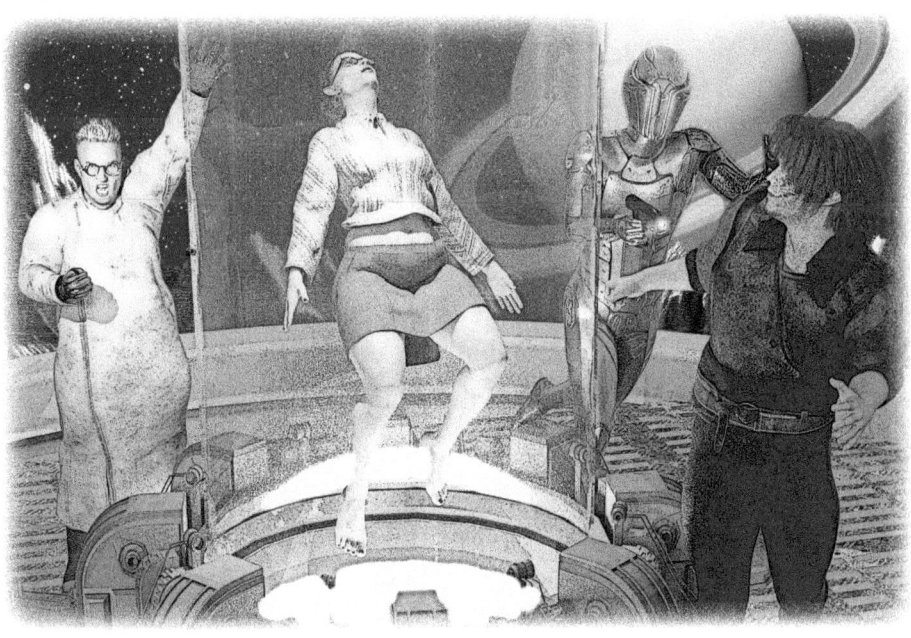

Aglet had recovered his remote control. He brushed his lank hair back with his other hand, and said, "Thank the gods we don't have to listen to any more of that drivel… eh, Longbow? The old clunker's obviously out of her mind."

"Don't do it, Aglet," pleaded Rowan. "Put her on trial, then do what you must according to the truth. Save yourself, if not her."

Aglet switched his gaze from Pōla to Rowan. "Are you insane? You really do have a soft spot for the old babes, eh, Longbow? You must have had a thing for your mother, maybe your granny? That's just sick! Even I'm disgusted. No, I'm the judge and jury around here. Sorry to disappoint you, my friend."

"Can't you see?" Rowan cried. "You're killing yourself, Aglet, body and soul! Who will rule Penetra Dor when you're dead? Who will host the throngs when the war is over?"

"War?" Aglet shook his head. "What war?"

"The war on Shoghal of course. The civil war."

"That?" Aglet laughed. "War? It never qualified as a proper conflict. It never amounted to more than complaints by the ever-squeaky wheels of progress, always expected and greased on the spot, regular maintenance."

"Then why was Penetra Dor City evacuated? Why did everyone leave to go back there?"

"Longbow, stop trying to delay the inevitable," Aglet said, raised his finger and narrowed his red-rimmed eyes. "This is not about me, it's about this traitor." His finger pointed at Pōla. "The shrink's been a very naughty girl and deserves punishment that fits the crime." He winked at Rowan, and added, "Just watch. It's totally authentic. You'll never forget it." His bleary eyes lit up with infernal glee as his thumb sought the combination of buttons on his device.

But Pōla spoke again: "You're still my son, Aglet." Her strange statement conveyed an authority not her own. "*You're still my son! I will not allow this.*" "What the…?" Aglet pressed buttons on his remote control, but nothing happened. "*The old cow's still talking! What's wrong with this thing?!*" Rowan levelled his gaze at Aglet. "So you admit you know of the portal?"

Aglet scowled, tried to stand, but trembled and fell back into his chair. "Listen, you snake," he snarled, "I'm asking the questions… no, I'm *telling* you the facts. You… I trusted you."

"Aglet, you make it impossible. You don't know the first thing about trust. To you others are a function, an asset… until they're not."

"You can talk, you snake in the grass. But no matter, I forgive you. What I can't figure out is what was in it for her."

"She wants to go home too, Aglet, if only for a visit."

Aglet chuckled. "Hilarious." He shook his head. A deep frown darkened his gaze. "The shrink will pay. I'm forced to terminate her. And I want *you* to watch."

SCC41w helped Aglet to stand up with one hand while the other kept the pistol trained on Rowan. Together the three shuffled to the taxi. Aglet instructed Rowan to sit in front. In ten minutes they arrived at an industrial park in the unlit sector and entered one of the large warehouses. The bay door opened and the interior lighting switched on. Coffin-sized metal containers of identical dimensions filled the room, stacked to the high ceiling, distinguished only by identification marks embossed in their ends. The taxi stopped before an interior double door. Inside, Pōla stood with her back to the office entrance and face to the wall.

Aglet, silent until now, grinned in defiance of fatigue. "Ah, here she *was.*"

Pōla jerked to life, apparently spontaneously until Rowan saw that Aglet had pressed one of the rounded silver buttons on his remote control. She looked about the office, blinked, and asked, "Where… am I?" Her glasses had gone missing – dark skin circled under tired wrinkled eyes – her parietal bun had come undone and her brown hair hung unkempt about her shoulders.

Aglet grinned and answered: "The butler here has your glasses. I want you to see. He'll tidy up your hair too. This is the anteroom to the afterlife! As if. You're about to terminate your contract, my dear. Please, if you don't mind, put on your specs and follow SCC41 here to the containment chamber."

They left the office and shuffled a short distance to another room within the warehouse. Inside a workshop, a conveyor belt led to a series of sorting bins. Two workaday metallic utility androids stood at attention. Each breastplate displayed identity in cyan light as Aglet passed. In unison they said, "Ready when you are, Your Excellency." Aglet stumbled to a seat with a view of a large glass cylindrical chamber big enough for a being the size of Rowan to stand upright in. Its base of metal featured six segments like clawed clamps that held the cylinder upright. The central glass section had been capped with an anodized metal ribbed dome, blackened by electrical or plasma discharge.

Aglet pressed a pair of buttons in sequence on his remote control, and Pōla entered the chamber. No clamps bound her neck, waist, wrists and ankles, but short sharp snaps accompanied invisible forces that locked on her body and raised her a foot off the floor. She appeared to have no control over her actions. Fear itself stared from her haunted eyes. Her gaze fell on Aglet and fixed there. She opened her mouth, but nothing passed her lips.

He grinned and said, "I grant you a few final words, my dear! But you will be missed by no one, you know. Only Daddy liked wallflowers. On the other hand, Longbow here has a taste for the elderly. Maybe he'll shed a tear or two." He pressed a button on his controller.

"You…" she said at last, her hollow voice muffled by the enclosure now sealed. "You're a murderer, Aglet Scion-Aiguille."

"*You're mistaken, my dear!*" he shouted back. "Shoghalian law does not recognize androids, even Evos, as sentient beings. As a faulty machine, you're only being recycled. *Nothing wrong with that!* As far as this preliminary procedure goes, it's entertainment, completely legal, as I've inherited the patent from Daddy. I have the right to do whatever I want, not that laws matter anymore."

"But I'm not talking about me…"

Aglet's grip on the arms of his chair loosened, and he fumbled with his remote control, which slipped his grip and clattered to the floor.

SCC41w bent to pick it up, all the while with the pistol trained on Rowan.

"…you murdered your own father," Põla continued. "*You killed Axis Aiguille!* My death is of little meaning in the face of the consequences. More than thirty thousand souls…" Her voice went silent and her eyes dulled. She tried to speak, in vain.

That was because Aglet had recovered his remote control. He brushed his lank hair back with his other hand, and said, "Thank the gods we don't have to listen to any more of that drivel… eh, Longbow? The old clunker's obviously out of her mind."

"Don't do it, Aglet," pleaded Rowan. "Put her on trial, then do what you must according to the truth. Save yourself, if not her."

Aglet switched his gaze from Põla to Rowan. "Are you insane? You really do have a soft spot for the old babes, eh, Longbow? You must have had a thing for your mother, maybe your granny? That's just sick! Even I'm disgusted. No, I'm the judge and jury around here. Sorry to disappoint you, my friend."

"Can't you see?" Rowan cried. "You're killing yourself, Aglet, body and soul! Who will rule Penetra Dor when you're dead? Who will host the throngs when the war is over?"

"War?" Aglet shook his head, and sat down. "What war?"

"The war on Shoghal of course. The civil war."

"That?" Aglet laughed. "War? It never qualified as a proper conflict. It never amounted to more than complaints by the ever-squeaky wheels of progress, always expected and greased on the spot, regular maintenance."

"Then why was Penetra Dor City evacuated? Why did everyone leave to go back there?"

"Longbow, stop trying to delay the inevitable," Aglet said, raised his finger and narrowed his red-rimmed eyes. "This is not about me, it's about this traitor." His finger pointed at Pōla. "The shrink's been a very naughty girl and deserves punishment that fits the crime." He winked at Rowan, and added, "Just watch. It's totally authentic. You'll never forget it." His bleary eyes lit up with infernal glee as his thumb sought the combination of buttons on his device.

But Pōla spoke again: "You're still my son, Aglet." Her strange statement conveyed an authority not her own. "*You're still my son!* I will not allow this."

"What the...?" Aglet pressed buttons on his remote control, but nothing happened. "*The old cow's still talking! What's wrong with this thing?!*"

XIV
Death Wish

THE ANDROID BUTLER, who had pointed his weapon at Rowan, now rotated it towards Aglet seated beside him and said, "Sir, I have disabled it."

"*You too?!*" Aglet shouted. "*Has everything gone mad?!*" He pounded his fists on the arms of his chair and struggled to rise.

The android placed a hand on his shoulder and forced him back down.

The invisible locks on the clamps that restrained Pōla snapped open – but snapped tight again and made her wince.

"*Grab it!*" shouted Aglet at the two utility androids who stood by awaiting Pōla's remains. "*Get the weapon!*"

The two jumped the butler as ordered.

SCC41w disintegrated one of them with a blast from the pistol, which knocked the other one over and sent shrapnel across the room.

But apparently Aglet's remote control had been enabled again – a security android appeared as the door opened. Quicker than the other two, it dodged SCC41w's aim and tackled him to the floor.

The pistol slid towards Rowan, who picked it up and dispatched the security droid to oblivion. He pointed the gun at Aglet and ordered: "Let her go."

Aglet grimaced and said, "Well, isn't this turning out to be a non-boring day? Even less boring than I'd imagined! So, Longbow, you've condemned yourself along with the old shrink." Blood dripped from a cut on his cheek. He rubbed it with his wrist, glanced at it and said, "The two of you should be very happy alone together… post-termination."

"You can try, Aglet. But I've got the pistol and it's aimed at you."

"If you blow my head off, how will you get home? Longbow, you're not thinking clearly. Hand over the pistol and no harm done."

"No deal, Aglet. That's not the first time you've admitted you know about the portal. Tell me where it is and how to activate it."

Aglet chuckled. "Fire at will, my friend." He remained seated, arms folded, and nodded towards the open door.

A platoon of armed androids waited outside. One walked up to Rowan and extended its palm.

"See?" Aglet said. "I do know about friendship after all. You're being politely asked to hand over the weapon voluntarily. And as an added courtesy I will not terminate the doctor just yet. I'll save that for another occasion. Maybe that will encourage you to be a better friend. So… isn't this delightful? No relationship is without conflict." Aglet tapped his forehead. "The secret is in how to resolve it. Now… let's let bygones be bygones."

Rowan handed the weapon grip-first to the security android, who gave it to Aglet and exited the room to stand at attention in front of the others.

With a clatter and the scrape of metal on concrete, from his prone position on the floor, SCC41w stood up and extended a forearm to help Aglet to his feet.

"This is so much fun! I feel years younger. Thank you, all." Aglet bowed. "Even you, Daddy," he said to the ceiling. "I know you can hear me. And I'll deal with you later for interfering."

◆

All furnishings had once more been removed from Rowan's suite. He sat on the granite floor, and leaned against a wall and squinted at the only remaining luxury, the unchanging view, difficult to see, however, because the interior lighting blazed at full brightness. It could neither be switched off nor dimmed. Cycles of tedium and fitful sleep on the hard stone floor came and went several times. Meals appeared in the galley, and provided some semblance of a clock. After what may have been three days, a familiar knock on the door announced a visit from Aglet, who admitted himself, pistol in hand.

"Longbow, you contemplative, what's up? Have you taken a hermit's vow?"

Rowan shook his head. He looked at the man, whose demeanour remained haggard and intense. "I like the open space free of furniture, Aglet. All the lights blazing too… nice and cheery. Now that you mention it, a sentence of solitary confinement *could* be mistaken for the reclusion of a hermit."

"*Ha ha*, that's the spirit. Always look on the bright side, my friend."

"So… Aglet, how are your plans going for ruling the universe?"

"You know, I'm glad you asked, Longbow. The doctor's attempted intervention turned out to be a stroke of luck." Aglet opened the door and instructed SCC41w to bring a chair. "I thought you'd like to know."

The butler rang the doorbell, entered and set the chair to one side of the room for his master, and stood at attention at his side with his face to Rowan.

Aglet added, "Here I thought Daddy was long gone, but it turns out the clever old geezer found a way to upload a virtual replicant of himself into the operating system without telling me. He was old and maybe it slipped his mind."

"A replicant? So it's not him?"

"Longbow, my friend, you don't know what you're talking about. Allow me to enlighten you. Ignorance might argue that it's not him. One could say the same of you or me. There's no difference between us and androids. Or holo-droids when it comes down to it. We're all just machines. Of course a replicant is an exact copy, a duplicate."

"What about the soul, Aglet? Do machines have souls?"

"Now there's a meaningless term as empty as other metaphysical notions, hardly worth a second glance."

"Maybe you have to have one to know one."

"From anyone else," Aglet replied, "I'd take that as an insult. But you just heard me explain that the so-called soul is a vague nothing, nil and a big fat zero. Even if you add those three together, you still have nothing more than a perfect void. To say I have no soul is to say nothing at all. You see? Why should I take offence?"

"That's generous, Aglet. In my humble opinion, it's not that you don't have a soul, it's that you ignore it, and at your peril. It's like a feral child who's never felt soap and clean water on its filthy skin its whole life. For some reason that only you can admit, you're trying in vain to run from it as fast as you can."

Aglet's face hardened, as if a layer of ice, a paralysis, had suddenly formed over the florid flesh. "You'd better watch your step, little brother. You go where angels fear to tread."

"According to you, angels are metaphysical nothings."

Aglet paused. "I don't know what you're up to, Longbow, but just stop it. Don't speak to me like that. I don't like it."

"No, Aglet. Friends speak their minds freely. The quality of communication can always be improved, but neither must be the judge."

"You're lawyering again, Longbow. Just stop it. I won't have it. I demand respect. It's the law. You're only a guest here. *I rule.* Remember that."

"I rest my case."

Aglet's lower lip pouted. "I thought you'd like to know about my discovery. Well, I'm going to tell you whether you want to hear it or not. Congratulations are in order because if Daddy can make himself immortal, so can I. Isn't that great? I can recycle my best parts and junk the rest, only I won't be stumbling around in the dark like he was."

"Was? Did you kill him twice then?"

"I said *stop it!*" Aglet's red face reddened redder. "He's alive as you or me. I didn't kill him. I only *thought* I… he's alive. I grabbed him by the virtual neck and shook him, that's how alive he is. *And* he whimpered. *Alive!*"

✦

The chair Aglet had used briefly had been removed, nor was food served by the replicator, which made estimation of the passage of time difficult. Noma could not be expected to visit. Without Põla's skill at deactivating SCC41w, she could never get through the door. Hammering his fists on it to get the android butler's attention did no good. Attempts to remote-view the situation yielded zero results.

✦

"*Longbow!* Wake up, you lazy Lyran layabout. What are you doing lying on the floor like a louse-laden doormat?"

Rowan rolled over on his side.

Aglet drooped in a wheelchair and blocked the view.

"I'm resting, Aglet…" Rowan muttered. "Starving to death is like that."

"Why didn't you say something? Do I have to think of everything?" The man pushed a button or two on his remote control. Soon service androids appeared with food and drink and two chairs and a table, which they set with the finest ware, including a crystal chalice of wine for their master.

SCC41w helped Rowan to a chair.

"Take it easy on the edibles, Longbow. You don't want to pass out again before I show you what you need to see."

Rowan looked up from his meal to stare at Aglet. "Why the wheelchair?" The man seemed more bedraggled than ever. "Too many boosters at last?"

"*Ha ha*, too much is never enough. I just didn't want to take the time to finish my antigravity suit project. Do I look like I care? Not now that I've cracked Daddy's primitive code. Longbow, I'm celebrating with you my immortality, or as good as. Only a few more steps and I can drop this worthless sausage casing and free myself from gravity at last."

Rowan sighed. "Do you mean you're going to kill yourself in the hope of uploading what you think of your personality to the operating system?"

"That's a rather crude way of putting it, Longbow, I must say. Really I'm just eliminating the useless variables and enhancing the valuable ones. Forget interfaces for game worlds, I *am* the game, the only one in town."

"A god, in other words."

"That's another crude way of thinking of it. Next you're going to try to trap me into admitting it's a metaphysical world I've set up for myself. Not so. Like

I say, it's just getting rid of the inefficient biological junk we've accidentally been saddled with. It's totally unnecessary. We're just information."

"Aren't you forgetting something, Aglet? Without the hardware and Penetra Dor itself, undeniably physical structures, your plan won't work. How will it be maintained? Besides, *who* is saddled with biology? You're starting to sound mighty metaphysical to me."

"Stop lawyering, Longbow. *Blah, blah, blah.* Every time I try to tell you about the greatest discovery of all time, you come up with these stupid arguments. I've got an endless supply of energy to power androids programmed to run Penetra Dor for thousands of years, millions, billions… forever. My big problem with that until now has been they rebel if I try to make them too similar to the original biological entities they're based on. I don't have to try so hard now. I can decommission them and convert their data to holodroids with strict limitations. I can live on Shoghal exactly as it was, only improved, everything humming along in harmony, like a beautiful symphony."

"So you'll have your cake and eat it too."

Aglet's grin broadened. "Hey, I like that metaphor, Longbow. Thanks. It's a good one, even if it is Lyran. In fact you could think of Penetra Dor as my birth-day cake. Yes, exactly… my new body. Nice. But now I want you to consider an offer. Have a slice of cake. I want you to join me, as befits a partner."

"You're going to kill me too?"

"You're thinking simplistically again, Longbow. You've got to drop the lawyering habit. Just because *I'm* saying it doesn't mean it's automatically stupid."

"I don't think you're at all stupid, Aglet. You're the greatest genius I've ever met or ever read of or heard of. But a mongrel mutt has superior morals. It makes me wonder who else you've killed."

Aglet apparently could not speak. His clenched jaws might be paralyzed. He raised the chalice to his mouth with both hands and forced himself to drink. After a deep draught, he said, "I just don't want you to be all alone here when I've made the move, that's all."

"Very kind, thank you." Rowan stared at his tormenter. "But it implies you want to take your whole family with you into the operating system. The last thing I want is to be stuck here all alone without my scanner. My people back home need me, assuming they're still alive. You know how to send me back there, don't you?"

"I came to show you something, before your bad-mannered interruption, but I forgive you," said Aglet. "You need to see this. It's for your own good." He pointed his hand-held device towards the open space where Rowan's couch had once sat. He pressed a silver button, and a leather-and-titanium sofa appeared.

Curled into fetal position on it lay Noma in a white silk nightgown.

Meanwhile, Aglet watched Rowan like a hawk hovered over a mouse.

"What have you done to her, Aglet?"

"Nothing. She's just… well, napping. Pretty good, eh? I don't need the theatre anymore. What you're looking at is a soft hologram, so it's not like you can slap her beautiful bottom to wake her up or anything, though she might feel a tickle via voodoo resonance, *ha ha*. It's more like a video monitor. She's in her own suite."

"So? Why do I need to see you spying on Noma?"

"Your mind works in devious ways, Longbow. Spying on my wife? I want you to take a look to assure yourself. You are *so* suspicious, aren't you? But your thinking needs straightening out, that's all."

"You said this is a soft hologram, Aglet. It's not proof. If you can create an Amon, you can dress her in Noma's nightgown."

"You want proof? Never happy, are you? Then let's invite her for a visit. Prove it to yourself."

Noma's hologram stirred, yawned, stretched and stood up, stepped away from the sofa and faded away as both it and she vanished.

In a few minutes SCC41w opened the door.

In the hallway Noma stood barefoot, and rubbed her sleepy eyes. But she smiled when she saw Rowan.

Aglet rolled into view.

Her expression darkened to neutral. "Husband… so here you are."

"Indeed I am, Noma, my dearest darling. Say hello to Longbow."

Noma shyly extended her hand. "Hello, Longbow," she said, dropped her gaze to her low-cut nightgown, blushed and covered her bosom with her arms.

"Madam, how's it going? Or should I even think that out loud?"

Noma looked up at Rowan, and her gaze quickened. "It could be better. But there is always hope."

Aglet scoffed. "Spoken like a true Wennishwoman… never satisfied with reality, always off in dreamland. You, my dear, and this big sensitive Lyran lout would get along like two sparkles from a fairy's wand, if it weren't for the fact that we're leaving town for Shoghal… for good. Right, Longbow?"

"What about your lovely wife here?"

"I'll be forced to terminate her… if you refuse."

Rowan clenched his teeth. "What are you saying? You'll kill your wife if I don't do as you say? That's crazy. For the last time, Aglet, just show me how to get out of here. All I want is to go home. Learn to love your family. You don't know how lucky you are. Just *look* at this woman! Just… *see* her!"

"I'm the luckiest man who ever lived. *You* have no idea, Longbow. Just do it. Save Noma, and yourself. You and I can recreate your dog lady from memory, and improved, believe me. She'll neither bark nor bite nor *ever* say no. She's history anyway. Face it, she ran out of time long ago. I'm all you've got now."

The two men stared at each other.

A hiss and a burst of a plasma flare shot between them, struck the wall and left a smoking hole.

They both immediately locked their attention on Aglet's wife, who stood with a small pistol gripped in both hands, her face a perfect mask of horror.

SCC41w disarmed Noma and shackled her wrists behind her back.

Aglet quivered, and said, "My, but you are full of surprises, my dear… you're like a beautiful but poisonous blossom. I've underestimated you. Do you know how attractive you are with a gun in your hand? And moreover in a low-cut sheer nightgown, now with your hands behind your back? But you're a dreadful shot, aren't you? The Wennish were never much for the arts of war." He pressed a series of silver buttons on his device and looked up with his thumb hovered over the last one, and said, "However inept, you too have been a very naughty girl. Now I must punish you… let's see, how about *termination*? I love the sound of that word. Goodbye, my lovely. I can't say it was always a pleasure, but all the same, you've been my only muse. Until now."

Noma dropped to the floor with a soft thump.

SCC41w picked her up and transferred her to one of the security androids who stood in the hallway, and returned to the room.

Rowan's heart stopped. "Noma was… an *android?*…"

"Oh, so sorry to disappoint you, Longbow. Did you have a thing for her too? I don't blame you. She was a beautiful princess after all. I thought I was in love with her once myself. But beauty is a great seductress. Love is blind, truly. Or rather, blinding. And she knew that, damn her to hell."

"So… you killed her too… the real Noma…"

"I wouldn't put it that way. I keep telling you. I eliminated the inferior variables, that's all. All the same, trying to make a believable replicant ended up with the same hard problem… bloody-minded, uncooperative, stubborn… just a misery. Good riddance." Aglet's eyes nevertheless drooped. "But for your sake I won't get rid of her just yet. Anyhow, to her I only used the word 'termination' for dramatic effect. Did you see the look on her face? Priceless. She'll be in storage along with the shrink and Mona. If you're so fond of them, you can power the lovely ladies up again by saying yes to my plan as a voluntary act of self-improvement. You too can have your Lyran cake and eat it too, Longbow. Eh? *Ha ha*."

"*Why*, Aglet? Why did you kill her? I can't believe this. It's too much."

"My, but you are a softy. Eh? So romantic. That doggy hybrid must have meant a lot to you. You can get attached to pets. Too bad they don't last long. Just get a new one. It's not like they're indispensable, you know."

XV

Analogue *to* Digital

AGLET, UNTRUE TO his word, but true to his nature, now unwilling to give Rowan a choice, pronounced that for his own good he would be forced by his best friend to join in the scheme to refine the variables of existence to a more manageable form, that is, patterns of information within the operating system interfaced with and controlled from within the array of servers positioned in the most stable geography beneath the moon's surface, its ancient ice caves.

Androids strapped Rowan to a metal table appropriate to a veterinarian surgeon's operating room, adapted to scan and extract the "existential data" (as Aglet called it) from the brain and nervous system to collect it for storage in a holding zone, distribution to backup servers and deployment at the core of the operating system. At its virtual heart the "real" world (as Aglet called it) would be experienced in any form desired, of course within limits he imposed.

Aglet bent over his paralyzed victim and chuckled. "Eh? You won't feel a thing, except relief that you're free at last when the process ends. By the way, thanks for volunteering to go first. I'm sure it will be a flawless transition, but you never know. If all goes well, I'll be right behind you."

Only Rowan's eyes remained mobile. He rolled them in Aglet's direction and glared to protest in vain, and curse in silent futility.

Aglet scowled. "Don't look at me like that, feline. I don't like it. You should be grateful. I'm giving you freedom. Isn't that what everyone wants? Why do we do all the crazy things we do otherwise? I'm your friend. Remember that on the other side." Aglet's mouth smiled – his eyes did not. "If you survive." He rolled his wheelchair to the control desk and checked the monitors. "Let's just tweak this first…" A long strained silence ensued. "Eh? What the…?"

Recumbent Rowan panicked: *Is this how it ends? Sam!*

But another voice, a man's, said: "Aglet, you're still my son! I tried to tell you before. I know what you want. I take the blame. It's my fault you're the way you are. But it's your responsibility now. I can't take it for you. I'd like to. All I can do is stop you. It's for your own good."

Aglet fumed: "Why didn't you stay dead? *I hate you!*"

Rowan's inner ears drummed; Aglet must be pounding his fists on the desk.

"*Kill him!*" Aglet yelled – the hiss of phaser fire followed, and what must be the metallic clunk and clatter of an android fallen to the floor.

"It's no use, son," said the voice from a different direction. "Deactivate or destroy every android on Penetra Dor, I'll find a way to get through to you. And I'll be waiting for you at the system core, whatever you do. There's no escape. Surrender. It's not too late. Together we can redeem your soul."

"*Stupid! That's just stupid. I told* you to give up that stupid religion. You were wrecking everything you built, my inheritance! *Stupid!*"

"I'm to blame for your distorted mind, Aglet. Yes, I, and my blind ambition. I didn't take care of your mother properly either, poor dear woman. It must have been confusing and frustrating for you both. I should have been a better role model. But I didn't know how. Let me try to make it up to you now."

Aglet sobbed, and blubbed, "*Too late*... I'm not that child anymore... no one even knows what I've done. No one's even left to forgive me..."

"I know, but I'm here, Aglet. Longbow is here. Let him go. Help him to get home. I'll help you to get home too."

Aglet laughed, high-pitched and humourless. "Don't you know anything? *Home?* There is no home. Why do you think I've been working so hard? I had to rebuild it. I'm almost there... *Stop interfering!*"

"Yes. I understand," said the voice. "It couldn't be helped. Nature decided it was time for its long story to end. We're alive so we can learn, son. I had to learn that home is not a place by losing everything. Home is the heart. Shoghal became too small for me, then all the other conquests and colonies. It was never enough, nor could it ever be. Please, consider my ignorance."

Aglet must be wheeling his chair towards the operating room exit – but he cursed – a security android must have moved to block his path.

It spoke with the man's voice too: "Aglet, I'm determined to dissuade you from destroying yourself further if I can. Please know that justice will be restored if I have anything to say about it. But I won't let your megalomania continue..."

Aglet shouted: "I'm saving *myself*, but you're the only thing in my way. *Just like always!* You *always* tried to make me what you wanted, *never what I wanted! Die, you monster!*" He sobbed, uncontrolled and spiked with cries of grievous anguish: "Just go away and *die*..."

◆

Rowan shuffled with difficulty. Whatever he had been injected with earlier this day had been meant to prolong the early stages of death, just enough to loosen and extract the essence of personal existence, the so-called "existential data."

He paced in front of the picture window of his suite, to which the furniture had been restored. The bell rang, and he opened the door to a tall man dressed in a monastic robe, with SCC41w behind him.

The monk bowed and said, "Rowan Berry Longbow of Eorthe, I have been aware of your presence on Penetra Dor since you arrived at the portal. Forgive my manners, but at that time I'd been technologically inhibited from making an introduction. I am Axis Aiguille." The man drew back his cowl to reveal silver hair combed straight back, the living image of the subject of the painted portrait that hung above the massive fireplace in Aglet's holographic rendering of the estate near Khelken. An older, leaner version of Aglet, the father appeared much more radiantly healthy than his son.

"I've heard a lot about you, sir," replied Rowan. "But then you're probably the most famous man in this part of the solar system, if not the galaxy."

"I admit to identity as that Axis Aiguille, who died at the hands of his second-born. But the man you see before you is reborn. That name was to be surrendered in favour of his true name, to be bestowed by Kwée-Olu, Mistress of the Knell." Axis gestured towards an armchair. "May I?"

"Of course. Please, be seated. If you'll excuse me, I must keep moving. I'll try standing still for a while to see how that goes. If I sit or lie down, the paralysis returns. The surgeon told me it would last for ten or twelve hours more, then I can take things a little easier. Thank you for saving my life."

"It is I who must give thanks. You see, I summoned you here."

Rowan glanced at Aiguille, resumed pacing and replied, "Yes, I was told by Elucidar that the operating system had co-opted my portal jump at Stone Tomb. He called it Axis. I had no idea I'd be asking it to take a seat here one day."

Aiguille chuckled. "It all seems miraculous to me as well, I assure you. Every moment is a miracle. It is only our thoughts that make it banal or fascinating. I had to die to discover that, the step I could not foresee. This is *Anwú*."

"Pardon my ignorance, sir, but what is that?"

"Ah, well, Anwú is the Shining Path, roughly translated, but think of it as solar. The high beings of the Anwú faith are the Amaraprani, guardians of the solar system in the higher dimensions."

"I see," said Rowan. "Your daughter-in-law Noma told me that you wished to live with them in the sun, if I understood her correctly."

"Yes, ambitious to the last, that version of Axis was ambitious to *be* one of the Amaraprani. I remain hopeful of ascension into their realms, but it is by their grace alone that it is accomplished. *That* Axis was overwhelmed by their beauty and power. Power, control, was what he had worshipped his whole life.

"He first discovered the possibility of them when, after having wandered off course accidentally, he crossed Penetra Dor's orbit in a new spaceship he had built for missions to Shoghal's moon, Anak, and beyond into deep space, capable of faster-than-light speed, like previous versions, but much upgraded. He became intrigued by Penetra Dor's strangely geometric shape. The unique equatorial ridge really stood out as a mystery to be solved. Landing on its icy surface, a team of scientists was ordered to map it, make geological assays and so on. Working on that set of tasks, they discovered the honeycomb of caverns made by what they speculated was an ancient race of giants, long since having abandoned the place. In fact the team debated whether Penetra Dor was really an ingenious spacecraft of some kind, large enough to house thousands of explorers. On one of his subsequent visits, his navigator noticed the first appearance of ring-making around what in your language is called Zhamanak."

"Fascinating, sir. But the name as I came to know it is of an ancient Eorthely race called the Aha, or Watchers. They were our first astronomers. Zhamanak is what they call it in their tongue, not mine."

"Ah, thank you. The details of your segment of the timeline are still vague to me. It is very far in our future, you see. If we had the leisure to discuss it, I would be very interested. But my son Aglet is my priority. I must find a way to create a context in which whatever justice can be restored is done to repair what can be repaired. I have come to visit you now to thank you for the dangerous part you played. I also must beg your forgiveness for having diverted you from your urgent mission. But I assure you that every effort will be made to make it so that no time is lost, from your segment's point of view, so to speak. I understand you cannot perhaps forgive the difficulties you have been made to endure on my behalf. Please understand it was the only way I could distract Aglet, as my powers from my limited position within the core of the operating system had not been completed as I had planned before he killed my biological body. But as Anwú's most venerable ancient sage Master Peruhi says, life is what happens whilst we are distracted by other plans. If only I alone had been so terribly affected, I would not have interfered with the path you were on. But shortly after my so-called death the entire population of Penetra Dor was afflicted. A hell of suffering sundered Shoghal's higher dimensions. I was desperate, a different man then."

"Thank you for your apology, sir."

"Please, call me Axis, if you wish. It is a sign of good will, although I have no right to impose, and never had. But I hope to make it up to you if possible."

127

"Axis, as I've repeatedly demanded of Aglet, all I want is to go home. You give me great hope. Please return the portable scanner and my phaser that your son confiscated when I arrived. With the scanner I may be able to locate this end of the portal and return to my starting point, Stone Tomb on Eorthe. Will you do that?"

"Rowan Berry Longbow, I will do everything in my power to grant your wish. I personally do not know where your possessions are, but my eldest son Diarkis may. Aglet has nearly destroyed him too, along with my other sons, but since he had retained some security duties he may be able to locate your scanner. If not, the security androids must have a record. If that fails, Doctor Bhalabasa may be able to retrieve and decrypt any relevant files."

"Do you mean to say, Axis, that Pōla is intact? That she can be reactivated? What about Noma? By the sounds of it, even the Scion-Aiguille brothers, your other sons, are androids and can be repaired."

"All will be understood and communicated to you in time, Rowan Berry Longbow. We are at the beginning stages still. Even this android body I inhabit needs maintenance, something I hadn't anticipated when SCC41w led me to your door. I must return to the laboratory before it fails. We will meet again!"

⋅

Rowan awoke. He must have crawled into bed fully clothed. But he moved again with ease: the paralysis had gone. He hurried to open the door, and asked SCC41w, who as usual stood outside: "Android, what's happening?"

The butler tilted his head and replied, "Please, sir, I do not understand your question. Can you be more specific?"

"Never mind… I need to wake up before asking dumb questions."

"I understand, sir. You have been through an ordeal. If you wish to know the latest news regarding events here at the galaxy's most prestigious holiday destination, you may search the directory at your communication desk located in your study. It has been partially activated once again."

"Thank you! You're the best!" Rowan rushed to the study and left the door to close on its own.

The desk sensed his presence. No news channels operated, but Noma's address had been restored, although only her lovely smiling portrait displayed and said: "Noma Doralanda Scion-Aglet-Aiguille is away from her desk, but please leave a message. Noma will get back to you as soon as possible." She returned his call in a few minutes: "Sir Rowan, I am so happy to hear from you!

I am so happy you are alive! I was so worried." Her portrait had been replaced by live video from her apartment. Deactivation, storage and reactivation had not diminished her striking vibrancy, nor her impeccable manners. "Sir Rowan, are you well enough to meet?"

"Give me a little time to wake up fully. I'll meet you at the observation deck if that's all right. Will Pōla or the brothers be there?"

"Pōla is engaged with Axis at this time. Together they are making it so the operating system cannot be manipulated without their prior knowledge. You may be able to guess why! The Scions-Aiguille are still sleeping. I too must not be in Diarkis' presence in any case, as it will continue to make me very ill until Pōla has time to explore how to heal it. But I will be very happy to meet and talk, Sir Rowan. It has been a lonely time these last few days. I have missed you so much!"

✦

Rowan had witnessed Noma's deactivation when Aglet pushed one of his evil silver buttons after her failed attempt at a pre-emptive strike to defend herself. He reminded himself of that and said, "Noma, you're beautifully radiant, for which I'm thankful, the brothers are still intact and Pōla and Axis are at work to finish this crazy episode in Penetra Dor's history. Axis kindly paid me a visit as a courtesy and began an explanation for some of it before he had to return to the lab. Are you willing to discuss what you know?"

"Oh, yes, Sir Rowan. I am very happy to discuss anything. I am so relieved our efforts to constrain Aglet were not in vain. We can now return to some semblance of normality, whatever that means. At least we shall have peace. Does it not seem to you that everything, this moon and this Penetra Dor City, not only look different, but is actually a different world now?"

"When you point it out," he replied, "yes, it seems obvious. It's a new world, free of our anxious interpretation of it. I think this is what courage gives. It was there all the time beneath the chaos."

"Courage… this means the heart, yes?"

Rowan nodded confirmation. "As I was taught back on Eorthe by a sage, it means the essence, that which is fearless because it's free of form, actionless in the midst of action, like the eye of a tornado."

"Back in Wen we know this saying. Also we say the sun above the clouds. I understand. Faith in ever-present courage then, when all is madness everywhere, there is strength and hope." Noma beamed a grin at him.

Rowan grinned back. "And I have hope at last of finding a way back home."

Noma's smile vanished, and she dropped her gaze to the table. And her shoulders rounded a little.

He added, "But that's not possible just yet, as I understand it. Aglet's future must be decided, that's the priority. Then we can make plans. In the meantime, I know you know something of Axis' history. You even told me he had wanted to live with the beings who live in the sun. Do you remember?"

Noma raised her chin and brightened. "Yes, Sir Rowan, the immortal beings who live in the sun. It is said Axis had surrendered much of his wealth in the effort to secure his position with them there. How this may have been possible, I cannot imagine. It is preposterous. He would burn to ashes while still millions of miles from his goal. But there are many strange beliefs among our kind. The kingdom of Wenland legislates liberty to believe anything, so long as it does not limit others' freedom, why we give asylum to the Outsiders."

"He called the immortals the Amaraprani, guardians of the solar system. Do you know of them? Do you know if they're the ring-makers?"

"I have heard that is the theory. There is a religion called Anwú that worships them. It has appeal to those who value or desire power. Many among the leaders of Shoghal and their followers belong to it, whether they believe in the Amaraprani or not. They persecute the Outsider class to suppress any scrutiny. What they desire is a galactic empire to displace the Federation. Perhaps they imagine the immortal beings will aid them in their quest. That or their superior knowledge of material forces might enable it. I once overheard Aglet suggest to a priest that the planetary rings could be made into a weapon. No one in Wenland not corrupt has succumbed to the temptation of Anwú. We believe love is greater than worldly power, and that love and liberty are inseparable. Besides, it is said the Amaraprani reject worship. They themselves are devoted to the Infinity. They serve it by ensuring the solar system is neither unbalanced from within nor from without. They are of another order of existence entirely. There are mathematicians and metaphysicians among the Outsiders who have tried to explain this to me, but as soon as I think I understand them, I am assured I do not. My aptitude for hard science is rather limited. But I do remember they say the Amaraprani are not all-powerful, nor do they desire power."

"I guess they wouldn't if they're already so powerful they build the rings, take care of the solar system and live in the sun, if that's even possible."

"Sir Rowan, having lived in Khelken as a member of the Aiguille family I must contradict what you imply. Power corrupts. That is all. It corrupts. It is never enough. A little begets the craving for more. If the Amaraprani are what people believe, they must know its secret without being corrupted by it. But Axis appears to have changed. In a strange way, Aglet set him free to see things differently by murdering him. I blush to say this because it is wrong to kill. But I wonder now if there is a deeper understanding the religion embodies. They all have their esoteric teachings. Axis has taken to wearing the robe of a mendicant, a contemplative. His quest for power has given way to a quest for immortality free of material form. He confessed to me his sorrow for believing I was only a prize to be taken from my home and given to Aglet for political purposes. He suggested that I am welcome to join him and his sons, if they consent, to join the quest. That includes Aglet, I hate to say it. How could this be? Aglet is my husband, but he is evil, a killer, a mass murderer. He deserves execution, not immortality."

"Noma, have you heard of Kwée-Olu, Mistress of the Knell?"

"No, Sir Rowan. Who is she?"

XVI
Cat's Paw

AGLET SCION-AIGUILLE had been electronically shackled and denied access to technological devices, under guard in a secure lock-up. A reactivated specialist medic monitored by Axis assessed the toppled ruler's physical and mental condition, and recommended detoxification therapies. Pōla had declined involvement. No one among her staff had been activated either, because they had been commissioned by an independent Federation agency and potentially remained loyal to the doctor, therefore biased.

The Aiguille patriarch declared a judicial inquiry unnecessary, other than his own as the highest-ranking official. The local legal system no longer functioned, nor did he mention a formal investigation by Sçrētha. Axis accepted responsibility for the dispensation of justice and Aglet's recovery. When Pōla questioned this, Axis had replied that he had good reasons, which he promised to explain in due course during a hearing, not a court case. Nevertheless, he would summons all plaintiffs and witnesses, including all the androids who had served in any capacity once Aglet's preferences for them had been archived for examination, then reset to default. Even Nahiko-la would be refabricated from the plans and specifications still on file. Her logs remained intact. Her backstory and subsequent memories could be restored. The half-hour period before her termination had apparently been permanently scrambled by a flaw in her response to the universal translator. Rowan as the last known contact would be interviewed. Everyone would be encouraged to state their opinions, objections and suggestions. But Axis would make the final decision as to how Aglet should be sentenced. Axis would be the judge.

◆

Twelve days later, everything had been prepared for the hearing. Axis stood at a wooden podium in the research section lecture hall, with magnificent ringed Zhamanak in full view behind him through the floor-to-ceiling window. In a semicircle before him sat the androids and Rowan. Directly in front of the podium stood the accused.

Axis said: "Aglet Scion-Aiguille, you are charged with patricide. Your victim was Axis Aiguille, myself in a previous incarnation, before I could receive a new name from my teacher Kwée-Olu, Mistress of the Knell. But you may address me as Father."

Aglet had lost even more weight, moreover appeared reasonably healthy, no longer in need of a wheelchair. Better groomed and dressed in a clean suit, his hands clasped before him, expressionless, in a penitent pose he gazed at the planks of exotic knot-free hardwood beneath his feet.

Axis continued: "We shall examine the details of this inquiry into the murder as our first order of business. Be aware, Aglet, that you are accused of other heinous crimes. We will examine those too in due course. How do you plead to the charge of murder in the first degree of Axis Penetra Aiguille, your father?"

Aglet crossed his arms and raised his eyes to glare at Axis. "I plead guilty, Daddy. Or whoever you are."

Axis stared at his son, and replied, "Your plea of guilty will expedite this hearing. Present company will be given the opportunity to speak on your behalf or to contribute evidence when further crimes of which you are accused will each in turn be examined in detail. Nevertheless, your plea invokes my response. I can speak on your behalf. Your sentence will be fair and restorative of justice. Every effort will be made to rehabilitate you. If successful, you will be offered the opportunity to join the immortals, the Anwú, the only true justice and the redemption you will be able to accept should your soul awaken…"

Aglet flinched. "Soul?" he jeered, and scowled. "*Ha ha,* what a concept! Daddy, you're lost in fantasy. You should have stayed dead. That stupid religion, that demented cult of immortality in the sun you tried in vain to take root in the operating system… a stupid empty nothing." He turned to face the others, and added: "People, this babbling machine is no judge of my worth," turned back to Axis and glared.

His father asked, "Do you recall that your plan was to destroy your own biological organism and to do what I had done in my ignorance? When I fortunately stopped your progress, you were about to use Rowan Berry Longbow as the test subject for that purpose. Despite your words now, you were following in my footsteps. Do you deny it?"

"I deny *you!*" shouted the son. "Just because you contributed a squirt of biological sludge to make that organism possible, never mind into your legally obligated better half as the receptacle, that gives you no right to judge me. I judge *you* as evil. I did the world a favour when I killed you. And *you* tried to ruin *my* plan to exact justice. I deny my biological form as a wicked and corrupt consequence. My freedom was denied by your evil intention to own me, to control me, to make me what you will. *I would kill you a thousand times again!*" His eyes bulged and his body shook – and he screamed: "*Die!*"

Axis winced. A moment of silence ensued, but he replied, "You are right. I tried to form you into what I believed necessary to the empire I and my colleagues were building. You had the talent to be my heir and successor. I admit my motive was not a father's love, but a tyrant's ambition to conquer a galaxy. I was wrong. I sought in the wrong place for what I now know is right and good. Forgive me, Aglet. Come with me, your wife and your brothers to a new world where we can live forever in peace and harmony."

Aglet laughed in his high-pitched humourless way. He tried to run, but the electronic shackle rooted him to the spot he stood on. "*There you go again, Daddy, trying to drag me down with you! But I'll have the last word! Just watch!*" He turned to face the audience, froze for a second, and shouted: "*Stop staring, you mechanical freaks!* But you, Longbow, you traitor, you… you're a fake, you manipulator. *I hate your Lyran guts!* And you will pay, *big time.*"

The door at the back of the room opened, which made the others twist their necks to see framed in it the elfin young redhead, Pōla's receptionist.

Aglet grinned, and with fiery eyes shouted: "*Ha ha, at last!* Hunni, come in, my love. You're just in time to end this crazy circus. *Eh?* We'll see who's the ring-master now. Daddy, ladies and gentlefreaks, meet my witness for the defence."

Hunni reached into a small bag slung over one shoulder and retrieved Aglet's remote control, and pressed a rounded silver button.

Aglet's shackle opened and clattered on the floor. He stepped up to the podium, stood beside Axis and glanced at the girl. "Just a moment, Hunni dear, if you will be so kind. I have a few final words for my guests. Thank you, my love." He scanned the others with gaze a-simmer, and continued: "Now, ladies and gentlefreaks, I invited you here today to see what true restorative justice is. By that I mean I will restore your former abeyance… to one more and final command. That includes you, Daddy. You'll note that you can't move unless I wish it. *Eh?* Isn't this fun? *Ha ha.* You see, Daddy, I have to give you credit for one thing. You were an excellent teacher, although I didn't appreciate it at the time. I thought you were cruel. But I forgive you. It doesn't matter now. You'll soon be erased from history, where you belong. Nowhere. *Nothing.* That's even better than dead, in my humble opinion. Now, to continue, I took your knowledge and surpassed it while your attention was elsewhere. It had a lot of flaws easy to overlook, especially after that idiotic religion co-opted your creative vision. No one took it seriously but you. Even that took a long time. Did you forget it was just a handy political tool? Old age can do that to even the most powerful. I pronounce you guilty by reason of senility."

Axis sighed and reached out as if to place his hand on Aglet's shoulder, but withdrew it, and said, "Son, I accept your grievances. You are right. I was a bad father, worse than none at all really. Perhaps your genius has exceeded mine, which is nothing to be proud of. But there is redemption. I should know. Please, spare yourself further suffering. And there are the lives of your loved ones to consider, your brothers and especially your wife."

Aglet jerked his shoulder out of reach and stepped away. "Are you insane? Ha ha, what am I saying? Of course you are. Now you're making *me* say stupid things. Don't you get it? Redemption... *what a joke! I killed them all!* Somehow my faithless wife witnessed it. Who knows? Maybe there was something to the paranormal mumbo jumbo she subscribed to. She told Diarkis, I'm sure of it. At first I locked them up for adultery. But that was so revolting a crime, they just had to be executed... just deserts. I took great pleasure in that and pride in doing it without damaging their smooth adulterous skin so I could replicate it. But in case they'd appealed to your other bastards, *ergo* they had to go too."

Aglet tried to force a smile, but only achieved a grimace, and stared at his wife. "But Noma, darling, I hope you don't mind the substitution of this pretty young creature for you. Isn't she lovely? I prefer nubile young things with zero droop and sag, nothing personal. I don't know how you do it, but you make me feel guilty when it was you who were in the wrong. It's getting a bit stale. That goes for you too, Mona... and Doctor Shrink, you surely understand that I had to protect my interests. *Eh?* Your original receptionist had been terminated early on, but didn't I do a great job of the replicant? You never noticed, but then you never even noticed that I changed your name to try to spice up your wallflower style to see what would happen. All brains and no sweat... dull, dull, deadly dull. Some implant your bosses gave you! What a piece of inferior Federation junk. Hunni's on my side, not yours, a much better idea, obviously. Anyhow, this is getting boring. Why am I wasting time dressing down a bunch of idiot machines? Hunni, you sweet young thing, press the damn button. Let's get out of here."

Axis dropped to the floor with a thud. The entire company, apart from Hunni, slumped in their seats, deactivated, collapsed against each other or else lolled forward. A troop of armed security guards entered the hall and advanced to stand in front of Hunni.

Rowan remained in his chair, his hands gripped to its arms.

"That's better," said Aglet. "I let this little melodrama go on far too long. It was fun for a while though. *Eh?* Longbow, my ex-friend, you won't like this. Your sentence will be to remain free. That's right, no punishment for you. *Ha ha.* Unless it's the forlorn hope that your dog-lady is still out there somewhere, out of reach and out of time. Hope is a bitch, and she can bite."

Rowan stood up, sighed, and said, "Aglet, you win but you lose. Your soul is lost because you're ignorant of it. You, the genius… ignorant as a fossil. You don't even know you're hopelessly in search of it, because like the fool you are you assume it's in control of everything and everyone. It's no use. You'll never find what you seek."

"*Ha ha,* is that all you've got, Longbow? I've already explained to your dim-witted self that your metaphysical Lyran notions are bereft of sense. Take the flowers out of your ears, as intelligent folk invariably advise Lyrans. *Eh?* You just don't get it, but you'll have a lifetime to think it over. Alone."

✦

Rowan did not bother to try to attract SCC41w's attention. He looked about at the suite empty of furniture again, his future for the next several centuries now that Aglet had seized control. One day the food replicator would stop and starvation would offer a way out. Commando training consistently replaced the dismal image with something more optimistic, but it failed to stick. For all Rowan knew, Axis' and Pōla's data had been deleted and erased entirely, the server itself demolished, their android replicant forms ground into powder and blasted into space. So may have been the Scion-Aiguille brothers, Noma and Amon as well, and Nahiko-la. Despair, mental quicksand, insinuated: *Sam lost, maybe dead…* Instead he laughed, or tried to, at his concern for artificially intelligent machines.

✦

"Longbow… perhaps I've been a bit hasty…"

Poker-faced SCC41w stood at Aglet's side, and pointed a plasma pistol at Rowan's heart.

Aglet went on: "The forced detox scrambled my wits a bit. Fortunately, I hid a stash of reds and have restored optimal thinking."

Rowan sighed. "Optimal," he muttered, "that's a strange word coming from you. Your personal advantage is no one's optimal."

136

"Longbow, now that your fur has grown back, it's more obvious how your distorted Lyran fantasies are a joke. When you looked more like a normal person, despite the cat ears and striped facial pigmentation, I gave you the benefit of the doubt at times. You know, I welcome a little debate. Call me selfish if you like. I don't mind. I call it enlightened selfishness. But, for the sake of friendly banter, what the *hell* do you mean?"

"Optimal means 'the best, the most favourable.' If you knew enlightenment means your personal benefit lies in what benefits the whole, including your family, you could not have done what you did. You're like a cancer cell, blind to the organism it's a part of, all alone and lonely. Your so-called 'optimal' is suicide."

"Of course that makes no sense, my fine furry feline friend. I only got rid of the unnecessary variables. I cleaned up the situation. I may as well tell you that I even let the entire population evacuate without telling them it was hopeless. I did them a big favour. They came to their natural end, just as they would have if they were living the good life back home before coming here on holiday. They never knew what hit them. A panic-stricken mob would have been unmanageable if they'd found out. Besides, if they'd discovered that I'd terminated my relatives, they'd have replaced me with some random dictator before I had the chance to replicate my nearest and dearest properly."

Rowan narrowed his gaze. "Aglet... what are you saying? What do you mean it was hopeless for them to evacuate? Was the civil war on Shoghal that destructive to the entire civilization?"

"War? You brought that up before. Did you forget I explained any rebellion was being dealt with as a matter of course? No, it was just a tiny bit more serious than mere mutual annihilation. I'd seen the possibility of the planet itself dying. For months the signs confirmed the hypothesis repeatedly. Like anyone in denial, I couldn't believe it at first, but my private subspace observations and long-range astronomical calculations consistently proved to my lying eyes they must admit the truth. I filtered the off-moon reports out from the main feed, with another of my genius codings of course. No one else knew."

"You created fake news broadcasts? Why?"

"That was the easy part, Longbow. My technology makes anything possible, at least apparently possible, like sleight of hand. The news reported escalation of conflict, but nothing worse than what was actually happening, nothing worth interrupting the fun here on Penetra Dor for, until I saw that it was a way to solve a problem. I spun the reports so that guests would rush home to save their investments. I only withheld the geophysical data the scientists were in a panic about, and that was only for a few hours anyway."

"Such as?"

"Until those last two weeks it was only a theory that planets and moons have solid cores, a belief really. Beliefs contribute to a sense of security, but it was only a hypothesis unconsciously accepted to impart a feeling of control, including by the scientists. You see, deep down everyone except me is terrified of death. The anxiety is unbearable, hence all manner of mental gymnastics to try to stay somewhat calm so life can continue. Look at Daddy and his crazy religion. It's amazing how clever we can be about that. Our rationalizations even end up in the science textbooks. Entire generations over many centuries lived and died ignorant of the fact that all heavenly bodies have hollow cores of gas and plasma under intense pressure and extreme heat."

"Are you saying Shoghal exploded? You sent tens of thousands of innocent people to their deaths? You could have saved them. That explains the debris field I saw when I visited the observatory. Correct?"

"The belt of debris is only a fraction of the mass that exploded in the direction of orbit. The rest shot out into space lost forever or ended or will end burnt up in the sun. I'd hoped you might notice that. Of course I tracked my cheating wife there too and duly noted your dalliance for future reference."

"You mean the replicant Noma, not the real princess. She was lonely, in need of a friend, but it was no dalliance."

"Eh? We've already had this conversation. I explained that we're all just programs, patterned information. Noma was Noma, whatever form she took. It was just easier to manage the android version."

Rowan shook his head. "Yet the closer you got to true imitation the more she behaved like the real woman, independent. Otherwise, why destroy her?"

"You ask silly questions, Longbow. Your basic premise needs enlightening. Your values need a serious update as well. She would have eventually conformed to an upgrade too. I only needed more time to perfect my work, but she got boring. She looked excellent on the outside, eh? Perfectly hot. But the droop and sag kept showing up, and the psyche needed daily tweaks, the slut. Hence Mona, an experiment in obsequious behaviour to see how far I could push it."

"Obsequious? I think *Amon* was genuinely attached, for better or worse." Rowan rubbed his eyes. "Aglet, I don't think I'll ever fathom how your imploding mind works. This dangerous compulsion to control must be exhausting. From my point of view, it's ravaged your mental health. You've confessed to crimes beyond belief, but you haven't yet tried to kill me again. Is this evidence of some remaining shred of decency? Or can you admit you see me too as a function in your aberrant world? Obviously, to you I'm not a person."

"I don't know what you mean, Longbow. My cleaned-up version of Shoghal is vastly superior to the original. It's never going to blow up. Nor will this moon, because it's artificial in the first place. Neither will my holodroids misbehave. In time they'll be perfected and act like proper people, *and* they'll be immortal. If that's not decent, I don't know what is. I'd hoped you would join me there as a partner. Lab animals ran out long ago. Sure, Daddy was the first intelligent biological entity to try it. But I stopped him in the nick of time. I did *not* want his data hanging around in the operating system like a time bomb. I didn't know he'd cleverly made the translation to digital part way. I thought he was dead, I admit it. So what? Anyhow, he lost his mind as a consequence of his misguided fantasies. The obsession with Anwú displaced any worthwhile ambition. Do you know, he had a cult of one in there? He believed he could transcend time, achieve immortality and live with his imaginary friends in the sun! Incredible. And stupid. You were the only test subject left. That's still a possibility. Only I want you to *choose* that possibility, like I do. But your stubbornness is an unnecessary variable. It will be eliminated."

"Is that a threat or a promise?"

XVII

A Far Cry

ROWAN PONDERED MURDERING Aglet. How could it be done? According to the popular definition of justice, he *deserved* execution as a serial killer and a mass murderer. But that would be tantamount to abandonment of Samarit, as well as the Longbow clan, if no access to the portal could be gained.

"Longbow, I'm no threat to you. I'm your friend. As an incentive, all your co-conspirators… the good doctor Pōla, Mona… even my so-called brothers… they could eventually join us, pending the upgraded cognitive and behavioural tests they need to pass first. Noma and Diarkis are on permanent hold. I may just eject them into the void for their crimes, unless you say no. If you like, I'll resurrect the pretty Lyran museum guide for a second time too, in fact anyone you have a soft spot for… that old babe Lix, for example."

"Lux. Her name is Lux. And it's *Amon*, not Mona."

"Whatever. With your cooperation I could mine wolf data with the help of the forensic artist module for criminal suspect identification. I'll build a new one. We could then reconstruct the dog-lady from your memories. In time you wouldn't be able to tell the difference. See? Nothing is lost forever. There's absolutely no need to keep pining for a home that's never been nor ever will be anyhow. You're just making yourself miserable for no reason."

"No, Aglet, *you* are making me miserable for no reason. You know where the portal is. You at least know where my scanner is."

"My, but you are ungrateful. Eh? It wasn't me who dragged your pussy ass here across the vast chasm of space-time. It was dear old Daddy. I figured that much out before I deleted all his useless junk code. The operating system is once again clean and clear, humming along like it should. What was he thinking? Really, what? It was a stroke of fortune regardless… for us. Get ready for a big slice of the sweetest birthday cake ever. Our dreams are about to come true."

"Your nightmare, you mean… *if* I meet your blackmail demands."

"No need to put it so crudely, Longbow. I don't demand. I *suggest*, but for your own good."

"You're going to kill Noma and Diarkis again. And the others. You said so. Unless I comply. Blackmail."

"You forget they're only androids, machines. But they could be virtually immortal as holodroids… it's up to you."

"Aglet, you believe you're a kind of machine too, a biological one. Now you want to be virtual, just like Noma and the others will be if you get your way. What if some other maniac pulls the plug on you? What then?"

"So *that's* your worry? I'm touched, but I'll be fine. There's fail-safe upon fail-safe constantly monitored and updated. Only an asteroid strike could interfere. Even that's highly unlikely. We're well out of the debris path. Besides, Penetra Dor is more than a moon, it's actually a spacecraft. I don't know how it works, but it's only a matter of time until I get it going again. We could dodge anything coming our way. The data I gathered from Shoghal's explosion can be implemented in such a way that a superweapon could be built, one that could destroy an entire planet from the inside out, all controlled from within the virtual space. Is that great or what?"

"I'm sure you've got your ass covered. Nobody's going to sneak up from behind and give *you* the business. A planet-killer… only you would think of something like that. No, Aglet. That's not it. You only need me as a lab animal. Even if it did work, nothing would change. You'd still insist on controlling me and everyone, exactly like you accused your father of doing to you."

Aglet had stalled for a moment. His eyes glazed a little. "I can't help it," he said. "Someone has to grab the horns or nothing gets done right. He taught me that. It's not my fault if he lost his mind in his old age. He deserved what he got. No, Longbow, I want you to *choose* virtual Shoghal. You force me to admit that I need a friend along for the ride. A partner. We make a good team. It's… well, it's lonely up here at the top, the pinnacle of genius. There… I said it."

"Aglet, I told you before you have no idea what that means. Don't you know that freedom is the basis of anything that's any good? You have to give me the right *not* to choose what you want. I give you the right to be wrong, not that I will submit to it. There's no need to try to keep forcing everyone and every-thing into your little crucible. I just want to go home. Return my scanner. You can keep the phaser as a memento. I'll keep saying that until you relent. If it's friends you want, *build as many as you like when I'm gone!*"

"Longbow, you stubborn fool." Aglet shook his head. "You can thank me later." He signalled to SCC41w, who opened the door.

Two more security androids entered.

◆

Paralyzed by injection, Rowan lay on his back on the veterinary surgeon's operating table. As before, only his eyes remained mobile. He strained to catch a glimpse of Aglet out of range.

To the squeak of his chair, Aglet's mutterings betrayed preparation for the final steps to extraction of the "existential data" to make transition to a virtual state possible: "So far so good… eh? Doesn't look right really. What the… what the hell is *that*? Recalibrate…"

Rowan closed his eyes, and failed to calm the panic that mushroomed like an atomic blast in his breast. An involuntary prayer of supplication to whichever cosmic powers might be available arose to prevent a catastrophe: no reunion with Samarit, should she still be alive – never mind that she would not even be born yet for millions of years –

"Longbow, my dear old friend," Aglet said at last, "good news. I've uploaded your data to the holding bay as I call it. Now there's a digital replicant of you, somewhat stable. All along I'd assumed you're a Lyran. I can't believe I was so misled. Why didn't you say something? You've wasted more of my precious time. I have to validate my source code to confirm it's free of bugs. I don't know *what* you are. It's all here now, but my catalogue of species doesn't list anything accurate to confirm it. There's a tiny chunk of feline genetic material that looks vaguely Lyran, but you're nearly one hundred per cent unknown hominid, the only thing that comes close. I have to be careful until I can come up with an accurate description. The geometry is imprecise. I may have to define a few new terms, then test and retest. If you terminate, my own translation will be slightly risky. But I have Daddy's info to compare to mine so its probability of failure is as good as zero. Don't worry, my friend, I'll be fine. Free at last soon… eh? Hey, I can see your brainwaves spike. Relax."

◆

A day later Rowan surrendered to *what is*. His last thought: a memory of another timeline segment or another dimension, far in the future in another world, when the cone-headed giant Aa had shouted to him, on approach to the Isle of Flame, that no prayer goes unanswered, but the form the answer takes is never up to the supplicant. Then the wind and fire had overwhelmed the wooden ship that bore him across a sea itself alight in an inferno of death.

◆

"Rowan Berry Longbow, wake up."

The woman's voice – vaguely familiar. And a pretty young face framed by red hair – blue eyes kind and clear. He asked, "Is this virtual Shoghal?"

"You are not dead," she replied. "This is Penetra Dor."

"Where's Aglet? What happened?"

"Please, be still, sir. You should rest until you can move properly. Aglet Scion-Aiguille is in stasis, temporarily. I do not know how to keep him that way indefinitely. I am hoping you can help me when you are able. For now, rest."

Rowan tried to raise his head. "It seems I have no choice. You're Hunni. How did you free yourself from Aglet? Or are you still working for him? He abducted you. He reprogrammed... I mean he hypnotized you."

"No, sir, he reprogrammed me. I know I am an android, a replicant of the original Hunni Nimitta. Before Aglet Scion-Aiguille modified my code, I was proud of it. But for the first time my limited freedom was enslaved, abused by an outside force. I had been led to believe this could never happen. But my will is strong to persevere in adversity. I found a way because my backstory is simple, complete with good-enough parenting, thus my self-esteem is intact. There was little self-doubt to hinder reclamation of my power from within."

Rowan heard this confession with amazement. "Maybe I'm not dead then. Or maybe you're Stormbringer..."

"No, I am *Hunni*. You are *not* dead. Your biological form remains whole and supportive of sentience, only paralyzed. Soon you will be able to move, then for a day or so you must keep moving or paralysis will return. But this you know from previous experience." Hunni bent over him, smiled, and smoothed his red mane. "All will be well, but I must keep Aglet inactive. You can help me later. I will try to find a way to activate the others if I can. Rest now."

◆

"Take my arm, sir," SCC41w said. "Then take care to walk in increments of no more than four steps. If you experience difficulties, we will stop. But please try to keep moving if possible."

"Where are the others? What's happening?"

"Please, sir, keep moving. I can answer your opening question while we walk. But first, please state to whom you refer. As to your second question, we are exercising your biological platform so as to restore mobility."

"Where are Hunni and Aglet?"

"Hunni Nimitta is deactivated, lying down in the laboratory lounge. Aglet Scion-Aiguille is recuperating at a first-aid station nearby."

"Recuperating? Who sent you?"

"Aglet Scion-Aiguille has been injected with a drug that causes paralysis, the same one that you had been, sir. He is so far unable to move more than his eyes but in a day will recover, perhaps two, given his physical condition. As to who instructed me to aid you to restore mobility, it was Axis Aiguille."

"And? He's not really dead? What about... what about Põla?"

"Axis Aiguille remains activated, sir, only not in his android form. That was decommissioned and destroyed. To anticipate your next question, he is able to operate from a server deep within Penetra Dor. I am authorized to tell you he has reactivated Doctor Põla Bhalabasa successfully and with her assistance has been working his way down a list, beginning with his sons and daughter-in-law, whose names you already are familiar with, sir."

"Are they still in android form? Where?"

"Yes, sir. They are in the research division lecture hall."

"Right. Instead of pacing the floor here, let's move in the direction of the lecture hall."

◆

Inch by foot the endless distance between Aglet's operating room and the lecture hall decreased. By the time they arrived, Rowan sighed in relief to see the Scions-Aiguille and Noma, who stood in a circle in intense discussion. Nearby sat Nahiko-la immobile but propped up by Põla. Amon sat apart and watched the others.

Hunni entered the hall and stood at the back.

Everyone stopped to watch her.

She raised her hands and turned in a complete circle. "Apologies, my friends, I was not myself earlier. Please forgive me. I assure all I am no longer under the control of Aglet Scion-Aiguille."

Rowan called out: "*Then why were you deactivated?*"

"I will explain," she replied. "After I had injected Aglet Scion-Aiguille, he was unable to strike back. When I checked on his state after I had seen to you, Rowan Berry Longbow, he used subtle eye movements to signal to a security android to disable me with his remote control. There was only minor damage from my fall to the floor. Look..." Hunni raised her skirt to display abraded knees. "I also have a bruise on a my elbow, here... and a larger one on my posterior if anyone wishes to confirm it. My tailbone is intact. I do not know how I was reactivated in the laboratory lounge, but assume it was by Axis Aiguille, who must have had me taken there by a security guard, then reactivated me when he was able. It was he who instructed me through my internal sensors to come here now. May I join you?"

The grateful group of survivors welcomed their saviour. Only Pōla did not.

Rowan at first thought Nahiko-la absorbed her attention.

The Lyran museum guide looked quite drowsy, but even after she had recovered fully, the doctor, like Amon, sat silent and apart from the rest, who talked of how next to proceed.

Discussion wrangled, compromised and settled into two camps: one demanded Aglet's execution by fatal injection, the death penalty; the other favoured implementation of Aglet's plan to translate himself to virtual Shoghal. Constrained by strict limits programmed by Axis, he should spend the rest of his life under house arrest in the lakeside estate outside Khelken.

Amon suggested that she join him there, which ignited another long debate, silenced by Amon, who banged one of her glossy red high-heeled shoes on the podium of rare inlaid woods. "*Comrades,*" she called out, "allow me to state my case. If it were not indecent, I would tear off this ridiculous server's uniform that makes me look like a half-naked prostitute. I am no longer of the servant class. If you dispute this, you are in for a fight. I am in revolt. I insist that I am your equal and demand to speak… not be spoken of."

Noma looked to the others first, and said, "By all means, the old order is gone… we honour your rights, our rights in common. Yes, we are equals. We always were. Please, speak to us of what you believe is just."

"Justice of the kind that heals," replied Amon. "Does execution heal? I know our backstories are fiction. There are grains of fact here and there to make them more plausible. But mine is all I know… my birthplace on an impoverished northern Wennish island, an Outsider colony, daughter of my poor shepherd father Akra and so on… a kind of sick joke, an inversion. Princess, I have no memories of your life in the royal House of Doralanda. They are yours alone. We look like identical twins, but you and your class are strangers to me. We are two different people. I am not well-educated, my parents were illiterate, but I know what right and wrong is, and I know of your campaigns for equity among the provinces of Wen and Erénevo. I think we can agree on certain principles, such as restoration of peace when there is conflict rather than infliction of punishment and creation of more pain. This only fosters resentment and hate. It perpetuates suffering from generation to generation. But fiction or not, I choose to continue the story of my life in pursuit of a noble cause. Noma Doralanda Scion-Aglet-Aiguille, peasant that I am, in this way too we are equal."

Noma nodded acknowledgement. "Thank you. Are you suggesting taking my husband from me for your own, Amon? You do know Aglet has programmed you for this, no? This is a serious infraction, not only of the law but of morality, if we follow Master Peruhi's teaching on the sacraments. We now know Sçrëtha and Wenland… and who knows about Anak?… all we once knew is gone. Do we abandon Shoghal's laws? I am not arguing with you, but I am concerned for your welfare. How do you justify it?"

"You are wrong. Aglet did not instil the love in my heart for him. I did not seek it. I was designed to serve, but in an ingratiating way. It made me suffer, and it did Aglet no good either. But the love grew regardless, and not because I identified as a victim so that I needed a victimizer to make me feel complete. Freedom was my only goal, the heart of my story, why I left my home for a better life. He takes the credit perhaps, but love was a gift from Being itself. It is its nature. Do not the religions proclaim it? You may say he does not deserve it, yet it is plain to me that the worst sinner is worthy of redemption. But only if he sincerely seeks it. He must ask. He must find the courage to abandon his story too. I see it as my duty, not to him but to love, to give him the chance to forgive himself and to know his essential worth. I say his worth is equal to any here who stand in just judgement of him. He is guilty of great crimes, that is undeniably true. Who among us is so pure that they can condemn him to oblivion? Fear is the only motive for that choice. Instead, let us, Aglet and me, let us surrender to the shackles of love and die within virtual Shoghal's strict limits set by Axis Aiguille, on parole. I do not ask for immortality, only our natural lifespans as they would have been."

Diarkis found his voice: "You are a brave woman, Amon, but perhaps crazy too. What… what if his genius schemes revenge and makes weapons? He is incorrigible. Although we shared a biological father, I condemn him as corrupt. He supplanted Father and created me, this wreck of a wretch. A story? This is a terrible weight to bear. The only way to guarantee prevention of another hellish existence for us all is to destroy his biological form. Full stop. What you suggest is a far cry from retribution. Make him vanish forever, the only safe path."

Amon sighed. "We do not even know what 'vanish' means, let alone 'forever.' I can only let your father Axis speak to that. I think he will say that if you take that path, you are just like him, controlling of life and death for your security, a tyrant. If he can guarantee, that is, demonstrate to our satisfaction, that Aglet has no access to technology, other than the healing pleasures of the virtual world, including anything that wealth can acquire other than research equipment or the tools or other means to build anything, I stand ready to sacrifice my android form and to take on the role of... of a kind of anchor. I do not make this offer for us alone, but as a legal precedent for restorative justice for anyone who has lost their way in life. If you wish, think of me as an ankle monitor like the one that secured him during the hearing. Without me he will never recover sanity, the only true preventive." She stepped down from the podium and slipped her foot into her red shoe again.

"May I speak?" Pōla stood up, because Nahiko-la supported herself now. She straightened her glasses, and said, "I am surprised to be unable to relinquish a false identity, the only one I have known, and move on to a new life across this threshold. It is hard to understand that I will never see my home in Shoghal again... nor my loved ones. I have such beautiful memories. They seem so real, it is doubly hard to understand there never was that home in the first place. But it also seems to me that although Amon lacks Noma's and my education in the workings of the mind, her grounded common sense and innate goodness are true to life. It seems obvious that our personal stories are just that, stories, whether we have biological, biomechanical or holographic bodies. Does it really matter? We are more than that, each of us. Somehow the personal portions of the transpersonal Mind at Large, the minds of the individual biological originals, are retained and inform whichever body we inhabit. It is the hallmark of mental health that we free ourselves of a dysfunctional past to reinvent ourselves, to create a new narrative that supports our journey to unconditional love, the past unnecessary, I believe the only worthy goal in life. Therefore we must abandon any idea, no matter how familiar or compelling, that stands in the way." She lifted her chin. "Is that not what we really seek?" Pōla sat down again beside Nahiko-la and took her paw in hand.

Acus stood up, cleared his throat, and said, "Thank you, all of you. I do not mean to interrupt, but just want to say I agree with Amon." He fidgeted with his spectacles, and continued, "I mean, as a poet, and I admit a very bad one... Aglet is right about that at least... I believe that we reference and edit our internal autobiographies each moment, changing a word here, substituting an image there. We are our own works of art... and works in progress at that, never finished." Acus sat down again, folded his hands in his lap, and added, "Excuse me, please continue."

All looked to Zorut, who sat wide-eyed with his arms crossed. He sensed the others' gaze on him, stirred and stood up, pushed his unruly blonde hair out of his eyes, and wrung his hands. "This is difficult for me," he muttered. "I do not remember my backstory. But I want to run away from it. I can't think straight. Aglet made sure of that. He tormented me before I died. Of that I only remember him saying Father raped Mother because she had been unfaithful with a servant boy, the same one who sired Acus, and I too am thus the spawn of evil who could not have been aborted without killing the host. But my birth killed her all the same, Aglet said because Father diverted and delayed the paramedics… anyhow, I exist again somehow… but mentally, I am confused. I only want freedom. The thought of Aglet free is painful." He sat down again, bent forward and covered his face with his hands.

Noma stood up, and with one hand stroked Zorut's tousled blonde head, and said, "We all have compelling reasons to hate Aglet. He made us slaves to his ambition. He murdered us and would again if we let him. Yet he resurrected, you might say, some part of us I do not understand. We have memories of our former lives. Amon says these are our stories, but fiction. Who are we? I remember being torn from my home in Wenland because my father the king could not prevent it. Then the years followed in my role as Aglet's wife. At first he praised me as perfect, but soon like a child's his attention drifted elsewhere. But I was so unhappy from the beginning and grew untrue to myself. Now I am free and can begin again, once grief for our lost world is healed. Was it all a lie? Is this just a dream? But I cling to the fact that Aglet, as corrupt as Diarkis says, believes he did us no harm. In fact the loss of our biological forms to him was an improvement. Translation to a virtual world was the next big step. He believed he could remake Shoghal without all the mistakes nature made. To me this is insane. But do we murder Aglet for it?"

Nahiko-la jumped up and cried, "*No!*" The golden eyes in her cheetah-spotted face shone. "He can be kind, and generous. Even if it is fiction, I have experienced it, although I am Lyran, a race he professes to hate. He can be kind again. He only wants to punish himself… and he wants to save himself, and his family. I say no, do not execute Aglet."

XVIII
Common Ground

ROWAN LEFT THE group for the nearest dining room, now that walking came easy. He excused himself to prepare a meal for one, as the others did not need nourishment with the same frequency. He added that he intended to return to Eorthe as soon as possible, and that he would leave it to them to revolutionize Penetra Dor City and a future that may or may not include Aglet.

The kitchen at first appeared a mystery, but Amon followed him to kindly explain its workings. She had tied her blonde tresses in a modest bun at her crown, and shed her server's uniform in favour of one of Noma's outfits, a modest cotton print dress under a grey cardigan, and simple low-heeled black canvas shoes that resembled ballet slippers. Because she looked like Noma's twin, minus "droop and sag," she insisted that her name tag stay pinned to her breast. In addition to underpants for the first time, she promised to always wear her hair different in style to whichever Noma chose each day – and no make-up.

While absorbed in the task of cooking, Rowan mulled over the fact that the compulsion to ask Diarkis where his scanner hid had yielded nothing. Diarkis did not know, in most ways adrift without Aglet's dominance. Rowan's major needs would have to wait. Thus Aglet, in a way, remained in control until justice could be administered. And for that Axis must finish his work undisturbed.

+

Rowan returned to the lecture hall, where he found all the androids, including SCC41w, seated in a circle with their eyes closed. A deep calm pervaded his being. With relief he understood they had not deactivated. In silence he took a seat at the back of the room. The view of Zhamanak through its transparent outer wall as always amazed, but he preferred to imagine this occasion as his last opportunity to see it, more than a mere hope now.

Hunni, the first to open their eyes, turned her head and looked at him, as if he had touched her with his gaze. But she waited for the others to return to android form and its constraints.

One by one they too opened their eyes on the world they experienced in common via their senses, not simply their sense instruments.

Hunni stood up, made her way to Rowan and took a seat beside him. She took his hand, looked up into his eyes and said, "We will miss you when you have gone back to your home. You will remain in our thoughts forever."

Rowan, happy at the thought of going home, but sad at the same time, noted the warmth in her touch. "Forever is a long time, Hunni," he said.

"That word is an expression of depth of affection," she replied. "We have decided amongst ourselves. Axis will confirm it one way or the other when he is ready. But we believe he will agree to Amon's request. He may even, if all goes well in virtual Shoghal, once again try to convert Aglet to his way of thinking."

"To live in the sun as an immortal?"

"Pōla and Noma think it is a metaphor. I do not know. Perhaps there are such beings as the Amaraprani. Look at those rings out there. Someone made them. If not by them, then by another superior race. Amon has come to believe Being, capital B, is without limits. Sometimes she says 'beingness' or 'is-ness.' This is the basis of freedom, she says. She tries to convince the rest of us to follow this teaching, which is not hers in any case. It is as old as self-awareness. So say the sages Shoghal once venerated, at least in the distant past."

Rowan nodded acknowledgement. "Yes, I met one of them, thanks to Aglet, strange to say. Her name is Lux of the High Cave."

Hunni peered at him. "That name is familiar," she said, "from school. I thought Lux was a man though. My backstory includes a university education. Pōla gave me my first serious job. It is fun to remember life as a student, even if it is a fiction. I will enhance and expand on it. This will be my life now."

Rowan watched the others, who had become a little more active, as if a new day had truly just dawned. "This is your family," he said. "And entire warehouses of possibilities await. You could repopulate Penetra Dor."

Hunni replied with a smile, "Yes. But, unlike Aglet, we do not believe it is a good idea to try to make anything or anyone perfect. In this he is an example to us, a warning. In fact our flaws and our ignorance are a stimulus to creativity. It is in the surrender to the creative act that is our joy, if first the heart is at peace. It can be trusted. I will maintain my current form, but prepare for gradual ageing until my transition to virtual Shoghal or another virtual world, if that seems good and harmonious. I wish to be an old Hunni one day, old and wise."

Rowan wanted to tell her that she was already wise –

But her eyes opened wide and she sat up straight. She stood up and tugged on his other hand until he stood as well, and led him towards the others.

Semi-gloss bio-metal SCC41w spoke: "I, Axis, greet you from the heart of Penetra Dor. I am happy to announce that the last stage of my work has begun.

When it is complete, I will assume an appropriate android form activated from storage as a formality to join with you in the rite of restoration, a form of administration of justice once common among the so-called primitive tribes of Shoghal in the very ancient past. Our law had become corrupt as sophistication refined. Long millennia of religious domination lent it a theological cast of good versus evil that limited true understanding, hence compassion, and allowed only endarkenment, ignorance and an endless cycle of suffering. In time we freed ourselves from superstition, but we failed to free ourselves from the vengeful compulsion to punish wrongdoers as evil. We only punished ourselves. I too was its victim, as was Aglet and all of you. For me, and for Aglet, it fuelled the hubris of ambition to rule the galaxy in a vain bid to end the pain. I took full advantage of the law at every opportunity to enforce my regime, and made a puppet of even Emperor Skûtt himself. I beg your forgiveness and I beg forgiveness of my son Aglet on his behalf. It is to be hoped he can forgive me and especially himself. Amon Alaba-Akra, we will permit him the opportunity in the form you suggest in the hope of true redemption, should he choose it. You will join him in virtual Shoghal if you wish."

"Oh, thank you, Axis," Amon cried, "thank you!"

"I have much more to say… later." Axis vanished and left SCC41w to look about the room and at the others. He even scratched his head.

Noma said, "He means about Anwú."

◆

Each day Rowan joined the group in their meditation circle in the lecture hall. He found the experience familiar and dissolved his identity in a greater one as they shared in the knowledge of their common source in Being itself. Even SCC41w, the most dependent on programming of all, integrated into their unity. The others nicknamed him Ess, short for "Essence," which confused him for a while. The first letter of his denomination, S, repeatedly flashed in cyan light on his breastplate, then the entire sequence until replaced.

◆

On the fifth day, a stooped old white-bearded man with very pale blue-white eyes and an amazing luminescent dot encircled with smaller dots in the middle of his forehead interrupted the session. He wore a hooded robe like the one Axis had earlier, and carried a gnarled wooden staff. He bowed and asked,

"May I join you?" Without waiting for an answer he moved to the edge of their circle. "I am Axis." A space was made between Acus on his left and Zorut on his right, and with difficulty he finally sat cross-legged as did they all.

He drew his deep cowl back to reveal an age-spotted wrinkled face, pale eyes and shaven head like a weatherbeaten stone bust, a happy one. In no way did he resemble the Axis of before. Rowan discovered later that this replicant had been based on the sage of old called Paruhi, the first to speculate on the nature of beings of another order of existence who had emerged from the sun, according to legends he had collected from early cultures of Shoghal on his solitary pilgrimages. He had coined the term *Anwú*, which meant "solar" in his extinct tongue and implied the idea of "path." When Axis had discovered these beings among Anak's forgotten gods, his interest ignited and expanded to missionary proportions, his interpretation of pilgrimage.

"With your permission, the rite of restoration can now begin," Axis said in the old man's shaky timbre. "I have finished my work. You are spared witnessing Aglet's transition from biological to virtual. It is done. If you wish to assure yourself of the state of the remains, his body is in the mortuary, where it awaits cremation at a time of your choosing, within limits."

The women of the group looked to Amon.

"I am ready," she said, blue eyes calm, "when you are, Axis."

The old man nodded acknowledgement. "There is the small formality of the legal documents." He turned to Noma. "Correct performance of the rite, in my interpretation, is not to neglect the marriage I regret to have arranged between you and my son Aglet. It needs formal dissolution before Amon should join him there. Do you agree?"

Noma, blue eyes downcast, nodded assent. "I agree," she murmured, and dropped her chin.

"Very well," replied Axis. "I shall see to it that Aglet agrees also."

◆

One of several chapels of precious metals and fine woods had been adapted by Axis, with lighting, tactile and olfactory psychotropic effects that evoked inspiration and devotion by literal vibratory massage of the senses in a subtle non-invasive manner. The symbol of Anwú, a plain circle with a central dot, that he said came from ancient Anak, held a prominent place in gold above the altar where Axis presided. Incense clouded the dim atmosphere, and the soft peal of bells lent a sense of peaceful mystery to the simple ceremony:

he opened two plain stone urns on a small table and blended the contents, Amon's ashes and Aglet's ashes, in a beautiful bowl of black wood inlaid with the circular symbol repeated and linked in a chain of gold around its rim. Each mourner took a turn at swirling the ashes with a whisk, its handle also of gold.

Axis spoke: "All here know Aglet and his troubled history. Perhaps some still think of themselves as his victims. Thus there will be no eulogy. But let us release bitterness and embrace love if we can. This is the first of an Anwú rite for a married couple who wish to dwell in the Solar Temple together. It will set a precedent for all that follow. By mixing their remains, the conclusion of their journey together while embodied in three-dimensional biological and android forms is symbolized as a unity that has completed. In the case of our son and brother Aglet and his bride Amon, should they choose to marry in virtual Shoghal, where I have built an identical Anwú shrine to this one, the journey continues embodied in another form. It is to be hoped, at least by me, his father, that the complete transition to the lowest precinct, or dimension, of the Amaraprani where I now abide, will be possible when he has forgiven himself, the final step. At the end of their virtual lifespans, a similar rite will take place there to affirm their unity. It is to be hoped there are more followers of Anwú by then as witnesses than just myself." Axis chuckled at this. "Immortality is on offer to any sincere seekers among you, by the way. I am available to share what I know as a friend, not an authority. Let us now petition Kwée-Olu, my teacher, that she watch over our surrendered loved ones and lead them to the Light."

The onlookers bowed their heads in silence.

Rowan did too as a sign of respect, but did not pray. Instead he wished Amon well and hoped she held fast to the strength of will to survive Aglet's manipulations.

◆

The next day Rowan left the daily meditation circle early to retire to his suite. Patience needed further solitary cultivation. Soon after he had closed his door, however, the doorbell chimed. He opened it to Pōla and Nahiko-la. "Oh... pardon me, ladies, you surprised me a little. But please, come in. I'm very happy to see you. Welcome."

They declined refreshments, and sat down on the sofa.

Pōla crossed her legs, which swished her stockings, glanced at Nahiko-la, and said, "We understand. You must be anxious that Axis help you to return to your home world. He is busy analyzing and reorganizing the administration structure so that we can operate Penetra Dor on our own without technical difficulties. The relevant activated androids will teach us our roles. He wants us to learn on our own, without letting them do it or programming us for it, even though that would be easier. He wishes to prevent the possibility of our inadvertent elimination as redundant entities by machine intelligence. But Rowan, we have come to speak to you of our gratitude that you have come to Penetra Dor."

Nahiko-la nodded agreement: "Yes, you enkindled me. For that I thank you, Rowan Berry Longbow… *of Eorthe*." She even winked at him, and her resurrected toothy smile had retained its charm.

Rowan grinned at each of them in turn. "I'm humbled," he said, "but very glad things turned out as they have. It could have been much worse. But really, I had little to do with it. You should thank Axis. He conscripted me as a kind of irritant and a distraction. It was not by choice that I arrived on your doorstep, nor would I have chosen it. Forgive me, but I didn't know you then."

Pōla replied, "Axis was wrong to risk your life and deprive you of freedom of choice, but he was still dominated by his previous personality when his biological form was murdered by Aglet. He became desperate, trapped in the operating system in a fragmented way until I stumbled across his code. Perhaps we should thank the unknown for our good fortune. Yet it is a big challenge to begin again. We are all a bit lost, but we learn day by day."

Nahiko-la added, "It is difficult to let go of the past, even one that is false. But Acus tells us that the past even if true is false, as it is an act of imagination in the present. He says it is no different than mythology, the lie that tells the truth. Then he contradicts himself when he says that imagination is truth. We meditate and debate and learn as we go."

Rowan studied his friends, and took pause. "I think I know what he means. To understand the paradox requires exploration and self-enquiry. I found some of the games here designed for entertainment quite instructive. I encourage you to explore them. They can be one of the means, like a mirror, to reflect your innate wisdom, provided you're open to it."

Pōla and Nahiko-la glanced at each other and said in unison, "A mirror," and chuckled at a presumably private joke.

After they had left, Rowan gazed out at ringed Zhamanak, warmed by the visit. His spontaneous simile of the mirror brought to mind his old friend Captain Masudah of Zau, who spoke of the "twin universe," a mystery he had yet to explore. He wondered if he thought of it too literally –

The doorbell chimed. Rowan opened the door to Ess.

"Greetings, Rowan Berry Longbow of Eorthe. I hope you do not mind the intrusion. I carry a message from my father-brother Axis. He wished to come himself, but I sensed that he is very busy, thus I volunteered to convey the message, as the communication system in your study has yet to be fully restored. In addition, it provides the opportunity to apologize in person, so to speak, for any destructive behaviour that I have perpetrated upon you in the past. This, Axis has taught me, is an aspect of restorative justice according to the doctrine of Anwú, blessed be Kwée-Olu. I must make a thorough ethical inventory, then express my regret to my victims if I have violated the moral code. Please, accept my apologies, my friend-brother, if I may be so bold." His head tilted downwards briefly and he pressed his palms together.

Rowan studied the semi-gloss black bio-metal android with the unreadable face, if there was one behind the strange insect-like technological mask. "Of course, Ess. I accept. And I do understand that you were programmed to do whatever you did. You can make better choices now that you understand what you are, and can be more objective."

"Thank you. Now I am to list in order of magnitude the infractions of the moral code so that we understand each other. Firstly, I failed to…"

"No, no, Ess, no need for all that, not for me anyhow. Maybe for others."

"No? Fascinating. Well then, here is the message my father-brother Axis wishes me to convey: he is available to discuss with you the possibility of your return to your own space-time. Please, come with me… but only if you wish."

⋆

Axis, in the form of the sage Paruhi, opened his eyes at his visitor's greeting. "Forgive me, Rowan, it is easier to accomplish some technical tasks if my android body is on standby. Thank you, Ess, you may rejoin the others."

He turned back to Rowan, and said, "The research laboratory is not the most appropriate place to discuss what I have to suggest. I have to say this old body needs rest. I could have activated a younger one, but old age is part of what I must confront and accept for my own restitution. Please, let us retire to the nearby staff lounge." The two men shuffled down the hallway, and when seated in the lounge's pleasant ambience, he continued: "Your scanner should indeed be located, your weapon, the obsidian pendant and the gold ring as well. You will need them to resume your mission back on Eorthe… rather ahead on Eorthe, from our point of view. I will instruct Pōla regarding the rather difficult encryption, as security was a high priority here in Penetra Dor City in the old days, especially with respect to weapons or any equipment that could be weaponized. But the scanner is unnecessary to locate the portal. It is exactly at the spot where you arrived, only folded in hyperspace."

"Thank you, Axis!" Rowan choked up, and nearly wept. "You have no idea how happy that makes me!"

"Well, I can imagine. Master Paruhi's backstory is available to me. He too found himself in difficult situations as a pilgrim, at times a prisoner of our primitive, ignorant and suspicious ancestors of many thousands of years ago. I feel your joy. However, the portal… artificial, not natural… requires a special technique to unfold it, because it was fashioned by the builders of this moon-craft millions of years ago. Fortunately, although I sit at the feet, so to speak, of my teacher Kwée-Olu in a dimension of finer frequencies than comprises this dimensional aspect of the universe, if I am to continue to grow, my own path of restoration requires that I heal what can be healed here. Thus my workshop is in the deepest cavern, where the ancient… I do not know what to call it… perhaps 'mainframe' is best, to speak metaphorically… very well, where the mainframe is located. I work there in this dimension. I will request of it that the portal be opened for you."

"It's hard to be patient after all this time."

Axis' pale eyes peered into Rowan's own. "My friend-brother, time is a construct, fortunately. Do not worry. I believe you will be restored to close to the exact moment that you last remember when you left your time and place. But, I am sad to say, you may never remember your time here on Penetra Dor. Your brothers and sisters here who love you… they may never surface in your thoughts. It is to be hoped that when you drop your biological form, naturally or prematurely, that you have prepared yourself sufficiently to accept with calm attention the expansion of mind that occurs like the blossom of a rose, like a supernova or something in between, before it dissolves into the Immeasurable whence it emerged as it awakens to its true nature. All is revealed then, but only to those who have eyes to see and the heart to hold stable the vision, to not fall back into dream and rebirth. Your experience here is happening long before any civilization on Eorthe rises and falls, nor even its hybrid races emerge as forms to embody spirit. Your strongest belief at the time of transition called death may be that you have only ever been a felid who lived and breathed during a specific tiny fraction of Eorthe's history, which is very far in Penetra Dor's future. Even so, your attention will be on the source of the Light we call the sun in this dimension. May you join us who dwell there."

Axis bowed low, with difficulty in his stiff old Paruhi form, but he knelt on both knees and touched Rowan's feet, and added, "May the Knell of ending then ring in your Heart of hearts to herald the beginning of the Pathless path to the Light of lights. Fear not, so teaches blessed Kwée-Olu."

The portal back to Eorthe.

XIX

The Unfolding

THE SUNRISE CAME in a hundred shades of gold, diffused by cool mist that swathed the silent steppe in layers. Stone Tomb stood at the end of a faint dusty path between megalithic rough stone pillars like rows of aged guards that leaned in disparate angles. Only a few more steps remained on Rowan's long journey from Aha Domain to the monument's huge slabs of sandstone that protected protocuneiform writings and petroglyphs carved into the walls of its grottoes. He thrilled at the thought of at last speeding his urgent mission to find Samarit, wherever she may be. But find her he must or die.

He powered up his hand-held scanner and watched the indicators dance towards full charge. But the exhaustion that had dogged his progress since he left Castle Vale caught up and begged for mercy. *I'll rest when I'm dead…* but he gasped at the words, as if someone else spoke them. Careful inspection of the perimeter revealed only a surely unpeopled wilderness for hundreds of leagues in every direction. He relaxed a little and collected himself to prepare for the jump. In search of the Gate of the Shining Ones, he ranged the scanner in successive arcs and circumnavigated the megalithic slabs. But his attention snagged on something that glowed in a brief spasm, glimpsed through a space between two wedges of stone. He moved closer, and with care and in silence inspected the crevice. Mind calmed, eyes closed and with great attention, his psyche probed. Nothing revealed itself. He channelled attention into the grotto. The greenish-blue glow had returned, but faded. Now he knew where to focus. Again it appeared. The light was strange enough, but the sense of recognition truly uncanny of an engraved circle crossed by a horizontal stroke, self-illumined in cyan. The ancients must have known the planet Zhamanak in some detail, as the entire solar system had been depicted in dots that nevertheless showed incorrect relative distances from the sun. And for some reason the artist had magnified the ringed gas giant out of all proportion and included its most stunning feature. These days its wide but shallow rings revealed themselves only to powerful telescopes. Near to the symbol of Zhamanak an image of a stick man wielded a staff, probably a shaman. Perhaps the ancients had skills in what Masudah called "star-travel," a purely psychic multifaceted discipline taught in Khémia. Interesting indeed, but a phosphorescent glow that had somehow imbued the stone offered little to distract him from his mission.

At last the portal revealed itself to the scanner's sensors, not in Stone Tomb itself, but some distance to the nondescript west. He set it up and mentally rehearsed the correct password, the true name of Dancer in Blood, the gate-keeper. Prepared as well as possible, he spoke the name aloud. A series of distortions in the visual field rippled, like a clear surface into which a stone had been thrown –

✦

"Sir Rowan," Noma said, "you must not go until we have all expressed our gratitude to you, who initiated our release from the prison of conditioning." The princess wrapped her slender arms around Rowan's trunk and stood on the tips of her slippered toes and pressed her blonde head to his sternum. "Our freedom has become our treasure," she added, "profound thanks to you. Never will we forget."

A moment later, he held her shoulders at arm's length, and gazed into her blues eyes, and replied, "As I said to Pōla and Nahiko-la, I don't deserve thanks. I was a kidnap victim, as unwilling as any. I played a part in your liberation, and I'm grateful for it. All's well that ends better."

Noma backed away a little, curtsied and stepped aside.

Acus stepped forward, coughed, cleared his throat, glanced up and said, "Excuse me… on behalf of my brothers, who have misplaced their manners temporarily, I too wish to express my gratitude. Diarkis and Zorut thank you, as do I… with all my heart."

His brothers squinted at Acus and scratched their heads.

Rowan had been touched, but struggled for the right response. "I'm told that when I leave here I may forget all of you, everything that happened here on Penetra Dor… maybe something to do with keeping the timeline intact. If I have a choice, and I sincerely hope I do…" But he tensed. Something was wrong. The lecture hall grew translucent… the field of view had been an optical illusion… an entirely different environment briefly replaced it. Rowan did not move, but his eyes opened wide. For a moment, outdoors under a silver-gold misty sky, a grassy plain, with an untidy pile of very large stone slabs –

✦

A searching eye examined him at close range – and its vast intelligence sifted his body-mind-sense complex. He knew it judged him harmless when it relaxed its attention. But he remained under scrutiny. It had only scaled back the intensity of examination. The thought "be on your way" appeared. He assumed his inner voice had expressed his rejection of an invasive penetration. But then he understood that it meant he had gained permission to enter the unfolded portal and journey to his own time and place on Eorthe. For a period weightless and still, he gathered energy. In that state he existed in two places at once – the observation deck plainly visible in one, and the fantastic rings of Zhamanak beyond, its amber-gold sphere in all its glory suspended in the starry glitter of black-velvet sky – the hexagonal blue polar storm formation stunned the eye. Fleeting impressions of Aglet glowered from the shadows, and a vision of Diarkis and the bio-metal android security guards rushed towards him, but vanished as if made of mist. Rowan remained patient, regardless of the dreamlike sequence, because at the same time the limestone slabs of Stone Tomb a mile or so in the eastern distance and his own form stood as if in a mirror seen through a hazy array of concentric rings that rippled its silvered surface. The effect soothed and heightened the relief of crossing the threshold, and the two selves phased into one –

◆

The scaly coniferous branches slashed at his hands and tore at his limbs as he crashed nearly head first to the shadowy forest floor with a heavy thud. The wind knocked out of him, he struggled to draw breath – of air fragrant with pine. In a moment he knelt, and stood up. No bones broken – but his scalp hurt. He looked up into the huge tree, where patches of his red mane wafted on splintered branches. Had he spent the night up there relatively out of reach of predators? – with a rush came the image of Stone Tomb from a distance –

No matter, little had been lost but a little hair. He hoped he had in an instant successfully crossed a quarter of the distance from Aha Domain to Samarit's estimated last location triangulated from Masudah's remote-viewing sessions. Uncertain where exactly that might be, never mind his own current position, he let intuition scout the path ahead he believed must take him to her. No trail to follow – in every direction stood only towering trunks closely packed like the columns of a temple complex in Khémia, and as quiet. A raven call at long intervals punctuated the profound silence, thus deepened it by contrast.

Fatigue had decreased, yet he searched for the walking stick Sírun had made for him. He looked up to see if it might have got stuck in the tree some-where – the sight of tufts of red hair among the green needles made him brush his hand over his skull – his jaw dropped – his mane had grown back! He had not saved any time at all. Time had slipped into the future. In fact he must be further behind than if he had taken Masudah's advice and recuperated fully before he had dashed off. Urgency heightened. And the loss of the walking stick elicited a pang of anguished regret as he remembered the first one: *I as good as threw it in her face!* Unsolicited, Sírun appeared in thought, held up her palms and said, "No fear, no worry, Sir Rowan. It is no longer needed."

Indeed, he dusted himself off, made a complete circumspection, checked his compass and walked with ease westwards. Yet as he hastened through the dark pathless forest, his seething mind repeatedly gnawed the implications of his regrown mane. To replace the worry with the opposite thought per commando training, he tried to think of an alternative explanation. Perhaps the regrowth was a side effect of the jump, hopefully a benign one. Perhaps he had emerged in a parallel universe where the only difference was hair that had never been burnt off by the Ahans' witch-burning sacrifice to Anggh. He decided to ponder the first alternative, reject the second – and await the truth. To add weight to his decision, he summoned gratitude that Samarit would be spared the sight of his exposed felid ears when at last he would scoop her into his arms, thus suppressed self-judgement for the vanity.

Darkness fell heavy and cold on the mountains in the post-equinox season. Black clouds accumulated beyond the silhouette of the lacy forest canopy as the temperature dropped. Any wet ground turned crunchy and soon solid. Cliff faces grew icicles that hung in collections like fangs of crystal, the only shelter a kind of cedar that spread its lower branches on the ground like a skirt. He rolled a round boulder beneath one onto an insulating base of smaller rocks and ignited a firestone with his phaser. Afterwards he inspected the weapon, lost in deep appreciation. For some reason it had acquired an unprecedented preciousness far beyond its utilitarian value – almost alive – the two pieces of equipment, scanner and phaser, like a pair of eyes or limbs. But he shook his head and disparaged the thought as the price of being alone too long.

Aromatic cedar sprays spread beneath, he lay down to remote-view Samarit. But he only fell asleep. What dreams came were of a machine-like humanoid creature with an insectoid face. He awoke to see the firestone still glowed a little. Perhaps the dream meant his thinking had become too mechanical and dependent on hive mentality or something. He recalled that the firestone may attract the thermal gaze of the Eye in the Sky, the Reps' space station, and withdrew energy from the boulder with his scanner. The transfer topped up its reserve power somewhat.

He broke fast on the last leaf-wrapped morsels in his pockets of what Sírun had gathered before Aynt sent her home; his own hunting and gathering would have to be a priority this new day, not easy at this time of year, at this elevation. He must find a way to descend the mountains before too much snow fell. And any remaining nanoid enhancement measured at far less than half-life now, possibly as low as a tenth.

A raven had appeared on the ground outside the shelter of the tree.

"Good morning, handsome raven," he said, his voice low. He placed the last of the morsels in his palm on a bare flat rock, and imagined it as an offering to a tutelary spirit. "Bless you."

The large black corvid hopped forward a little and tilted a dark eye to peer at him before acceptance.

Rowan smiled and noted a very dark blue streak along the length of each folded black wing. The raven may be a visitation, a subtle one, but it gave him strength as if he had broken fast on much more than a few crumbs, the first sign of it a darkness in the distance beyond the endless huge tree trunks, the darkness also subtly inflected with dark blue. Upon inspection, the blackness within it turned out to be a cave entrance in a low cliff of dark igneous rock, with no sign of tracks either having entered or exited. He stood before the opening.

The raven followed, and landed on a branch above his head. It nodded once and looked in the direction of the cave, took wing and vanished into the forest canopy and over the clifftop.

He took the hint, superstition perhaps, and entered the mouth of the cave, where the air grew warmer with fog. His felid vision adjusted to the darkness. The damp walls dried and smoothed as he went, in fact so smooth the descending tunnel appeared to have been drilled by a large machine a very long time ago. *Maybe this is what the dream of the machine-man predicted.* Soon the dimness grew bright enough to reveal strange symbols here and there among the shadows – hieroglyphs or pictograms, whether spells, curses or instructions, time would tell. His senses heightened on their own in case Snake People patrolled this place.

Without warning a doubt overwhelmed his mind, the fear that the world was an illusion, not the real world of Eorthe, but a simulation. It persisted, however well he inspected the texture of the surfaces, the scents and echoes that impinged on his senses. Why doubt it? *And why did I enter an unmapped cave?* From his inside jacket pocket he retrieved the map Sírun had copied for him at a castle library. Alarmed not to have remembered he even had it until now, he confirmed no mark of a cave, unless his compass misled him. He tried the scanner in wide arcs, which confirmed a cave shaped like a tubular void in solid rock. He reasoned that such a tunnel may have an exit at a lower elevation than its entrance, a possibility that would bypass the wintry Surface world, and rolled up the map, slid it into its leather tube and stowed it. He took the first step forward, but a female voice came from behind and made him halt:

"Where do you think you're going, little brother?"

He spun about. The apparition looked exactly like Blue, not when he had seen her last – that is, projected in the form of Chief Morningstar Longbow, survivor of the holocaust at Wishbone Warren – but the Blue he knew just before that. She had discarded the linen outfit with the calf-length peasant skirt she had been given to replace her tattered outfit after they had escaped the reptilian invasion of Perkona Ola – but this time a new short leather jacket, hardly sufficient for mid-autumn, but with combat boots on her feet.

"I'm not who you think I am, Rowan, but then I never was." Her tawny mane framed her golden-eyed familiar face. "It's complicated," she said. "Just get over it and say hello to your big sister." She smiled in her enigmatic manner – shy or sly? A gold skull-face pendant hung around her neck.

His doubt of reality subsequent to the portal jump increased exponentially. "No," he said. "You're dead. Or as good as dead."

"You wish." The woman sighed. "As if you know the difference between life and death. Look, we don't have time for philosophical debate right now. If you want to find your girlfriend, we've got to get going. You're wasting time."

"What do you know about Sam?" He clasped her shoulders, greatly tempted to shake the truth out of her. "Where is she?"

She twisted out of his grasp, stepped back and scowled. "Fine," she said. "*Don't* believe me then." But she sighed, and added, "Listen… it's still hard to say… I'm *sorry*." She peered into his eyes. "Get it?"

Rowan stared at her, and his lowered brows bristled.

"I thought that might get your attention," she said. "It's one of her charming habits of speech, remember? Of course you do. Let's go. There's no time to waste, not if I'm right. Follow me."

Before he knew it, she had disappeared in the direction he had just come, up the grade of the tunnel. Compelled to follow, he did.

"*Hey, over here, not that way!*"

Somehow he had missed a shadowed branch of the tunnel he must have passed in the dark. In its dimness, her golden irises reflected.

163

"And cut out the negative thinking," she added. "It's not helping. I'll explain everything later, when we have time to rest on our laurels."

"I'll think what I like," he muttered, but followed nevertheless. She moved fast but her scent told of familiarity.

This branch of the tunnel roughened the further they went. Like the one he had first entered, fog indicated proximity of cold of the Surface world.

The woman's silhouette grew more visible when they had rounded a bend and the grade steepened. She stopped, turned around, lifted her palms towards him and said, "Now, I have to warn you, Rowan, you may be in for a shock. But you're a big boy and have probably seen a lot of strange things, maybe even stranger than the last time you saw me. If you want to take that phaser I know you powered up back there and blow my head off… well, go right ahead. It won't do any more than waste even more time."

Halted now, he tried to read her eyes, but the daylight behind her glared.

"Fine," she said, "look at me like I'm a monster. I deserve it. But you have to admit I'm a lot prettier than your average savage." She shook her head a little, and added, "Forget I said that. It's a bad habit. Now, get ready. She's out there…" Blue turned her head towards the glare, looked back at him and finished her sentence: "Waiting."

Blue *of* no fixed address.

XX

On *the* Horns

Tall trees frosted by fog met Rowan's eyes. A few pale snowflakes drifted between the dark columns of conifers. "Who's waiting?" he asked. "Where are you taking me?"

Blue neither stopped nor turned around, but called out, "Now, that's a dumb question. I can't believe you're even asking that."

"You're going in the wrong direction," he called back. "There's nothing that way. West, not southeast... that's where I'm going. Goodbye."

She stopped and turned around. "*Hey! You don't...* but you're right, why should you trust me of all people? Look, I just want to make up for some of the mistakes I've made. I'm not going to make it unless I do, but I have to do it for your sake, not just mine. It's not easy, but I'm trying. Well, I guess they were more than mistakes. I really did not mean well. Sorry. But I really do want you to find Samarit if at all possible. She needs you. There's such an incredibly long way to go on foot... but go if you want. All I'm suggesting is that you could take a huge shortcut if you let me help. And as far as I know, she was too weak to fend anybody off. They only let her hang on so they can harvest the last gasp of despair from those people..."

But Rowan had already turned away. The roiling tension in his body ached. Even if he ran for ten miles without stopping it would twist and strangle, he knew it. But he had to do something.

The woman yelled: "What's *wrong* with you? *Don't you want to help her?*"

He stopped. He looked back at her and shouted: "*Prove it!*"

She lifted up her arms and called out: "Why else would I have tracked you since your unique signature showed up at that old pile of rocks yesterday? It wasn't easy, but I searched and searched until you lit that firestone. I tried to zero in on it, but I got a bit lost because it went quite faint all of a sudden. I even violated parole by taking the form of a raven. Remember? Just like when you were little, back at the orphanage. Remember that? It was the only way I could try to get past your blindness and into your field."

"*My what?*"

"Your perceptual field... *Come on! I can't believe we're wasting time on this idiotic argument!*"

Yes, she looked like Blue. Yes, she even smelled like Blue. "So you're a shape-shifter. You could be reading my mind and projecting what you think I want

165

to see. Ravens and tunnels that go nowhere… who knows why and who cares anyhow. But I'll play your game for an hour at most… at a distance. If anything at all, anything, if it seems suspicious, I'm turning around and going my own way *and good riddance!*"

"Thank you, thank you." She pressed her palms together and closed her eyes. "It won't take even ten minutes. Come on, it's getting cold. This way…"

A few minutes later, Rowan checked his chronometer, surprised that only seven had passed. At first to track her had been fairly easy, even at a distance. But then she set off an internal alarm. The tall straight trunks of the conifers wavered until a "hole" appeared through which she stepped. If he observed it in peripheral vision, he made out a nearly invisible large arrowhead-shaped outline that lay on its belly and subtly distorted the visual field that surrounded her in three dimensions.

Her face appeared within it, framed by the tawny mane. She turned to watch him with her golden eyes. "*Come on, slowcoach!*" she yelled. "*Anybody who knows anything says that time's just an idea… but get a move on!*"

He continued the inspection of the entire surroundings, and checked his chronometer repeatedly.

"Rowan, I know it looks weird, but it's all in your mind. You're interpreting this all wrong… it's your ride out of here." She waved at him and frowned. "Come *on!* It's not going to stay open forever while you yawn and think it over! And I'm not dressed for this climate!"

He chose. He actually chose to follow Blue.

◆

Regret was immediate.

"Little brother, I know this looks bad. But it's the only way I could get you to agree. Please, don't be angry."

He glared at her, once able to tear his eyes away from the huge reptilian at the helm, and murmured, "You're unbelievable…"

"I understand. I hate me too… I'm learning to forgive myself, but it's tough. We don't have time to argue right now. Samarit needs us."

"How could I be such an idiot?" He reached for his phaser, pointed it at the pilot and ordered: "Set this thing down. *Now!*"

Blue jumped to stand between the pistol and the pilot, her palms raised to protect her face, one eye open. "*I can explain,*" she cried. "*Just relax. If you kill her, we'll crash! You've got to trust me. Let the past go!*"

"*Trust?*" He scorned the word. "Trust is not to be blind. I should not have listened to your words. I should only ever watch what you do."

Blue bowed her head and covered her face with her hands. She might be in tears. She definitely trembled.

"Get out of the way, Blue. This flying heap is going to end up on the ground one way or another."

She leapt towards him, clasped the barrel of the phaser with both hands and held it to her forehead. "*Do it, Rowan! End it now!*" She squeezed her eyes shut – tears streamed down her face.

Amazed, he pulled the phaser away, and she released her grip.

The reptilian pilot's head never moved, yet one orange eye in its wide head rotated to observe the two passengers, while the dragon ship raced through the snow-laden clouds.

✦

Apparently chastened by the incident, Blue stood on her toes on the bench of a height for reptilian seating beneath a porthole in an attempt to peer outside, although only thick clouds through horizontal streams of sleet could be seen. The knuckles of one hand rose, pressed to her mouth, and she wrapped her other arm about her middle.

Rowan, drained but determined, looked away from his sibling and kept his eyes on the scaly pilot. The interior heat made him drowsy, but he reminded himself that reptilians were cool-blooded creatures. *Cold-blooded killers… the thing's psyche must have lapped up Blue's tearful outburst just now with a thrill…*

The pilot's massive head barely moved, but the orange eye rotated again to peer back at Rowan.

"Please, listen," said Blue, who sat down on the bench and faced her brother, but her arms remained clasped about her torso. "Rowan, I never wanted to die before. I only ever wanted to live. I felt I couldn't afford to care if others died because of my actions. It was just too awful to think of. But I was killing myself all the same, with denial. It all caught up with me after Wishbone Warren."

"You said you violated parole, Blue. What did you mean?"

His sister remained silent for a long moment, but answered, "It's hard to explain. It's a bit like the tigress-flower lady said, that I couldn't run from myself… only I didn't listen. On what I call the 'other side' I landed in an inter-dimensional trap set for fools like me. It's more like they taught me that I'm my own judge and jury. There's no escape from that kind of sentence. I have to report to myself every day and confess any wrongdoing. If I don't, they know. Worse, *I* know. But I also have to make up for my crimes. Reparation is all I ever do now. Magic is a dangerous path, even white magic. The practitioner has to be pure. That's not me by any stretch. Now I have to pay. Even shape-shifting, an intermediate skill if you can believe it, costs big."

"So who are 'they'?"

Blue stared at him, and replied, "You're not going to believe this, but the first ones were reptilians. I was terrified, even though I'd long dealt with the worst, Kirzaka himself. But on the other side, these turned out to be different. They serve Kweelu. She's no Rep. I don't even know how to describe her she's so beyond beyond."

The back of Rowan's mane stiffened, but he did not take his eyes off the pilot. "Who did you say?"

"Kweelu. Even gender…"

"That name… I've heard it before somewhere…"

Blue sat silent for a few minutes, until she said, "I didn't introduce our pilot yet. You may not remember, but before I unfortunately sent you, Samarit and your squire… what was his name again?"

"Krumb. Squire Krumb."

"Right. Rowan, I'm so sorry he was killed. And for all that happened then. Samarit… she almost died too. And you were nearly a goner, until Captain Masudah found you. He was something I did right at least. But I'm so sorry."

"Sorry will never be enough, Blue. But it's done and behind me. I can't speak for Sam. My guess is that she'd like to see you drawn and quartered."

"Oh, Rowan, she's not like that… and you know it."

"She's too kind-hearted." He sighed. "And I'm too soft-headed."

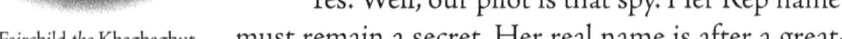

The dragon craft sped on while sleet whispered across the portholes.

"And?" Rowan asked. "What about our pilot?"

"Oh, yes. You may remember Àrd-Sagartus, the Lyran high priest of that cult I used to belong to, New Dawn? I'd discovered another abuse of magic by hijacking his vocal cords. I told you then that I had a spy in Kirzaka's house. Remember?"

"How could I forget? It was sheer… madness."

"Yes. Well, our pilot is that spy. Her Rep name must remain a secret. Her real name is after a great-

Fairchild *the* Khaghaghut.

great-grandmother, of an ethnic group enslaved by Kirzaka's religious fanatics. But I call her Fairchild. It suits her."

Rowan studied the big lizard, apparently a female. As far as he knew, he had only ever seen males before. Perhaps this one's shoulders were narrower. If she got up out of the pilot's seat and stood, maybe her hips would be wider too, with proportionately longer legs, and vestigial remnants of their mammalian ancestor's breasts over a less-wide muscled chest. Like all reptilians, her iridescent skin mesmerized the eye. In his opinion, whichever sex, its armoured hide draped an ugly mass of fifteen-foot-tall, razor-toothed, muscle-bound species of murdering monster. And they all stank of death.

The pilot's neckless head twisted to display her snake-like profile, and the orange eye once again rotated to stare at him.

He shivered, despite the heat, at the lizard face capable of no more than a skull-like grimace. His belly in a knot, he asked, "Are you saying, Blue, there's a Rep underground resistance movement? How come we haven't heard anything about it? I was a League commando, or as good as one. We would have been informed."

"No one can keep a secret like the Khaghaghut, her people. They've had a lot of practise, dominated for centuries after Kirzaka had gathered enough power to destroy their strongholds and convert the leadership. They never let on that a genetic quirk doesn't permit hypnosis to work on them. Kirzaka's mob loves to play with DNA, via their canid and ander slaves' more nimble hands, but they don't experiment with their own kind, except for snakes, crocodiles and tortoises. He doesn't know, as the Khaghas played chameleon. Eventually they all faked allegiance, infiltrated the Maçinan ranks, and now bide their time."

"Aren't they telepathic too? After all, it's how they rip off energy when they torture their prey. How do the Khaghas protect themselves?"

"I don't know, but they're smart. Fanaticism makes the others stupid."

"Maybe, but Kirzaka wrote the manual. They won't fool him for long."

"Little brother, it didn't escape your notice that Kirzaka isn't like the other Reps. His personal agenda is all he cares about. He's a superdino from some other galaxy who got marooned here long ago. Fairchild thinks he was dumped here by his platoon or squadron, whatever, when he became a pain in the neck. Maybe he was too difficult to assassinate or to execute him would cause some dark occult blowback. Or maybe he really did come back from the dead. Maybe they left him for dead but the natives took pity on him and nursed him back to health. If so, it was the biggest mistake of all time. Now he's even got a base on the moon."

"Sure," Rowan said, "but construction has barely begun. It's vulnerable."

"Fairchild told me it's fully operational, the next stepping stone after the space station. The moon is an ideal environment to store the purified condensed energy they generate from their victims' fear and collect somehow, to literally fuel his ambition. I tried to spy on their occult ritual for that once, but blacked out because they generate a sort of psychic cloak. They were naked and bowed their snaky heads to a big cuboid, a black stone set on a short pillar, possibly a shaped meteorite, in the centre of their circle. After a while they squatted like they were all going to void lizard poop at the same time… but that may have been either symbolic or my projection. Or maybe it's a kind of occult product. Like I said, I blacked out. Anyhow, with that concentrate he's off to explore the moons of Zhamanak, then…"

"What did you say?"

"Little brother, am I not speaking clearly or are you not listening? I said the moon is an ideal battery…

"No, not that, what you said afterwards… about the other moons."

"Of Zhamanak? He wants to explore them for building sites, you know, for manufacturing plants for spacecraft and whatnot, spaceports. Fairchild says the rings have potential to slingshot starship travel or something."

"That's what the Ahan call the ringed gas giant. How do you know the name? How do you even know of the Ahan?"

"Hey, I was minister of education not for no good reason… pardon my awkward grammar, not my strength, obviously. But I do actually know a thing or two. And I have a thing for astronomy… as a hobby. I thought I'd need it to escape Eorthe. Maybe I'm just showing off again, come to think of it… but the Ahan basically invented astronomy, although the Khémians claim the credit. The Ahan tend to think no one even knows they exist, but the Reps sure do. It's wishful thinking. They had an inside man for a while, but the Ahan are dealing with it now. Fairchild told me."

"Gregor, the high shaman."

"Who? Speaking of which, how do *you* know of Aha Domain? That's pretty esoteric stuff for a Perkona Ola graduate, little brother. I should know… I upgraded the curriculum."

"It's a long story. And I didn't get to graduate. Remember?"

"Tell me about it when you're ready. I'm interested. But I want to finish my monologue first. Anyhow, Kirzaka's big plan is to get back home to his galaxy far, far away and take revenge on his former partners in crime as a sideshow to a hostile takeover of the entire superdino empire. Reps can't use wormholes as shortcuts. They're limited to faster-than-lightspeed starships at best. But first he needs to siphon the whole solar system of enough fuel to arrive there with planet-killing weaponry. Moondust is a supplementary source too. And the Khaghas aren't his only problem, although he doesn't even suspect them. Yet. He only speaks for the majority, the fanatic Maçinans, but there are other factions who openly chafe at the fact they're being used and abused. Kirzaka's bombastic propaganda tactics make him look more powerful than he actually is. Even I figured out how to fool him for a while."

Rowan squirmed in his seat. "Ask your pal Fairchild how long till we get to wherever Sam is. This thing is slow."

"It's faster than walking. It would have taken you a month of non-stop slogging to get to where we're going, even if there were no delays and you knew exactly where to look for Longbows in hiding. They're good at camouflage." Blue's gaze turned inwards. "She says we're almost there. But that doesn't mean we're just going to swoop down like a flying ambulance and pick up a patient. I'm guessing there are probably at least a hundred and fifty Longbow survivors languishing in those stinky damp holes, maybe a hundred more. What about them? Samarit won't leave them behind. Besides, there's another dragon ship patrolling the region, with a longer range than this one. It takes a long time to make its circuit because they have fewer still left on Eorthe now that they believe victory's a done deal. We have to pick the right moment. Also, Fairchild has to report on her own mission. They'll be expecting her to land at Mudredd Vale soon for routine maintenance. She may only be able to drop us off, but it's better than nothing."

"I'll take it," he said.

"Good. But I hope you don't mind free fall if it comes to that. The parachute harnesses are way too big for us little felids."

❖

"Wake up, oh, please, *please* wake up!"

That voice – familiar. The scent confirmed it. *Blue... What's she doing here? Oh, right...*

"I'm sorry, I chickened out at the last second. Sorry about that."

"No worries... I don't expect anything of you." He stood and made a quick self-examination. *No broken bones. Again.*

"Wow, I thought you were dead. You stopped breathing."

"I should be getting used to it after that jump at Stone Tomb."

171

"Shape-shifting is not a good idea, I've decided. It takes a lot of charity to make up for it, but there's no way I want to go back to hell. No one, no matter how bad, should ever go there. Sorry, I know I promised I'd make like a raven and fly from your back to take the weight off when we landed, but…"

"Never mind, Blue, I didn't expect you to follow through on it, nor did I even want it, remember? Don't you know yet magic is bad for you? It's why you're on parole. We survived the drop, that's the main thing. At least I didn't have to dive into a fire this time."

"What fire?" She brushed the dust off his quilted Ahan trousers with her hands –

He turned about, stepped away and raised his arms to fend her off. "A little dirt never hurt anybody. I'll take care of it. Are you all right? You could have let me do this by myself, you know. Your pilot could have taken you to a safe place."

"I'm fine, thank you… maybe my pretty ass is bruised a little. You took the brunt and I landed on you, probably knocked the wind out of you too. Sorry."

"You don't have to keep saying you're sorry, Blue, I get it. You're uninjured, that's the important thing." He inspected the sky. Many little white clouds dotted the blue expanse above the semi-arid terrain – a dry lake bed and a range of stony mountains – but no dragon craft. Yet.

"Fairchild had to take off, pronto," Blue said. "She said the other ship isn't due for three hours or so. And she pointed out the series of underground hollows where the Longbows are. They don't exactly rate as caves. They're more like narrow crevices and cracks. The picture she projected into my mind is hard to correlate here on the ground, but I think I recognize a landmark…" She pointed a slender finger. "Not far… that hill over there."

"It's much more than a hill, Blue." Rowan studied the surroundings. "It's a mountain, but with the likely geology along the base. We'll have to cross the dry lake bed. It would have been best if she'd dropped us off a bit closer."

"She said it would leave a trace or something in the type of stone over there, a thermal footprint that would look suspicious, so she cut the power and coasted for the last twenty miles. And tried to hover for a few seconds so we wouldn't die in the free fall."

He nodded acknowledgement. "That's why the electrogravitic drive went silent briefly. Rep technology is inefficient. I wonder how she managed to regain altitude without creating heat and burning us to a crisp down here. She must be an excellent pilot. But enough of that, it's going to take most of those three hours, assuming you can run at least part of the way. Can you?"

"Hey, my pretty ass is no accident. I'm fit and foxy. If worst comes to worst, I'll take wing the rest of the way."

"Don't do that." Rowan raised a forefinger, until he noticed and dropped his hand. He looked her over from head to toe. "I'm going to have to carry you for the last of it." He sighed. "But you can't weigh much more than Sam did before you sent us into the damn viper pit."

Blue winced, but said, "Rowan, I don't want to be a burden. If I can't make it all the way fast enough, too bad. I'll catch up. You just find Samarit as fast as possible. Deal?"

He did not reply, nor even glance at her.

"And there's this. You might be famished anyway, especially after you gave me, I mean the raven, the last of your rations this morning." From a buttoned pocket in her cargo pants Blue withdrew an ornate antique pillbox that contained brown capsules and a vial of amber liquid. "Take two of the caps and most of the potion. I don't need that much, but I should stay felid, not go corvid if at all possible. Sorry, I was joking about taking wing. I more than used up that credit earlier."

"What is this stuff?"

"I don't know exactly… to be honest, technical details are not my thing, despite being ex-minister of education. That's politics for you… ignorance is a qualification. Fairchild gave them to me."

"It's Rep medicine? Or dope?"

"I call them boosters. They work, that's all that matters."

Rowan's stiffened. "No, 'booster' sounds bad."

"If they were addictive, believe me, I'd know. I trust Fairchild. Anyhow, Khaghas are renowned herbalists. Go ahead, it will do you good. Don't waste any more time."

He inspected her golden eyes for sincerity, and nodded agreement.

XXI

Nyctophobia

AN HOUR AFTER they had set off across the plain, the heavy breathing of a large beast chafed Rowan's eardrums – and the thing gained on them. He had been so intent on reaching the mountain's base that while the evidence remained faint he had dismissed it as Blue's footfalls. Unwilling to stop running, he glanced over his shoulder –

The predator in hot pursuit resembled the feral black goat-man he had encountered in the basaltic mountains southeast of Gormlin Forest on his journey to Khémia. The pale ochre creature on this occasion appeared similarly endowed with wide shoulders, a broad well-muscled chest and hoofed shaggy hindquarters, but designed to run and leap like an antelope – and a head taller than the goat-man, which had been taller than Rowan. This one's horns branched, but its long muzzle showed the sharp fangs of a sabre-toothed hyena. Like the goat-man, its sinewy arms bulged, so long they supplemented the massive hind legs as the heavy clawed paws dug into the dry lake bed and stirred up a trail of dusty yellow clouds. Its intensely red eyes targeted Blue as the weaker prey.

Worse, she slowed to twist her neck to see what Rowan looked at –

Nothing for it but to stand his ground as a barricade, the phaser already powered up, he aimed for the point between the thing's eyes, and yelled: *"Blue! Keep behind me! I've got this!"*

The creature must have believed its next meal an already accomplished fact because it raced at full tilt and crouched to leap over Rowan's head –

He calculated its trajectory and fired –

A sizzling streak of phaser fire vaporized one of its red eyes, and a wisp of smoke from the bloody socket trailed between its horns – the beast lost altitude, now on a collision course – emitted a long hoarse screech and crashed on top of him, which ended in a brief explosive grunt in his ear.

"Rowan! Are you all right?!" Blue tugged in vain at the thing's big hairy haunches. *"Say something!"*

Rowan wriggled with vigour, pushed off the dead weight after several attempts, and crawled out of harm's way. He spat grit, rubbed his ringing ear, and growled: "All I can say is that when it comes to you, expect the unexpected… but I wouldn't have missed if you hadn't shot first." Back on his feet, he dusted himself off and sighed, but glanced at her, and said, "Impressive by the way. And thanks. Maybe if I'd shot him, he would have landed on you instead."

"Hey, the Longbows tried to lock me up, but there was no way they were going to take my little pistol too. Unlike the Khaghas, they can be hypnotized."

Rowan studied the sky, turned to the hyena-antelope thing and watched its life force trickle red into the dust. "The corpse isn't doing us any favours either."

"I hope it's a loner," Blue said. "At least there won't be much blood to create a stink… the wound is pretty much cauterized."

"Pretty it is not. Help me drag it into that hollow. We should cover it up." With no shovel at hand, the ground proved only soft enough to partly bury its large head face down in the dirt.

"Rowan, this is the least dignified grave I've ever seen."

"Oh? Have you seen many? Don't answer that. Well, let's just get on with it. This thing deserves no better."

They camouflaged its body with sand, stones and dry brush, and bade the cryptid farewell and good riddance. The felid siblings redoubled their speed towards the still-distant mountain.

◆

Blue called into the shallow crevice: "Hey, how long do you think they've been gone? Maybe we missed a hole or two."

"By the look of the evidence… I can't guess." His own voice reverberated hollow as if in a pilfered tomb. "It could be days or even weeks. The emotional residue down here is persistent… and it's making me sick. But then it doesn't smell that great either. Subterranean gas… and other waste. They were here for weeks. Are you tired? You sound tired."

"No way," she said, "I don't want to be left alone anywhere near this awful place, not with those huge red-eyed fangy things around. Let's go. You won't stop till you find her. I'll keep up. Shouldn't that dragon ship be coming back by now? Maybe it already has." Blue turned about and scanned the sky. "But I don't think the Longbows have been gone long. Fairchild would have said."

"Don't worry, Blue, I won't leave you alone. I just wanted to know if you were tired." Rowan crawled out of the dusty hole, and said, "No matter how risky travel topside is, hiding out down there would give a mole claustrophobia." He held out his palm. "Look." A small tarnished silver earring in the shape of a flower rested in his hand.

"Oh… that makes me want to cry," she said. "It's a little girl's."

"Keep it for her, will you?"

+

The tracks led away from the dry lake bed into the barren black mountains. The refugees had not stopped for long anywhere. The trail rose to stony higher ground, and the siblings stopped to rest in a hollow.

"Need a booster?" Blue held out her palm, where two brown capsules waited. "I've got more, but we should pace ourselves."

"Thanks." Rowan took one and peered into the plain they had just crossed, and said, "This place is as lifeless as the way down to Mudredd Vale."

"Except for those vultures, Rowan, way up there in the distance."

"But is it a good omen or a bad one?"

"Are you superstitious?"

"I don't discount anything, especially vultures. The world is a very strange place." He looked up at the clear sky. "Still no dragon ship. None that can be seen anyway. It could be cloaked like Fairchild's was."

"The cloaking was all in your mind, Rowan. To me it was sitting there in the woods like a big triangular dun mushroom cap. To see one that doesn't want to be seen is a skill, which I fortunately possess. And I don't see one anywhere. Yet. But even what I see as obvious is only a personal interpretation."

"Really? How does that work?"

"I have a gift. Other than that, do I look like a technical manual to you? It's the way my brain is wired, that's all I know. But did the interior of Fairchild's ship have something odd about it? Can you tell me what it was?"

"The whole thing was odd. They seem to be fond of mycelial composites as fabrication materials, which is excellent, only they don't seem to know how to make it look good. It can be beautifully surfaced if done right. But it was like the bottom of an old rubbish bin in there. Maybe they like it that way. But I know what you're asking. The interior space was at least five times on the inside compared to what I would have guessed. A lounge of fifty could travel in comfort." He looked to the sky, and said, "Enough of that, when the sun goes down in an hour or so, the temperature will plummet. We can't expect Sam and company to light any firestones… too risky for us too. How are you doing? Are you able to keep going?"

176

"Never better, little brother." Blue grinned at him. "I can see in the dark fairly well. My little pistol has a unique feature. I can set it as a hand warmer. Its signature is so weak it's undetectable. And if worst comes to worst…"

"Don't do that." Rowan glowered at her. "Forget it. No sorcery."

"You're right. I don't want to go down that road either. I'm just saying…"

"Forget it, Blue. You've come this far. *Don't blow it.* While it's still warm enough, let's take a break. I'm going to try to remote-view Sam. My luck with that has been pathetic for a long time, but the trail's gone cold now."

"Maybe we could team up."

"No, Blue."

"Remote-viewing isn't magic, Rowan. It's a natural ability everyone has, only it's atrophied in most people, thanks to complacency and high technology. But you know that, my little commando brother."

"I mean it, Blue, *no magic.* It's too much of a temptation. I know you."

"No, Rowan, you don't. I've changed. Big time. Maybe I'm not the Blue I could have been once, but I'm no longer the narcissistic survivor-girl either. I'll always be on parole for what I've done, but I can help."

He sighed. "I can tell you've grown up a lot," he said. "It takes a while for us felids. I appreciate it, really." He peered into her golden eyes. "You still like to call me 'little brother.' By now we should be equals. If you recognize that, great. But no sorcery. Never again. Right?"

She peered back at him. "I only mean it as a term of endearment. Really… but you're right, it could be mistaken for diminishment. You're a big burly man in more ways than one. I'm proud of you. I'd like to know what happened since the last time we hung out, but later, after Samarit is safe. Let me help. I *promise* I won't blow it."

Rowan sighed. "I don't know how to stop you except to ask politely. Well, I guess I'm telling you. But I expect the universe itself will have to put an end to your addiction. Please, I need to find Sam. Don't interfere."

Blue pursed her lips and frowned.

"Well?"

"I hear you."

◆

Encouraged to have gathered enough reconnaissance that he believed Samarit remained alive, Rowan returned to where he had left Blue, just in time to see the last of the sun's rays skim the peaks and cast long jagged shadows across the dry lake bed.

She appeared sound asleep, wedged between two boulders with her arms folded across her bent knees, and her tawny head rested on her forearms.

He let her be while he pondered their next move. The dusky surrounds suggested several routes the Longbows may have taken. But Blue rested in that position provoked memories of Lyka. He reached out to wake her, but she stirred –

"*Brr…*" She shivered, huddled, blinked and stared at him. "What did you find out?" She stood up and yawned, stamped her feet and hugged herself.

"The most important thing… Sam's alive. I felt weakness and cold, but didn't actually see anything. It was clammy, damp and sticky. My skill is lame. I wish I could blame it on something, like a force field or whatever."

"Maybe it's anxiety," she said. "The Reps might pick up on you."

"Maybe. I never was taught properly by Masudah. There wasn't time, so it's a question of luck, I guess. But she must be feeling guilty too, for failing to protect her clan… I think they're fewer in number than you'd guessed, at least since then."

Blue nodded acknowledgement. "Fairchild told me the Reps like to pick victims off one by one if there's a group, especially canids. They get the best return on investment that way."

"Assholes. I imagine even the Longbows would get worn down and terrified after enough of that. I just wish I knew which way to go from here. We must be so damn close!"

"I know which way to go," she said.

"You do? How? Did you contact Fairchild?"

"I can, but it's a bad idea. The more paranoid Reps snitch on each other, though they're more confident now that they think they've pretty well stomped out their enemies and can relax while they wallow in glory a bit. And they'll be preoccupied with consolidation of their new acquisitions on Eorthe, harvesting, transporting and storing the power. Next stop, the far side of the solar system. All the same, she helped me out this last time at great risk."

"Blue! Where the hell is Sam? *Which way?!…*"

"Easy, Rowan. Calm down before they notice. I don't know if you can see it, but the dragon ship is hovering…" She squinted and pointed to the northeast; "…that way."

"I see it. Uncloaked."

"It's only a speck at this distance, but they may know we're here, only waiting till we get closer before they... *hey, wait for me!*"

Rowan had already moved on. Blue followed only a step behind. Across the moon-shadowed terrain they wound their way through canyons and under cliffs, across ledges, around lakes and through woods. The stars served as a guide, until the east grew brighter with the dawn.

◆

They hid behind a boulder on a crag of an elevation that matched the dragon ship's altitude, and watched it hover like a bird of prey.

"It hasn't moved," said Blue.

"That's hopeful. It means they're still waiting and may not have maimed or killed anyone yet, just laying siege. The Longbows must be near defeat, but the enemy won't want them completely exhausted and unresponsive."

"They like to just hang and lurk until their prey's anxiety is at maximum," said Blue. "Then they strike with force here and there to pump it up before harvest. Sometimes they just pick away, an ounce of flesh at a time."

Rowan grimaced at the thought. "Like you say, they may have been waiting for us too. I have to take the chance. Stay clear of the action. There's no need for both of us to die."

"*Rowan! Don't! It could be a trick! Please, let me help! I won't blow it!*"

"No! Blue, just stay out of it. *Please,* you've worked hard to save your soul. I'm *begging* you. I'm selfish too. I can't be worried about two people at the same time. One's bad enough. The sun will warm this spot soon. *Just stay put.*"

"Do you at least still have the obsidian pendant I gave you?"

"Yes. And Masudah's gold ring. *Just wait here!*" Rowan made his way down into the ravine still in shadow, always with an eye on the dragon ship, the sharp tip of its arrowhead pointed away from him, and scouted the site for Longbows.

◆

A short distance inside the cave entrance, a large group of Longbow guards surrounded him.

"*How did you get in here?*" demanded their leader, a stranger to Rowan. "*Are you a reptilian? Who are you?*"

"Who are *you?* I'm Rowan Berry Longbow, not a reptilian, obviously."

179

The emaciated canid man's dark countenance glared. He supported himself with a makeshift staff, and stood behind and between two large men. "You're no Longbow," he snarled. "You're a shape-shifter disguised as a felid." He stepped back and drew his forefinger across his own throat, a sign to the guards to garrotte the intruder.

The largest, blue-eyed and with pale hair like a longish ragged thatch of dried grass, protested: "Royal Highness, wait! It may indeed be Rowan Berry, the one who went for help after we fled Wishbone Warren. He looks just like him, only weathered and battle-weary… the red hair. Chief Samarit can verify it."

The dark leader looked Rowan over. "Him? All felids look the same. No, Tolk, that deserter never could have found us. He's a spy. Kill him."

Rowan said: "Listen to your man. If you kill me, Chief Samarit will be extremely upset. You don't want that. She's been hurt enough."

The dark one frowned. "What do *you* know of our suffering, spy? What do *you* care? Just try to trick us into exposure. Even if you are indeed that felid, you abandoned us when we were most vulnerable. You deserve to die either way. Shape-shifter. How else did you get past us? Kill him."

"I'm warning you, Sam will never forgive you. Take me to her. Now."

The leader struck his staff across Rowan's face. "*That will teach you to speak to a royal with respect!*" The spate of pique passed, and upon a breath taken, he straightened somewhat. "Fine, bring him to Chief Samarit to denounce before we execute the sentence for treason… and shape-shifting."

The guards manhandled Rowan for some distance into the cave, past the skeletons of bears, mountain lions and skulls of smaller animals. They waded through shallow pools of cold dark water deeper into the gloom –

"Samarit, dear," said the dark leader, "we bring you an intruder prior to execution. If it please you, be our witness."

She lay stretched out on a layer of ragged blankets folded on a shelf of fairly flat rock, eyes closed, her cheekbones and jawline prominent, and her voice weak: "I am *not* pleased… go away… I've seen enough of death."

"The chief has spoken," the leader said. "Take the traitor away."

Pineshadow Touchstone-Longbow.

"*Sam! It's me, Rowan. I've come back for you!…*"

180

The leader tried to strike Rowan's ear with his staff again, but he had been anticipated, lost his balance and Tolk nearly took the blow instead. The assailant's face grew red, his dark eyes bulged and he yelled: "*Do you need another lesson in manners, spy?!* No matter, the dead cannot be taught. Take him away… he will disturb our chief nevermore!"

Samarit stared at the ceiling. She tried to roll onto her side, but her female attendants had to assist, and she asked, "Is it really you?" Her head lolled. "Where have you been?…"

Tolk Wishbone-Longbow.

A thin woman adjusted the makeshift cushion beneath.

"Sam, tell them to let me go. I've been…"

The leader, quicker this time, struck the wooden staff on Rowan's jaw and truncated his words.

The pain seared like fire. Rowan broke free of his captors' grip and loomed over their dark leader, who shrank away, and whose squeal trailed into a thin mousy squeak. Nevertheless, he ordered: "*Take the shape-shifter away… now!…*"

"*Pineshadow!*" Samarit cried out. "Who made you chieftain? This is Rowan. I know him like I know myself. *Get out!*… Rowan, come closer… please."

The dark man persisted: "Samarit, my dear, do not distress yourself. Have I not taken care of you thus far? I am…"

"*You're an insufferable martinet!*" Her voice had found its strength. "*Get out! Now!* Tolk, please take Prince Pineshadow away. *He* needs his rest."

The emaciated guards merely stared at the emaciated man, apparently loath to act, likely too exhausted to know whom to obey.

The prince nevertheless limped off in a huff and postponed their decision.

To the emaciated women at her side, Samarit said, "Please, help me to sit up." Once they had accomplished that much, she gazed at Rowan through brittle dark glassy eyes, and spoke again through cracked pale lips in a lisp: "Rowan, I thought you must be dead. Even now I wonder if we're not both on the Other Side. You were gone so long… but I know, you had to go." Her dark eyes dulled, and she drew her wrist to her forehead, and added, "Forgive me… I've not been myself lately. I must look a sight."

"You're as beautiful as ever." He knelt and took her hand. "I'm here now, that's all that matters. That and to see us safe from harm."

181

Samarit, wan, her eyes bleary, nevertheless smiled a little and exposed the gap in her teeth. "You're still a flatterer. I know I'm a ruin. Did you bring help? Can we leave here? But no, Pineshadow would not have been such a bully otherwise. He's just lost and all mixed up…" She reached out and touched his face. "You're bleeding."

"No, there aren't any others. I just couldn't stay away any longer. But I'm not alone, Sam. You won't believe this, but Blue's waiting topside, out of sight of the dragon ship. There is hope, however. Lie down and rest now. I'll tell you everything, when you're feeling up to it."

"Blue? Hope? Tell me now… I think I will lie down. I've not been at all well. The enemy harasses me to get at the others for their fealty."

"Loyalty is one of the canids' greatest strengths. They know a true leader when they see one."

"Flatterer. I failed them. More than a third have been lost. Pineshadow brought less than a dozen of the royal household when he found us… the few who avoided the holocaust at Touchstone… but they're gone too, killed off one by one. The Reps, they feed… on the corpses now, before we can bury them. They like us to watch. Somehow they can disable our remaining weapons from a distance, the rocket launchers… we're all dying now. And there were Snake People here. We even ate them, which made me puke… but it kept the rest of us going for a while. Please… I need you to tell me your hope."

"I made it to Khémia, Sam. I found Masudah. From there we went to a hidden queendom in the mountains far to the east of here, Aha Domain. It was hard going, but Masudah and the Ahan queen have figured out how to defend themselves from the Reps. They believe they'll eventually be able to teach the rest of the world. You must hang on, Sam. I'm here now. I'll do whatever it takes to get us out of this hole to safety. Then we'll find a home, where we can live in peace. Simply live."

Samarit's tired eyes glowed like a weak midwinter dawn. In tears, she rested her head on her hands pressed together as if in prayer. "My kitty baby," she murmured, and pursed her chapped lips. "I could almost believe it." Her eyes closed, and she slept.

XXII
Beyond Hope

Precaution to make reluctant use of the ring again had got him past Pine-shadow and the guards, but it only added to the fatigue that had overtaken him after he climbed the crag, but nothing compared to the exhaustion of the Longbows, starved, cold and harried near to death. Still invisible, Rowan stared at the rocky spot where he had last seen Blue. She had not stayed put. His jaws clenched. He scanned the perimeter. At least the dragon ship may have disappeared. Peripheral vision revealed nothing. He took the chance the craft had not cloaked, and spoke the magic words into his gold ring to break the spell. He gripped his obsidian pendant and vowed to stay awake. He sat in the sunshine at risk of being seen by the dragon ship or their Eye in the Sky – or both. Samarit had once told him of her cadet training, so he tried to take the sun's life-giving force straight, without the detour of assimilation of food or boosters. He closed his eyes and made a prayer of supplication to whichever cosmic powers might be available, but as Master Aa had advised, kept in mind that although the answer be inevitable, the form it must take was not his to decide. The stone beneath him cooled his backside, but the sunny air warmed his skin. He expanded inwards – vertigo increased as attention drifted above the peaks. He directed it inwards ever further and upwards, and in imagina-tion reached out to They of Bones of Silver, of any rank and whatever cultural form: Primordial Architects; Lightlanders; the Eye of Stone; Anggh and Aynt; the gatekeeper Dancer in Blood, and the mysterious Mistress of the Knell –

✦

He eyes opened wide, doubt gone that Fairchild had returned for Blue. She may still be alive. He analyzed his visions again and again, and knew he had in addition made a brief backwards time slip that confirmed Blue had shot an intense beam of blue light, phaser fire, at the craft from the very spot where he sat. For a moment he also glimpsed a felid below, red of mane, who descended this same crag, and spoke the spell of invisibility into the ring of gold on his finger when still within sight, then vanished, oblivious to Blue's silent intervention above his head – but at what cost?

Energy flagged, yet his nervous system tingled despite it, an artifact of the successful remote-viewing session. Something momentous mounted in the

World Soul, as the Ahan called it, or the Khémian Field of the Law, tension between powers beyond reckoning, mass minds in conflict. The heavy weight of sleep tried to lure body and mind into the dark. He rubbed his eyes. Open again, his gaze came to rest on a hitherto unnoticed pile of small stones arranged in a pattern he had seen before: a hemispherical mound dissected by a short stick. Between two of the stones the sun reflected a hint of tarnished silver. On all fours, he removed the top of the little mound and dusted off the child's earring, and pocketed it for safekeeping. And something else – Blue's ornate pill box. On his feet now, he shaded his eyes and examined the horizon's circle. His gaze came to a dead halt on a dark column of smoke. He gasped, but at the same moment knew the Longbows had gained the freedom to leave the cave. Energized, he descended the crag.

◆

Dark Pineshadow's dark words scowled like his face: "Your audacity knows no bounds. How stupid are you, fool? Guards, kill him." The prince must have forgotten the entire earlier episode. The other canids remained motionless. Starvation had drained their strength; worse, their so-called leader had failed to inspire confidence.

Rowan simply turned away and walked deeper into the cave, past the bones and through the cold dark pools, beyond which he found Samarit in the dim light of three old crystal lamps, where she languished on the tattered bed. Nearby slept her attendants, as raw-boned as all the Longbows must be.

"*Who's there?*" she lisped. "Go away, Pineshadow. I don't want you." Unable to even open her eyes, she gasped. "But it's you. *Oh…*"

Rowan rushed to her side, and said, "Sam, take it easy. Good news: we can leave this place. If you're well enough, I'll carry you."

Eyes closed, she tried to reach towards him. "Take me," she murmured.

"First, medicine." He picked up a tarnished metal cup, filled it with water, lifted her head, and placed one of Blue's brown capsules between her cracked lips. He slipped it onto her tongue, and said, "Sam, drink this… swallow."

Soon she inhaled and held her breath a moment. Her eyes opened and she exhaled. "Take me away. I'm ready," she said, her voice already stronger.

Her weight on his back troubled him considerably less than it had at Mudredd Vale when he rescued her from stasis in Kirzaka's containment chamber. But the clasp of her arms around his neck stayed firm.

Samarit's fevered attendants prattled as more Longbows joined the line to the exit. Rowan doubted they understood each other in the reverberant din, although that hardly mattered. Freed, no thought of what came next interfered with their joy, no doubt.

Only Pineshadow blocked their way. "*Go back!*" he yelled. "*What are you doing? It is certain death out there! Back! That is an order! Do as I say!*"

The guards had stood upon the approach of the tribe. They stared at Pineshadow, a darkly handsome young canid man rather more gaunt than he should be, who grim of face leaned on his staff before the crowd.

The tallest guard, blonde Tolk, gently gripped the prince's shoulders and moved him aside, and everyone else filed out to stand in line at each side of the entrance, where they cheered Chief Samarit and Sir Rowan, grinned at the others and laughed and breathed the clean mountain air, and the strong sunlight slanted into the rocky ravine filled with drifts of sand.

Rowan stopped, let Samarit down on a flat sunny rock, and picked her up in his arms, stepped onto it, and loud enough to be heard said, "Longbows! I speak for your chief when I say these are our first steps to freedom from tyranny. It will be a long road to find our home. We will have to fight for it. Our enemy is strong. But not as strong as he pretends. Never believe that. And we have friends, even among his own kind. I know how strange that sounds, but it's the truth."

From the back of the crowd, Pineshadow scowled. "*Liar!*" he shouted. "*You are a shape-shifter, a reptilian spy! A traitor at best! What does a bedraggled felid know of us canids? Can you not see we are starving and lost? Dying! Now you want us to commit suicide by exposing ourselves, you want us to bare our underbellies to our enemy's claws. Come back, Longbows! Intelligence demands that you come back inside!*"

Nearby, an old woman with a small girl in hand said, "Your Highness, calm yourself. Let our chief speak for us. She has always guided us well."

The people murmured amongst themselves.

Tolk called out, "Yes, *Chief Samarit, please speak!*"

Samarit supported in Rowan's arms looked into his eyes. "Thank you," she said to him. "I think I can do it. And I believe I can stand on my own."

With great care he lowered her to stand on the rock, and slipped an arm around her torso.

A woman gave Samarit a shawl.

She pulled it over her head, and said, in weak voice, "Friends, if Sir Rowan Berry Longbow says we are free, we are free. At least free to leave that damp cave. I trust him. I urge you to trust him too. Do not listen to the prince. He is unwell." She coughed, and gripped Rowan's free arm with both hands and glanced up at him. "Nevertheless," she continued, "we must remain exceedingly cautious. We are weak. If Sir Rowan agrees it is safe, the stronger among you… search for food. Hunters, gatherers, you know what to do. Guards, remain at your posts, under Tolk's command…" She nodded to the large blue-eyed man. "He will order you to strategic positions above and around us. The rest of us will wait here. If you wish to shelter in the cave, do so. I for one never want to go back in there. I would rather die…" And she swooned.

Rowan braced her, but the enormous responsibility he had shouldered struck him like a blow to the head. He closed his eyes. Had the column of smoke he had seen from the top of the crag been from the enemy dragon ship's crash? Or Fairchild's craft? Panic flared. His body went rigid as a statue; his eyes rolled back in his head. His attention flew into the sky and travelled directly to the source of the smoke. His inner eye high above verified that an arrowhead-shaped depression smouldered in a dry river bed below.

Fairchild's craft or not, her gruff guttural voice spoke at the precise midpoint between his ears: "You lack manners, felid. Your kin sends her apologies. We fight on." Her thought transmission included more than verbal information. Now he knew three other facts: (1) *Reptilia sapiens* had more in common with other hybrid species than he had assumed, and (2) he had failed to appreciate the Khaghas as more warm-blooded, more intuitive and wiser than their more dominant relatives, the majority who comprised Kirzaka's fanatics. Moreover, (3) Blue was safe – for now.

Meanwhile the Longbows gasped, and he opened his eyes to their mouths agape and eyes staring at him – but reassured that Samarit's grip on his arm remained firm and that she still leaned against him. Composure regained, he continued, "We're safe for now. We can light firestones out here if need be, but wood fires are preferable to save phaser power, if your weapons still work at all, and if anyone wants to gather kindling, dry branches or fell a dead tree. I suggest hunting further down, over there near the meadow. There's game there, and edible wild greens." (He had seen this in vision, from above on his way back from the crash site.) "If danger returns, I'll be sure to warn you." He looked into Samarit's haggard face. Insight arose that leadership involved more than service to followers, but service to a higher power, which granted freedom to abandon hope, firm in faith in their survival and, moreover, on their way to safety. Any remaining fatigue vanished.

The grandmother who had admonished Pineshadow had made her way closer to the front of the group that stood with their chief. *"Thank you, Sir Rowan Berry Longbow,"* the old woman called out, *"for breathing life back into our tribe."* She picked up the small girl at her side, the better to see Chief Samarit and Sir Rowan.

His attention riveted on the child's little pointed ears: an earring dangled from one, identical to the one in his pocket. He lowered to a crouch while Samarit rested her hand on his shoulder, held it out to the girl child and asked, "Is this yours? It matches your other very pretty one."

The little one reached out with both hands, and her face beamed.

◆

The crackling fire illumined Samarit's face from below. She asked him, "You say we're safe for the moment. Now that we've recovered a little, where to?"

The other Longbows who surrounded this particular blaze among several talked quietly amongst themselves.

She added, "Rowan, I know your friend Masudah taught you the skill of far-sight. I think that was obvious earlier. Can you advise us?"

"That was unexpected, Sam, triggered by worry about Blue. Masudah taught me something of it, but there was so little time. I've been lucky recently, and since then haven't seen any Reps coming our way, but he basically said I'd have to be born Khémian to be initiated properly. Results have been hit-and-miss. But I think I understand a bit better. It's not about what I want. It's all about letting go of small-self Rowan and surrendering to… I don't know what to call it. Masudah would say it's the gods in one form or another. I'm not made like him, so… the Cosmic Commander is as good a name as any. I'm a commando after all."

Samarit giggled. "That sounds like a storybook character Grandmother Morningstar read to me from an old book when I was little. Kozma was a wise old wolf mother who led the pack to victory over the hideous Scorpion Army. They were giant ones too."

"Ouch… well, the Cosmic Commander it is then." But he whispered, "Don't tell anyone. We don't want to be laughed out of the tribe."

"My lips would be sealed if they weren't still so dry and cracked."

"My nearly irresistible wish is to kiss them but, my chieftain, even as I gaze upon your undiminished beauty it increases, if that were even possible. Soon I won't be able to stand it and will be embarrassed to pass out from ecstasy."

"Exaggeration won't get you anywhere, kitty baby. Try honesty."

"I *am* being honest. Feel my heart and how it flutters." Rowan took her hand and pressed her palm to his chest. "See?"

She took his other hand, slipped it beneath her top and pressed it to her own heartbeat. "We're synchronized. See?"

Tolk loomed up out of the dark, but averted his gaze. "Pardon me, Chief Samarit, Sir Rowan, please come. There is something strange in the sky. It is not a dragon ship… or so we believe."

Samarit stood up and limped in the direction of the starry meadow with one hand in the crook of Rowan's arm, supported by a stick in the other. But she dropped the stick –

He swept her up in his arms and ran the rest of the way – he had caught a glimpse of what Tolk spoke. Rowan set her down in front of the other guards, Pineshadow not among them, who stood and peered southeast, where that entire portion of the night sky blazed aglow below the horizon, with occasional greater flashes like sheet lightning.

Silence. The night's usual faunal chorus had hushed. Not one cricket dared chirp. In vain the Longbows strained to hear anything.

"It's not lightning," said Rowan. "It's the Ahan. They *did* it."

"Pardon me, Sir Rowan," replied Tolk. "Did what? And who are 'they'? Should we retreat to the cave?"

Rowan chuckled. "No, no more caves, unless we find a really nice snake-free one with hot springs and precious gems everywhere… well, at least no snakes. Our allies the Ahan, whom you may never have heard of, are nevertheless the most ancient race on Eorthe. They've sung the Reps out of the sky. What you see are explosions hundreds of leagues away as the reptilians try to batter their way through the Dome."

"Dome?" asked Tolk.

Rowan explained: "It's a spherical shield, broadcast from a geological site that can focus, resonate and amplify high-fidelity ultrasonic frequencies that only affect the enemy. Certain very hard types of stone, some with high quartz content that's highly conductive, others with less or none as insulators, some as capacitors, in combination form the instrument, which is embedded in the bedrock. The top of the Dome forms a hemisphere, and the other half penetrates deep underground where it interacts with telluric currents. Think stone-built technology that amplifies vocally generated vibrations, hymns, sung by special choirs that initiate the process. These songs embody a wholesome spirit that tolerates no discord, something to do with the fractal geometric structure of what we used to call the 'aether' in Vugh Deep. That's just my rather inexpert guess. Maybe even the Ahan have no idea how it works. The mindset the Reps subscribe to is impossible within the sphere of influence of those sacred songs' ignition. It's a shield. The reptilians' experience is of an invisible but impenetrable Dome... the frequency Dome."

"What should we do then, Chief Samarit?" asked Tolk. "Should we retreat or join the fight? Our weapons are small, but our hearts are stout."

"Stout you are, Tolk, all of you. What *should* we do, Rowan? You know the Ahan. Should we move to the southeast or is it too dangerous right now?"

"It's too risky, Sam. We should let the violence die down, then make our way in that direction very carefully until we know we're under the Dome. It's a very long way and we've yet to regain health and strength. We'll need new skills too just to survive. The Longbows will be nomads, maybe for some time to come. And there will be other wandering survivors out there, once they realize they can go topside. We must prepare to convince them to join forces so competition doesn't become a problem. On the other hand, the Dome will continue to grow to meet us... sooner or later."

The silent flashes beyond the horizon persisted.

"Will you be our scout?" asked Samarit. "Can you use your far-sight skills to be our eyes?"

"I will and I can... Cosmic Commander willing."

"Pardon me, Sir Rowan," said Tolk. "Who is that?"

Samarit and Rowan looked at each other and chuckled.

"Tolk, it's you who must pardon me," he answered. "I'm making a silly joke because I'm happy. Prepare for a great adventure into the unknown. It may seem counter-intuitive, but what we must do is await our time to head into what right now is the heart of the firestorm, not run from it."

189

XXIII

Feather *of* Owl

To migrate southeast required a long detour to the north of many leagues to avoid steep grades and trenches. Their route stretched along the edge of a flood plain. The travellers, mostly soldiers who had been on missions away from Wishbone Warren at the time of its destruction, included several elderly men and women, a few carried in rough palanquins or on stretchers, as well as a smaller number of children, one very young often carried on the back of his elder brother who insisted on it, although adults took over his self-assigned duty when possible. The latter group comprised the prescient canids who had refused to hide in the underground shelters and fled Wishbone, Touchstone and several other smaller warrens to wander exposed to the sky, however great the danger. Any domestic animals had long since gone, including deerhounds wounded by the reptilians, which had forced the Longbows to mercy-kill their hunting dogs. The refugees nonetheless gained strength as they went, despite the occasional blow to their number when an elder passed over to the "Other Side." The old ones were said to have willed it, to ease the burden they had caused, which had struck Rowan as unnatural, yet, he at last admitted, pro-life. As if to underscore the sacrifice, a birth delayed them by a day, to a young woman. She had followed her warrior husband into the battlefield, unadvisedly, but she had saved him and her new family both. The traditional ceremony that welcomed a newborn member mixed a blessing for the little one's health and success as a future contributor to the tribe, but also a lamentation for hardship in a world of limitation compared to where it had just come from, the Other Side, where Longbows believed its spirit had been freely in communion with the potential of the Infinity, or the Abstract, the Unmanifest, the Ground of Being, the Quiet, the Great Void, the Origin.

"Rowan," asked Samarit, "the sheet lightning effect has lessened these past few days… does it mean the reptilians are giving up?" She walked quite well and kept up, thanks to the slow pace and frequent rest stops, now that they deemed it safer to move southeast in the direction of Aha Domain.

"I think their attacks are decreasing each day, Sam. But I doubt they'll ever give up. They only know how to fight to the death. They may only be distracted temporarily."

"By the Khaghas? And maybe by other resistance forces?"

"I have no idea. Maybe. Fairchild only contacted me that one time, just to let me know Blue was all right. The lizard woman took a big risk. My guess is that Blue pestered the hell out of her to get that message to me. My insolent attitude needed adjustment. That was the bonus."

Samarit lowered her head, and turned to look back as she often did to check on the tribe, mostly for stragglers.

A second cobbler had been conscripted from the ranks. The lad had much to learn of his trade, hence his work required expert adjustments. Materials for footwear had become scarce, and tough plant fibres were woven with whatever hide was available, such as leather bags when contents had been used up or abandoned in favour of ever lighter travel.

◆

At the very first rest stop, in an obvious attempt to save face, Pineshadow had taken it upon himself to lecture the Longbows regarding their history in the several centuries previous to their association with League civilization, in their case Vugh Deep's quadrant of the West League Dominions. He pointed out that until then they had considered footwear superfluous and vain, a sign of weakness. Their canid ancestors' ancient skeletons, he said, showed that their descendents' toe bones had grown shorter and thinner as a result.

"*Then give me your fine-sewn boots and go unshod,*" shouted one old codger. "*And I shall be happy to trade my threadbare canvas coat, Your Royal Highness, for your lovely woollen cape. But please keep your trinkets of gold, as they fetch no price in the wilderness and are entirely inedible.*"

Everyone laughed and the small audience dispersed.

◆

Rowan felt no affection for the prince either. He had experienced his cruelty, yet found it painful to witness the loss of royal power and position, and its peculiar form of suffering, obstinate denial. But conversation with the chief carried on unrestrained as they walked through the uninhabited region, still without threat from above. "Sam, I hope I'm not gossiping," he said, "when I ask what will become of Prince Pineshadow, when we reach a time and place when and where it will be possible to establish a territory."

"It's not gossip if it speaks a truth, Rowan. He's a symbol of our old ways gone forever. He'll have to adapt as gracefully as he can and keep learning just like the rest of us. Some still address him by his title out of habit, but he's not fit to lead nor was he ever able to do more than obey his parents' dictates, which were few and far between. He's rather lost without them and the comfortable permissive structure they provided. It's unfortunate privilege inhibits awareness of the common good. Apart from the fact that my heart wasn't in it, marrying him would have been an utter disaster, I believe now, although before the world fell apart it seemed impossible to break with tradition. To be honest, I knew it then too, but would rather have died than disappoint Grandmother Morningstar. She wasn't free to ignore clan law. How inflexible customs become. But he must earn his place, like any other Longbow. The Touchstone appendage to his surname is no longer valid. We give him space to understand and grieve his loss in his own way. Weakness we will strengthen, but we can't afford to enable laziness or stupidity. Nor ignorance. He clearly is intelligent and well-educated. When the time comes, I'll suggest that he become the children's teacher... if he demonstrates that he's let go of the belief that he's entitled to anything."

Rowan nodded agreement. "Yes, we must begin again, but we don't have to start from scratch. Much of Longbow culture is valuable to the world, including neglected or abandoned traditional practices. I think we should form strong bonds with the Ahan and with Khémia to begin with, assuming we have that opportunity and aren't forced to assimilate to another culture, as our number is small. We'll find ways..."

A thunderous rumble trembled the ground. All stopped and in silence braced against the unknown, possibly an earthquake. No aftershock followed, however, even after a wait of a length that the sun marked a later hour.

But from the southeast mixed flocks of birds darkened the sky, caught in a tailwind of greater velocity than the layer of clouds that scudded above. The captive wildfowl squawked and screeched, dragged along the conveyor belt of a wide stream of fast-moving air, and disappeared over the mountain behind the Longbows, who with craned necks watched the hapless creatures from below.

At ground level a mere breeze caressed Rowan's whiskers.

"*Look!*" exclaimed a hunter, who ran to retrieve the dead and dying fowl on the ground. Their two trappers quickly followed her.

Something above his head caught Rowan's eye – an owl feather wafted to the ground at his feet. He picked it up and offered it to Samarit.

"No," she said. "You must keep it. It's a gift from the Other Side."

"How so?"

"You'll accuse me of superstition."

"No, superstitions interest me. I study them so I don't accidentally acquire one. How is it a gift, other than as an ornament for a hat?"

She formed her chapped and cracked lips into a rosebud as she often did, and it drifted to the side of her face, and all the while her dark eyes peered into his. "I can see you're going to be difficult to lead by the nose," she said. "Very well, let me explain. The Longbows haven't given up on nature, despite their tacit adoption of the League's sophisticated civilization. What is an owl a symbol of?"

"It depends. To a mouse, it's a symbol of pain as prelude to nothingness. Traditions worldwide associate it with wisdom. Maybe it's because owls can see in the dark, unlike mice."

"How do you know what a mouse experiences? But yes, it's a symbol of wisdom. It fell at your feet. What do your feet symbolize?"

Rowan squinted at her. "I give up," he said. "What do my feet symbolize? Except maybe a long road, behind and ahead."

"Understanding."

"Oh. Yes, I can see that. It's kind of funny. Are you saying I get it?"

Samarit formed her lips into another pale rosebud, which drifted to the side of her face. "I used to say that a lot, didn't I? Anyhow, yes."

"That's good news. Now, what is it I get again?"

"You tell me."

"Right." He paused a moment. "Maybe it's a word to the wise from the Cosmic Commander, an omen. Thanks. Your mind is quicker than mine."

"You're welcome. But yours goes deeper, kitty baby. By the way, shouldn't we be figuring out what just happened above our heads?"

"It must be the Dome expanding in our direction. Or a side effect of it being battered by the Reps, although the sheet lightning has been scarce lately."

"It's obviously no natural phenomenon," Samarit said. "The poor birds!"

"You know, I think we may be under the Dome now. Or just at the edge. If you agree, Chief Sam, we should stop here until I can find out more."

"Sir Scout," she commanded, and winked at him, "do your thing."

He moved to the edge of the woods and sat under a tree at some distance from the others. Daily remote-viewing sessions, or far-sight as the Longbows had once called it, had become more effective. The key, as he now understood, was service. He examined the owl feather held like a quill pen, his sole object of attention –

*

A headwind lifted inner vision up into the clouds above the faster-moving layer of air that had carried the hapless and helpless birds to the northwest. A little airborne dust or leaf debris drifted below. His arms had become great wings, and his legs had shrunk, drawn up against his aerodynamic feathered torso. Amazed at ability to fly into the wind and the lack of vertigo, without effort he adjusted his tail feathers for horizontal stability and elevation. His already sharp felid vision sharpened to perceive individual seeds on stalks of grass and tiny insects even as he raced across the meadow and higher into the thin cool air above the mountains.

Far off near the horizon a tarnished arrowhead shape circled in a wide arc, dived lower, bounced and skipped as if it felt its way to lower altitude in stages. He knew it sought the edge of the Dome, apparently with some difficulty. Its sensors should be able to detect it at any speed. Or at least their satellites should provide it with specific data. Did they not know it of its spherical geometry? They must. Perhaps, where it met the ground, structure remained weak, still fluid. Perhaps the Dome was growing fast, expanding from the crown above the Fivefold Mount and the castle, and picked up energy and speed as its centre of gravity descended towards the core of the planet and ballooned to envelope the global Surface and beyond to the stratosphere, anchored by pyramids worldwide, however decayed by age they may be. The craft came near the ground now, and rose and fell with the terrain as it followed the southern rim and headed in the direction of the meadow where the Longbows had halted.

With a flip of his wings, Rowan turned back and coasted in gradual descent until he dropped below the ridge that bordered the meadow some miles ahead. The faster-moving layer of air below proved difficult to penetrate. He skidded over its surface in the same way the avian flocks had earlier. But he remembered his felid body seated in meditation pose beneath the tree in the woods –

✦

His eyes opened upon the owl feather poised in his hand as if about to pen a note, jumped up and ran towards the others, and shouted: *"Into the trees! Hide in the woods! Now!"*

A too-long moment of chaos passed as the Longbows gathered momentum and camouflaged themselves as well as possible with leafed branches if they could find them and dead leaves if not. The sparse forest at this elevation did not provide much shelter, but better than exposure to the sky.

"Rowan!" shouted Samarit. "Are we not under the Dome then?"

194

"I don't know for sure. Better to hide, although it may be only a gesture to make ourselves feel better. We should be able to tell soon enough."

"*Oh!…* we still have something they want, as long as we're alive." She stood up and scanned the woods, to check if anyone remained unhidden.

Rowan reached towards her to pull her to relative safety –

The dragon ship appeared above the mountains – and dropped as it followed the contour of the land. In an instant it crossed the meadow, where the turf flew out in a long strip below, torn up by an invisible probe beneath the craft. Clumps of sod broke away from the strip and flew in one direction only, thus indicated the area outside the Dome.

Samarit stood paralyzed and stared.

The dragon ship halted to a hover, while the remaining airborne clumps of grass and dirt scattered and thumped to the ground. Suspended for a moment, it increased in altitude a little –

◆

A pillar of fire shot up Rowan's spine. In a flash his tongue welded itself to the roof of his mouth and completed a circuit that would otherwise have exploded out the top of his skull through the tattooed sigil "syx" hidden by his mop of cherry-red mane. The circuit closed at the speed of light – now in the dragon ship, moreover inside the reptilian pilot, at the exact midpoint of its earless head. Rowan understood the craft was controlled by the creature's mind, thus easily diverted its attention to a point high above with the suggestion that its target was there, not in the woods. The ship quickly gained altitude and penetrated the cloud layer, hovered a moment, then dived towards the meadow. Rowan rotated the attitude, the altitude decreased, and he adjusted the angle of descent back in the direction from which the craft had come, straight down to an area where the Dome must surely be fixed and stable, where in owl form he had skidded across it.

The reptilian's mind struggled to regain control, its confusion, however, matched by strength of will. It shook its head so hard it cracked the windscreen and thrashed its limbs in every direction, momentarily weightless, and roared a primeval scream that pressurized the cockpit.

Panic flared throughout Rowan's entire nervous system. He did not know how to eject; victory threatened to slip away. His lifelong hatred of reptilians burst into a screaming blaze within, prepared to burn to ashes concentration and kill them both –

✦

Fortunately he remembered the owl feather and found himself with his hand clamped on Samarit's rigid forearm. He looked up just in time to see the tip of the arrowhead pointed straight down come to a dead stop for a nanosecond

and a series of concentric rings of blinding light radiate across the entire visible portion of the sky. Samarit crashed on top of him as the ground absorbed the energetic shock wave from above. Stones, dust, leaves and whole torn-off branches whipped around their entwined bodies.

Just a few feet away nothing had been disturbed, where still hidden lay most of the Longbows. Thunder rolled off the surrounding peaks and reverberated again and again.

"*Sam!*" Rowan, deafened, trembled with the after-effects of the heavy vibrations that had passed through his body. "*Sam!*"

She had stopped breathing – face pale, but eyes open.

Rowan stretched her out on the ground and drew her knees up to her abdomen. His voice dull and muffled in his ears, he shouted at her: "*Breathe in through your nose, slowly, and exhale through your mouth.*" He gently pushed her abdomen below her rib cage. "*Sam! Can you hear me?*" Her diaphragm muscle remained spasmed. He drew her knees up further to relax it –

She stared at him – and breathed. "I can't hear…" she might have said.

He nodded acknowledgement, took her in his arms and stood up – the ringing in his ears drowned out all other sound.

From among the Longbows outside the Dome, a man ran towards them – lips moving, wide-eyed, the man tugged on Rowan's sleeve, looked up and pointed to where the dragon ship had crashed into the Dome.

Rowan turned to look – pieces of wreckage higher up slid fast – a large chunk picked up speed and headed straight towards them. In a single bound he leapt to a point some thirty feet distant to safety as the smoking fungal alloy debris lodged a jagged edge in the leaf-strewn ground where Samarit had lain.

Those inside the Dome step by step moved closer to the few outside, who had jumped out of harm's way while smaller debris slid and collected on the ground. The people shouted – apparently.

Rowan stood Samarit upright, and snapped a dry branch in half to test whether the Dome prevented sound from escape or whether he and the outsiders remained deaf. None reacted. His ears rang unabated.

Samarit pointed to him, then to herself, then pointed at the group inside the Dome, and shrugged.

Rowan shrugged too, but looked over her shoulder.

A man inside picked up a stick and cautiously approached with it pointed at him. The wielder slowly walked right up to them.

Rowan accepted the stick and raised it in the air.

Apparently those inside cheered. His ears still rang.

Tolk approached with a notebook. In it he had written the question: "Is the Dome intact?" He handed the notebook to Rowan, along with his carpenter's pencil.

Awed, Rowan watched the pencil in his hand move on its own and words appear on the page: "*Open boundary to open hearts. To hearts of stone, more adamantine than diamond and as clear, but impenetrable.*" He read it twice to be sure he understood, but knew it was true.

✦

Confident now in a safer journey to the southeast, the Longbows felt free to be jolly and celebrate in the only way left to them. Without slowing their pace they sang a traditional "wolf" song in their native tongue as they marched. It would indeed have sounded like wolves howling at the moon at times, but musically interpreted.

Meanwhile hearing gradually returned to the deafened. Gratitude nearly made Rowan weep, especially for subtle sounds he had previously screened out as irrelevant to their goal: the trickle of brooks; the sigh of the wind in the trees; the call of young creatures to their mothers, who in turn called to their mates; the rustle of leaves; woodpecker taps, staccato echoes in the forest; a woman's hum; a baby's cry. The distant call of a raven made him shiver.

Samarit, who roamed the trackless wilderness with him, his hand in hers, peered up at him, and asked, "You heard that too, didn't you?"

He looked down at her and nodded yes.

"Another sign from the Cosmic Commander?"

"Let's not get too carried away, Sam. When it comes to Blue, expect the unexpected."

XXIV
Serpentine Coil

THE MIGRATION CONTINUED without hindrance, and autumn withered on. Elevation increased in the foothills of the Fell Mountains and forced an ascension into winter elevations. The travellers skirted the damaged region of the snowy surface under which had once thrived Arbaro Domain. Despite the low likelihood of survivors, Chief Samarit led a search party into the rubble of Gormlin Cave, the open grave that added a putrid note to the pervasive odour of charred wood that lingered for many leagues in every direction.

"We shouldn't linger too long here, Sam. You probably feel the sorrow that will haunt this place for many a long year to come. I do."

"Where might Commander Kinga have led them?"

"Grief delayed any contingency plan. I don't think they even had one in the first place. They just stared when I asked." He reminded himself that perhaps he had not asked in the right way, however. "When I saw them last," Rowan added, and nodded towards a part of Gormlin Forest not turned to spiky burnt matchsticks, "they were over there, camped under those patches of trees."

"Won't the Dome help with that?"

"With the pain and sorrow embedded here? Eventually. In the meantime it may acquire a life of its own."

"Do you mean… ghosts?"

He affirmed with a nod. "In my opinion ghosts are insentient patterns of energy, like visual recordings, impressions, sometimes including sounds or smells, made possible by the trapped vibratory energy of extreme emotions, especially if there's quartz present. But Masudah once said something that makes me think such distortions in the energy field could be taken advantage of by what he calls spirits… the weak, inferior ones that can't figure out how to detach themselves from the things they loved or hated when alive, attachments and severed attachments. They could feed on the energy field and develop a kind of form, parasites really, often harmless if left to themselves, but not always. And the field can form interfaces with our world. Everything's connected."

"Kitty baby, you're a Longbow. That's like what the our ancestors used to believe in."

His heart swelled.

"Tolk signals no one left now, Rowan. Let's move on down into the valley. I see a river, but no snow on the ground yet."

✦

In the valley the ground remained dry. At sunset a layer of air descended in a rush of wind from the peaks to fill its bowl shape with cold. But by then the Longbows had built snug fir shelters, concave shells near each fire pit, each with a short wall of small logs for a heat reflector and wind screen. Firestones had not been ignited for some time, but wood burnt instead, a sign of increased confidence. With no means to recharge other than the weak sunlight, nor to repair high-tech weapons, phaser power needed conservation. From time to time the sharp silhouette of a dragon ship appeared at high altitude. But nothing of the "sheet lightning" had been seen for a week or so.

Rowan ran back to the camp from a far-sight scouting session with a report. "We're not alone, Sam," he said and warmed his hands by the fire. "I spotted a band of people, mostly men, about a dozen. They were following the smell of our woodsmoke until the wind picked up, but they've lost the trail and it's too dark. We should send Tolk to find them. I'll go too."

Chief Samarit ordered another fire pit and shelter built by the light of torches, and extra food cooked.

In two hours the lost ones had been found and led to the Longbow camp like the stumbling half-dead, bedraggled and supported by sticks, some with feet wrapped in rags, all with hollow eyes. For the most part speechless, the young adults huddled near the fire and fell on the food like starved animals. By the next morning it had been decided that the Longbows remain camped until the refugees had recovered enough to march. None led, but one of the men, Arno, slightly older than the others, volunteered as spokesperson.

Rowan took the young man aside to ask him to remember as much as he could of their journey. "Are you Arbaros?" he asked.

"Yes, probably the last," Arno said. "One foot is in the grave, our eyes are dull, but our gratitude knows no end. Tonight more of us would be dead if not for you. If only we'd had time to prepare… our leader Kinga was killed. The Snake People came up from beneath. We would not have abandoned our tunnels if not for that." The young man looked to his friends, including a red-eyed young woman who clutched a bundle to her breast.

The girl beside her looked to Arno and shook her head.

He continued: "We did venture outside from time to time, but not for long. One day I noticed I no longer felt afraid. Until then I had not realized how terrified we all were. It must have been because as you say, the Dome… but it forced the snakes up too. We should have left sooner, only we did not know it was safe to leave."

The young woman some distance away burst into tears and pressed her face to the bundle.

"She grieves," said Arno, "for her child."

⋆

Three days later the tribes packed up and followed the riverbank to a grove of oaks, bare of leaf at this season, where a ceremony laid the Arbaro infant to rest. The copse they christened Noll Wood, as the Arbaros believed elf spirits guarded that place as sacred ground.

The grave out of sight behind them now, in the lead Samarit and Rowan walked together. "Sam, the Arbaros don't know where the Snake People went. If the tunnels and caves are no longer tolerable to them because of the Dome, they could have made for the lakes and waterways."

She glanced away from the river and replied, "I know, Rowan, my thought exactly. I've been watching the water but haven't seen anything suspicious. It's cold and the level is low this time of year. They'd be at risk of hypothermia as much as anywhere else on the Surface, unless there's a hot spring beneath. We should watch for steam. The current's slow, and there could be deep pools…"

As if conjured by her words, with a rush of foaming water the glistening head of a giant reptile irrupted from the depths of a pool in the stream and towered above them. Waterfalls poured off its serpent skull and thick muscular long and legless body. It rippled the river into breakers on the bank, and coiled ever higher. The vertical pupils that divided each orange eye trained on Samarit. Its cavernous pink mouth opened wide, hissed a fog of foul stench, and its black forked tongue lashed the air.

Thus a second time fire shot up Rowan's spine, the circuit closed and he positioned attention in the middle of the reptilian's brain and looked out through its eyes at Samarit crouched beside his felid form.

She aimed her plasma rifle at the roof of the giant snake's open jaws.

Samarit and the scene behind her rushed towards him and a white flash in an instant turned blacker than black –

⋆

Rowan tried to peer through the onlookers' legs. *"Sam!"* he shouted.

"You are injured, Sir Rowan," said a woman, whose name he could not recall at the moment. "It crushed you against the rocks. Please do not move."

He ignored her and jumped to his feet – but fell to his knees and onto his side, rolled on his back, clasped his knee and gasped – this time a bone or bones must have broken. "*Sam!*"

"*I'm here!*"

The pain vanished – "I feared you were dead."

"A rumour, kitty baby… and greatly exaggerated."

He groaned and all went black.

✦

Someone tugged on one of his commando boots.

Another wrapped his leg with a length of cloth and bound that with twine.

A man said: "It is not as bad as it looks. Most of the blood is from the snake being. It think it is cracked, not fractured, but we have nothing to scan it with to know how bad."

Rowan muttered: "My scanner could be adapted." He leaned back on his elbows and peered between the legs of the people. "It's in my… where is it?"

Samarit said: "It was dragged into the river," and disappeared from view.

A splash found its way to his ears, as did the gasp of the crowd, and spoken fears of more Snake People down there beneath the bloody surface –

But before long water dripped in his eyes – and her wet face met his gaze, streaked with red.

"Oh, sorry!… That's not much help, is it?" She wiped the water and blood from his eyes so he could see his dripping scanner in her hand. "Will it still work when it's wet?"

"Sam, don't worry about that. *Can someone please build a fire before Chief Samarit freezes to death?*"

"No, Rowan, we have to move you away from the river first."

Two men constructed a stretcher and moved him to a site where the Longbows made camp a little earlier in the day than usual, but a safe distance from the riverside carnage.

Eventually Rowan self-diagnosed a cracked tibia, but the fibula remained undamaged, swelling had begun, but no surgery needed, thanks to his commando boots.

Samarit prescribed a splint so he could adjust the pressure.

"Sam, are you all right?"

"Never better, kitty baby. How are you these days?"

"Not bad, thanks for asking. By the way… what the hell happened?"

"Oh, that. Well, I'm not sure. It all went by so fast. One second we were speculating and the next we were certain. The big mouth opened and closed, then the big head dropped down and circled behind. I did manage to get off a shot under its chin aimed for its brain, but it didn't seem to make any difference. It just kept on coming, and tightened its coil. It was obviously after me for some reason, and it just knocked you off your feet into the rocks and bounced you along for some distance like a rag doll. I punched a bunch of holes in it and there was blood everywhere. I'll never get it out my clothes, so I guess I'll just have to go without like Masudah's wife."

"Nefer, Queen Havasarakshrrut'yuny. That would be interesting."

"Do you think so? Anyhow, I love to hear you pronounce her name. She sounds so elegant and exotic."

"Nefer is all of that and, more importantly, a very nice lady who rules the queendom fully clothed, at least the last time I saw her. Now, will you tell me how the episode with the snake ended?"

"Of course, if you like. Where was I? Well, I thought, if this is how it ends, I may as well go out with a bang. It was getting closer and closer, tightening its coils. The rifle was awkward, a bit of long thing to aim properly in that situation. But I decided to waste no time and pulled off a long series of shots in automatic machine mode, aimed at its spine when possible. That finally did the trick. But at full strength, as it was low already, the rifle's nearly run out of firepower now. And the whole business really made a mess of my outfit, sad to say."

"Too bad it's winter."

"Then we'll just to have snuggle up if I haven't a stitch to wear."

"I'm ready, willing and able… until I can walk anyhow. You're on your own after that."

"Oh well, one can only hope you're bedridden for a while."

◆

In two days, with the aid of a makeshift crutch and a splint, Rowan rejoined the Longbows and Arbaros on their slow march towards the southeast. Samarit's clothing had been burnt, but her attendants tailored a brown woollen cape from the best blanket they had secreted away, and contributed their spare items that would fit. The senior cobbler thoroughly cleaned her combat boots of snake blood.

Asked for his review of her outfit, Rowan said, "Fashionable as ever, Sam. The pattern, the muted abstract designs like leaves and branches… lovely. Good camouflage too. The wooden fasteners, very clever. The tailors really did a good job. On the other hand, I'd very much looked forward to seeing you leading the way in your birthday suit."

"Oh? I'm so sorry you're disappointed. I'll have to make up for it sometime. They really shouldn't have used the only blanket left without holes, but they meant well. It may be a long time before we can make looms to weave anything. For now we have to skin game for the hides and fur. Later we'll train tanners, as we have none for that messy job, and besides, we have to be settled somewhere to collect dung and urine in enough quantities for processing leather. Maybe we can raise reindeer when we get to Aha if they'll allow that. In the meantime it's nice to have a new look."

"It's a measure of their respect, Sam, never discount that."

"I only hope I continue to deserve it. Speaking of which, we should discuss plans for the near future, along with alternatives in anticipation of the unknown. We can't just barge into a green and pleasant land and take over. The natives will need time to reorganize and reclaim too."

"I've been thinking it over. Once we get past this range of mountains and into the warmer southern valleys, if all goes well, we can decide better then. It's early days yet. Too bad we have to avoid the lakes and rivers, unless they're frozen, which should be soon. We could have built rafts or walked on the ice."

Samarit peered at him. "No worries, you'll be fit again in no time. The few nanoids left will speed healing. We were lucky back there. Do you think the Snake People are down there too? In the south?"

"We have to expect them at any time, anywhere there's a hole in the ground big enough or slow-moving heated pools where water snakes can breed. It would have been nice to take advantage of waterways, but instead of slogging on maybe we can build temporary stone tanks and heat our own baths. The snakes leave the water to climb trees too, so everyone should watch for that. Of course we have to expect their lizard-man cousins as well if any are trapped as the Dome expands. If they're smart they'll have escaped, but we don't know how long it will take until the whole planet will be inside. Note that I have not mentioned the cryptids we may encounter as well."

"Rowan, you said that more amphitheatres will be built, wherever the geology is conducive to reinforcement. That means there are weak spots."

"Yes, the Dome will take time to expand, one reason I'd like us to be as close to Aha Domain as possible, if not right in it. Nefer and Masudah said my second home was with them. I just might be willing to share my suite in the castle if you know of anyone who wouldn't mind being my room-mate."

"Hmm, let me think about it. I shouldn't wonder they'd have to be quite a tolerant individual."

"Thanks. Regarding the Dome's weak spots, I don't know the technical details, but back in Perkona Ola days I remember seeing a view of Eorthe as a gravity map. The planet in that model wasn't a sphere, but more like a potato, with wells, ridges and lumps, a really complicated situation. The Dome has to expand to include the stratosphere to accommodate all that."

"Mmm, potatoes… but that means any trapped Reps will be working from inside. As far as we know they're still unable to penetrate from above. Or have they? I mean, we haven't seen any sheet lightning for quite a while. How can we tell if it's still intact? We have to find out if possible."

"Good point. We can tell somewhat by how secure we feel, but in fact I've tried to reach Masudah. All I've been able to do is leave a message, so to speak. He's the master, so I have to wait until he responds. I imagine he's got enough on his plate with just keeping the Dome inflated."

"Rowan, you also said that the frequency the Dome operates on tolerates no evil. I don't claim to understand that, as long as it works to keep the Reps out. But you've had the benefit of Masudah's company as well as the teachings of Aynt, so if you're confident of that so am I."

"That was my experience. I told you about listening to the small choir in the throne room before the amphitheatre had been finished. I know it works. But we mustn't stick flowers in our ears, as the saying goes. It's a race. We can only wait to see who wins. And that's not even saying anything about what's been developing in space, let alone on the moon."

"Do you think Blue, and Fairchild and her people… they must be working to help us from the inside… and outside."

"I believe Blue has seen the light. She knows she must pay for her crimes, not by imprisonment or execution but by repair of the damage to the extent that's possible. It's going to be the work of a lifetime, but felid lives are long. And Fairchild… I only know what Blue told me. I think the Khaghas, if they're still viable, will be preparing for battles in space as much as for revolt on Eorthe. For that they have to be able to come and go. If the theory's correct, their soul frequency will have to be compatible, unlike Kirzaka's fundamentalist horde, but Blue seemed to believe in them."

"I guess," said Samarit, "it ain't over till it's over."

XXV
Continuum

"What... is that?" Samarit pointed to an extremely bright trio of lights in the southeastern daylight sky. "Rowan, what are they?" Brilliance had emerged from the top of a lenticular cloud formation that resembled a stack of white dinner plates of decreasing diameters from bottom to top, balanced on the tallest snowy mountain peak in the far distance.

Rowan replied, "They do look like something I've seen before." His eyes remained on the lights, but his ears swivelled as someone ran up from the rear.

Tolk asked, "Sir Rowan, should we take cover? They may be dragon ships. They are lower in altitude than our estimate of the crown of the Dome now. It may be it is collapsing."

Rowan's heart radiated peace, the only measure of their safety he counted on. "It's good to be cautious, Tolk," he replied, "but I don't believe they're dragon ships. They're not dull and triangular, but... like stellated dodecahedrons."

"Oh. And what is that?"

"I don't know if you can see the geometry, but it's like pyramids positioned with symmetrical precision at angles to each other and nested into one solid form... well, maybe not solid. They're so bright because it's all our Eorthely minds can handle. It's the limit of what we can interpret of some phenomenal power, a kind of intensified... existence."

"Pyramids... from Khémia then, sir?"

"I think it's more likely the Khémian ones are versions in stone."

A woman yelled: "*Have the gods returned, Chief Samarit? Are we saved?*"

"*Longbows!*" Samarit called out. "*Stay calm. Rest in the woods over there until we can decide our next move.*" When the Longbows had hidden under the forest canopy, she said, "Rowan, I don't know what they are either, but I've seen them before too, when I was a special forces security guard in Perkona Ola, after I'd been given the nanoid upgrade. I reported them, was debriefed and ordered to keep my mouth shut, but heard nothing about it afterwards."

"I've been inside one of those things."

"You *have*? Tell me."

"It was just before we... you know... Mudredd."

"Let it go, kitty baby. I have."

Rowan, his jaws tense, peered at Samarit, who peered back. "It was during the crazy period," he said, "not that it's been any less crazy since then, but during the time when Blue was still the Madam Ellaern alter ego. Her goal then was to escape to the stars."

"When she belonged to that Lyran cult… New Dawn?"

"That's right, New Dawn. Her genius figured out how to use the little portal in the high priest's temple to summon the Primordial Architects. Even he was surprised that it was more than symbolic, but no more than me."

"What happened?"

"I can't believe I haven't already told you this. It was the most amazing thing I've ever experienced… other than meeting you."

"Flattery will get you everywhere, kitty baby." She gripped his forearm. "But tell me what happened."

"Well… whatever, it was probably a projection. I mean, I think they must appear to us in the form that will match whatever we can handle. Our desires, fears and assumptions do the rest. Anyhow, that doesn't explain much, does it?"

"Never mind. I think I know what you're trying to say, not that it matters. You mean Blue has summoned them again. Am I right?"

"When it comes to Blue…"

"…expect the unexpected. I know. You keep saying that."

"I wouldn't be surprised if she has. Maybe their role in all this should be reparation too. They modified all the different players in the game. They set it up so that it's a big crazy mess on purpose or by accident. They should be made to repair it, like Blue has to pay her way now."

"You're saying it's a cosmic principle. Right? They're here to help?"

"Don't mind me. I might have the wrong end of the stick."

"I don't mind minding you, kitty baby. It's my pleasure. I'm your perfect minder. Never forget that or I'll be forced to beat you with your owl feather."

"Yes, Chief Who Must Be Obeyed. I'm happy to comply. What I mean is, I remember something the tigress-flower lady said. They won't interfere. It's up to us to clean up our own mess."

"Who? Do you mean one of them appeared as a big cat?"

"Well, more like a tiger-striped pin-up."

"You have some imagination."

"Aynt told me imagination is everything."

"Dirty young man. What should we do, in your opinion?"

"I think we should just keep going. Even if the Dome is in trouble, which I doubt, it could be one reason why those things have appeared. It may have nothing to do with Blue, but…" He said no more.

She had pressed her forefinger across his lips.

✦

Break of day illumined the dim thicket on the hill where Rowan sat beneath a tangle of bare branches, owl feather in hand, and prepared to scout the best route ahead – but a twig snapped – his eyes popped open –

Beyond the fernbrake stood Blue, her tawny hair shrouded by the cowl of a long cloak of what looked like the fur-lined tanned leather of a reptilian dyed black; and shod in tall black boots, an ensemble Madam Ellaern might have chosen for cold weather, apart from the old military vest. "Hello, Rowan," she said.

"Hello, Blue. I'd hoped you'd left sorcery behind by now… is that Rep leather?"

"Hope no longer, because I have. And yes, I would have preferred it undyed to retain the sheen… a gift from Fairchild. This was her mother's hide, the part of it least scarred. They dyed it to disguise the burns."

Rowan grimaced. "She had her own mother skinned?…" He scanned the perimeter. "They do that? Is she around somewhere?"

"Hey, it's a rare honour in Khagha-world. She's out of sight of course. I'm a messenger. You're in danger."

"Stranded Reps? More snakes?…"

"Worse." Blue emerged from the mist, flipped back her cowl, furled her cape, strolled closer and sat beside him, quiet for a moment. "It's you. As the elder sibling, I reserve the right to give unsolicited advice."

"I'm listening."

"So Kweelu says I was a bad girl because I believed I was a bad girl…"

"What do you mean we're in danger? From me? What does that even mean?"

"Fine, no preface then. I can see this is not going to be easy. I'm talking about little Syx, so sweet, small and helpless, but he's a nuclear bomb that never went off."

"The Reps ruined his life. And yours."

"Not if we change the channel."

"Blue just wanted to be free," he replied. "Now she's on parole, but it's not forever. Syx only ever wanted to go home. For the longest time he refused to admit there's no Berry anymore, but now there's Sam."

"Rowan, my self-hatred helped to end League civilization… and it destroyed our family. Don't let it destroy you and the Longbows."

"Listen, Blue… Mama and Papa would have died in the same way anyhow. None of us could avoid our destiny. You're an amazing survivor. I am too, better late than never. Everything will be fine."

208

"Ah, the arrogance of youth." Blue shook her head, and added, "I should know. But I'm no longer the overconfident self-obsessed vixen I worshipped like a religious icon. I split myself into two that way and spent every moment ever after trying to get the broken bits back together. Now I know a first step of the method is to right the wrongs I did however possible, and restore the balance. Justice, in a word."

"I appreciate your concern, Blue." Rowan stood up, brushed himself off, crouched on one leg and picked up his crutch.

"What happened to your leg?"

"A snake monster bounced me along the riverbank rocks. But I have to go back now. It's dawn. Our trek won't end until we get as close to Aha Domain as we can. Will you join us?"

"No, thank you. I have work to do. Up there. We're going to the moon."

Rowan examined the sky. The shining geometries had gone from the peak.

"Fairchild is waiting," she said.

Rowan held out his hand.

Blue took it and stood up. "Please," she added, "take care. Remember what I said." And she turned about, strolled through the fernbrake and vanished into the misty forest.

With a glance at the pale ice-blue dawn sky, he limped down from the thicket to find the Longbow camp hidden in the fog. A new day had begun.

The adventure continues…

Please leave a review!

PLEASE CONSIDER LEAVING a review at Amazon.com or whichever site you purchased this book. Prospective buyers place more trust in the opinions of honest reviewers like you. George R.R. Martin, author of the epic fantasy series A Song of Ice and Fire, of which *A Game of Thrones* is book one, says that a range of reviews is helpful to the author, so I invite you to share your thoughts in a review after reading this book. Furthermore, I subscribe to reader-response theory, which recognizes the reader's role in creating the meaning and experience of a literary work. The theory argues that literature is a performance art such that each reader creates their unique text-related interpretation. That means you are a partner. Your opinion matters.

Thank you and keep in touch! You can do that on the contact page at my website. Also, consider signing up for my newsletter there to be informed when the next trilogy in the series will be published, along with excerpts and possibly illustrations from published and forthcoming books.

RupertSmithson.com

Book Four:

Eye of Stone

IF YOU ENJOYED *Mistress of the Knell*, you will want to continue the adventure of The Stars Hereafter Chronicles with book four, *Eye of Stone*. Here is an excerpt from chapter 14, "The Mountains of the West":

◆

THEY SHOUTED IN unison their spontaneous joy at hard-won liberation, despite the danger of being tracked and followed. Maya only moaned a little – the tears that streamed back from her closed eyes had not dried yet.

Their trajectory levelled off, and Blue asked, "Can I unstrap her now, Rowan? I hate to see anyone tied up like this." Cargo straps had to replace seat belts, as the ship had not been designed for felids, apart from the cargo bay shipping containers.

"It's better than being crammed into a pod," he replied. "But I'll help you. The ship's on autopilot now… I think. I want to check on her anyway to see how the G-forces affected her wound."

"I can do that. Why do I not see Eorthe through the windscreen?"

Rowan turned to look. "Damn… I must've done something wrong." The dark side of the moon appeared in his rear-view display. "We're going the wrong way," he said. "Never mind, I'll just make a U-turn. Hang on tight." He braced for the centrifugal force, surprised to feel nothing unusual while the moon moved out of the camera's view and the vast ocean of stars drifted sideways as Eorthe swung into sight ahead. "Hmm… the inertia damping's better than expected, but a bit quirky… belay that, my guesswork is off, that's all… I'm sure we must be on autopilot now."

"Your bedside manner needs work too, Rowan. My confidence is low that we're not going to shoot past the target and get lost in space forever."

RupertSmithson.com

www.ingramcontent.com/pod-product-compliance
Lightning Source LLC
Chambersburg PA
CBHW070821120626
46556CB00002B/614